THE
LEGACY
HUMAN
Singularity 1

Susan Kaye Quinn

East Baton Rouge Parish Library
Baton Rouge, Louisiana

For information visit
www.SusanKayeQuinn.com

March 2015 Edition

Edited by Bryon Quertermous
editing.bryonquertermous.com

Cover Design by Dale Robert Pease
www.walkingstickbooks.com

Formatting by Polgarus Studio
www.polgarusstudio.com

ISBN-13: 978-1508557494
ISBN-10: 1508557497

When transcending humanity is the prize, winning the Game is all that matters.

Seventeen-year-old Elijah Brighton wants to become an ascender—a post-Singularity human/machine hybrid. But when he competes in the creative Olympics for the right to ascend, everything he knows about his world starts to unravel.

to Liz
for loving Eli first

ONE

I want to ascend so badly, I can taste it.

It's bitter and metallic, like the acrylic paint spread before me. It's beautiful and beckoning and untouchable, like the shimmering rose skin of my patron, Lenora, who hovers over my work, tasting it in her own way. Her fingertips barely graze the paint, sensing its color and texture and scent in a way that is utterly inhuman.

Because she's not human. Not anymore. She's *ascended*—vastly more intelligent, compassionate, and enlightened than any human could be without the procedure. I'm just one of those remnants of humanity the ascenders left behind long ago.

Lenora leans in toward the painting in that sudden kind of motion ascenders sometimes have. Her cascade of red curls brushes my cheek... and raises goose bumps on my arms.

I hold absolutely still.

This is the closest she'll come to touching me. Anything more would be... *wrong*. Ascenders and legacy humans don't do that sort of thing, at least not legally. I tell myself the instant full-body alert is just because I'm a seventeen-year-old guy who's definitely straight—anything vaguely female would get this response—but it doesn't help that Lenora's body is pure fantasy. Sculpted cheeks. Curves that irresistibly draw my gaze. Lips that beg for me to draw each perfectly rounded part. The red curls have to be synthetic—ascenders don't have hair—but their softness still heats my cheek. There's plenty to desire in the bodyform she's wearing now, but lust is a pale reflection of the thick, complicated feelings I have for her.

Feelings no legacy should have. And no decent ascender would return.

It's wrong to want her. Or really, just delusional. But my fingers ache with the need to touch her, just once. She's close enough that I easily could.

If only ascendance were equally within reach.

Once again, I taste the bitter nearness and yet absolute unreachability… of her. Of ascending. Of everything that means anything at all.

Lenora leans back, her hair no longer touching me: it breaks the spell. "It's lovely, Elijah." She always uses my full name, just like my mother. Which is disturbing enough, but it also reminds me that Lenora was born long before any human now alive. "I like it. But you can do better."

I fight hard to keep my disappointment from showing. Which is ridiculous because I need her to *hate* the painting—or at least dislike it enough that she'll let me keep it. I won't tell her I'm selling it, but black market medicines aren't cheap, and those are the only kind my mother can get now. Yet I can't help wanting Lenora to love my work anyway.

I search the delicate palette of her skin for some hint of what she truly feels. Her cheeks are currently the color of a white rose blushing pink, and tiny flashes of silver dart just below the surface, making them glisten. That means *something*, but learning to read Lenora's emotional state is the kind of color study I could spend an eternity trying to master. I think the rose means she's relaxed yet excited, but the silver flashes... I just don't know.

"I was only messing around with some color," I lie, swinging my gaze to the carefully blended shades of green in front of us. I went through a dozen canvases before I could capture the spectrum of the rainforest in just the right balance—good enough to be worth something on ArtNet, but not so good that she would want to keep it. But she's right, of course. I can do better. A lot better. Fantastically, inspiringly better... only I can't control when that creative madness strikes. It's more like *possession*. I don't remember it afterward, I just find the result smeared in front of me. Madness rendered in paint.

Most people would call that kind of black-out a mental problem, not a gift. But to Lenora, it's the entire reason she became my patron two years ago.

"I'll do better next time," I say, knowing I can't guarantee any such thing.

She steps back to examine my work from a distance. Her costume is more ridiculous than normal: full body armor, balloon pants, and a gleaming silver helmet on top of her curly red wig. My patron likes to dress up, but I truly wish she wouldn't. Ascenders playing human isn't exactly a compliment. And everything about it is exaggerated, like she thinks it's hilarious. An outrageous purple feather dances on top of her helmet, jerking and twitching in the breeze, as if it agrees with me. The feather is a wild thing held captive, an adornment to be tossed aside when she's ready for the next one.

I squirm on my stool. That thought's dangerously close to home, given I need my patron—her support, her approval, her understanding of my art—far more than she needs me.

I don't say any of this, just give her outfit a bemused look. "Sixteenth century conquistador?" I guess. "Planning to make some conquests today?"

A hint of a smile tugs at her lips, but she's still examining my work. "No, I simply enjoy the feather."

More squirming. "It clashes with the hair. Red and purple. The colors of passion and divinity."

"Or blood and royalty." She's toying with me.

Then, lightning quick, she strikes a pose, as if she has an invisible sword held before her. She lunges toward me. I throw up my hands in mock terror then fling them wide, allowing her to pierce my heart with her imaginary blade. The motion unbalances me, and I tip off the stool, falling to the floor. From there, five different kinds of brightness compete to blind me: the metallic shine of the dustless floor, the natural light beaming through the glass ceiling, and the multitude of glints from silvered art cabinets, brushes, and easels. Lenora's sun-drenched studio is perched on a cliff at the edge of Seattle, and from here, even the decaying legacy city towers seem to sparkle.

I wince more at the gracelessness of my fall than the glare.

She laughs.

I stare, unabashedly smiling at the sound. I haven't heard her laugh in this bodyform yet. It's taller than the last one, with more ample curves and more delicate limbs, both of which I greatly appreciate, but the laugh... it's almost musical.

I blush when I realize her laugh is directed at me. "Glad I could amuse you today." I get up, set the stool on its feet, then snatch my painting off the easel and turn to leave.

"Elijah," she calls, the music in her voice softer now.

I hate that I automatically check my determined stride. But leaving in a huff is an idiot move anyway. Orion's normal chit-allowance—the one every legacy gets for playing by the rules and living off the ascender's largess—barely covers enough food to keep you moving. Forget art supplies, not to mention black market meds. And I can't sell my works if I don't have paint.

I slowly turn back to Lenora. Her perfect face is marred by concern, as if hurting my feelings actually pains her. And I believe it's completely genuine: ascenders are far more empathetic and understanding than the human animals they've left behind. It's not that they're all the same, as if linking up to Orion turns them into hive-minded household bots. Ascenders are definitely still individuals—they're just *better* individuals than any human in all of history has managed to be. At least, that's how it is with Lenora: she's the only ascender I've met in person. But everything I've ever seen on the legacy net shows it to be true: ascenders care far more about everything from eliminating war to fixing all the environmental damage done while humans were in charge. And to top it off, they caretake the few legacy humans like me who are still around.

The ascenders do a much better job of running the planet than humanity ever did.

"I'm so sorry, Elijah," Lenora says, regret making her voice heavy. "That wasn't kind. Let me take another look at your work, treasured one."

I can tell by the way her skin pinks up in a wave that she means well—but the endearment rubs me the wrong way. It reminds me why I'm allowed to exist. I'm the treasured relic of a humanity that used to fill the planet as common as dirt. Then the Singularity came along, and the vast majority of people ascended, or died trying. The eighty percent who survived managed to accelerate the evolution of the human race by changing irrevocably into something else. Something *better*.

Only there were some who refused the gift of a nanotech-enhanced brain: artists, philosophers, religious men and women of all stripes. Creative types who feared the loss of that creativity, not realizing ascenders were better even at that. The dissenters opted out. But they didn't just doom *themselves* to a life of inferiority—they doomed every generation to come after. Because you can't have an endless supply of humans, breeding like rats, continuing to ascend, and growing the immortal population forever. So it wasn't long after the Singularity that the dissenters lost their right to choose.

I've cursed my great-grandfather for that more than once.

Now I'm his legacy: preserved for the pure, unadulterated genetic code in my cells. The ascenders kept humanity from going extinct, just like the revived rainforests I render in paint and pixels. They care for us, feed us, and treasure us. We are their origins. The only problem with being part of a living genetic museum is that you're not allowed to change.

But it keeps me alive. Which, generally speaking, is better than the alternative.

I take a deep breath, swallow my pride, and hold up the painting for Lenora's inspection. She's my patron; I'm not supposed to sell my works without her permission. ArtNet's one of the few legacy marketplaces ascenders visit, but there's no reason for an ascender like Lenora to slum there. The real art markets are on Orion... which is inaccessible without a patron. She says I'm not ready for that, but maybe she wouldn't mind if I sold a few things on ArtNet in the meantime.

I take the risk. "I know it's not great, but what do you think? Could it fetch a few chits on ArtNet? Some other ascender might not have as discerning taste as you." I hope that doesn't sound too bitter.

"Don't be absurd, Elijah." She takes the painting from me before I realize what she's doing.

I try to decide if I should put up a fight.

She regards it again. "I love all your work." She looks at me. "Each is a small part of you, and I cherish them all, just like you, treasured one."

The pet name again. I bite back the words that want to leap out: *Don't treat me like a child. Or worse, a...* I don't even want to think the word.

I smile instead.

She gets that momentary flickered look, where she flutters her eyelids, and I know she's consulting Orion. Of course, she's always in contact with the collective knowledge net—I only notice the flicker because I've studied her a lot. *Study* probably isn't the right word: I can fill sketchbooks with drawings of her bodyforms from memory. The flutter means she's checking in with the collective in a conscious way, opening herself up to them and them to her. She's described it before as a communion, but not in the religious sense: believing in a higher power is one of the endearing flaws of legacy humans. Ascenders tolerate it, with airy disapproval, like all our flaws. Most of the time.

The moment is past. "Consensus is that a work like this, original art from a treasured one, especially the representational irony of preservation rendered by a legacy artist, would command about a hundred chits on Orion." Her expression softens, as her iridescent purple eyes focus on me. She's altered them to a shade darker than her feather. "Would that be a fair price, Elijah?"

I blink, confused. That's way more than it would fetch on ArtNet. Like ten times more. "So, you're all right with me selling it?"

"I will buy it from you."

"Um…" I've missed something, but I'm not sure what. "You already own it."

"You would not be looking to sell it, if you didn't need the money." Her voice is soft with compassion. "And I can't bear to part with any of your works. It seems a fair exchange. Do you agree?"

Embarrassment flames my face, but I can't afford to say no. "Yes."

She rewards me with a dazzling smile that sweeps away my embarrassment. "Good! I've already transferred the untraceable chits to your account."

Untraceable. She's already figured out the money's going toward something illegal. And yet she's breaking the law, no questions asked, all because it's what I need and she wants to keep my art. She's always been generous, always given me exactly what I need, effortlessly and with grace, but this… I don't have words for this thing she's doing for me. I don't believe in angels, but if I did, Lenora would have to qualify.

I am so hopelessly lost when it comes to her.

I concentrate on handing the painting to her, resisting the almost overwhelming urge to touch her. Hug her. Make some excuse to get closer. It shames me to want something from her that no decent ascender would give. A pet can kiss its master, but the master won't kiss back. Not the way I want her to. Lenora is buying my art because she's kind and decent… and all my base human brain can think of is putting my hands on her.

And how soft her ascender lips would feel.

"Thank you." My words are hushed. There's shame in my eyes, so I drop my gaze to the floor.

She takes the painting then whisper-walks with ascender speed past me. She's gone before I can look up. When I turn, my painting sits on the easel. A half second later, a soft sound, one I can actually hear, announces there's someone at the front door of her house.

That's probably my cue to leave. Maybe I can find my dignity before I go.

I take my time strolling from the studio to the gathering room. Maybe I can steal a few more minutes of Lenora's time when she's done at the door—I'm due for another lesson anyway. The curved walls of the gathering room swoop up to an arched ceiling, which always confuses my human eyes. I'm sure it's pleasing to ascenders—every part of Lenora's house is a work of art. There's no bathroom or kitchen, which keeps my visits short, but the entire building is an inspired mating of form and function. Like the energy port in the gathering room that appears to be an electric flower. Or the chrome chair in the net room that's the shape of a Mobius strip but actually serves as a holographic portal. I saw Lenora using it once—I had arrived early for our lesson, and she was still bathed in its blue glow.

There's a bedroom in the back somewhere. According to the legacy net, ascenders use them for maintenance, down time, and vacations. I've never seen it. Probably never will.

I cruise slowly through the gathering room, keeping

my distance from the household bot gliding along the two-story-tall window. It's not humanoid, just one of the non-sentient kinds. It cycles the window through a cleaning mode, flinging off any offending dust particles that dare to alight. The whir of the bot's air filters masks my footfalls, but it still detects me as I pass. I don't move fast enough, so it queries me.

"Can I get you a refreshment, sir?" The bot knows I'm human, so it doesn't try to transmit messages to me, but Lenora told it to treat me like an ascender. Which means I can ignore it. I pick up my pace, careening around the corner to the front door, only to pull up short when I see who's there.

Another ascender. And Lenora. And they're...

I drop my gaze to the glistening steel floor under my feet. I didn't know Lenora had taken a second. Most ascenders pair, of course—some forever, some just until they find someone more compatible. I would have realized Lenora had an ascender lover, if I'd thought about it for more than two seconds.

I'd never let myself think about it for more than one.

Now I'm frozen, awkward, while they embrace in the doorway.

I peek up. They're still hand-to-face, absorbed in each other. They haven't noticed me yet... which means they're engaged in something a lot deeper than just *hello*. I cringe as a swirl of color dances over his skin and flows into hers where they touch. Ascenders are hooked on all kinds of sensory input to begin with—as far as I can tell, they're outright sensation junkies—but when they're physically connected to each other… well, I'm not exactly sure what they're doing, but Lenora's reaction is enough to make my skin heat.

As I watch, Lenora's second lazily opens his eyes and trains them on me.

I give a start as I realize I'm caught. My eyes automatically avert again, but the only way out is through the door. The one they're standing in front of.

I grit my teeth.

It takes ten interminable strides, but by the time I reach them, he's released her. I'm sure Lenora's second is attractive for a male—all the bodyforms are. He has the classic, rugged kind, the one that projects a physical prowess that's almost laughable given the strength their bodyforms naturally possess. He strikes me as all wrong for her. Shoulders too large. Face too pretty. Eyes too cold with the way he's giving me a look that could freeze steam midair.

Or maybe that's the look I'm giving him.

"Oh," Lenora says. Her voice is thick, like whatever haze he's induced in her is still buzzing. "Elijah."

My stomach curls into a knot that makes me want to punch something.

"I'm just leaving," I say, looking at him, not her.

His amused annoyance makes it clear I'm one step up from the household bot.

"Marcus, this is my artist-in-residence, Elijah." Lenora's voice has lost its tremble.

I give him a nod. He ignores me and returns his attention to Lenora, lifting a hand back to hold her cheek.

It's clear from the way he's looking in her eyes, his facial expression: he's transmitting something to her. Talking to her, ignoring me.

I manage not to snarl. "I'll work on a new piece, starting tomorrow," I say to her.

She nods absently, absorbed in whatever he's saying. He pulls her closer, re-engaging in their embrace. It leaves enough of the doorway clear that I can slip out. Which I do as quickly as I can.

Turns out, I left my dignity behind after all.

TWO

I jam my boot into the door of the tram to keep it from closing.

It screeches but lets me board. I leave the rusted-out platform behind, but my face is still hot from the encounter with Lenora and her second.

I stalk down the aisle between the rotted seats. This is a *legacy-only* tram—just stepping inside means trading the pristine world of household bots chasing dust particles for the grimy world of what's left of humanity. The car is empty except for a girl with bedraggled hair in front and a twitchy guy in the farthest seat back. The girl's eyes are wide—she can't be more than fourteen—and she quickly ducks her head, avoiding my anger-filled gaze.

I sigh. She probably thinks I'm storming down from a high. A lot of legacies bliss out on whatever makes them forget they're the hairy ape evolution passed by... and they're no fun to be around when they're coming down. The police bots keep everyone from killing each other—most of the time—but there's still a lot of humanity that fails to be even close to human. Their redeeming quality is their DNA, not their behavior.

The girl really shouldn't be traveling alone.

I smile at her, but she keeps her head down, hunched over a weathered brown satchel that looks rough enough to be gray market trade. She probably bartered another legacy for it or traded her chit-allowance. Definitely not bot-made, in any case. She's clutching it like I might steal it straight out of her trembling arms. I stride past and take a seat far enough away to not seem like a threat.

I wonder which dingy Orion-sponsored housing complex she lives in: some are tougher than others. Legacy cities may not be much, but they've got nothing on the barbarism of Oregon's dissenter reservations. The holograms I've seen are pretty horrific: roving bands of crusaders, cult camps, and no police bots to stop the bloodshed. Seattle may have its share of human dreck, but at least the life expectancy is more than thirty.

Rain drizzles down the windows as the tram lumbers along the line. By now, Lenora's glass ceiling must be flecked with a thousand tiny puddles haunting her from above. Ascenders have an aversion to water of any kind. Not that there's any danger of frying or browning out. Some bodyforms are even built to swim. The net says it's more of an instinctual thing. A voice buried somewhere in the depths of their artificial cortexes whispers, *rain is dangerous*. Like the human fear of the dark—even though it's not the dark that kills you, but the things hiding in it. Maybe Lenora's gone to the net room and buried herself in the cognitive physics studies that take up her time when she's not making mystical landscapes with holo paint.

Or maybe she's in the bedroom with her second.

I glower at the seat in front of me: it has a crack with the padding bleeding out. It's not the kind of thing that will get repaired. The ascenders give us just enough of everything to stay alive—minimal food, adequate shelter, and all the free virtual reality simulations you could want. The upkeep on a legacy-only tram doesn't figure in the top million things important to them. I'm sure whatever Lenora and her second are doing, I'm just as long forgotten.

I'm so absorbed in my thoughts, I almost miss it when the twitchy guy lurches past me. He's holding the seats as he goes, whipping his head back and forth. A jolt of alarm rips me out of my fixation on the seat: *he's a reality-freak*. The side-to-side thing… either he's really admiring the scenery or he's trying to trigger a refresh on his virtual. Only the guy isn't hooked up—which means he's lost his totem, and he still thinks reality will bend to his wishes.

He pauses at the girl's row and scowls.

I'm up out of my seat before I can think. If he believes he's still in virtual, who knows what he'll try. The girl is trying to melt into the side of the tram, holding her flimsy satchel like a shield. I surge forward and catch the guy just as he goes for her. I shove him hard, and he goes down, catching his jaw on the edge of the seat. He's stunned enough that he stays down.

"Come on." I gesture the girl out of the seat. My stop is coming anyway.

She shakes her head.

"Do you want to stay here?" I ask, giving a pointed jab of my thumb to the downed reality-freak.

She shakes her head again, but it's more of a quiver. Then she edges across the row. I help her up, but she jerks back from me. The freak is up on his hands and knees.

I hoist him up by the arm. "Sorry, man. Didn't see you there. Why don't you have a seat?" I shove him into the row next to us, rough enough that he stays. He looks up at me, dazed, then goes back shaking his head.

Great.

I hustle the girl past him. We make it to the exit just as the tram stops. The rain holds its breath as we spill onto a street darkened with it. The girl's in such a hurry to get away that she trips and splays out on the pavement. I don't know where she thinks she's going—this is *my* stop, not hers, and there's nothing here but business more dangerous than the reality-freak. As she pulls her satchel from a puddle, it spews out a couple dozen paint brushes, all different sizes and bristles. Lots of legacies do creative work, but that's way too many for her own use. I bend down to help her, but her soft brown eyes squint with suspicion.

I back off and stand up just as the tram pulls away. It floats her hair into her face. She blindly gropes for the rain-soaked brushes. I don't need any new brushes—Lenora provides me with everything I need—but my mom could use a few. And I just earned a hundred chits I wasn't expecting.

"I don't suppose those brushes are for sale?" I ask.

She swipes the hair out of her face and examines me with an eye that would do a grizzled gray-market trader proud. Then she gives me a short nod.

"How much?" I appraise them, but it doesn't matter. I'll get some no matter what.

"Half a chit." Then she adds quickly, "But they're all real sable!"

"Is that right?" Half a chit is a lot for synthetics, but a real-fiber brush is worth more than a month of allotment chits. I own a few, but only because Lenora bought them. If the girl actually had sable brushes, she wouldn't be selling them for half a chit.

"Unless you need synthetics," she adds more quietly, ducking her head. "I've got those, too."

"I'll take those two." I point to the fan brush in her hand and a dagger-tipped one still in the puddle. My mom will love them, even if they're not real sable.

The girl hands them over and digs out her phone. I authorize payment with a quick, "Transfer one chit," while it reads my face. The girl beams, staring at her phone as the chit goes through. I stuff the brushes, handle down, in my back pocket.

The next tram trundles toward us in the distance. The gray blanket that hangs overhead threatens to drop wet misery on us again, but the tram will be here in less than a minute.

I gesture to the remaining brushes still scattered on the ground. "Are you okay?"

She gives me a shy nod and hurries to pick up the rest.

I wait until I can see the tram is empty, then I smile my goodbye. The girl keeps ducking her head, but I get a small glimpse of a smile. I make it to the overhang of the nearest building just before the skies loosen. I stick to the shelter of the abandoned storefronts as I stride away.

All the buildings in this part of town are supposed to be empty—abandoned by legacies and ascenders alike. I can't decide if that's ironic or fitting: Seattle was ground zero for the Singularity a hundred years ago, not that you could tell now. Shadows lurk in the corners of the boarded windows, all carefully calculated to mask the lively black market inside. The Orion-sanctioned gray markets are all within the city. Most ascenders long ago moved away to sunnier places, and the few who stayed behind live at the outer rim. That leaves a dead zone in the middle. Perfect for black market trades, intentionally or not. And with the ascenders, you never know. They could have some advanced-brain-level reason for allowing the black market to exist even while pretending it doesn't. Figuring them out is beyond me.

I hurry down the street. A half mile later, I reach a door that's the same as all the others. I slide back a panel and let the camera read my face.

"Sun Tzu," I say to it, hoping I get the pronunciation right. Cyrus always picks the most unpronounceable passcodes. The door clicks unlocked. The screech of the hinges echoes down the street, and I hope there's not a police bot within hearing range. I slip inside.

The cramped shop is a cross between a tech wonderland and biohack exhibit. Cyrus tells me it was once a shoe store, but now it mostly looks like a junkyard of the illicit and bizarre.

"Eli, my man! I didn't expect you until later." Cyrus doesn't own the place, he just acts like it. He's big in a muscular way, and a good three inches taller than me—both of which might be intimidating, if he wasn't practically family. His parents were murdered for chits in the complex he grew up in, and he's been a pain in my side, and my best friend, ever since he moved in with his grandfather next door. When the old man passed, Cyrus became the older brother who beat on anyone who pushed me around. And there was no lack of that in our childhood.

Cyrus is standing behind the glass display case, holding some hardware. He gives it over to Riley, the actual owner, who raises a leathery hand to wave. Riley's been in the black market trades more years than I've been on the planet.

"Hey, Riley," I say. "How's business?"

"I'm still here, ain't I?" He shakes his head, like that's the stupidest possible question. Riley's tech takes the shop off the normal surveillance grid, but that's no guarantee someone won't leak his operation. "No thanks to you," he adds, giving me a dirty look.

I know how much trouble I bring into his shop, so I just nod.

Cyrus strides around the end of the glass counter case. It's littered with implants, some subdermal and simple, like phones and vision enhancers, some more serious mods, like a heart and a slimy thing that looks like a liver.

All of them are Class One felonies waiting to happen. But they're nothing compared to my black market meds. If the ascenders had any idea Riley was trafficking in genetic drugs, we'd all be exiled from Seattle. If we were lucky. The ascenders don't normally practice capital punishment for the legacy dreck in their cities, but "putting down" a dangerous human isn't unheard of.

"Hey Cyrus," I say as he approaches, glad for the distraction from Riley's glare.

Cyrus is giving me a disappointed look. "Man, where's your painting? I can't fence something without the goods, you know?"

"I sold it." The last thing I want is to say *who* I sold it to—I'll never hear the end of it.

"Sold it?" He looks hurt. "To who?"

"I'm sorry, Cyrus. I'll give you your commission, I promise."

He waves that away. "I don't care about… wait." He cocks his head to the side and examines me like I'm a refurbished implant someone's trying to foist on him. "You didn't… you gave it to her, didn't you?"

"I didn't *give* it to anyone." I should just come clean now. He'll drag it out of me eventually.

"You *did*," Cyrus says like I just admitted to it. "You gave your hot patron your painting. Man, what am I going to do with you?"

"I didn't give it to her!"

He shakes his head then slides his arm around my shoulder, holding me in a classic one-arm Cyrus-giving-advice hug. I'm tempted to shove him away, but it'll be over faster if I don't.

Riley ignores us and flips through a tiny screen he's pulled from his pocket, but Cyrus still drops his voice. "You gotta get over this thing with your patron. It's just sick, man. You need to get yourself a real girl, the all-human kind. One that's soft in all the right places, you know?"

The sensation of Lenora's faux red hair brushing my face comes rushing back. "She's soft," I whisper before I can pull the words back in my mouth.

Cyrus looks horrified. "You know that for a fact?"

"No." I shrug his arm off and push him away. "I'm not a wonder hack like you, but I read the net. I know basic tech. Their bodyforms are just as pliable as—"

"Eli!" He throws out his hands. "She's an *ascender*. You're *legacy*. I know—" He stops, sighs, and lowers his voice. "I know you want to be her second, man, but it's not going to happen. It doesn't happen. Ever. With anyone. You'll never be anything more than... than her *domestic*. And that's no good, bro."

A *domestic*. A human pet. Useful for companionship... and less noble purposes. It's one of the few things that legacy law prohibits. I don't know if the ascenders have laws against it, but the only thing that's worse in the legacy world is to interbreed.

I glare at Cyrus. "Remind me again why you're my friend."

He gives me a pleading look. "Because I'm the one who's going to finally get you a *real* date."

I blow out my anger in a long sigh. I know Cyrus is

just looking out for me, but he hates the ascenders. I get it: he has a talent for tech in a world where all the best tech is banned, and the only legal trade open to legacies is handicrafts like the girl's brushes. There's a reason Cyrus is in the black market, not the gray one.

I roll my eyes at him rather dramatically. "I think you date enough girls for the both of us, Cy."

He puts a hand on my shoulder. "And that's something that is supremely sad. A tragedy. A travesty against the brotherhood of teenage guys everywhere." He straightens, full of mock outrage. "Who am I? A tech-head. No better than a bot, except I have a keener sense of style. You, on the other hand…" He gestures to my clothes, which consist of black work pants flecked with paint and a shirt that's starting to fray at the edges. "Look at you! You've got that downbeat, artsy look going all day long. You're moody. And you flipping *paint*, man. You're a *creative*. Girls lose their minds for that stuff, and you just waste it. You're killing me."

I can't help the grin. "I can get you a really good deal on a paint-spattered shirt."

He covers his face with his hands. Behind them, he mutters, "I weep for what's left of humanity."

I have to bite back a laugh.

He drops his hands. "So tell me the truth, bro. Did you sell it? Because I've got the meds if you've got the cash. You know I'd lay down my life for your mom, but I can't front the money for this on my own."

And that's the real reason I put up with Cyrus—not just because he can get my mom the meds she needs, but because Cyrus *would* do anything for her. And she loves him like a son.

"No, no. I've got the money." I pause a beat. "Lenora bought the painting. A hundred chits." I grit my teeth, waiting for the backlash.

It doesn't come.

Instead, Cyrus's eyebrows slowly inch up his forehead. "A hundred chits?" He draws out the words. "Are you sure you didn't do something for her other than... *paint?*"

I hit him. Not hard. Just a punch to the shoulder. It bothers me that it happened without me even thinking about it. He cringes under the blow, hand clamped over the spot. But he's laughing. Shoulders heaving with silent hilarity.

Tears are forming in his eyes. "Okay. Okay. Oh man... you are so messed up."

"Do you have the meds?" I'm considering the possibility of disowning Cyrus. Or strangling him.

"I told you I do." He limps with exaggerated injury back to the counter where Riley is still ignoring us. Cyrus pulls out a black case the size of a small paintbrush tote, sets it on the counter, and pops the lid. A mist of condensation floats up and drips down the side. Inside is a single syringe, frosted with the coolness of the case.

"The guy said this should be tailored to that sample of your mom's DNA," Cyrus says. "He mentioned something about nanite vectors and B-cells, but gen tech isn't my specialty. Honestly, I'm not at all sure about the tech on this, Eli. But he says it's relatively safe, and it will eat that strange brand of leukemia your mom has."

"That's what he said the last time." I peer into the box. The syringe contains a whitish liquid that will soon be injected in my mom.

"It's experimental, Eli. There are no guarantees." Cyrus sounds pained when he says it.

"I know." And like that, I've forgiven him. It's a huge risk for him to even get this stuff for me. I don't know where it comes from, and I don't want to. Not knowing allows whoever's doing the genetic engineering to stay hidden from Orion. The ascender laws restrict legacies from all kinds of adaptive technology. We're living relics. Our purpose on the planet would be literally snuffed out if we polluted the "genetically pure" strain of our humanity with *any* kind of internal technology, but gen tech is the worst offense.

At least that's the excuse they give for letting my mom die from a disease they could cure if they wanted to.

"It's eighty chits, Eli," Cyrus says softly, like he's not sure I really have the money.

I smile. "Not a problem."

He looks uncertain, but he raises his payscanner to process my picture anyway. "Transfer eighty chits," I say into it. The look on his face says that it went through. He nods.

The presence of actual chit-transactions in the room draws Riley's attention.

"Hey, kid," he says, rubbing the graying bristles on his face. "You should bring more of those paintings around. I can get you some good prices on them."

I nod. "Thanks, Riley. I'll think about it." He's right. I

should get busy on some more works, in case this treatment doesn't pay off. The last one gave my mom a low grade fever for a few days, but that was it. And if Lenora will buy more of my stuff, I'll have as much money as we need to keep trying until we find one that works.

Riley leans his elbows on the counter. "Cyrus showed me your stuff. You've got some talent, kid."

I lean back, not sure where this is headed. "He did?"

"Yeah." He taps his handheld screen and brings up something. "I saved the picture, just cause I liked it. Seemed like something special."

He turns it to me, and I feel the blood drain out of my face. It's a painting of a boy puppet drawn up on strings suspended in the air... and it's mine. One of my fugue works, the kind I can never create when I'm conscious. This one convinced Lenora to become my patron—she thinks I have a secret genius that I need to bring out, but it's just the madness of the fugue. And if she knew that, she'd drop me. There are dozens of legacy artists in Seattle, all vying for a patron. She doesn't need a crazy one. The puppet boy stares at me from Riley's phone, like the fugue is mocking me with how little control I have over it.

I shoot a glare at Cyrus, and he's got a worried look on his face. He only saw it briefly. I didn't even know he took a picture of it, much less shared it with his boss.

"Eli..." Cyrus says apologetically, but Riley cuts him off.

"No, it's really good," Riley insists. "I mean, I don't

know art or anything, but it seems like… I don't know. It makes me sad and yet kind of happy." He gives a little chuckle. "Like I said, I don't know art. But I watch the Olympics on the net. You could compete in the art division with something like this. Get that patron of yours to send you. It's coming up again, isn't it?"

My face heats instantly. Because the Olympics are right around the corner, and the last thing I need is Riley wondering why I haven't done exactly that.

He doesn't seem to notice. "That'd solve all your problems, right? I mean, with your mom sick and all—"

I can't speak. My words are choking on a rising volcano of anger.

Cyrus hastily snaps the lid down on the meds and rushes around the counter to grab my arm. "Come on, Eli." He tugs me away from Riley, who's lifted his hands in confusion.

"What?" Riley asks. "I'm just saying—"

"Yeah, we know," Cyrus cuts him off. "The Olympics are *fantastic*."

My mouth is flopping, but no words are coming out. I let Cyrus pull me backward toward the door.

"Let's go take this to your mom," he says quietly to me.

I close my mouth and turn to shove open the door.

The rain pelts my face, hitting like ice and turning to steam.

"Eli, I'm sorry—"

"You *showed* him." The betrayal is roiling through my chest. Lenora and my mother both have seen my fugue works, but they don't know how they're made. That I black out. Cyrus is the only one I've ever told... and only because he found me passed out after making the *Puppet Boy*. But he should have known better than to show it off.

Once people see it, they'll wonder why I don't make fugue art day in and day out. Why I didn't try for the Olympics. And with my mom sick... they would do exactly the math Riley just did and wonder what secret I'm keeping. Eventually someone would find out about the blackouts. And that would get back to Lenora... and then I would be done. With her. With art. With everything that makes life worth living.

I don't look at Cy as I stalk toward the tram line. I gain speed as the steam inside me gains pressure.

"I didn't know he'd... Eli, wait up!" Cyrus jogs to catch up to me.

The rain paints my face. Anger seethes through me. At Cyrus. At Riley for so blithely suggesting I could save my mom with my art. At the ascenders who refuse to cure her.

The truth is, if I could just master this insane ability that sits at the edges of my fingertips, unreachable, I could have it all. I could take my art to the Olympics. I could win—I *would* win. I know it. Like every legacy and ascender on the planet, I've watched the games. I know what it takes to win. A fugue painting would get me the gold. And the winners of the Olympics get the one prize that means anything in our world: *ascendance*. Not just for them, but their family as well. The ascenders would take my mom, strip the genetic disease out of her body, and we would both get the procedure. We would become ascenders... and live forever.

Only we won't. We'll never have any of it.

All because I can't paint worth a damn when I'm actually awake.

I punch the door of the tram before it has time to open.

THREE

I cradle my aching hand against my chest and stare out the tram window.

My rage has simmered to surliness, but Cyrus still keeps to the far side of the car. My clothes are damp, sticking to me from the humid mid-morning drizzle and adding to the misery. We don't speak as the car lumbers toward downtown.

Taking my frustration out on the tram door didn't change anything but the color of my swollen knuckles. No matter how much I rage, all of it—the fugue, Lenora, the Olympics—is just as out of reach as before. And none of it is Cyrus's fault. In fact, without him, I wouldn't have the one thing that matters: hope for my mom.

By the time we reach the city, the anger has leached out of me. Our tram stop is a ramshackle station that barely keeps out the rain. Holes have been punched in the skylights by age and winter ice. Cyrus follows me with the box that might contain a cure for my mom. That's what I really need—all the rest are just distractions.

Cyrus stops me at the entrance to our apartment building. My mom and I live on the fifth floor, but Cyrus spends as much time there as he does in his own apartment across the hall.

His face is scored with worry. "Eli, I really am sorry about—"

"You know what? Forget it, Cy." I breathe out the residual traces of my anger. "I shouldn't have gone off on you. It just gets to me sometimes."

Cyrus nods, ducking his head then looking up. "Truce?" He tilts his head toward the apartment upstairs. "I don't want to go in there all pissed at each other, you know? Your mom doesn't need to see that."

"Yeah, I know. Besides, I might need your help someday. In case I need a date."

"Might?" he asks incredulously. "You would be hopeless and pathetic without me."

I shake my head. "Come on."

The building bot reads my face and lets us in. The lift is working again, so we save our breath and take it up. I scan open the door to our apartment, but I don't get two steps inside before I stop in my tracks. I hear voices from the back room. My mom's room.

Cyrus nudges me from behind. "Art man! You're blocking the door."

I narrow my eyes. "There's someone here."

He frowns. "You expecting company?"

I shake my head and stride toward the back. I'm nearly up to a full run by the time I reach my mom's bedroom and pivot inside, one hand on the door frame.

There are two men standing on either side of her, hands on her shoulders and head, eyes closed, whispering. The only thing that stops me from launching myself at them is the gentle smile on my mom's face. I grip the door frame and yank myself to a stop. The squeak of my shoes on the wood floor makes my mom's eyes slide open.

She blinks, like she's trying to process why I'm gaping at her from the doorway. The men are still speaking, their words floating across the room.

"...forgive you your sins and lead you to everlasting life."

That's when I figure out who they are: *Christians*.

My shoulders slump just as Cyrus appears at my back, holding the box. His eyes go wide. If there's something worse than bringing illegal gen tech into the apartment, it's bringing in religious people. The last thing we need is someone ratting out my mom for running an illegal church in legacy housing. The ascenders tolerate individual faith—legacies can believe whatever they like, and ascenders have a keen appreciation for individuality—but organized worship is a banishing offense. The purges after the Singularity decimated most religious institutions anyway, but by the time the legacy cities were formed, the ascenders made it clear: if the remnants of humanity wanted to live in some semblance of civilization, they had to play by the ascenders' rules. That's how the dissenter reservations got their start, but that's no place for us. Even if the living conditions weren't horrific, we need to be in Seattle, where there's a decent black market—I can't get the meds my mom needs in Oregon.

Cyrus's sucked-in breath draws the attention of the two men. One is Asian, the other a light-skinned Latino, but they both have the kind of peaceful look that's quickly fading from my mom's face.

"Come on in, Elijah." Her voice rasps with fatigue.

"You shouldn't be out of bed, Mom." I say this because I can't say, *What are you thinking, bringing Christians into the apartment?* It's bad enough she has a shrine with all kinds of icons and dying saints in the corner of her bedroom. Gathering together with other believers is flat dangerous. And she knows it.

She waves me off, but it makes her teeter. The men shift their hands to support her.

"I can't rest *all* the time," she says. "Besides, these fine young men brought me something I need even more." Her voice weakens as she speaks.

I want to go to her, but I'm rooted in my spot, angry that she would take this risk right when I'm trying so hard to get a cure for her. Cyrus goes to her instead, slipping through the doorway and past me.

"Hey, Mrs. Brighton," he says cheerily, dropping a kiss on her cheek and nudging his way in between her and the men. He takes her by the elbow and gently leads her away from her religious partners-in-crime. "How are you feeling today?"

"I'm fine, Cyrus." She says it like a protest to his help, but she lets him escort her to the rumpled bed in the corner. "I'll sit, but you two have to let us finish up here.

We're almost done, and I don't want these boys to have wasted their time."

The "boys" are both mid-thirties. They're not quite old enough to be my father, but I'd rather have my mom dating younger guys than praying with them. Not that she's ever dated… with the exception of my father, who doesn't count. He was gone before I was born, and she refuses to speak of him—no pictures, no stories, no lineage maps to show our Legacy Descendent line. I didn't realize there was something wrong with that until some kid on the playground called me an *inbred,* and I punched him in the nose. I was only seven, but I already knew that was the worst kind of insult, and there was no way my mom did that. The only decent explanation for no paternity records was that my father was a dissenter. Which still made him a piece of work: stealing into a legacy city to knock up my mother then disappearing again.

I don't blame her for not having much interest in guys since.

Except now… when she's bringing them into the house to pray.

The two men are still standing where they were, whispering to each other, clearly as awkward with the situation as I am.

I edge my way into the room, finally. "Mom, we have some medicine for you—"

Her fingers slice the air and cut me off. "When we're finished, Elijah."

I purse my lips. Cyrus backs away from her bed,

having helped her ease into sitting on the edge. I can't believe she's insisting on ancient religious rites when I have actual medicine for her. I tell myself it's the disease: she's been too frail for too long. It's taking a toll on her, and she's reaching for the religious stuff like it's a lifeline. But it's not: the only thing that's going to cure her is the gen tech. And that's if we can find a therapy that will actually work before it's too late. My stomach twists... because my greatest fear is that it's already too late. One look at her tells the story: the disease is ravaging her voice, hollowing out her eyes, and stealing the delicate beauty she's had all my life. I remember being frustrated as a child that I didn't have the skills to render my mother's beauty in paint. Now, just as I'm starting to become somewhat competent in my art, the disease is slowly destroying her. I suddenly know my next painting will be of her, full of the life that's being drained from her body.

The Asian man approaches her with a small gold-colored tin. He opens it and pulls out a wafer. I recognize it from the stash she has in her shrine. She was always a believer, but the crazy religious stuff didn't start until she got sick, almost two years ago now. We've been through treatment after treatment, with me getting more desperate with each failed attempt and her gaining new icons each time. But I didn't realize she'd taken it up a level—a dangerous, illegal level—to having people gather in the apartment. Which makes me wonder how long they've been coming around when I'm not home.

One of the men holds up the wafer to her. "See the

Lamb of God, who takes away the sins of the world."

"Lord," my mom replies, "I am not worthy that you should come under my roof, but only say the word, and my soul will be healed."

"The body of our Lord Jesus Christ." He places the wafer in her hand, and she lifts it to her mouth. I shift from one foot to the other and glance at Cyrus. He's frowning deeply. I nervously check the window. It would be just my luck to have a police bot hover by.

The man hands her the gold tin, and it appears they're done. I sigh with relief as the men say their goodbyes to my mother and make their exit with tight smiles.

I kneel by her side while Cyrus sets the med box on her nightstand. He'll have to do the injection; he always gets the instructions from his supplier about how to administer it, but that's not why. I couldn't poke a needle in my mother if my life depended on it. My hands would shake, there would be crying—mostly mine—and half the life-saving meds would end up on the floor. It would be a disaster for both of us.

"Mom," I say, looking up into her watery blue eyes. "Cyrus has a new medicine. His guy says it's the latest gen tech, tuned to your DNA. Best stuff available. It's going to make you feel better." I'm not sure if I'm trying to convince her or me.

"Oh, baby." She puts a cool, too-thin hand on my cheek. "I'm going to die. You need to make your peace with it. I have." She leans backward, easing into the super soft pillow like it's a sharply carved rock.

I close my eyes, briefly. *Please, no. Please don't fight me on this*. I hear Cyrus's feet shuffle away, backing up to give us room.

I open my eyes again, looking hard into my mom's weary face. "You're *not* going to die. Not while I have anything to do with it." I fight the tears because I know they won't help. My mother is a passionate painter in her own right and clings to an ancient religion that I don't understand, but she's not sentimental. If I cry, she'll just comfort me, like I'm a child. She'll be strong. She'll tell me she loves me, and then I'll fall apart.

We've done this before.

But none of that will convince her to let Cyrus inject her with the meds.

"You have to get better," I say, forcing a calm in my voice that I don't feel. "You can't quit now, because I still need you. My art is apparently weak and uninspired, and you're the only one who can give me a half-decent critique and help me improve."

"Did Lenora say that?" She frowns, half-angry. That's what I want. I need her to fight.

"You know how they are," I say, knowing she doesn't. She's never met Lenora. Or any ascender, as far as I know. "Arrogant. Think they know better than us, even in the arts. *Especially* in the arts. Sometimes I wonder why she even took me on. And I haven't produced anything like the *Puppet Boy* since she became my patron. I'm not going to keep my position if I keep disappointing her."

Lies. All of it. But I know it will piss her off. The only person who loathes ascenders more than Cyrus is my mom. She makes an exception for Lenora, but only because she keeps me stocked with canvases and paint.

"That's absurd," she says, half sitting up again. "She's your patron. She should know that it takes time. You need more time."

"I know, but—"

"No buts!" Her thin shoulders are starting to shake. "She made a promise when she took you on. She *has* to keep supporting you. That's what being a patron means! She can't just abandon you in the middle, right where you're starting to come into your own. You're at a critical stage, Elijah. You're just beginning to reach your potential—"

She's getting too upset now. I put a hand on her arm, to slow her down. "She hasn't said anything like that yet."

"But she *promised,*" my mom insists. Her voice is shaky but a little calmer. "How are you supposed to afford your supplies on Orion's chit allowance?"

"Exactly," I say quickly, before she can ramp up again. "So, here's the deal. This medicine Cyrus brought will help you. It's not a cure, but it will at least help you fight it off for a little longer." More lies. I'm desperate for this to finally be an actual cure. "And I need your help right now, to keep my position with Lenora, so I need you to stick around as long as possible." The tears are coming again, so I hurry up to finish the pitch. "So just let Cyrus give you the meds, okay? I need this."

That last part is one hundred percent true.

It's always been just the two of us, me and my mom, all the time I was growing up. When Cyrus moved next door, I gained a brother, and she gained a son. But they're all I have. Everything I've learned about art—about *life*—I learned from her. Before the sickness, she was the strongest, most beautiful, most caring person I knew. Even now, she's dealt with all the endless days of her slowly dying body with more patience and stamina than I ever could. All my dreams of ascending and being worthy of Lenora are just that: *fantasy*. Right here, in the grimy reality of Seattle, all I really have is my mom, my best friend, and my art.

I can't let her give up.

I know that's what the icons and the gold tins and the men in her room are really all about: she's ready to die. And I can't let her do that. If I have to tell her lies to keep her fighting, I will. Because *I'm* going to fight for her. Me and Cyrus both. All the way to the end.

She looks in my eyes for a moment, and I have the sense she's seen through every lie to the truth: that I really do need her not to die, not now, not any time soon. She sits up the rest of the way and gives me a nod.

The relief is like a gushing waterfall through my body, and in that moment, I'm sure this time it will work. This is the one. I want to hug her, but I don't want her to change her mind. I grasp her hand instead, give it a gentle squeeze, then move back.

Cyrus swoops in and has the syringe out in no time. "Okay, Mrs. B, you should probably lie back for this. I actually need to give you several small doses. It's going to take a little while, so you might want to get comfortable. Maybe flip on the net? There's a new show called the Secret Life of Household Bots that's so incredibly stupid,

I swear I snorted coffee out my nose when I was watching it last week."

She smiles and lays back, pushing up the sleeve of her shirt and offering him a vein.

I scrap any plans I ever had of strangling Cyrus. I just might kiss him when he's done. In the meantime, I back slowly out of the room, keeping it together until I can reach the hallway.

I make it to my room before I let the silent sobs shake my body.

FOUR

It's been two days, and I haven't left the apartment.

Our grocery allotment has been bot-delivered, and I haven't wanted to leave my mom's side, even to get those pastries she likes from the gray market. I've been either painting or keeping an eye on her. She's always liked to watch me paint, and since I'm painting *her*, it works well. She gives me pointers, and I let her, even though I've mostly outgrown her help these last two years under Lenora's tutelage. But it reminds me of the million other times when my mother and I sat, side by side, her canvas covered in art as beautiful as she was, mine splashed with a childish attempt to keep up.

If nothing else, I'm glad she's seen me come this far.

Most of the time she sleeps, and then her face relaxes into angelic smoothness. I try to capture that innocence on the canvas—I lighten the dark circles under her eyes, keep some of the red flush of her fever, diffuse her face with a soft glow that draws the eye and makes it lift from a background that's swirled with the darkness of her disease.

Sometimes I lose track of time, and when I look over at the bed, she's lying too still. I have to resist waking her, just to make sure she's okay. I watch for the slow rise and fall of her chest, holding my own breath until I'm sure she's still with me. Then I return to creating a healthy version of her that restores the beauty ravaged by her disease.

Acrylics are unforgiving, with a limited amount of time to work before it dries, so I go through a lot of canvases before I get it right. This last piece is as good as I can make. Better than almost anything I've done before, at least while conscious. I walk away from it, afraid I might be tempted to mar it, chasing perfection. I should take it to Lenora, but I spend extra time cleaning my brushes instead, pinning them up to dry next to the new ones I bought from the girl on the tram. Maybe after this treatment, my mom will feel up to painting again. When I'm done stowing my paints, I clean the kitchen, even though we've hardly eaten anything. By the time I'm rearranging the boxes in my mom's closet, I realize I'm stalling.

I step quietly to my mother's bed and touch the back of my fingers lightly to her forehead. She's still feverish, and it's getting worse. Cyrus says that's a good sign. Her immune system is in a furious battle with the leukemia. But all I see is the dampness turning her fine blonde hair dark as her body tries to cool the fires of the fight within. I don't want to leave her, but Lenora is expecting me for our tutoring session. And I have a new painting for her now. I'm not sure if I can bear to give it over... but I'll need the chits for more meds soon. Even if this round works. *Especially* if it works. My mom will need follow-up care to ensure the disease is gone for good.

A soft tone from the front room says Cyrus is here. I tell the building bot to let him in.

I'm still standing by my mom when he quietly shuffles into the bedroom.

He hovers just behind me. For a moment, he's silent. Then he asks, "How's she doing?"

"I don't know if I can go, Cy."

"She'll be fine. Go do your painting thing with your patron. I got this covered."

I turn to him, still uncertain.

"Go on, get out of here." He throws a thumb over his shoulder. "I didn't take the afternoon off to look at your sorry face."

I give him a grim smile and glance at my mom. "Message me if anything changes."

Cyrus doesn't answer, just lifts a chair from the end of the bed and sets it quietly next to the head. He settles into it, waving me out of the room. Not wanting to wake her with any more conversation, I leave.

The tram ride is silent. The clouds brood over downtown, threatening the mostly vacant towers with more rain. I hold the painting of my mom in my lap, isolating it from the vibrations of the tram. The travel case Lenora bought for my mid-sized works probably cost more than two months chit-allowance all by itself. And that's cheap compared to the meds. I'll have to sell this painting of my mom, even though the idea makes my stomach clench. I tell myself I can always paint another one. At least I know Lenora will hold onto it. And at the rates she's willing to pay, I should be able to afford any meds my mom needs.

When I reach Lenora's house, I wind through the lush vegetation that crowds the outside walk. Peeking between the heaping branches of the trees is a commanding view of the Olympic mountains in the distance. The tranquil beauty of it settles into me. I understand why Lenora made her studio almost entirely from glass and set it up in the clouds.

The building bot knows me, so I state my name, and it slides the front door open. I find her in the studio, and for the first time in days, a smile cracks my face.

She's bent over a vase of roses, face buried in the yellow blooms, fingers spread through the petals and stems, each seeking some kind of contact. She's smelling them, sensing them, getting drunk on whatever the myriad sensations are that she can draw out of a simple bunch of flowers. A swirl of pale yellow color seems to leach from the flower petals straight into her fingers, and her whole bodyform is flushing with waves of golden-red. A stray beam of sunlight falls on her arm, sending flashes of sunfire skittering across her skin as it reacts to the heat.

I've never seen anything like it, so I keep quiet and watch.

She has no hair today, no costumes. Her feet are bare, and her normal lightweight shift hangs from her shoulders and hugs her curves—the filmy fabric is standard wear for ascenders. It must have some property that interacts with their skin. Every square inch of their bodyforms absorbs a full spectrum of heat, light, sound, and chemical composition: ascenders taste the world in ways I'll never understand.

I don't see why they bother with clothes at all—they certainly don't need protection or warmth. But I'm glad for the slight nod to modesty—their bodyforms still have all the external body parts of a human, a conceit from the time when they were still flesh and bone. And Lenora's beauty is already more than my human senses can handle. I don't think I would be able to speak coherently if she walked around naked all the time. Not that the sheer fabric hides much—the banquet of colors rippling across her body shines through. Supposedly, the ascenders see more than just the colors. Whatever they see, it must add in some way to how they communicate, on top of the thoughts they can broadcast, bodyform-to-bodyform. I can only guess what she's feeling—whatever it is, it's in no way *bad*, given the look on her face.

She's so immersed, she still hasn't heard me step into the room. Maybe she has her audio inputs dialed down. I decide to test that first, just because sneaking up on an ascender isn't particularly safe.

"Do I even want to know what that feels like?" I ask, loudly, from the door.

She jumps clear to the other side of the studio in one leap. Ascender reactions are so lightning fast that when they're startled, it's like a mini-explosion occurs in their body. The left-behind roses rock hazardously on the table. She zips back, rights them, then finally looks to me.

It's all I can do not to burst out laughing.

"Sorry." The wide smile on her face tinges delightfully with a purple ripple of embarrassment. "I was a little preoccupied."

"I guess." I'm grinning ear to ear.

The ripples of golden-red from her encounter with the vase settle into a more muted glow. She blinks a couple of times, extra slow, like she's still in the thick of the experience. Finally, her gaze finds the painting case hanging from my hand.

"Did you finish a new piece?" The excitement in her voice makes my heart lurch.

I take a breath. "Yes. This one is… well…" I can't put the feeling I have about painting my mom's beauty into words. Especially when the chances are against her ever looking this way again. "It's different." I settle for that.

Lenora steps toward me. "Let me see." It's not quite a command, but it doesn't occur to me not to obey.

I pass my thumb over the sensor lock, and the case opens. I carefully slide the painting out, easing the case to the floor and holding the canvas up for Lenora to see. I watch her face as she takes it in, not sure what I want to see. If she disapproves, she might not buy it from me. I need the chits, but even more… I know it's one of my best works. If Lenora was willing to buy the rainforest piece, she'll have to want this. Only I'm not sure I want to sell it.

She doesn't say anything, just steps closer. My heartbeat kicks up a notch. She passes her fingers over it.

Her movements are so precise she can touch it without disturbing even the finest brush marks. She examines her fingers and whatever microscopic traces are there, as if the depths of the painting can somehow be found in its molecular structure. I wonder if she sees things, meaning and intent, that I can't even see myself.

She's ascended, not magical, I remind myself. Although sometimes I doubt it, with the effect she has on me. And the ascenders are closer to being true gods than the icons in my mother's shrine.

"What I don't understand," she says, finally, "is why you've painted your mother."

My throat closes up. "I wanted to…" The words are like mice scattering before a cat. "I wanted to remember how she looked before." Lenora knows my mother is dying. She has to know the untraceable chits are for illegal meds. But I don't want to voice how desperate I am to keep my mother alive. Lenora's an ascender, and ascender law is what prevents my mom from getting a true cure. Outright rebellious talk risks exile. And an end to those black market meds.

Lenora drops her hands and looks in my eyes. She's standing so close I can smell the faint scent of roses on her. "This one is very precious to you," she says softly.

I swallow. "Yes."

"It's beautiful, Elijah," she says, dropping her intense gaze to the work instead of me. "Your love shines in it. I think it's some of your finest work so far."

I can't speak for a moment. She loves it, which is exactly what I want to hear, but that means she'll keep it, which makes my stomach twist. "Thanks," I manage.

She looks up. "You'll want to keep it, of course."

"I… what?" It's so unexpected, my brain can't process it.

She steps back to admire it further. "Elijah, it's a deeply personal work. I can't possibly take that from you. Even the idea is repellent to me." She holds a delicate-fingered hand out toward the canvas. "There is so much… *potential* locked inside you, Elijah. Do you see what a leap you took here, when you reached deep inside yourself? I can't possibly overstate how important it is for you to focus on that and take it to the highest possible level."

I'm nodding, but inside, I'm squirming with guilt. She sounds like my mother. Even though they've never met, the one thing they've always had in common was a fervor for me to develop my art. Even as my mother is dying, it's the one thing she'll keep fighting for.

"But if I leave it with you, you must promise not to sell it elsewhere." Lenora's eyes are bluish-purple today, and they bore into me. "*Promise* me, Eli."

She called me *Eli*. My mouth hangs open, but I quickly shut it. "I promise."

"I'm your patron precisely so you do not have to worry about these things. I will credit your account with a hundred extra chits for each one of these you create for me. I will only keep the ones you can part with. Just *create* them… that is all I ask."

I nod, mute, mostly because my throat is thick with emotion.

She gives me a small frown. "We don't need to discuss what you use the chits for, Elijah." There's a warning in her voice, but all I hear is my full name again. And I'm disappointed. "That's none of my business. But your art *is* my business. It's more important than... than I think you realize." She hesitates, like she wants to say more, but is holding back.

She has my full attention now. "What do you mean?"

"Just that you're on the verge of something here, a movement forward, and I want you to focus on that as much as possible."

"Okay." There's more she's not sharing.

"In fact, I think we should put aside our lesson today."

My face must show immediate disappointment because she hurries to add, "Oh, we're definitely *painting* today. But I want to turn our focus to this deeper spring you've tapped into. I want you to paint your mother again. For me, this time."

She rushes with ascender speed across the room to the cabinet of supplies and pulls out a canvas easily twice the size of the one I brought. In a blur, she's back at the easel, then she returns to the cabinet for a palette and paints.

I watch her flit back and forth. "I guess we're in a hurry to do this?" She's never been so *animated* when it came time for our lessons.

She freezes in place, two tubes of paint in one hand and half a dozen brushes in the other. "You must seize upon it when it's here, Elijah."

She's talking about the fugue state, even though we've never called it that. She must think I'm finally mastering it, tapping into that potential through my own effort, rather than some kind of random fit. But I know it was really nothing more than an ardent desire to see my mother beautiful again.

I sit at the ridiculously large canvas she's set for me. "This is… quite a lot of real estate." Suddenly, my body shivers even though the studio is warm with baked-in sun. I don't even know where to start with this.

She pulls a stool and sits very close, distracting me further. "I want you to have plenty of room to explore." She sweeps her splayed hand across the face of the blank canvas. "No detail is too small. I want you to dive deep and see what you find there."

I take a breath, pick up the pencil, and hover over the canvas, trying to decide where to begin.

"No," she says, pulling the pencil from my hand. "Paint only."

I look at her, wondering suddenly if it's possible for ascenders to go crazy. Like, actually short circuit their electronic brains. "What?"

She leans closer, looking directly into my eyes. The tiny pixels in her iris shift and contract, darkening the color and dilating her pupil. "Just try, Elijah."

I'm lost in her eyes for a moment before I force myself to turn away. I pretend to carefully choose a brush from the tray, but really I just need some distance from her in order to think coherently. I mix some colors, buying time. She wants a picture of my mother. I just spent days watching her in the throes of her illness and possible cure. Her face is etched in my mind.

I should be able to do this.

I start with the eyes, but they come out dead-looking. Or near death, as if they're peering back through a veil drawn across the afterlife. I try blocking in skin tones instead, forming a rough shape for her face, but it's likewise sickly gray. Next, I layer in some color, but it turns to angry red, a mix of fire and ash. This supposed portrait of my mother is quickly turning into some kind of demon.

"I can fix it." My breaths are becoming shallow.

Lenora doesn't move. Or speak. She's fixated on my work. My hand shakes. I grip the brush harder to quell it and turn away again to avoid her intense gaze.

The front door tones. In a whisper of movement, she's gone. I set down the brush and press my hands to my face, rubbing my eyes and sucking in relief. I don't know how she expects me to do *anything* with her hovering over me like that. I try to clear my mind and focus on this beastly work in front of me. How am I going to make something of this mess? I may have to scrape and start over.

Then a thought drifts through my mind. *Who's at the door?*

As soon as I think it, I know it must be her second. *Marcus.* I'm up and heading toward the front before I realize what I'm doing. I stop and look back to the easel. I should stay here and work. I should ignore the idea that they're probably embracing at the front door again. Not think about why he's here. Not picture the swirl of color that will sweep her skin when she touches him.

Yeah, right.

I use soft footfalls to sneak out of the studio, the brush still in my hand. I find them in the gathering room, and I'm quiet enough that they don't notice me right away. The rush of seeing them *not* touching makes me smile. Although they're having some intense discussion, judging by the flashes of dark blue curling up and down their arms. I can't hear the words they're transmitting between their bodyforms, but whatever they're talking about, it's serious.

Before I can decide if I've seen enough, they both turn at once to stare at me.

I hold up the brush. "Um… not quite sure the direction you want me to take this."

"I'll be a few more minutes, Elijah," she says. "Please continue without me."

Marcus glowers at me. He's barely dressed, the same lightweight shift as Lenora, only the male version leaves his upper body bare. A dark wisp of gray curls across the light beige skin of his chest, and I take it to mean impatience for me to leave. Which, naturally, makes me want to stay. But I can't come up with any plausible excuse.

I give a short nod and slump back to the studio.

The monstrous picture of my mother on the easel is a horrific contrast to the one I painted at home, which leans against the glass nearby. The paint on the new canvas is already drying. I try to mix in some white to lighten it up, but it just brings a chalky pallor to my mother's face.

I'm going to have to start over.

I stomp to the cabinet, grab some rags and acetone, and return to the canvas. I start with too little solvent, so it simply smears. I drench the rag and rub harder. Paint bleeds through the rags. The fumes burn my nose. The color has turned to mud and leached onto my hands. I search for a clean part of the rag to wipe my fingers, but the acetone stings my skin and there's grayish red on everything. In frustration, I throw the paint-laden rag to the floor.

Then I feel it. Like the rush of a train coming behind me, all noise and impending doom. I turn, as if I can actually ward off the fugue by facing into it...

My mother is painting. I can tell it's her by the shape of her head, even though I'm behind her, and the room is blurred with hazy sun. Her blonde hair is longer than it should be, falling in waves down her back. She turns to dip her brush into a palette filled with nothing but blues. Her face is unlined, bright with youth, no dark circles under her eyes. She's radiant with a beauty so bright it hurts my eyes. Her gaze flits over the colors on her palette, choosing and dabbing with a small wiggle in her brush. I would know that movement anywhere. I spent years watching her. Painting with her. Dab. Blend. Wiggle. Just like I remember, but this is too real to be a memory...

I'm on the floor.

I don't remember falling.

A paintbrush lies in my upturned hand, on the steel floor in front of my face. Its blue paint glistens in the sun. Suddenly the floor disappears, and the room spins. Cool arms hold me. With horror, I realize that Lenora's second is carrying me like a baby. I struggle to get free, even though with one wrong twitch, he could crush my bones.

He sets me down. My legs buckle. I fall into a chair that has appeared next to me. I blink and look up, my limbs trembling. Lenora's second stares at me with cool, calculating eyes. Lenora stands behind him. Her skin is a tombstone gray, a pallor that hides all her emotions… but her eyes are wide with alarm.

I look at the paint brush still clutched in my hand. A shudder spasms it. I lean to the side, peering around them, afraid of what I'll see on the canvas across the room.

Breath rushes out of me.

The fire and ash of my mother's face have been turned into an inferno of death. A blue spirit rises out of it, wrapped in delicate white wisps, arms spread wide. It's a rendition of my mother more beautiful than any memory. It's nothing I've ever seen or even envisioned. And it's luminescent with something greater than reality.

Just looking at it makes me want to weep.

It's mine. I know it is. My heart seizes as I realize why Lenora is alarmed.

I've just created a fugue-state painting in front of her second.

FIVE

I'm entranced by the impossibly beautiful painting I've created.

My head is still fuzzy from the fugue, but it's obviously the best thing I've ever made. My attempts before to render my mother's beauty in paint were like a child's scrawl compared to this—the fine spun colors of her face alone have a transcendence that lifts from the canvas.

I made that. It was in an insane fugue state, but still—some part of me was able to create *that*. Deep inside, the love of the work wrestles with a creeping horror of what it means.

My gaze swings back to Lenora's second.

"How are you feeling, Eli?" Marcus asks. His name comes back to me as I stare up into his tar-black eyes.

I command my still-shaking limbs to calm while I straighten in the chair. "I'm fine."

He inspects me with a piercing gaze, which doesn't help my mental state. I flit a look to Lenora, but she's holding back.

"You seem to have made some rather rapid progress with your skills." Marcus glances at the two paintings of my mother, an object lesson in what I can do when awake and when insane.

Insane is definitely better.

"I suppose." I narrow my eyes. Has Lenora told him things about me when they're locked in their fevered embraces? Am I pillow-talk between them? The idea makes me grip my brush harder.

He's still studying me, measuring me in a thousand inhuman ways, but none of his thoughts show on his face. Or his skin, which has gone to a carefully neutral gray.

He gives a short nod. "He's ready to compete."

Lenora comes to life, suddenly lurching forward. "No! He's not ready."

"The evidence would suggest otherwise."

"Ready for what?" I ask, but my heart is racing. They're talking about the Olympics. I know they are. My mind is spinning... the Olympics are almost here. Is it even possible?

Marcus ignores Lenora's angry looks to give me an arrogant smirk. "For the art division, of course. Unless you have a hidden talent for dance as well?"

Every hair on the back of my neck rises, and I slowly stand up from the chair. His bodyform is taller than me, but not by much.

"I paint." I can feel the pride of it, but I don't care. There's nothing wrong with dancing, but Marcus is mocking me, challenging me.

Lenora moves between us, and I don't miss the protective stance she's taken in front of me. It's both insulting and makes my heart swell. Her back is to me, but whatever words she's transmitting to Marcus banishes his smirk.

"He's not ready," Lenora says, obviously speaking aloud now for my benefit. "I'm still working with him to bring out his potential. He needs more time." Her new bodyform puts her a few inches shorter than him, but she's not backing down. A fanciful image of them fighting jumps into my brain. If it came to blows, I honestly don't know who would win. Lenora's bodyform is more graceful, but they both have the hidden strength of ascender tech on their side.

"He doesn't have more time." He's speaking to Lenora, but the words are meant for me. "The competition is in days. The boy is nearly eighteen. Next year, he won't qualify."

He's right: this is the last year for me. Not that I ever thought I would have a chance to go, but once I turn eighteen, I can't compete. The ascenders want their gold medal winners to have the best chance of surviving the ascendance procedure, and after eighteen, the risk of death starts to go up. The family members are allowed to ascend, no matter their age, as a courtesy to the medalist. It would be cruel to force the winners to leave their families behind.

This is my one and only chance. For both me and my mom.

Marcus locks his gaze on me. "What do you say,

legacy? Do you think you have something worth contributing to Orion?"

Lenora whips her attention to me. Her frown brings a flush of anger to my face. With all that talk of my "potential," all I see in her eyes is fear and doubt. Her skin is still carefully gray, hiding her emotions.

Of course, she's right—I'm nowhere near ready.

A thought scrapes at the back of my mind: there was something *different* about this fugue. I've always blacked out before, but this time... that memory or hallucination or whatever-it-was of watching my mother paint... it has to mean something. Maybe it's a sign that something about the fugue is changing. That maybe I can learn to control it.

I meet Marcus's expectant look. "I'm ready."

Lenora throws an icy glare to Marcus then steps forward to take my face in her hands. I'm so shocked, my body seizes up, and I nearly tumble backward. Her fingers are cool and soft as satin on my face. I'm completely distracted by the sensation and miss the first few words of what she's saying.

"...but you mustn't rush it," she says. "You have to have patience, Eli, not push beyond what you're ready for."

Eli. My name on her lips torments me. Her purple-blue eyes are close and concerned. Her face is so near, I could lean forward and kiss her right now. But her lips are drawn into a tight line of disapproval. And I can't imagine Marcus would tolerate a kiss, even if I could steal one.

"You were the one rushing me five minutes ago." I

stay in her embrace even as I protest with my words.

"It wasn't five minutes ago, Elijah." She drops her hands from my face. The alarm is back in her eyes. "You painted for an hour."

An hour. I forgot there's always a time loss with the fugue. Only this time, she watched it happen. They both did, watching me paint in a trance for an hour then end up on the floor. She and Marcus both have to know something is seriously messed up with my process.

I have absolutely no idea how I can possibly master something that hits me like a freight train, but I have to try. It would bring *everything* into my reach. Including her.

"I can do this, Lenora. Please. Let me do this. I'll prove it to you."

"No." For a second, the gray pallor of her skin flickers, and a ribbon of darker gray trickles across it… then it's gone. "I'm not going to let you attempt this when you're not ready. I won't sponsor you." She gives me a stern look. "And you can't go without my approval. I will terminate your patronage."

Breath escapes me, but the hurt is still trapped inside. She means it: she would cut me off if I even tried to go. My mind can't wrap around it. Does she have so little faith in me?

Or worse: maybe she's afraid I'll actually win.

"I will sponsor you," Marcus says.

My shoulders jerk. I had forgotten he was there. Then his words sink into my brain as Lenora turns on him.

"You will not!" She stabs a finger at him.

He looks amused. "A dozen others will gladly step

into my place. Orion is already buzzing with what he's done."

Her bodyform tenses. The dark gray ripple shudders across her body again. For an instant, I think she might actually attack him. Or maybe just slap him. But slowly her shoulders drop until… she just looks defeated.

Which makes me hate Marcus even as he's giving me the one thing I truly want.

He softens his voice and ducks his head closer to her. "Better me than someone else. I'll watch over him." He lifts his gaze to look at me. "Are you ready to compete, legacy?"

"Yes," I say without hesitation. But I hate the slight tremble in Lenora's shoulders as she gives up. She brushes past Marcus and exits the room with a speed that leaves a stirring of air in her wake. I hope it means she won't forgive him. Although I don't know if she'll forgive me either. And if I don't win, I lose everything… including my patron.

A long moment stretches, while Marcus and I both watch the door. Then a look of determination settles on his face. "The competition is in two days. Which means we're rather short on time. We should relocate you to Agon right away."

"Agon," I say, making sure I heard him right. "You mean the Olympic Village. In California."

He shakes his head and has a pinched up look, like dealing with a human is already more trouble than he expected. "We must leave immediately."

"Like *right now?*" I suddenly realize I can't just pick up and leave Seattle to join the competitors in sunny

California. Who would take care of my mom? Cyrus can't watch her full-time, and she doesn't have any other family. It's just the two of us.

Marcus regards me coolly. "Whatever your concerns are, they can be handled. I'm your sponsor now. Whatever you need, I'll provide. But your actions from this moment forward will reflect on me, and word is already spreading through Orion that you'll be in the competition, so I'd prefer if we didn't waste time—"

"It's not that simple," I cut him off.

Marcus's shoulders tense. I have the feeling he doesn't expect me to talk back.

"I can't just leave my mom." Does he know about her sickness? Ascenders tend to know *everything*.

"Your mother will be provided for, obviously." Then he pauses and frowns. "I can see you're not adequately prepared for this. We can remedy that once we reach Agon, but for now, you need to trust that I want nothing more than for you to compete. And win. I have resources at my disposal that you're probably not aware of. Whatever problems you foresee, I am certain—"

A pinging sound from my pants pocket cuts him off. He pulls a face, and the carefully controlled, steely gray tone of his skin darkens.

I hurry over to the easel to set down the paintbrush that's still in my hand and still wet from creating something I have no idea how to recreate. My miraculous painting innocently challenges me from the canvas while I dig out the phone buried deep in my pocket. It pings again as I check it.

My heart sinks as I read the message from Cyrus.
Come home now.

SIX

I fly down the winding streets of Lenora's outer-rim neighborhood.

I catch the tram just as it's leaving the station. I pace the length of it while I try to get Cyrus on the phone for the fifth time. It just keeps ringing. I sprint the entire two block stretch between the station and my apartment building, taking the stairs three at a time up all five flights. I can barely breathe by the time I reach the top. It takes the building bot three tries to recognize my voice and let me in.

I run to my mother's room, but she's not there. My heart is ready to burst out of my body.

"Eli!" Cyrus calls from down the hall. "We're in the bathroom."

In a blur, I'm there. I see now why Cyrus wasn't answering the phone. He's got my mom in the bathtub, immersed in water, with her head propped against the far end. Her white nightgown floats in odd puffs where the air is trapped and clings in other spots, revealing her withered body underneath.

"What happened?" I ask, my voice trembling.

My mom's eyes are closed, and they twitch under the paper-thin skin of her eyelids. She must be caught in some kind of dream.

"Her fever spiked." Cyrus is breathless. His shirt and pants are soaked with water. "She was burning up. I had to cool her down. I know you don't want her going to the hospital, but her fever was insane. I had to do something." His broad shoulders bow with the weight of this.

I briefly place a hand on his bent back. "You did the right thing, Cy." I edge past him—there's barely room for the both of us in the tiny bathroom—and kneel by the side of the tub. My mom's skin is flushed, glistening either with sweat or water from the tub.

"Eli," Cyrus says softly from behind me. "We should take her to the hospital."

"We can't." My eyes start to pool water. "They'll find out she's been taking gen tech."

"But once she's there, they'll have to do something," Cyrus says with exasperation. "They'll have to give her antibiotics to fight the infection. Or treat her somehow…"

But I hear the doubt in his voice. They *should* do something to save her. But they won't. He knows it as well as I do, or he would have taken her there already.

"Eli, I'm… I'm so sorry…" His voice is choked.

I look up. His face was already wet, but now there are tears as well as bath water. I stand and grip his shoulders, struggling to keep us both upright on the slippery floor.

"This isn't your fault. I'm the one who wanted to try this, okay? And the fever is good. That's what your guy said— the fever means she's fighting the disease. Right?"

He nods, but the worry seizing his face belies it.

I clap my hand on his shoulder, once, and let go. "She's going to make it through this." I say it with conviction, as if I can believe it into being true. "I have a sponsor for the Olympics, Cy."

"What?" His face transforms like I'm the one having feverish dreams.

My mom moans. I ignore him and drop a knee to the floor by the tub. I press my fingers to her forehead. She's still crazy hot. My heart pounds in my ears and panic starts to climb up my throat. Maybe the gen tech will kill her before it cures her. Maybe she won't last long enough for me to rescue her with ascendance. I have no idea how I can possibly leave and compete with her like this. Her eyes blink open at my touch. She seems surprised to find herself in the tub. The water sloshes up the sides, startling her further.

"It's okay," I say quietly, my hand still on her forehead. "You're okay. Cy brought you here to cool you down."

She takes a shuddering breath. "Elijah." Her voice flutters. It sounds like her life is escaping right out of her body, carried on that breathy sound. "I was afraid you had gone away." She lifts her hand out of the water and lays it, cool and clammy, on mine, which is gripping the edge of the tub. "I think it must have been a dream."

"I just stepped out for a lesson with Lenora."

She nods her head in approval, eyes half closed. Art is the one thing she would forgive me being absent for.

"And... I've got some news." My voice trembles. "I'm going to the Olympics." I give her a smile, but it's probably more farce than a grin.

Her eyes blink open. "You're going to compete?" Her frown gathers water and sends it trickling down her face. I've never discussed the idea of competing with her—it just never seemed possible—but I know what she thinks of the Olympics. And it's not good.

"Mom, I have to. It's the only thing that..." *That might save you.* I can't force the words out.

She turns, half rising out of the water, her hand locking onto mine. "You do *not* have to, Elijah. Ascending is dangerous. I don't want to lose you!"

"Almost no one dies," I say, knowing that won't convince her at all. "And they'll take you, too." That part is a whisper.

"No!" Water splashes around her as she struggles to sit up in the tub.

"Mom, don't." I grip her thin arms as gently as I can. They're burning hot under my palms. "You need to stay in the water until you cool down."

"I *will not* allow you to do this for me, Elijah." She struggles for a split second more, then she gives up and sinks back against the white-tiled edge of the tub. "You *know* I don't want anything they have to give. And I won't let them have you. You're just starting to come into your own. Your art, Elijah..." She closes her eyes briefly, and I can tell this is taxing her when she can least afford it.

"I'll continue my art. I promise." I say it, but her eyes stay closed, and I know it doesn't matter.

I shouldn't have told her. I knew she would object: she despises how the ascenders use art to judge who's "worthy" to join them. But I can't help thinking that, once her son was one of them, she would have to change her mind. She would have to see all the good they do. And how nothing would be closed off to me anymore. I could make art, literally, forever. I could do *anything*. Even if she refused to ascend with me, she would qualify. She would no longer be legacy. Which would mean I could cure her. Strip her of the disease that's killing her. And that's just the beginning. I could master the fugue and fulfill all that potential she's convinced I have. I could show Lenora I'm worthy of being more than just a pet to her. *Everything* would be within my reach. And eventually… given enough time… I could convince my mom to join me. We would *both* live forever.

With that possibility dangling in front of me, I can't let her die in a bathtub. No matter what she says.

She sucks in a breath and struggles to open her eyes. "You will lose the one thing that belongs to you, Elijah. The one thing that matters."

I sigh, and silently curse the ancient religion that's convinced her of this. "Mom, you won't lose your soul when you ascend. That's just superstitious talk."

"You don't know that. You don't know…" Her voice is fading. Her eyelids flutter. "You don't understand… so much, Elijah. I won't let you compete. I won't allow it."

But her voice is weak.

My gut is twisted in knots.

Her eyelids slowly close. "You're so special. My Elijah. You were created to… to do great things…" Her voice fades, and under her closed eyelids, she falls into that feverish dream mode again. I'm afraid I've taken whatever energy she had with this pointless argument.

"Mom." I blink back tears and give her arms a small shake.

Her eyes open again, but only half way. "I can't lose you to them. Not now." Then her voice fades again, like she's falling asleep, and her eyes drift closed.

I hold my breath and watch her. The water laps at her body as her chest slowly rises and falls. I wait until I'm convinced she's not… dying. That she's just fallen asleep.

I stand, half drenched like Cyrus.

He rests a hand on my shoulder. "Eli." The word is laden with the ones he's not saying.

I turn to him. "She's going to hate me, Cy."

A grimace tortures his face. "No, she's not. She loves you, man."

I look back to her, drenched and already hovering near death. "How can I do this? How can I even think of going off to compete and leaving her like this?"

His hand squeezes my shoulder. "If you really have a chance to do this, you've got to take it. If anyone was meant to compete, it's you."

I take a deep breath. "I don't know. She's going to hate me for even trying this. If I manage to win, if I become of one *them*… she's going to hate me more."

"At least she'll be around to hate you."

I nod. My stomach is a spasming ball of guilt. But he's right: I have to do this. Maybe, eventually, she'll forgive me.

"You know what I'm going to hate?" Cyrus says, his voice lighter. "*You* as an ascender. I mean, for the love of all that's tech, you're arrogant enough as it is."

I laugh, even though it feels like the tears are going to gush out if I do.

"But you know I'm all in on this, right?" he adds softly. "Whatever you need, man, I'm here to help."

That chokes off my laugh. I know Cyrus is suspicious of everything the ascenders do—and not just because he makes a living off skirting their laws. His grandfather was a believer, just like my mom, which meant he was always looking over his shoulder for a police bot. The fact that Cyrus is willing to help me with this…

I give him a small nod. "I need someone to help me figure out how to win this thing, Cy."

"Is there a way to cheat? Because I'm an expert at that."

I smile. "No… at least, I don't think so." Although if there is, I have no doubt Cyrus will find it for me. "But I think I know how to make sure my mom is taken care of while I'm gone."

"Oh?" Cyrus glances at my mom's trembling body in the water. "How's that?"

"My sponsor." I take a deep breath as that sinks in. Marcus is possibly the last person in the world I would want for a sponsor, but I can't afford to be picky about who sends me to the Olympics. "I don't know why, or what's in it for him, but I think my sponsor wants me to win as much as I do."

Which makes no sense, but the ascenders rarely make sense. They're capricious, and like Cyrus says, they always have their own reasons for things. The vagaries of the gods aren't meant to be understood by mere mortals. Whatever Marcus's reason, it probably has very little to do with me and everything to do with some ascender drama that I'll never understand. Maybe once I ascend, I'll figure it out. For now, I don't care.

Cyrus's eyebrows lift. *"Him?* So your hot patron isn't sponsoring you?" He folds his beefy arms across his chest, like he's not sure I'm telling the truth anymore.

"The point is, he says he can get us whatever we need to do this."

"Whatever we need?" Cyrus's interest goes up three levels. The ascenders may have their own interests at heart, but Cyrus is right behind them with that.

I scowl. "Meaning help for my mom, not a way to feed Riley's black market trade."

Cyrus grunts, but he nods. "Sounds like you need to get your shiny pants sponsor over here and see what he's good for."

SEVEN

It's been twenty minutes since I called Marcus, and he's still not here.

I pace the bathroom, all five feet of water-slopped floor and tension, while Cyrus and I wait for Marcus to show. But each minute that ticks by, each nearly-silent slosh in the tub while my mother fights her fever, convinces me Lenora's second will change his mind. That this is some kind of cruel ascender prank. Or more likely, a spat between ascender lovers, where I'm an inconsequential pawn to be cast aside the moment they link up in one of those otherworldly embraces.

My teeth grind as I pace.

I wonder if Marcus was serious about the other ascenders, the ones who would sponsor me, even if he didn't. How would I find them? Maybe I could go through ArtNet. I certainly can't contact Orion on my own. Even if I could, the Olympics are almost here. I can't imagine making this work so quickly with another ascender. It's like they exist in another world, separated by tech and time and space from the one inhabited by the unwashed remnants of humanity.

Because that's what we are, no matter what pet names they call us.

It's taking too long.

I'm about to lose hope, when I hear the faint swish of the front door opening. Only I didn't tell the building bot to let anyone in.

Cyrus's voice jumps in from the front room. "Hey! Ever heard of—whoa." He's never seen an ascender in person, as far as I know. Most legacies haven't.

With a quick glance at my mom, I hurry out to the front.

Cyrus is staring gape-mouthed, but not at Marcus: there's a humanoid bot behind him, dressed in nursing scrubs. It looks like an ascender, except for the uniform metallic-blue tint to its ungendered bodyform, which indicates it has low-level sentience. I've never seen one in person before, either, but I know it's a huge step up from the standard med bots at the hospital that normally care for legacies.

Marcus ignores Cyrus's stunned expression. "Eli, I trust this level of home care will be sufficient for your mother. I understand she's in the last stages of her lymphoma."

My mouth runs dry. He's so casual, as if this isn't a death sentence that his kind has placed on her. Yet, I can't hate him completely. He's brought the finest in human medical care right into my home, away from the prying eyes of Orion's health care system. *Private* homecare. It's something I could never begin to afford—

only the most pampered domestics have them—and Marcus is tossing it to me like it's a speck of dust he's brushed off his shoulder.

"That will be fine," I manage. "Thank you."

"Where is your mother?" Marcus asks.

I gesture down the hall, and the med bot glides by, its eyes roused to attention now that it's been given a task. I watch it close the bathroom door, and a nameless fear lurches my heart. I'm three steps down the hall before Marcus's voice stops me.

"Eli."

I loathe the way he calls me *Eli* when Lenora will only use my full name. I force myself to turn back.

Marcus's skin tone is back to a more normal beige— he's not masking his emotions anymore—and a streak of dark blue intensity flashes across it. "You will need all of your attention for the competition."

Cyrus stands next to him, still wide-eyed, but he gives me a small nod of agreement. My brain tilts sideways at the sight of the two of them, side by side, urging me on.

"I understand," I say.

"Do you?" Marcus asks coolly. "Somehow I doubt that. But your mother will be well cared for, and we need to leave. That is, if you're fully committed to the competition. I can't sponsor you otherwise."

"I'm committed," I say, grinding it out. I don't trust Marcus. *At all.* Whatever is behind his eagerness for me to compete, it's not an appreciation for my art. He's getting something else out of this. I don't know what, but at this point, I have no choice but to take what he's offering. "When do we leave?"

"Immediately." Marcus's impatience shows in more flashes of blue intensity across his bare chest. I can even see the streaks of color through the thin fabric of his shorts. I'm really hoping at some point he'll decide to wear clothes.

I gesture to my best friend. "I'll need Cyrus to come with me."

Marcus doesn't look at him. "Mr. Kowalski may come. You can bring any support you wish, but we must leave now."

Cyrus frowns, finally breaking out of his shock to give Marcus the critical eye he deserves. "What's the hurry?"

Marcus gives an elaborate sigh, which rubs me five ways wrong. Ascenders don't breathe—sure they can suck in air, but it's just one of their five thousand ways of sampling the world. *Sighing* is pure drama.

I'm not impressed.

Marcus glances at Cyrus but returns his steady-eyed stare to me. "You are at a distinct disadvantage. Most of the competitors have been at Agon for months. I had to make a special petition for your late entry. There was much resistance. You need to prove them wrong by coming up to speed as quickly as possible."

He thinks I'm going to embarrass him. My ears get hot. "Fine. I'll just grab some things—"

"You cannot bring anything with you. Besides, everything you need will be provided." Again the sigh. "I can see you have even more to learn than I thought. If Mr. Kowalski is ready, he can come. Otherwise, you'll have to manage without him."

Cyrus's eyes are wide again. Marcus is serious: he wants us to walk out the door this instant.

I shake my head at Cyrus. "I can't ask you to just drop everything and follow me—"

"Shut up. You'd be lost without me." Cyrus runs his hand across his face then tosses a smirk to Marcus. "Besides, shiny pants here says he'll provide us with everything we'll need. You'll want me to help you out with the particulars on that."

I grin. Cyrus will find a way to pilfer some kind of tech from Marcus's largess. Which just might keep Riley from firing him if he runs off with me to the Olympics for a while. It won't be too long—with the competition starting in a couple of days, we'll know soon enough whether I've won or not.

"I've already arranged for transport." Marcus dashes to the door so fast, I barely see him go. Then he stops suddenly at the threshold, gripping the doorframe and waiting. I'm afraid he'll put a dent in the frame with his apparent frustration. I get the feeling that, unlike Lenora, he doesn't deal with legacies very often. And I'm beginning to realize that my view of ascenders might have been colored, just a bit, by spending time with one who *chose* to live near legacies. As much as they supposedly treasure us, most ascenders stay far away.

Cyrus glances back to the closed door of the bathroom, where my mother fights her fever and her disease... and where a slightly sentient bot is probably providing better medical care than either of us ever could. The torment on his face tears at me, but he shuffles toward Marcus waiting at the door, watching to see if I'm following.

My shoes are suddenly filled with lead. I can't say goodbye—it will only upset my mother again, and I'm not sure I'll be able to leave. She'll despise me when she wakes up to find I've gone for real this time, and for something she's explicitly forbidden me to do. But while the bot can tame her fever and keep her comfortable, it can't give her the one thing she needs: a new life.

I turn back to Marcus and Cyrus at the door and wrench myself forward.

Not saying goodbye is the least of the things I'll need her forgiveness for.

The rain has lifted, and stark sunshine glares from every water-beaded surface. We speed toward the outer rim of Seattle in a taxi bot Marcus summoned. The taxi's dust-free shininess speaks to the ascender clientele it normally serves. Legacy humans are stuck with the tram, sun-powered bikes, or our own mortal shoe-covered feet.

Marcus, Cyrus, and I are speeding toward a rail station I've heard of but never seen. It's an ascender-only high speed line that connects Seattle to Los Angeles. Ascenders usually travel over the net, uploading to Orion then downloading to a rental bodyform—Lenora takes several trips a year that way—but the high speed rail lets ascenders take their custom bodyforms on travel instead.

After all, they're sensation junkies. They live to soak up those enhanced inputs, and rental bodies apparently aren't as good for that—at least, that's what Lenora tells me. Ascenders get where they need to go with high-speed rails and taxi bots and personal flight craft for more remote destinations.

The weed-cracked roads outside the cities are left to the humans.

Not that we use them much either. Highways still crisscross the country like a skeleton left to bleach in the sun, and oil flows faster than ever with new ascender tech, but after the Singularity, personal cars and the fuel infrastructure they need died from lack of use. The ascenders found better and cleaner ways to travel, as well as a dozen new methods of producing energy. If there's one thing the ascenders are good at, it's making sure the power stays on. Then they built a half dozen legacy cities around the world, designed just for their treasured humans' biological needs—food, shelter, waste treatment, and medical care. The ascenders figured we would stay put. Not that they actually care what humans do—they don't lock us into legacy cities any more than people lock rats into a sewer. The police bots just keep the human rats out of the ascenders' sparkling-clean cities and let the humans nest wherever they can scratch a living from the earth.

The truth is legacy humans don't travel because there's really nowhere to go.

Our choices are basically dissenter reservations, the nomad tribes, or going it on your own... in descending order of brutality. The nearest reservation is in Oregon—you can live there if you want to call "home" a place run by religious zealots who like to publicly stone heretics and sinners. At least the reservations *only* regressed to the barbarism of the medieval era—the nomadic tribes went completely pre-history. Now they're hunting in the rejuvenated forests of the Midwest and following the buffalo herds the ascenders resurrected. The tribal humans don't seem quite as barbaric as the theocrats who run the reservations, but my personal theory on that is there's so much ascender-restored natural habitat now, that the nomads never actually run into one another.

Seattle's not great, but it's the only legacy city in North America... and the only civilized place for humans. Legacies only travel because they've been banished from the one place worth living. And it's a home I'm about to leave—all so I can join a tiny enclave of legacies competing for the right to ascend and *stay* in the gleaming all-ascender city of Los Angeles.

The rail station is spotless, filled with tarnish-free reflective surfaces. It's smaller than I expect, just a check-in kiosk and a sheltering room, until I realize the train is actually below ground. We take a lift that drops us down one level at a stomach-clenching speed.

The train itself makes my stomach knot even tighter. Its narrow nose points like a supersonic needle toward a darkened tunnel. Faint accelerator rings glow within the darkness, waiting to hurl the sleek maglev train to human-unfriendly speeds.

Cyrus looks like he's going to lose his lunch, and we

haven't even boarded yet.

Marcus must be more perceptive than I thought, because he takes one look at us and says, "There are special accommodations for humans. You will not experience much discomfort."

Much.

I swallow, but there's nothing to wet my suddenly-dry throat.

Marcus moves too fast again, reaching the train in an instant. He sighs his impatience as Cyrus and I drag our dirty human sneakers across the stainless steel platform. I clap a hand on Cyrus's shoulder, and we pick up the pace.

The train door slides open upon our approach, and inside are a dozen liquid-metal-looking seats. They're spaced widely apart. Marcus sits in one, and it ripples to conform to his body. Cyrus and I hesitate.

Marcus holds up a hand to stop us from sitting. "Your seats will be here in a moment."

Just as the words leave his mouth, a low-sentience humanoid bot arrives carrying what looks like a coffin: human-sized, sleek metal, it's a pod that could contain even Cyrus's broad shoulders. When the bot reaches two nearby seats, it taps the backsides. They relax their shape, like they're made of mercury, shuddering liquid metal until they settle into the form of an angled bed. The bot hoists the pod onto the now-solid surface of one, and the coffin pops open. It has two identical halves, each filled with blue, shimmering jelly and a couple of restraining straps. The bot separates the two halves and places one on each angled bed. They're like little baths of gel waiting for us.

I almost gag at the sight of it.

Cyrus voices my thoughts. "I don't know what you have in mind here, Marcus, but there's no way I'm getting in the goo."

"That's fine," Marcus says dryly. "Your human tissues are certainly capable of withstanding the three-g forces, but I doubt you'll enjoy the aftereffects. The trip is eight minutes. The choice is yours." He straps himself into his seat, and it shifts with him as he settles in.

I know ascenders can dial back their senses when they choose. I know they have bodies that can withstand all kinds of forces, shocks, and temperature swings. The net says they're even hardened against mid-level EMP attacks. Maybe someday I'll join them… but today, my weak, human body is all I have.

I climb in.

Cyrus still looks like he might throw up.

I'm surprised when the blue gel doesn't squish between my fingers or cling to my shirt. It's more like an infinitely soft cushion that moves with me, helping me ease into the half-coffin that is apparently going to be my seat for the ride down to Los Angeles.

The assistant bot stands by. My legs are encased in goo, but I'm loathe to lay back into the rest of the gel.

"You must secure the harness in order to activate the gravity seat," it tells me, with a tinny voice. I'm pretty sure its level of sentience doesn't come with emotional expression, but it still manages to sound impatient.

I don't want it deciding I need assistance, so I clench

my teeth and lay back. The slight chill seeps through my clothes and makes me shudder, visibly.

"I don't know about this." Cyrus's expression is the one he reserves for ocular implants and people who try to cheat Riley out of his chits.

"It's not so bad." I wrestle with the harness, looping one strap over each shoulder, then securing them to another between my legs. When I click them together, the straps tighten and yank me back into the gel lining the seat. Cyrus's eyes get big.

"Train departure in two minutes." The soft, feminine voice of the train echoes in our empty train car.

"You can still punch out, Cyrus," I say. "No hard feelings, man."

Cyrus grunts and gingerly puts one foot in his gravity seat. He makes several more noises of disgust, such that I nearly choke on held-in laughter by the time he gets the harness on and is locked down, just as I am.

"Shut up." He leans his head back and looks at the ceiling. There's nothing to see. He's just avoiding me.

Marcus has that fluttered look, the one I've seen on Lenora. He's consulting Orion about something. Or possibly communicating with Lenora. For a moment, my heart lurches, and I think that maybe she's forgiven both of us. I also realize I'm leaving without saying goodbye to her as well.

"Is she coming with us?" I ask Marcus, before I think it through or rein in the hope in my voice. I don't want him to have any idea how I feel about her. But he knows exactly who I mean.

"Lenora offered to join us," he says coolly. He comes out of communication with the Orion and looks sideways at me. "I told her not to."

Like that, my face is hot. I shouldn't say it, but I do anyway. "She doesn't have to listen to you."

He turns forward again, adjusting in his seat. "She doesn't have to. But she knows as well as I do that she would just be a distraction."

A chill washes through my body. *She knows.* She knows that I hang on her every word, that I count the minutes until I see her, that… she distracts me more than anything on the planet. My mind is a torment, trying to decide if this is a good thing—maybe I distract her as well—or a horribly, disastrously bad thing. *She knows, but it doesn't matter to her.* I'm just her pet.

My lack of response makes Marcus turn and pierce me with his gaze. "You'll need all your focus to win, legacy. You *do* want to win, don't you?"

"Yes." I stare my conviction into his eyes.

He gives me a short nod of approval and turns forward.

If Marcus's reason for helping me is a puzzle, his relationship with Lenora is a complete mystery. If Lenora knows I have feelings for her, he has to know as well. Or does that even register in the millions of thoughts that run through his electronic brain? He's a god, and I'm a hairy monkey. Lenora's little anthropological project. Her pet. And if I ascend… I'll be the newest ascender on the block. Probably no threat at all to those who ascended a hundred years ago.

Maybe.

I have no idea how they really think. All I know is that, for now, he's my ticket to getting everything I want and need.

Including his second.

The assistant bot has disappeared. Cyrus gives me a nod then settles his head into the cool embrace of the gel. A small tone signals the train is about to pull away from the station. It doesn't shuffle forward. It doesn't rock softly on the magnetic fields that levitate it before easing into the tunnel.

It screams forward like a rocket.

My head slams back into the gel, and the harness is the only thing keeping me from cracking my skull on the top of the metallic casing. The gel squeezes me, starting in rhythmic waves at my toes and working up my body. It's like I'm inside a giant boa constrictor, traveling the length of its digestive system.

It goes on.

And on.

And on.

I keep waiting for it to stop, but the lights of the tunnel just flash by in pulses faster and faster until I shut my eyes against the onslaught. I forget to breathe, and when I remember, I can't. The gel is pressing on all sides, giving my lungs nowhere to go. I quickly learn to time my breathing to when the squeeze has passed my midsection, squishing the blood in my body up to my head. I don't think I'm going to pass out... but I want to. It seems like an eternity, but it's probably only three or four minutes when the acceleration starts to ease. It's barely noticeable at first, and then more and more, until I'm free enough to move. I chance a look at Cyrus.

He's pale as death. One blink. Two. That's all that lets me know he's alive.

Marcus is still sitting casually in his seat, apparently no more discomfited by the g-forces than a gentle ride on the tram.

Suddenly our seats tilt up to nearly vertical and pivot, rotating so we're facing the opposite direction then lowering again. After a blessedly pressure-free moment, the train starts to decelerate, pressing us once again into the seat. It builds until it's as strong as before and stretches for endless body-crushing minutes. Finally, we break out of the tunnel. Blinding sunlight stabs through the train windows. A standing guard of palm trees whizzes by as we decelerate into a sleek glass-and-chrome station.

We've arrived.

EIGHT

"Welcome to Agon."

Marcus stands at the entranceway to an enormous complex. He's waiting for me and Cyrus to emerge from the taxi bot. I stumble, my legs still shaky from the maglev ride. Cyrus's awkward amble says he's about the same. The hot summer air is so dry it instantly parches my lips. Cyrus and I both gape and shade our eyes against the sun-burnished steel of the building. Five enormous, swooping domes rise and fall, glaring white hot against the faded blue sky of California.

I've seen the Olympic Village before, of course, but only on the net. The games are held here, in the same location, every year. The original Olympics died after the Singularity, like so many other things. With nations eliminated by Orion, there wasn't much to represent, and the *faster, higher, stronger* motto of the original Olympics was hopelessly outdated by ascender tech. But once the choice for ascendance was taken away, there arose a need for exceptions to the rule. The legacy net isn't clear on whether it was to keep legacies happy or some other reason—parsing ascender motivation is a constant guessing game—but soon after, the creative Olympics were born. Legacies have been competing for those few slots every year since.

From above, the domes form five rings, a holdover from the ancient symbol of the five regions of the world. Now the rings represent the four creative performance areas—drama, language, visual, and aural—plus a fifth ring for the intersection of the arts. There's no fifth competitive category, so the fifth building of Agon connects all the others, serving as a common area for the agonites.

Agonite. An official competitor who's taken up residence in the Olympic Village. Something every legacy artist dreams of being, and which, to my still wide-eyed astonishment, I am about to become.

I've never seen the inside of Agon. Documentaries of the competitors' lives fill the legacy net for weeks leading up to each competition, but what goes on inside the Village is strictly off limits. Only when the agonites take the stage does the legacy world get to see what they have planned for their performances. I have no idea what information makes it to Orion. But this is their show— I'm sure they see far more than we're allowed.

Marcus leads Cyrus and me through the frosted glass doors of the entrance to Agon. A sweep of artificially cool air bathes us. Cyrus's eyes shine with anticipation. My heart pumps excitement through my body.

We don't get far.

Past a small receiving area, two security bots stand

guard by a set of tall metal doors. The bots are six feet of hardened steel and conspicuous armaments. They're humanoid, and supposedly have low-level sentience, but mostly they're walking guns. One arm sports an entire armory of shock and beam weapons as well as the more lethal kind with bullets, while the other arm is left barehanded for physically constraining anyone foolish enough to confront it.

Above the doors they're guarding, the four arts are inscribed in Latin: *musica, artem, storia, drama*. A tall ascender and a legacy boy who has to be an agonite are being scanned by a blue light emanating from just above the door. It traverses them quickly head-to-toe. The security bots merely watch, but I'm sure if something's wrong with the scan, they'll spring into action before the agonite has a chance to blink. The boy bends under a hushed but bitter chastisement from his apparent sponsor. Whispers of "focus" and "time" float across the room before the doors open, and the two of them slip inside.

I figure that's where we're headed, too, but instead, Marcus leads us to a smaller door on the opposite side of the room. There are no security bots, and he simply swipes us through. Inside, it looks like a med bay, only without the beds. In their place is a shimmering steel pod that reminds me of the coffin-like gravity seats, only this one is twice as big and floats upright. It's six inches off the floor held up by some kind of maglev field.

My stomach clenches just looking at it.

"I am sick of ascender tech *already*," Cyrus grumbles

under his breath.

I nod but keep quiet as a door on the far wall slides open, and another ascender strides in.

His male bodyform is sleek, less bulky than Marcus's overly-masculine form, and he's dressed in a blue one-piece uniform. It drapes lightly on his body, but it's not sheer, leaving only his hands, feet, and face to reveal the colors shifting across his skin. The medium brown color has subtle waves of deep purple rippling underneath, like he's been infused with lavender. I have no idea what that means, but the holo rings of the Olympics floating on his uniform make him look very official next to Marcus's casual ascender shorts.

The new ascender ignores me and Cyrus. "Good to see you, Marcus. Stirring up trouble again, are you?"

My eyebrows arch. I flash a look to Cyrus then watch the two ascenders carefully. First, they're talking out loud, which means they want us to overhear. Why? I have no clue. Maybe that's the rule here at Agon. Second, I wonder if Marcus is some kind of ascender bad boy... and if that's why Lenora might be attracted to him.

I don't like it.

Marcus simply holds up his palm. "Leopold. I trust you'll treat my agonite well."

"Of course," Leopold says. "I wouldn't keep my position if I was anything less than completely impartial."

Then they touch palms. It's obviously not the same kind of touching Marcus shared with Lenora at her front door, but they're sharing some kind of information. Maybe something secure, like an access code, so they can't just transmit it? Maybe transmission isn't allowed inside Agon, and that's why they're talking out loud? Whatever it is, it's over fast. Just a brief blink of eyelids, a touch that lasts a half second, and they're done.

Marcus nods as if their touch verified something for him.

Leopold looks at me for the first time since entering the room. "Elijah Brighton, you'll need to remove your clothing and step this way."

"Remove my... wait, what?" I look to Marcus for confirmation.

Leopold looks on with amusement then flits with ascender speed over to the pod.

Marcus lowers his voice. "Just do what the intake officer says."

I'm embarrassing him. Which I shouldn't enjoy quite so much, given I need Marcus's sponsorship. I manage to keep in the smirk.

"I'm just... verifying that I heard him correctly," I say, louder for Leopold. I drop my voice again. "Take off my clothes. Like, *all* of them?"

"I told you before that you wouldn't be able to bring anything with you," Marcus says tightly. "That includes clothing, any internal devices—which I sincerely hope you do not have—and any biological agents that may be destructive to the other competitors."

"Biological agents? Like a virus? I'm not sick—"

His eyes dilate and grow darker blue. "Viral weaponry is easily hidden, given the alarming number of biological entities your human forms harbor. And not everyone enters the games to win, Eli."

My eyes widen. Cyrus gives me a nod, which only trickles unease through my stomach. I shuffle over to the pod where Leopold waits for me. He's pulled up a virtual control panel that hovers in the air just outside the pod.

While he manipulates the controls, he says to me, "Leave your clothes on the floor. I'll have a bot take them away and fabricate a uniform in the correct size before we're done."

I start to unbutton my shirt, decide that's too slow, then pull it over my head and drop it on the floor. As I'm working off my shoes and pants, Leopold keeps swiping through the screens. The pod suddenly hisses, which makes me jump, then it cracks open like two halves of an egg. A blue mist oozes from it, coating the floor around my now bare feet.

He's still talking. "Once you step into the decontamination chamber, make sure all parts of your body are inside. It will close and cycle through a series of tests and scans, as well as flush you with scrubbing agents."

The blue mist licks at my toes, and my stomach feels like a pile of snakes. I drop the last of my clothes and stand naked and shivering in front of him.

"You can enter now," Leopold says with impatience, like I should have jumped into his pod of scrubbing agents with joy the nanosecond I had my clothes off.

I swallow and glance back at Cyrus, who's giving hard looks to Leopold and his tech interface. I gingerly hold the cool edge of the pod and slide inside. The mist obscures some of the inner casing, but there's clearly a corrugated shelf at the bottom with space for two human feet.

While I'm stepping up, adjusting to make sure all my parts are inside the chamber, I hear Cyrus speak up. "What are the dangers of this procedure?"

Leopold answers like he's lecturing a child. "There are no dangers. Unless your agonite has an artificial heart he failed to disclose on the intake forms or any kind of implant—"

A hiss of gas cuts him off, and the chamber clamps shut around me. It's dark for a moment, then a blue light flicks on.

Leopold's voice comes through a tiny speaker hidden somewhere behind the mist. "Place your hands flat on the plate in front of you."

The mist starts gushing into the chamber, filling it with churning blue clouds that I can't help but breathe in. It tastes of bitter antiseptics and chlorine, and it clears out my sinuses like I'm breathing straight rubbing alcohol. I rub my face only to discover the blue mist is sliming me with some kind of coating. It starts to cling to my eyelashes. Belatedly, I close my eyes to keep it out. I fumble to place my hands on the plate. Cold metal handcuffs snap over them, which jolts my eyes open again. Sure enough, my hands are locked down on the plate. The coolness of it infuses and numbs my skin.

"Hey," I say loudly, wondering if the pod is equipped with a microphone. "What's the deal with—"

My words are cut off by a row of needles jabbing into

my wrists.

"Hey!" I hold my breath, but the pain doesn't come. The needles are injecting something, or possibly draining blood, but they're painless. The mist starts to thin, and a blue ring of light pulses from the top of the pod to the bottom and back again, scanning me. The needles retract from my wrists, replaced by pressure for a moment, and then that is gone as well.

Leopold's voice comes through the speaker again. "Please hold your hand still for the stamp."

"The what?" I ask.

"Your implant." The irritation in Leopold's voice makes me imagine Marcus outside the pod, cringing at my ignorance. "It identifies your art, gives you access to areas you're authorized for, records your intake procedure and various other things. Hold still so it takes well the first time. I assure you it would be better not to have to remove the implant and repeat the process."

I gulp and hold my hand as still as humanly possible. "Um... okay."

I expect a jab from below, like the needles, but instead a brilliant blue light beams on the top of my left hand. It forms the shape of the Greek letter *alpha*, and my skin smokes a little. It freaks me out entirely, but I manage to hold my hand still until it's done. The blue light switches off, but my hand still glows, the new neon tattoo adding its own pale light to the dim interior of the pod. A blast of warm air from below steams off the gel that coats my body. A hiss precedes the cracking open of the pod once more. My ears pop, and my legs are shaking again as I step down. I grip the side to keep upright.

Cyrus shoves a blue uniform that feels like weightless silk into my hand. "You okay?" His face is open with concern, and he grips my shoulders like he's afraid I might fall down. My hand feels numb, and there are nearly invisible bandages where the needles stuck me, but overall, it was more freaky than painful.

"Yeah," I say, a little wheezy from the mist. "I'm fine, just…" I turn the stamp on the back of my hand toward him. "…getting a tattoo."

He huffs a laugh.

I shift away from him and bend to step into my uniform. It's all one piece, like Leopold's uniform, and glides over my skin like it's made of air.

"You will need to remove your clothing as well, Mr. Kowalski," says Leopold.

I jerk my head up to look at Cyrus. His shock fades quicker than I expect, and he starts to shuck off his clothes.

"Doesn't hurt, right?" he asks me, like he expects it to hurt like crazy, and he wants me to lie to him.

"No more painful than watching you paint." I cough out the mist that still coats my lungs.

He snorts. "Hey, I don't *need* to paint. I can get girls the old fashioned way."

"Bad jokes?"

"Pity dates." He climbs into the pod.

It hisses and closes around him.

I'm struck by how many things I can never repay Cyrus for.

NINE

Agon is shaped like the spirals of a snail laid on its side.

Marcus leads us deep into the center. The curved and winding corridors are strangely empty. The spotless steel floors and swooping white walls remind me of Lenora's apartment: the ascenders sure like their walls without edges. Doors line the hall, each with a small window. Most are dialed opaque, but Cyrus and I sneak looks into the ones that are clear. One room is mirrored, obviously a dance studio. Another is a tiny closet with a desk and chair. They're both vacant.

We reach a large, windowless door, and Marcus points to its scanner. "Your imprint gives you access to the Lounge twenty-four hours a day, but I recommend only visiting at meal times." He gives Cyrus and me stern looks. "In fact, you should restrict yourselves to your room or your studio, and when you must travel, don't go alone."

I think Marcus's electronic brain has had some kind of short, but Cyrus's face locks up, like he's been given a signal to arm for battle.

"You think Eli's in danger," he says. "From who? The other competitors?"

Marcus regards Cyrus anew. "The stakes are high for the agonites. This is their one and only chance to attain all the benefits of the ascender world. The prospect of failing and returning to their legacy cities, after coming so close, is daunting."

"Yeah, well... somehow I'm sure they'll manage to carry on with their insignificant human lives." The frost in Cyrus's voice hikes my shoulders up. His ascender-loathing is going to mess this up before we even get started.

But Marcus ignores him. A sweep of gray darkens his chest. "Your competitors will stop at little in their efforts to eliminate you." He pauses. "There have already been two deaths this year."

"What?" Alarm trips through my body. "You mean... somebody's killing the... but, I haven't heard anything about that on the net." I wrack my brain, thinking back on previous Olympics. I vaguely remember agonites dropping out before the competition, but I don't remember any deaths.

"It's always kept quiet until after the games," Marcus says, coolly. "Faced with losing, it's plausible some agonites would take their own lives. At least, that's what the families are told. Given the amount of pathology inherent in human creatives and the pressure of the games, it's not difficult to believe."

"You ascenders are a real piece of work, you know

that?" Cyrus is pissed.

I hold my hands out to Marcus. "He doesn't mean it like that."

He lifts his chin to look down his nose at me. It's a challenge. "The games are a dangerous business, Eli. I assumed the risk was worth your mother's life. Or are you having second thoughts?"

I stand straighter. "I'm here to win."

Marcus nods approvingly. "The stakes are high for the agonites, but they're even higher for the sponsors. And the ascender world at large."

My eyebrows hike up. "So what exactly *are* you getting out of this?" I can hardly believe I get to ask him flat-out like this.

"Once you cross the threshold of Agon, you become a possible future ascender," he says. "But the games are not merely, or even primarily, for the benefit of the legacies. The law strictly restricts the sentience of new forms, and the ascender population has been essentially fixed since the final ascendance. However, the hunger— or psychological need, one might say—for reproduction is still very strong. The games provide an outlet for that need. It's not just the chance to discover a new talent; it's the ability to create a new life. The winning sponsors garner tremendous social status, but all ascenders benefit—not just from the entertainment, but from the emotional release of bringing new ascenders into the world."

Cyrus looks disgusted. "So the legacies who win... they're like baby ascenders?"

Marcus nods. "And what would you do to win the right to bring a new life into existence?"

Cyrus pales and glances at me.

The thought of being Marcus's "baby" makes me slightly nauseous. Along with the idea that somehow I'm only truly *alive* once I ascend. "So... great. The winners are the newest ascender on the block and everyone's happy. But it's not like you can rig the competition." I can't help a glance at Cyrus, who is back to looking like he's girding for war. "I mean, everyone just has to do their best and—"

Marcus cuts me off with a dead serious look. Tendrils of black wisp across his chest to punctuate it. "Do not underestimate what the sponsors will do to sway the competition. The fact that tampering with the games is a capital offense is only a slight deterrent."

"Capital offense?" I lean away. It's never occurred to me that ascenders might commit crimes against other ascenders. I had assumed they were above all that. "Wait... I thought ascenders lived forever."

"Capital punishment for an ascender isn't death, Eli. It's permanent storage."

Not sure what that is, but it sounds bad. "I'm guessing no one wants that."

"No. Most sponsors stay within the law." He waves off my confused look. "You can study up on the regulations tonight. For now, no physical altercations, no altering your implant, and no tampering with security of any kind. Those will get you thrown out of the competition."

I give Cyrus a warning glance. "That shouldn't be a problem."

Marcus's coloration is back to a more normal brownish-pink. "There are also *legal* ways to influence the competition. Watch out for anything that distracts you, anyone who shows an undue interest in you, and any attempts to destroy your confidence. Orion considers surviving such attempts a reasonable measure of your character and focus."

I'm thinking my confidence is already on the ropes, given I have no idea how to master the fugue... and no chance of winning without it.

Marcus glances at the still-closed door to the Lounge then tilts his head to the scanner. "Log yourself in. Bring your food back to your room. Less mingling with the other agonites means less opportunity for mischief."

I wave my hand at the scanner. My implant pulses blue light in the shape of an alpha then the door slides open. Every agonite and support team member appears to be inside.

Hundreds of people cluster in twos and threes at the tables. There are a few ascender sponsors but mostly agonites. It's a parade of the four colors of the games—the blue of my uniform, as well as green, yellow, and red for the other arts. The competitors are eating and talking, but there's not much laughing. The noise is still impressive, bouncing off the hard walls and floating up to fill the two-storied room. Screens on the walls rotate through selections of all the arts: vids of dancers, panned images of drawings, silent renditions of musicians playing. Suddenly I'm wondering about the ones not pictured—the ones who were "eliminated" so these ones could win. My attention is drawn back to earth by a small shriek and a clatter of something crashing to the floor at my feet.

"Oh! I'm so sorry! Oh my gosh! I didn't see you!" The frantic rambling is coming from a petite, dark-haired girl in a red uniform next to Cyrus. She's Arabic, with delicate features and dark brown eyes. Her lunch tray is on the floor next to a smear of sandwiches, a smashed piece of chocolate cake, and two cups that have spewed their orange contents.

Cyrus is wearing half the liquid. "It's okay. Really."

"No, no, it's not! I'm such a clumsy—oh no!" The girl covers her mouth with both hands, her eyes going wide with horror as she takes in Cyrus's uniform. "I've ruined your uniform."

She looks like she might actually cry. I stare in amazement.

"Hey, now," Cyrus says softly. "I'm sure these shiny pants sponsors can spare another one." He's at least a couple feet taller and probably a hundred pounds heavier, but Cyrus is in full charm mode now. Which makes my chest tight. We don't know this girl. She appears about as threatening as a kitten, but that could mean nothing.

Marcus hangs back, watching her carefully, but not moving to interfere. Maybe there's a rule about that too. I make a mental note that I *really* need to study up on this stuff. Soon.

The girl drops her hands from her face and shakes

them out. She seems to be blinking back tears. "I'm sorry. I promise I didn't mean to. It's just... just..." She takes a breath and looks up into Cyrus's eyes. "I'm not normally this... this..." She's drowning in some kind of panic that mystifies me.

Cyrus touches her shoulder gently, calming her. "I promise you, I've survived much worse than an attack by orange juice."

Another girl in a red uniform arrives at the first one's side, and says, sharply, "Basha! What are you *doing?*" She tugs the girl none-too-gently away from Cyrus, eyeing him like he's a lion intent on eating her friend. Her eyes are liquid brown, and her skin is the color of slightly melted chocolate, but the softness ends there. Her cheeks are high and carved, and her teeth are white and fierce behind full lips. The arch of her bony fingers makes it look like she's going to take Cyrus with her bare hands.

He steps back. "I was just—"

"No, no, Kamali, I'm fine, I'm fine," the petite one says, patting her arm. "It was my fault. I wasn't looking where I was going."

Her friend Kamali is lean to the point of ridiculousness, but she towers over her short friend like an angry, brown tree. She finally takes in the mess at our feet and seems to put it together. Her alarm steps down a few notches, but she still levels suspicious looks at Cyrus, then me, then Marcus. It's the ascender among us that finally turns her warm brown eyes cold.

"Let's go," Kamali says to her friend, taking her by the shoulders and guiding her away. The way she moves—

contained, purposeful, with a grace that's unnatural—has me watching her until they're obscured by the sea of colorful uniforms.

"That was really strange," I say finally. Cyrus is watching them, too, and I don't like the look on his face. Like he wishes the short, Arabic-looking one—I think her name is Basha—would come back.

"Generally speaking, you won't need to worry about agonites from *drama*, or any of the other arts," Marcus says, speaking for the first time through the whole event. "You're not competing against them, and most are too focused on their training to engage in espionage. I would, however, avoid anyone in *artem* if at all possible." He splays a hand toward the food line, and we slowly make our way that direction. "You are new, and that will automatically garner suspicion. It will get worse as we near the competition."

Hot stares follow us as we make our dinner selections—fresh-roasted turkey and salad greens, far better than the processed meat and canned vegetables in our grocery allotment in Seattle. Cyrus and I get our dinners packaged to take to our room. On the way out, I glare back at the sea of faces tracking us, especially the ones in blue *artem* uniforms.

My competition. I wonder who they are. Artem encompasses all the visual arts, so they could be working in any media, not just paint. Everyone is young, of course. Given the fact that you can only compete once, most are close to the eighteen-year-old age limit, to give themselves the maximum advantage. I wish I had paid more attention to the current crop of Olympians before Marcus's sponsorship suddenly dropped into my lap.

Marcus leads us again through the spiraling maze of hallways. I'm completely lost. He finally stops at a door and instructs us to log ourselves in. It's a small apartment, just a couple of beds, a couch, a large screen on the wall, and a bathroom.

"Your screen has access to all the Olympic regulations." Marcus purses his lips. "Make sure you understand them. Your studio will be equipped with everything you need by tomorrow morning."

I take it all in, then turn to Marcus. "Thank you. For everything."

He arches an eyebrow and seems to be holding back a smirk. "I'll return tomorrow."

"You're not staying? Here at Agon, I mean?"

The nascent smirk fades away. "Sponsor contact is limited to specific training hours. Previous experience has shown that too much sponsor presence at Agon can lead to an unfortunately high loss of agonites."

That makes me swallow.

Cyrus sweeps a look around the room. "Is Eli safe here?"

"Your room and your studio are the most secure," Marcus says. "There are no cameras or recording devices allowed—to keep competitors from gaining an unfair advantage over one another—and you are the only ones with access. Even I cannot enter without your permission."

Cyrus raises an eyebrow. "Good to know."

Marcus tips his head to me. "I'll stop by your studio tomorrow afternoon to check on your progress." He turns and leaves us alone in our new apartment.

The door barely slides shut before Cyrus is doing something that's probably illegal to our screen.

"Do you really think the games are as dangerous as Marcus makes out?" I ask.

"Either that or he's trying to scare us." Cyrus throws me a look over his shoulder, but his hands are busy manipulating the virtual controls of the screens. "And I don't see the upside there for him."

"Agreed," I say with a frown.

"I'll study the rules, bro," Cyrus says, eyes back on the screen. "You hit the sack."

"Just don't tamper with the security, like Marcus said. Or pirate any ascender tech until after I win. Deal?"

"I won't take anything they'll miss."

I snort and turn away.

"I call the bed on the left!" he says, not looking at me or the furniture.

"Whatever, man. They're identical."

"Obviously not. Or I wouldn't be calling the superior one."

I shake my head and rummage through the small closet by the bed on the right, finding toiletries and some softer, woven clothes that look like sleep pants. Only when I'm cleaned up, the last vestiges of the mist coughed and spit out of my lungs, and settled into my ridiculously comfortable ascender-tech bed, do I realize: Cyrus's bed is closer to the door.

If anyone comes through, he'll be there to greet them first.

TEN

Cyrus left his humor back in our apartment. Not that I blame him.

I don't think either of us slept last night. Now that I'm staring at the blank canvas set up in my studio, I'm wondering why I ever thought this was possible. We've been here two hours, and there's not even a pencil mark on it. I get up from my stool and stalk the perimeter of the room. It's small, not even fifteen feet on a side, just three walls and a side with a sink—pacing the edges is almost like spinning in place.

"Does that help?" Cyrus asks.

"No." I keep stalking.

"Carry on, then."

I reach a wall and drive my charcoal pencil into it like I'm killing a vampire with a stake. It just slides in my hand; the wall is impenetrable. I let loose a growl and glare at the streak of carbon black it leaves behind: the only *art* I've accomplished so far.

"Does that help?" Cyrus asks again.

"No." I smudge the carbon with my finger,

succeeding only in blackening my fingertip and making the mark an even uglier tarnish on the perfect, dirt-resistant, ascender-tech wall. Slowly, as I watch, the wall hums. The sound is so minute, I almost don't hear it. The smudge loosens, then spreads, then breaks into microscopic pieces that will eventually lift and drift away, leaving the surface clean once more.

Even my frustration can't leave a mark behind.

I turn to Cyrus, but I can't look him in the face. "It's hopeless."

"That's the spirit," he says drily.

I look up. "I'm serious, Cy. There's no way I can do this. I don't even know where to start."

"I'm no expert, but I'm going to guess that stabbing the wall isn't it."

I sigh. "I don't even know what I should be working on. Maybe if Lenora were here—"

Cyrus comes to life. "Okay, look." He covers the floor of the studio in three strides and stares me down. I shrink a little under his glare. Not to mention his oversized form towering over me.

"I may not be your hot ascender patron," he says, "but *I'm your friend.* I actually give a crap about whether you win this thing. And this is no time for your mopey, moody, *I'm-an-artiste* drama."

"I'm not being moody!" Then I realize what I sound like, and it makes me even more depressed. I glower at him.

Cyrus grabs hold of my shoulders. "Don't think I'm above punching some sense into you. Because I will. For your mom."

I push him away but not hard. Just enough to get some space. I scrub my face with my hands then bang my head back against the wall a few times. I stop and draw in a deep breath. "For my mom."

"Now you're talking." Then he starts to pace.

"I can't paint a gold-medal-winning piece on demand," I say.

Cyrus stops and gives me a sharp look, like he's ready to hit me.

I hold up a hand. "But... I can when I'm in the fugue state." Cyrus has known about the fugue since the *Puppet Boy* painting, the one he showed to his boss. Like an idiot.

"So, the key is figuring out what triggers the fugue."

I nod.

"How many times have you done this fugue thing?" he asks.

"I don't know—six, maybe seven?"

"How can you not know?" he asks, like maybe I really am crazy. Because, *obviously*, I should know how many times I've passed out and made great art while unconscious.

"It's been going on my whole life," I say defensively. "Since I was little."

"Okay, fine. How many times do you remember doing it? For sure."

"Five."

"The only one I've seen is the *Puppet Boy* painting."

"That was the fourth," I say. "The fifth was at Lenora's, when I painted a picture of my mom as some kind of spirit. That's the one Marcus saw. Before that was a picture of a woman I've never seen, another one with a field of flowers, and the first one was an abstract. I didn't even think it was anything, but my mom kind of freaked out about it at the time. I was seven. That's the first time I remember for sure, but there might have been times before that." I shrug. "Maybe my fugue art was developing just like my regular art. Only on a completely different plane."

Marcus nods, thoughtful. "Doesn't sound like they have any kind of theme in common. Or even a style."

"They're all in acrylics," I offer.

"Do you paint in something other than acrylics?" he asks, eyebrows fighting each other as his face contorts.

"Not normally." Acrylics are fast-drying and unforgiving... and difficult for detailed work. All of which makes it a medium conducive to performance art, like the Olympics, where time is a limiting factor. Serious artists work in all mediums, but most compete in acrylics.

"Okay, you're the artist. You tell me. What do they have in common?"

"They're brilliant? They're eerie and move people? They... wait." A thought pushes on the edge of my mind. "Every time the fugue came before, I blacked out completely... except this last time. I had a vision of my mom, only it didn't feel like a vision. It felt... *real*. But she was completely healthy and a lot younger than she is now. I was watching her paint."

"Okay, that's a start." But Cyrus sighs like he's frustrated. He stomps over to the easel and stares at the canvas. He picks up a pencil. "Tell me exactly what happened the last time. Back it up, like five minutes before. Walk me through it, step by step."

I come up behind him and take the pencil from his hand. He looks back at me, questioning. "Lenora wouldn't let me sketch first. She took away the pencil."

Cyrus nods.

I face the canvas and wave the pencil in front of it. "I try to paint my mom from memory, but it's coming out horrific."

"What's Lenora doing?"

"She's hovering over me, distracting me, making me nervous." I turn my head toward the studio door. "Then Marcus comes to the front door." I slowly walk to the studio door, replaying that scene in my head. "I snuck up on the two of them. They weren't touching." I give Cyrus a sheepish look. "They were talking. You know, silently. Transmitting their thoughts back and forth, or whatever they do. Lenora sent me back to the studio." I slowly turn and step back to the canvas. "I realize that what I have is a mess." I pretend to wipe paint away. "I get the acetone out, but I'm just making it worse. Everything's smearing. I throw the rag on the ground." I mime the action, then look over my shoulder, back at Cyrus. He's watching me intently. "Then I feel it coming."

"The fugue?"

"Yeah. It's like..." I fumble for words. "Like a mountain collapsing on you. You hear the rumble first. The rush. The sense of it. Then it hits. And you're out."

"Then you paint?"

"I guess." I frown, tugging at the memory, but there's just a blank spot where time should be. "I had the vision of my mom painting, then the next thing I knew, I was waking up on the floor."

"What were you feeling right before the fugue hit?" he asks.

I close my eyes, trying to picture it. "Frustration. Anger. Embarrassment. Longing. It's like an ache in my chest, a hole I can't fill." My eyes pop open. "Jealousy."

"You were jealous of Marcus. Because he was with Lenora."

"Jealous of Marcus. Jealous of everything he has. But it was more than that… like there was this *other me* who could produce great art, and I was jealous of *him*." I spin away from Cyrus and dash to the fully-stocked paint cabinet. I use my implant to unlock it and fumble with the paints, the palette, the brushes, juggling them all in my haste.

Cyrus steps back, watching me. "Can I help?"

"No." I'm trying to hold onto that feeling. The aching hole in my chest. The extreme desire to fill it. With paint. With control. With something beautiful and real.

I sweep away the pencils lying next to the canvas and make space for my palette and the tumble of tubes. I'm mixing and blending and dabbing. I move back and forth—palette, easel, palette, easel. I dip, wiggle, sweep, just like my mom. As soon as I think of her, though, all the jealousy flees, leaving just the hole. It's like air escaping a balloon, deflating all at once.

I stall out.

There's nothing on the canvas, but a smear of angry reds and tortured grays. Just like the inferno of torment I created before the fugue in Lenora's studio.

But nothing more.

I throw the brush to the floor. It skids across the room, leaving a bloody trail in its wake.

"Eli—" Cyrus says, then stops.

I lurch toward the door and scan my way out into the hall. My vision is blurred with pathetic, angry tears. Or maybe my frustration has reached such epic levels that it's literally blinding me.

I stumble past the other doors. The windows are all dialed down. I picture other artists, ones who have some control of their art, working inside. They're painting or sculpting, practicing their showpiece for the competition. Not only do I not have a showpiece, I don't know if I can even paint anymore. It's as if my Muse is real, an actual creature that lives inside me, possesses me... and now it's gone. I stride past the doors, looking for one where the window is clear. I want to bang on them and demand the true artists let me in and tell me their secrets.

How do they master the beast?

My rational brain knows that most of these studios house different artists: musicians, actors, singers. They're not all going to be painters, and they probably don't have this insane split personality like I do. But my irrational brain is convinced every single one is hiding a painter who is superior to me in every way... who holds the key and can give me the secret... right up until I find a door with a clear window.

And it's not a painter inside.

It's the tall girl from the Lounge.

I tell myself her nudity is just an illusion: she must be wearing some kind of leotard that matches the creamy brown richness of her skin. But my face heats anyway.

I stare, mouth open, and watch her dance.

She lifts from the ground as if weightless. Her legs leap into an impossible stretch, and her arms carve the air with delicate strokes of grace and strength. This is how humans would fly—if their bones were made of gossamer steel and their muscles were exquisite lines of female beauty. I can't hear the music, but I don't need to. She spins, arms splayed like wings, then she takes another soaring leap that turns her into a human butterfly taking flight. When she lands, her bare feet quickly kiss the floor and depart again.

I don't breathe.

I have only one thought: *I need to paint her.*

"You have got to be kidding me."

I startle and blink rapidly at Cyrus. *When did he arrive?* I have no idea what he's talking about.

"*Now?*" he says incredulously. "Now… when we're training for the Olympics… now is when you decide you like human girls?"

"I… what?" My gaze is drawn back to her. She twirls past the window, so close I catch my breath. She keeps spinning, oblivious to us. I gesture to the window because it's obvious. She's amazing to watch. Anyone would be affected. *Anyone.* "I'm just admiring her… form." I stop because I know how it sounds, and that's not what I mean.

"Yes, you are," Cyrus says with high amusement. "I'm going to have to call a maintenance bot to clean up the drool."

I'm strangely embarrassed, but I shouldn't be. It can't be wrong to watch beauty like this and be moved. I fling my anger at him. "You can't tell me you don't think she's incredible."

"Well, sure," Cyrus says, peering through the window and pretending to give her a serious look. I know him well enough to see this isn't going to end well for me. "She is tremendously hot. And anyone who dances naked gets a serious *yes* vote in my book."

I briefly squeeze my eyes shut, then tip my head up to stare at the ceiling, searching for patience. When I look back to him, he's barely holding in his laughter.

"I'm not interested in *dating* her," I say with as much disdain as I can muster. I peer through the window again. She's still doing it. Still creating beauty in movement like it's as simple as breathing. "I am, however, very interested in painting her." I say it like a starving man might be interested in his next meal. Because, suddenly, that's how it feels to me.

Necessary. And urgent.

Cyrus sighs. "Man, you are one strange bird."

I ignore him. But then we're both startled by a face appearing in the window.

It's the short Arabic girl from before—the one who splashed her drink all over Cyrus then freaked out. She's barely tall enough to peek out the window.

She disappears, and a moment later, the door slides open. "Hey!" she shouts over the blast of music from inside. "You guys came to visit! Hey, Kamali, look who's here."

I frown and look past her. Kamali stops, somehow graceful even in her half-completed step. She glares at us. I bite my lip, not wanting to be the cause of her stopping the dance any more than she obviously doesn't want us interfering with her training.

We're interfering… just what Marcus said to look out for.

"I'm sorry," I say, quickly. The music dies, and my voice suddenly carries into the room. "We don't mean to interrupt."

"No, don't be silly!" The petite girl smiles to reassure me, but her smile grows even broader for Cyrus, who is strangely quiet. She sticks her hand out to him. "I'm Basha. I don't think I ever introduced myself. So rude! But I was worried you were… well, you know. This place…" She leans forward, conspiratorially. "It's completely *nuts.*"

Cyrus grins as he holds her hand. Too much of both smiles and hand-holding, I decide.

"Well, it is filled with a bunch of *creatives,*" he says.

"I know, right?" Then she starts counting our sins on her fingers. "Moody. Demanding. Messy. Can't keep track of time."

"Don't forget arrogant."

She looks up at Cyrus like he's her sudden soul mate with this insightful bashing of creative types. "You are *so* right."

"Hey," I protest. "Standing right here, you know."

Cyrus shakes his head like I'm hopeless, but I ignore him because Kamali has just joined us. I swallow. She has slipped a uniform over her nearly-nude leotard, making it a lot easier for me to keep my eyes on her face—which has a carved beauty of its own. Tiny beads of sweat glisten on her forehead. Her dark hair is pinned tightly behind the nape of her neck, and her liquid brown eyes are almost too large for her sculpted face... but they're gorgeous.

Even though they're glaring at me.

"I'm sorry," I say again. "You were..." *Amazing.* The compliment sticks in my throat. There's no way I can say it without having it sound wrong. Or having Cyrus make it wrong. "You were training. We didn't mean to interrupt."

"Why are you here?" she asks. Her voice is flat. Demanding.

Wandering the halls? Looking for my Muse? Finding you? I can't think of anything to say.

Basha saves me. "I'm sure they're just heading to lunch, right? I promise not to dump our drinks again all over... um..." She shakes a finger at Cyrus, like she can't remember his name. I'm pretty sure he never offered it.

"Cyrus," he says with a grin. "The *artiste* is Eli."

"Great! Cyrus and Eli are joining us for lunch." Basha announces this like she's the Queen of the Olympics and has just laid down a decree, daring any to disobey. Then she hooks her arm around Kamali's and drags her into the corridor. "Let's see what fresh *drama* there is to be found in the Lounge today."

Cyrus is all smiles as he follows the girls down the hall. I have no choice but to join them, not least because Marcus said we should stick together. But the truth is I'm already calculating ways to ask Kamali to model for me.

I think she might be just the inspiration I need.

ELEVEN

Agon is still a maze I haven't deciphered.

But the girls know the way to the Lounge, and I'm sure Cyrus does, too. He studied the maps and tried to explain them. All I could see was a mass of giant centipedes in some kind of death dance: four of the five Olympic rings have spiraling main hallways with studios and apartments sticking out like a thousand tiny legs. The fifth ring is filled with the Lounge on the inside, and the competition stage and stadium on the outside.

It must be the lunch hour because the place is jammed. Cyrus leads us to the food line, bending to hear Basha's running commentary of the artists and their support teams: where they've come from, what kind of art they're known for, what odds the legacy net is placing on them. There's no official betting on the games allowed—at least for legacies, who knows what the ascenders do—but that doesn't keep people from speculating.

Kamali is behind me in line, not saying a word. I try to catch her gaze, but she's studying the selection of vegetables intently.

"...and when *you* dropped into the competition," Basha gushes, capturing my attention as her words spill over onto me, "well, everything just got turned upside down."

"Why is that?" asks Cyrus. "I'm mean Eli's art is great, but he's just one more competitor."

"He's a dark horse," Basha says, knowingly. "Came into the competition late, no established artistic record... of course, there's the *Lady in the Light*, but that's just one piece."

"The Lady in the Light?" I ask.

Basha turns her wide brown eyes to me. "Isn't that what you call it? I mean, that's what the net was calling it. Well, not the *official* net," she says with a sly grin. Then she catches a dark look from Kamali and clamps her lips tight.

"I think she means the painting I did for my patron," I say to Cyrus. Marcus uploaded the fugue painting of my mother to Orion, but I'm not sure what Basha means by the "unofficial" net. I can see the gears in Cyrus's head turning. If Basha's tapped into some kind of black market Olympic book makers, I'm sure Cyrus will be all over pumping that information out of her. It's the kind of thing he would have done already, if he weren't focused on helping me figure out how to win.

We use our implants to pay for the food and weave our way through the multi-colored crowd of uniforms to find an open space to sit. Frowns and glares follow us the entire way. Once we settle in—Kamali and I on one side of the small square table, Basha and Cyrus on the other—Basha is back into full gossip mode.

She points with her fork, like it's a mini-taser. "See that cluster of *drama* over there?" I glance over my shoulder at a group of four red-uniformed girls. "They're from Rio. All of them in the same family. All dancers. Their mother was an agonite who came in second. They're *all* competitors, not just support."

Second place. It has to be the hardest loss to bear—the gold medalist goes on to immortality, while the one who was just slightly less brilliant goes home. Often their patrons abandon them, looking for someone else to sponsor. Someone who can still compete. The ascenders have all of eternity to score a winning agonite; legacies only get one shot.

"Is that legal?" I ask. "To have that many competitors from one family, I mean." Rio is the main legacy city in South America, and it's not unheard of for second-generation agonites to get sponsorship. After all, talent runs in the genes. Chances are even better if one of their parents was well-loved by their patron. *A domestic.* My mind floats up the offensive term, but I shove it away.

Basha gives them a glare, like their mere existence is a crime against art. "Not technically. They think they're increasing their odds by packing the field. But it doesn't really matter." Basha sniffs and turns her gaze back to me. "Everyone knows Kamali is going to win *drama* this year. Even the book makers."

"I believe it." I sneak a look to her.

She stabs her vegetables with her fork, half-heartedly

pushing them around. "Don't jinx it, Basha." Her voice is quiet, but I hear a tremble in it.

I frown and ask her softly, "Is it dangerous to be the front runner?"

Kamali stops torturing her food to look at me. "It's worth it."

I nod, but a strange feeling takes up residence in my chest.

Before I can decide what it is, Cyrus pipes up. "Well, I'm glad we're in *artem*, then. Eli would have no chance against Kamali."

I hear the humor in his voice, but Basha nods, like this is a given.

"You guys need to worry about *that* guy." Basha uses her chin to point out a nearby gang of three blue uniforms.

Cyrus gives them a long look. "I know that guy in the center. Eli?"

I check him out. "He's from Seattle, I think." I vaguely remember him from one of the legacy Art Fairs when we were young.

"Aaron Thompson, seventeen and three-quarters years old, resident of Seattle." Basha leans forward and lowers her voice. "Both his parents were agonites. They competed against each other, lost, and... decided to have a baby instead. There's more than one way to win ascendance."

"What?" I draw back. "You're kidding. You mean they had a baby just so it could compete?"

Basha nods wisely, and I'm surprised to see Cyrus

nodding with her.

"Not the first time it's happened," Basha says. "Pretty creepy, if you ask me." She shrugs. "Or maybe they just fell in love. Drowned their post-competition sorrows in each other's arms."

"That seems more likely." I'm vaguely horrified at the idea of parents conceiving a child just to have hopes of ascending themselves if it won.

Basha looks askance at me, then turns to Cyrus. "Is he always this straight?"

He smirks. "Unfortunately, yes. Painfully so."

Apparently, I'm going to be the source of many jokes between the two of them. I give Cyrus a pre-emptive glower.

Something catches Basha's eye. "Oh, hey!" she bursts out. "Delphina, you made it!"

A short, angry-looking girl stands next to Kamali's chair, arms crossed, giving the evil eye to Cyrus and me. Her uniform is yellow, but it's torn and blackened with stripes of charcoal. The ripped pieces of fabric have been repurposed as bindings that shorten the arms and legs, with another strip twisted and wrapped around her forehead as a lumpy bandana. The effect is ragged and somehow defiant. The black smeared on her eyelids and lips adds a fierce touch.

Kamali leaps up from her chair to hug Delphina. The difference in their heights means Kamali has to bend down to wrap her long arms around her. Cyrus gives me a one-eyebrow lift, and I'm not quite sure what to make of it either. It's a pretty enthusiastic hug for just being friends.

When Kamali releases her, Delphina asks, quietly, "What's with the *artems?*" She says it like we're dangerous animals that were mistakenly let out of the zoo. Her hand lingers at Kamali's waist.

My puzzlement about Delphina turns into an instant dislike.

Kamali shakes her head. "Basha invited them."

Delphina releases her and sits down to join us. I just now notice she has a red apple in her hand. She carefully places it on the table, like it's a cryptic challenge. I don't understand it, but I don't like it either.

Cyrus puts out his hand. "I'm Cyrus. This is Eli. We're new here. Don't want any trouble."

She regards his hand and slowly takes it. The shake is brief, but somehow Cyrus has managed to diffuse whatever bomb was waiting to explode inside her.

"Delphina is in *storia!*" Basha's exuberance seems unaffected by the tension. "She's a writer."

"A spoken word artist," Delphina says, like she's bored. Only there's a million watts of dangerous energy underneath it.

"She's from *Paris*," Basha says, like that explains everything. Paris is one of the legacy cities known for producing top competitors year after year, so I suppose that it does.

"You must have a good shot at ascending," I say, trying to make a truce.

"Why else would I be here?" she asks, stone-cold.

I'm about to concede the arrogance factor of creatives

to Cyrus for all time, when Delphina cracks a tiny, secret smile. But it's not directed at me… it's for Kamali, who's just shaking her head in response. I'm annoyed with the secret language between them—which would be fairly ridiculous, except I already feel a connection to Kamali. Or rather my Muse does. Kamali feels… *important* to me. Somehow key to making this all work. It's just a gut feeling, but it's strong.

"So…" says Cyrus, trying to break the tension again. "Where are you and Kamali from?" he asks Basha.

"Oh, we're from Paris, too," Basha says, like it's no big deal. "Kamali comes from a long line of Parisian dancers, but I'm just a legacy girl trying to—" She stalls out and looks at something over my shoulder. "Uh oh."

Delphina's curses are as colorful as her outfit. "I could have told you the *artems* would be trouble, Basha," she says, harsh but quiet.

"Eli," Cyrus says, warning in his voice.

I twist around to see what they're talking about. Aaron Thompson is stalking up to our table, flanked by his support team: two very large guys who weren't chosen for their intellect. I rise up from my chair. Whatever issue Thompson has with me, I don't want him bringing it to the rest of the table. Cyrus has come around, so he's in between Thompson's crew and Basha. I have no idea what's about to go down, but I'm regretting having any of it near the girls.

Thompson stops just out of arm's reach. He stands with his feet planted wide, arms folded. "Elijah Brighton." He cocks his head to one side. "Never thought I'd see you here."

"Never expected to be here." I scramble for some clue as to who this guy is. His dark hair is long and straight and tucked behind his ears in a slick way that certainly says *artiste* more than the ragged brown mop on my head. I only get a haircut when my mom has a chance… and when she's well.

Thompson takes a step closer to me. "Aren't you that kid who was always sketching boats?" His blue eyes shine with menace. "Imagine that. Boats. In Seattle."

My memories start to fill in the blanks: Thompson, the local prodigy, son of two agonites. Thompson, winning all the junior art fairs. His art was so good, he had a patron by age ten. I was sixteen before Lenora took me on, and then only after my mom circulated *The Puppet Boy* on ArtNet—a fugue-piece that I haven't been able to replicate since. Thompson's been making Olympic-level art since he was a kid. He should have nothing to worry about—yet here he is, harassing me. Like Marcus said, distracting the competition.

Two can play this game.

"I like painting boats," I say, playing up the dark horse angle. "Simple. Unassuming. Easy."

He chuckles and glances back at his goons, who are having a laugh at my expense, too.

"Good choice," Thompson says. "I hear ascenders like boats. They like water, too. Here's a tip: why don't you paint the Dead Sea for your showpiece?"

It's too bad that being an Olympic-sized jerk has no bearing on whether you win. A burning need wells up inside me to take the gold away from this guy. If he loses, he gets to disappoint his morally-challenged parents, the ones who had him just so they could ascend.

If I lose, my mom dies.

"I've already got something... *unexpected* planned for the showpiece," I say, coolly. "I guess you'll have to see it when everyone else does. On stage."

His eyes turn cold, and the smile falls from his face. He leans in closer. "When I heard you had a sponsor, I said to my friends..." He gestures to the two thugs whose muscles bulge under their uniforms. "...who is this Elijah Brighton? Then I remembered: your mother's a two-chit paint-slinger. Had a patron for a while but couldn't keep him. And your father... oh, that's right. No father on your birth records."

My fists curl up. I don't know what he means about my mother having a patron—she tolerates Lenora, for my sake, but she's never had one of her own—but I know exactly what he means about birth records. My mother doesn't even have relatives in Seattle—but that doesn't stop the rumors. Another memory dredges up: the playground, a tall kid, arrogant even at seven. *Inbred.* The word-memory still sends a shiver through me. I remember Thompson's nose crunching under my fist.

I'm ready to bloody it again.

Cyrus puts a hand on my shoulder and whispers in my ear, "Regulations, Eli."

Throwing the first punch will get me kicked out. I let loose a slow breath, packed with anger.

Thompson snorts a laugh. "C'mon, Brighton. Can't

imagine an inbred like you worries about regs too much."

Cyrus's hand clamps tighter.

Thompson leans closer, within punching distance. "How is your mother? I hear she's not feeling so well."

My eyelid twitches, and Thompson's smirk grows.

Suddenly, Delphina appears out of nowhere, stepping around me and forcing her short body in between me and Thompson. "Why don't you find some different puppies to eat, *artem?*" she says up into his face. Her voice has no fear, and Thompson actually leans back.

He jerks his head, motioning her aside. "This isn't your problem, *storia.*"

"Massive jerkwad bullies are everyone's problem," she says. "You see, I think your threats are as empty as your head, *artem*. As empty as your *pants*." Thompson's mouth falls open. The power in her voice just grows. "As empty as your mind, which they'll find when they try to ascend you, and all they get is an echoing shell that walks and talks like a man, but has no heart. No soul."

Thompson clamps his mouth shut, his jaw working. Her words ricochet around in my head. There's silence as the Lounge collectively holds its breath.

She spreads her hands wide and looks him up and down. "You see, I'm five foot nothing, with a headband and attitude, and you're one of three, six foot two, with fists to match. No one— and I mean no one, *artem*—is going to believe I threw the first punch."

She pulls back a fist. Thompson's eyes grow wide, and he takes a stumbling step backward, out of her reach.

I'm struck dumb with awe.

Delphina relaxes her arm, flicking her hand. She's shaking him off like so much dust. Her gaze never leaves Thompson's face, but her words are for me. "Get out of here, painter boy. We got this."

When I don't move, Cyrus shoves me a little. "Go," he says, between clenched teeth.

The thought of leaving burns shame in my chest. But I can't afford a fight. And leaving means Thompson no longer has someone to taunt. No fuel for his fire.

I turn and stride away, embarrassment flaming my cheeks. I strain to hear any signs of a scuffle, a fight sparking in my absence, but I don't dare look back.

I hear nothing but the hushed murmurs of the Lounge slowly coming back to life.

TWELVE

I stumble out of the Lounge and into the hallway.

The fire in my face, the shame of Thompson's taunts and Delphina's rescue, spreads down to my chest and consumes the air in my lungs. Because he's right: I have no right to be here. I don't have a long line of competition-level artists in my family. I have some kind of freak gift I can't control. Being here is an accident. A waste of time. I should be home with my mother, caring for her in her final days. Obeying her dying wishes, not going against everything she believes just to reach for a prize I don't have a chance of winning.

Because there's not going to be any ascendance for her. Or for me.

I stop my headlong rush down the hall, realizing I have no idea how to get back to my apartment. The long hall outside the Lounge is lined with images: vids of gold medalists of the past, showing snippets of their winning performances. One displays a dancer, a classical ballerina like Kamali. *Anatalia Petroli* flashes across the screen as she levitates from the stage, creating beauty with her body by moving through space. Kamali belongs with her picture next to Anatalia's, that much is clear.

I touch the image, and it resets. Replays.

Anatalia is an ascender now. One of the billions that will be watching and voting on Kamali's performance. Next to Anatalia is a painter. *Heinrich Schubert* is halfway through his work, his brush sweeping across a painting I can already tell will be incandescent when it's finished. Better than anything I could create outside of the fugue state. I step back and scan the line of ascended artists, a Hall of Fame literally immortalized by taking these legacies and ascending them into what passes for gods in our world. I notice one is darkened. As I step closer, I see it's an actor. His performance is frozen, the expression on his face pained. It wrenches emotion out of me, even without the moving vid of his performance. I touch the screen, to see if I can bring it to life. Nothing. Then a chill sweeps through me—he must be one of the winners who ultimately lost. Who won the games, but didn't survive the ascendance procedure... and paid the ultimate price for his ambition.

My mouth is suddenly dry. I step back.

"Are you all right?" Kamali's voice is a whisper next to me. I jerk away, startled by her sudden appearance. The burning embarrassment floods back. I straighten and try to recover some dignity.

"I'm fine. I just..." I cast a look down the hallway. "I'm not sure how to get back to my apartment." Then I frown, realizing she's alone. And that she came after me. The embarrassment wrestles with a small glow caused by that thought.

"I can show you the way."

"Where's Basha?" I ask. "My sponsor said you shouldn't wander off alone. You never know when some creep like Thompson is going to show up." Obviously, I'm not supposed to be on my own either… but I was driven out of the Lounge. She came voluntarily.

"I'm with you." She gives a tight smile.

I quickly return it, the glow becoming a little brighter.

"Besides, Basha wanted to stay and keep an eye on Thompson."

"Did he hassle you? Or was he just after me?" I'm worried about Cyrus, but I don't say anything.

"Just you, I imagine. You're the only real threat to him. Getting your support team thrown out could be detrimental to you, but it could also make you more determined to win. There are all kinds of double and triple strategies." She shakes her head, her pretty lips turning down. "That's what the competition does to legacies. Turns artist against artist. Makes people like Thompson do things they probably never would otherwise, all to have an edge."

I frown. "I'm pretty sure Thompson was a jerk *before* the Olympics."

Her lips turn up into a small smile. "You're probably right. I just hate seeing people turned into something they're not by the games."

I think about Marcus's warning: someone was willing to murder to influence the games. Then again, I'm not sure how much to trust Marcus. He might just be trying to scare me.

I don't say anything to Kamali.

"Anyway," she says, "I don't pay attention to that stuff. I'm just here to dance."

I'm glad for the change in topic. I point to the wall. "You're going to be up here soon. I just know it."

She studies the wall, scanning the faces, but she doesn't say anything.

I wonder if I've said something wrong.

Then she drops her gaze to her delicate hands, which are playing with one another. I stare at them: I could just draw her hands and be happy. When she looks up, her eyes are wide and timid. Like she's holding something sacred inside, and she's not sure if she should share. "Cyrus said you wanted to paint me."

I suck in a breath. "He did?" I hope like crazy he said I wanted to paint her *on canvas* and not in a hundred other ways that only Cyrus could make sound dirty.

She frowns. "He said you were blocked. That you needed some inspiration for your showpiece and that you thought... that maybe I could help."

I'm still holding my breath, so I let it out. "Would you do that for me? Model? I mean, you don't even know me—"

"I know what it's like. To not be able to access your art. It hurts." She grimaces then gestures to her left foot. "Last summer, an injury benched me for several weeks. I couldn't dance. It was a dark time. The pain of the sprained ankle was nothing compared to that... emptiness. I wouldn't wish it on anyone." She pauses.

"Besides, I trust Delphina."

Delphina. She made a bully twice her size back down. The fact that she stood up for me makes Kamali think I'm someone worthwhile. I'm not sure how I feel about that, but Kamali offering to model is a gift I won't refuse.

"It really would be a tremendous help if you modeled for me."

She gestures down the hall, and I fall into step beside her. Her movements are graceful, even when she's just walking. I try hard not to stare. After a few turns, I recognize that we're in the ring that houses both my apartment and my studio. And probably hers as well, because I didn't go far before stumbling upon it.

"It's very kind of you to help me," I say, "but I don't want to take you away from your training. Maybe I can just grab a sketch pad from my studio, then we can go back to yours? You can dance…" I swallow, thinking about that. "And I can sketch."

She nods. We're silent until we reach my studio. I scan in and grab a half dozen pencils and a large sketch pad from the cabinet. After a quiet walk filled with itchy anticipation on my part, we arrive back at her studio.

She peels off her uniform. I busy myself with paying close attention to choosing a pencil, just to keep from staring. She slips off her shoes, but instead of dancing, she starts warming up. I give myself permission to watch, hand poised over the blank sketchpad. As she dips and bends, she's entirely focused. It's like I've ceased to exist… which is freeing. My hand whips over the page, catching a moment when she's bent to the side, arms reaching like fluttering feathers. I flip the page and sketch another position. This time I focus on the lines of her muscles, detailing her slender but powerful legs. The lingering embarrassment at her near-nudity finally fades. I'm grateful for every curve that is revealed. That she holds nothing back.

I fill five more pages before she stops the warmup and walks toward where I'm sitting along the back wall.

"Do you want to see?" I ask, holding up the sketch pad.

"No."

I try not to be crushed by that, but she gives me a small smile and ducks her head. I think maybe she's embarrassed. Not of dancing nearly naked in front of me. But of having her picture drawn.

It makes me grin.

As she pulls up the holographic music controls from a panel in the wall, I ask, "Have you always danced?"

"Yes. Honestly, I don't remember a time when I wasn't dancing." She carries on with the music selection then stops and turns to me. "You know, sometimes… I'm afraid."

I'm riveted. "Of what?"

"That if I stop dancing… or if I can't… that I'll die." She stares at her bare feet. "That sounds crazy, doesn't it?"

"Not at all."

She looks up and gives me a small, uncertain smile.

It's like a beam of sunshine. I hold up my hand. "Just… hold that. For a moment."

She frowns, ruining it. "Hold what?"

But I still have it in my head. I flip over the page, sketching just her smile, like a delicate Cheshire cat beaming from the page. I grin. "Never mind. I got it."

Curious, she drifts toward me, peering over the top of my sketchpad. I hold it flat against my chest, hiding it.

"I thought you didn't want to see." I hope she knows I'm teasing. My heart pounds, uncertain now whether I want her to see it or not.

She scowls at me, but it's playful. "I want to see it when you're done."

My grin returns. "Deal."

She nods and floats back to the music controls. Before she can start it up, I say, "You don't have to worry about dying, you know."

Her hand freezes midair. Slowly, she looks back to me. "What makes you say that?"

"I have a feeling about you. Winning, I mean." I intend it as a high compliment, but her face shows no reaction. "Have you always wanted to ascend?" I add, wondering how long she's been training for this one shot at literally being able to dance forever.

"No." She turns back to the music player. Her fingers move then stop. The music hasn't started yet. I'm about to apologize for saying the wrong thing, even though I'm not sure what it is, when she says, "Delphina convinced me to compete."

Delphina. I have a small stab in my chest that I recognize as jealousy. I'm a little dumbstruck by that. How can I feel that way about someone I've just met?

But it's there, pulling at me with a piercing need to know: what exactly *is* Kamali's relationship with Delphina? Are they... *together*? Or just friends?

When I don't respond, Kamali peeks over her shoulder.

"She's special to you," I hazard, not sure if I want her to explain how.

Kamali turns to face me and crosses her arms. "She's special to a lot of people."

"Why?" I ask, although I have an inkling.

"You saw her."

"She's... inspiring?" I guess.

"She puts into words things I can only begin to think on my own."

I nod. I can't deny she has that power. Words are obviously her talent, or she wouldn't be here competing with them. "Do you think she'll win?" Suddenly the possibility that we might all win occurs to me. We're all in different arts—*drama, artem, storia*. It could happen. And what would it be like to have forever to explore a relationship with Kamali? Or Delphina? Or other artists like them?

It sparks a fierce longing deep inside me.

Kamali hasn't answered my question. She stares at me a moment longer, then turns back to her controls. "You ask a lot of questions for a painter."

Before I can respond, music blasts into the room. She steps away from the controls to the center of the room. I'm still struggling for a comeback, wondering if I should shout over the music, when she starts to dance.

It destroys every other thought I have.

She moves constantly, leaping through space, one long, continuous dance made of a million tiny movements of beauty. I sketch furiously. Time suspends. I'm not sure how much of it actually passes, but my hand starts to ache. The pages flip by, consumed with sketched snapshots of her, capturing all the different ways she moves, stretches, leaps, and wrenches beauty out of thin air.

I'm a little light-headed.

I think I'm forgetting to breathe.

I shake out my hand, rubbing away the cramp, and I'm about to dive in again, when there's a loud banging on the door that thumps over the music.

Through the window, I see... *Marcus*.

THIRTEEN

I am so busted.

I sprint to the door of Kamali's studio, where Marcus waits outside with an expression that sends tremors through me. I try to open the door, but I can't. It's keyed to Kamali's implant. Fortunately, my rush across the room has caught her attention, and she hurries over to open the door.

Marcus doesn't come inside, just grips the doorframe. He's traded his sheer shorts for a one-piece uniform that's blue like mine, only he has the holo rings of the Olympics floating next to the airy fabric. His clothes obscure the coloration that must be raging across his chest, but it spills out the high collared neck and creeps up to stain his cheeks the color of spilled blood.

"Marcus, I can explain—"

He cuts me off with a raised hand. Cyrus is behind him, looking contrite. But it's not his fault I'm not in my room *or* my studio *and* I'm hanging out with another agonite. Marcus motions me out of the room, giving a suspicious glance to Kamali that makes me want to jump to her defense.

But I don't.

"You have a visitor," Marcus says quietly. "Your patron is waiting by your studio, but since you're not there, there's no one to let her in."

"Lenora's here?" My voice pitches up. I shoot a look at the sketchpad in my hand, hanging open with detailed drawings of Kamali's body in every possible pose. I quickly flip it closed and shoot an apologetic look to Kamali.

She's coolly taking all of it in.

"I have to go," I say, lamely.

She nods.

I leave with Marcus, keeping pace with his too-fast stride down the hall toward my studio. Cyrus catches up. After a moment of silence, he and I both try to speak at the same time. We stop.

Before we can try again, Marcus cuts in. "I warned you about distractions, Eli."

We round a corner. "She's not distracting me."

He gives me a look like he can't decide if I'm lying or simply stupid.

I briefly consider telling him the truth—that she's my inspiration—but that feels strangely personal. Cyrus is right: the ascenders have their own motives, and there's no telling what they are. Whatever Marcus's reasons for sponsoring me, I don't want it to affect Kamali in any way.

"I doubt you know who your true friends are, Eli," he says. "Or your enemies."

We turn another corner. Lenora stands outside my studio, halfway down the hall.

Marcus drops his voice. "Don't put me in a position where I have to defend your actions to the Olympic Board."

"I'll do my best to keep you out of trouble," I say, sarcastically. Maybe he knows about the incident in the Lounge. I remind myself that ascenders tend to know *everything.* Thompson must already be on his radar.

We arrive at my door and Lenora's side.

"I'm sorry I've been away, Elijah." She's as beautiful as always... and dressed up again, this time as an angel not a conquistador. Her dress is fashioned from gossamer, a dozen sheer layers arranged like rose petals around her body. Her coloration pulses through at the sleeves and chest, where the layers are thinnest—she's flushed pink with excitement. A golden shimmer skims up to her cheeks, adding an otherworldly touch.

"I would have been here sooner..." She gives Marcus a glare that sends satisfaction coursing through me. "But I was delayed."

Cyrus darts suspicious looks at both of them.

"I'm glad you're here." I key open the door with my implant and sweep an arm out. She steps inside. Marcus and Cyrus follow us in.

I gesture with the sketch pad. "I've been doing some work, getting ready for the competition." I set it down, hoping she won't want to see.

"Eli," she says softly and steps close to me. "I'd like to speak with you. Alone."

My heart skips a beat.

Marcus's tight expression confirms that *he's* the one she wants gone. "She's not here to help you, Eli. She's here to stop you from competing."

I frown, hoping he's wrong, but the golden flush in her cheeks dims with his words.

His expression grows colder. "The only reason she's here is because patrons have rights even sponsors can't deny. But remember this: I'm the one who believes you have what it takes to win. And I'd like nothing more than to see you ascend."

Lenora presses her lips together and locks glares with Marcus.

My stomach churns in an angry storm of bile. I'm just a pawn in whatever their little game is. Which makes me wonder how all this would change if I actually won.

"I'll be outside if you need me." Marcus turns to leave.

Cyrus folds his arms and doesn't budge from his spot by the door. Lenora acts as if he isn't even in the room. I wait until the door slides shut behind Marcus.

"Is it true?" I ask her. "Are you still trying to stop me from competing?"

"Elijah." She lays a cool, perfect hand on my arm, but I flinch away. She frowns. "It's not that I don't believe in your talent."

"Really? Because it looks an awful lot like that."

Cyrus is keeping quiet, but he gives me a small, supportive nod.

Lenora's delicate fingers lace and unlace. I don't think I've ever seen her... nervous. "Marcus is ambitious. Our world is very different from yours. I know it's hard for you to understand, but if Marcus sponsors a winning agonite, he'll become even more influential than he already is. He'll be able to sway others in a way he can't now."

"That's fine by me. As long as I ascend, I don't really care what Marcus gets out of it." In that moment, I include *her* in that. I don't really mean it, but it hurts—badly—that she doesn't want me to compete.

"There are things you don't understand at work here," she says.

"I think it's pretty simple, actually." Bitterness is a poison working its way deep inside me. "When I ascend, you don't want Marcus getting all the social status instead of you."

"That's not true." She stops the torment working through her fingers. "Marcus is right. Patrons have rights. I could claim you for my own, if I wanted to."

"But you don't want to." The poison plunges into my heart.

"I can't."

"Why not?" My heart twists with the pain of it.

She's so close now, I could reach out and touch her. I want to sweep my fingertips along her perfectly sculpted cheek and tell her how ascending means everything to me. That we could finally be together, as equals—

My thoughts cut off when she touches me instead. Her hand on my face.

Her eyes lock with mine, so close. "Eli... Eli..." Her fingertips are tiny islands of cool against the sudden heat of my skin. Breath is frozen inside me.

"You are so special." Her voice is low, whispering. "You don't have any idea how true that is. Come home. Stay with me. Become a true artist-in-residence. We'll work on your art together, and when you're ready, I'll take you to the finest shows in the ascender world. I'll give you anything you wish, just please come home with me now."

Her words have worked the poison free of my heart. She's so close... close enough to kiss. "There's only one thing I want," I breathe out. Does she know?

"What is it? Just tell me. I'll give it to you. I promise."

A loud cough breaks the spell.

Cyrus scowls at me from the edge of the room. I blink and lean away from Lenora's touch. I'd completely forgotten he was there. Completely forgotten my purpose for being here, all because there was a whisper of a chance of being in Lenora's arms.

The shame of that makes me take a step back. "My mom is sick. She *needs* me to ascend. If you cared for me at all, you would sponsor me yourself." The poison creeps back in. Lenora may want me as a pet—her little human *domestic*—enough to offer me money or patronage or whatever I could ask for. But she clearly doesn't want me as anything more than that.

Her perfect lips turn down. "I can help with your mother, Elijah. I can get her the best medical care. I can even..." She pauses, her eyelids fluttering. She's communing with Orion.

My eyes go wide. "You can even *what?*"

She focuses on me again. "I might be able to find her a cure. I would need some time."

"What do you mean *find* her a cure?" As if the cure for my mother's illness is just misplaced under a bed or in a drawer somewhere. "You ascenders *have* the cure. You just refuse to give it to her!" Anger is making me shake.

"Eli." Her voice is a gasp, heartbreakingly soft. "Eli, I know. It's monstrously unfair. Which is why I would need time. To find a way around the rules. It can be done. I'm sure of it."

"How sure?" Cyrus says coldly, still at the far side of the room.

She keeps her focus on me. "I can't guarantee it. But I will do everything in my power to make it happen. If that's what it takes."

"If that's what it takes... to keep me from competing." The chill in my body reaches my voice. "Tell me the truth, Lenora. Why is it so important to you that I not compete?"

She hesitates. "Because you might win."

"Why is that so bad?" I wince at the plaintive tone in my voice, but I'm almost afraid she'll tell me the truth. That I'm good enough for her to love as a domestic but not as an ascender.

"I'm afraid you won't live through the procedure." Her voice is soft, like this is a confession that embarrasses her.

But I'm not buying it. "Only one in a hundred medalists don't survive... what's the real reason?"

She opens her mouth, hesitates, then closes it. "I

promised your mother that I wouldn't send you to the Olympics."

"You what?" My mind is reeling. When did she talk to my mother?

"From the beginning, it was our agreement. Part of your patronage." Her hands are tormenting one another again. "That I would help you develop your art, but under no circumstances was I to sponsor you for competition."

"I... what..." My mother hates the Olympics, but I can't see her making a pact with Lenora about it. My mother barely tolerates the fact that I have a patron at all. The only reason she allowed it was because she was sick—with a disease ascenders like Lenora refused to cure. But my art was too important. My mom wanted me to have someone to help develop it, even after she was gone.

Lenora watches me struggle, the golden glow of her skin dying under waves of wispy gray.

Finally, I manage to say, "Why didn't you tell me this before?" Is Lenora lying to me? My mind is breaking into pieces trying to figure this out.

"I never expected you to—" She cuts herself off, and I realize why.

"You never expected me to qualify." The words are bitter in my mouth.

Lenora holds her hands out, pleading innocence with them. But all I can think is how she's not telling me the truth. Even now. "Elijah, please. Your mother wants you to come home. We both think it's better for you to continue to explore your art there."

My mouth drops open. *"Did you go see her?"* My fury spikes to a new level. My mother is in the throes of fighting off her illness, and Lenora is trying to *use her* to stop me. All so she can keep me for her *pet*.

"I want you to *stay away* from my mother." I turn my back on her, mostly because I don't want her to see the tears that are threatening to spring out of my eyes. "I think you should leave now."

"Eli, please—"

"He said it was time for you to go." Cyrus's words are clipped. "Last I heard, this space belongs to Eli. He decides who comes and who goes. I can call security if you'd like."

I can't believe I'm letting Cyrus throw Lenora out, but I am. I stare at a spot in the floor and focus on reining in the torrent of emotions rushing through me.

The whisper swish of her feet across the floor finally forces me to look. The door slides open, and Marcus waits just outside. She brushes past him, but he catches her arm and brings her back. Ribbons of dark gray are writhing across her body, but with his touch, they dissipate. He strokes her cheek and gently presses his forehead to hers. She relaxes into him, eyes closing. A flush of pink swells through her body, flowing into his, and they're locked in one of those ascender-only embraces. The kind that left her breathless before.

The kind I can never have with her.

The door slides closed.

I ball up my fists. My body is one rigid cord of anger.

"Something about this doesn't make any sense—" Cyrus stops as I stomp past him to the half-paint-smeared canvas—my pathetic attempt to conjure a work worthy of ascendance. I drive my fist through it, smearing paint up my arm and letting out a guttural sound. It only amplifies my rage. I fling the canvas against the wall. It splatters the ascender-tech surface with paint. The canvas falls to the floor.

Then I feel it: like an incoming hurricane has sucked all the air out of the room behind me.

I turn into it. "Cyrus—"

I'm in a brightly lit studio. All glass, everywhere glass. It reminds me of Lenora's house, but the man seated before me is human. His gray scraggly beard carries flecks of the blue lilies he's painting. I slowly realize that the stone floor is cold on my bare feet as I inch toward him. He doesn't see me. His strokes are minute, deliberate. The work itself is spectacular. Familiar. I know this piece, but I can't place it. It's old, like the man. Ancient. Beautiful. Masterful...

"Eli!" Cyrus's face is in mine. He's shaking me. "Eli, wake up!" He has me by the shoulders, squeezing so hard it hurts.

"Hey, ease up!" I struggle away from him, but my limbs don't work right. Like I'm half-asleep while standing up.

He releases me, eyes wide. "You're back."

"Yeah." I reach my hand up to rub away the ache at my temple and stop when I see a brush. There's paint everywhere. On my hand. On the brush. On my arm. My other hand is covered in it, too, swirled hues of darkened red, like I've been finger-painting in blood. "Oh no." I look up at Cyrus and see Marcus standing behind him.

They're both eyeing me like they think I've gone stark raving mad.

I slowly turn around, a sense of dread crawling up my back.

The canvas is drenched in paint. Reds and browns and oranges. I have to blink several times before I can bring it into focus.

It's a muddy hole with a body in it. A slender brown body splashed in blood and lying bent like a doll that has been dashed to the ground in anger. A broken doll. Even before I stumble over to it... even before I search the tiny, perfect details of her lips, her fingers, the spindly strong lengths of her legs... I know.

It's Kamali.

And she's dead.

I drop the brush.

A wave of vertigo sends me to the floor after it.

FOURTEEN

I can't get the painting of Kamali out of my mind.
Cyrus and Marcus helped me get back to the apartment. It's not far, but the aftereffects of the fugue are worse this time—I don't know why. Maybe because Cyrus yanked me out of it. And I don't miss the fact that it's happening more frequently now: that has to be a good sign. Maybe there's hope of mastering it, but right now, it's all I can do to lie on my bed and wait out the shakes. The ascender-tech sheets don't know what to do with my tremors: they keep moving away, then coming back, trying to adjust. It ripples a strange pattern in the shiny fabric. I stare at it, but in my mind, all I see are Kamali's dead eyes.

The painting is disturbing and chilling... and, without a doubt, my best work yet. Her eyes alone are some kind of magic. They stare at me from the canvas, as dead as her broken and lifeless body but, at the same time, they're alive with some kind of ghostly movement. As if she's accusing me from beyond the grave. Kamali spoke of how not dancing would feel like death to her. My fugue state just put that into acrylics. It's logical, and maybe she really is my Muse. It still disturbs me.

I force myself to sit up and listen to Cyrus and Marcus as they debate our next move.

"Sketching the dancer brought something out of him," Marcus is saying quietly. "Arrange for them to spend more time together."

Cyrus has his arms folded with his back to the giant screen in our room. "I thought you wanted him to stay away from other competitors."

"He needs to stay away from *Thompson*," Marcus says tightly. "If the girl is his Muse, that's different." He glances at me. "I want you back in the studio. The Showcase is tomorrow, and I want you to practice this piece. Expand upon it. See where you can take it."

I glance at Cyrus, who is stony-faced. Somehow Marcus hasn't figured out that this isn't something I can do on demand, and Cyrus hasn't enlightened him.

"Maybe I should save *The Broken Artist* for the competition." My rough voice should be a clue that I'm not entirely recovered yet. Plus it's hopeless for me to try to reproduce the painting. Not that I'd want to, even if I could.

"The name certainly fits." Cyrus gives me a steely look, like he thinks I'm the *Broken Artist*. Which is also pretty clearly true.

"Besides," I say, swinging my legs off the edge of the bed and blinking away the vertigo. "I thought the Showcase was just a pre-game exhibition. Only the competition votes count."

"*Everything* counts." A swirl of blue next to his collar says I'm testing his patience. "From the moment you are born, the records of your training, your patrons, all of it weighs in. Every aspect of your life is already being discussed, analyzed, and interpreted by the viewers, in person and over Orion. The competition is still the biggest influence on the vote, but everything from your birth records to the Showcase can sway voters."

I stand up on unsteady legs, but they hold. "Yeah, well, I hope this isn't hinging on my birth records. Because then we might as well go home."

Marcus shakes his head. "Your petty human concerns will all be swept away once you ascend. From the ascenders' perspective, it's all about discerning your potential. You have to demonstrate your essence."

"*My essence?* What does that even mean?" My head's still fuzzy from the fugue, but Marcus isn't making any sense.

He seems annoyed that I'm not getting what he's saying, but it would help if he stopped speaking in riddles. "Your essence is that essential spark within. The one you bared while creating the *The Broken Artist.*"

Cyrus and I exchange a look. Marcus is talking about the fugue state. He thinks it's just some kind of internal "spark" I can tap into at will. Or somehow "bare" to the world, like it's a switch I control rather than a possession that controls *me*.

I grimace. I'll be lucky to master the fugue state before the final competition, much less the Showcase. "Look, I don't think recreating *The Broken Artist* is the way to go for the Showcase. It's a little… I don't know… *disturbing* for a Showcase piece, don't you think?"

He gives an elaborate sigh, which seriously rubs me the wrong way. "That is *precisely* what you want in the Showcase. Your human senses are extremely limited in this regard. You need to trust me when I tell you that the more radical your art, the better. You have to push boundaries. They're looking for something that will jump the gap."

"The gap?" I rub my temples, trying to clear out the fuzz, so I can have a hope of understanding what Marcus is telling me.

"The very large chasm between your present state and the ascender you will become," he explains, like this should be obvious. "Your competition art needs to be something that transcends your human restraints, the biology that's holding you back."

"How am I supposed to do that?" My head is definitely pounding now.

"Forget about human art—every ascender is an artist, and that's the standard they will be judging you by. Ascender art explores what it means to be ascended and how that is different from the humanity we've left behind. You need to reach for that. There's a reason why we have these games, beyond fulfilling that residual need for creation."

"To make up for ascenders who die in hideous hyper-rail accidents?" Cyrus asks. I think he wants Marcus to leave so we can get to the *real* strategizing.

Marcus gives him a look of disgust. "Ascenders don't

die in accidents."

"Right, you upload. Sorry, I'm just a stupid human. Carry on."

Marcus shakes off Cyrus like he's an annoying fly. "There are a small number of ascenders who take their lives or otherwise have to be put to storage, thus leaving room for replacements. But that's not what I mean."

Cyrus arches an eyebrow at me. I return it and immediately wonder what would make an ascender want to end their guaranteed immortal life.

Marcus keeps talking. "The main purpose of the games is to find the spark. The ascender within, waiting to break free. You have to move your audience by baring it. Ascenders are somewhat obsessed with the idea of this spark... past what is truly rational. It drives more than you might suspect."

"And this relates to the Showcase piece how, exactly?" asks Cyrus.

Marcus gives one of those dramatic sighs that usually makes me want to punch him, but for once, I understand it. Cyrus doesn't get it, but I do: I have to *move* them. Demonstrate the ascender within. And the Showcase will be just as important for that as the competition.

"The Showcase," Marcus says, "is the counterpoint to the competition. The day of the competition you'll have to bring everything you have to your art. It's your peak performance. But in the Showcase, you're given room to experiment. To show the breadth and depth of what you can do. It should be a piece fundamentally different from your competition piece and that illustrates another aspect of your potential."

Cyrus and I exchange quick looks. This is all kinds of messed up. If I manage to induce a fugue for the competition, the result will be completely random. There's no way to plan a Showcase piece that will balance it. And whatever I pick, the result isn't going to *move* the ascenders who are watching. Except maybe move them to laughter at how awful it is.

"Fantastic," Cyrus says. "You got that, Eli?"

"Sure," I say, even though I have no idea what he means.

"All right, then," Cyrus says to Marcus. "Why don't you let Eli and me take it from here?"

Marcus frowns. "We still have much to discuss."

"Sure, sure we do," Cyrus says. "How about you come back after dinner?"

"Cyrus just thinks I need to rest some more." Seems like a handy excuse.

"Perhaps I should call for a med bot." Marcus's frown digs deeper into his bodyform's forehead.

I work up a smile for him. "No, I'm fine. I'll take a quick nap, then hit the studio, okay?"

"We've just had our limit of ascender assistance for the day," Cyrus throws in.

I give him a warning look, but Marcus is already headed for the door. He pauses at the threshold. "I'll check back with you in the studio after the dinner hour."

"You got it, boss." I give a small wave.

His frown is almost a scowl by the time he leaves.

The door slides shut. "So what are we actually doing?"

I ask.

Cyrus's hands are up, already tapping into the screen. "Figuring out how to cheat."

I scowl. "I thought you were going to help me with the fugue."

"I'm thinking it'll be easier to just eliminate the competition."

"Cyrus…"

He smirks as his hands fly over the holographic controls. "Relax, bro. I'm not going to poison Thompson's soup. I just want to know who you're up against. Maybe mess with the competitions' heads. Throw them off their game."

"I don't know." It's one thing to try to master my own art. It's another thing entirely to tamper with someone else's.

Cyrus gives a low whistle, looking at the screen. "Man, you are one popular guy."

I shuffle over. Cyrus has a dozen vids going at once. "What do you mean?"

"I mean, a good chunk of the darknet thinks you've got a chance at winning this thing."

"Darknet?" I ask, eyebrows raised.

Cyrus smirks. "Basha linked me in. It's like Riley's black market net back home, but this one's worldwide. Anyway…" He points to a table of statistics. "Three-to-two odds of you taking the gold."

The table of numbers swims in front of me, the squiggles barely comprehensible. I can't decide if it's the aftereffects of the fugue or the dizzying idea that I might win.

"They don't know about the fugue." I gesture to the screen. "Otherwise, I'd be the long-odds bet, not the favored one."

"Does Lenora know about the fugue?"

"I'm not sure if she realizes I pass out and go into this whole hallucinogenic state. She knows I can't produce that level of art on demand, for sure. The first fugue I had in front of her was with Marcus there. Regardless… you should probably bet against me. You'll clean up."

Cyrus frowns and swipes the stats away. "Your attitude needs an adjustment. And the ascenders aren't stupid, Eli. In fact, I'm pretty sure they know more than we do. Which includes your ascender girlfriend, sorry, *patron*."

I grit my teeth. "I think it's clear whose girlfriend she really is."

"Right." Cyrus narrows his eyes. "Then tell me why she's trying so hard to stop you from competing."

I look away, heat rising in my cheeks. "Look, I'm not proud of—"

"Eli." Cyrus's sharp tone makes me look back. "She doesn't want you for a domestic. She's working way too hard on stopping you for it to just be that. Man, that doesn't even make sense. If that's what she wants, she'll have plenty of takers—"

He stops at the look on my face.

"Not that you're not *awesome* enough to be a domestic," he says, dripping sarcasm. "But there's something more going on here. If you weren't so…" He gestures up and down at my clothes, still splattered with bloody paint. "…messed up, you'd see it. When this is all done, I'm sending you to therapy or something. Right now, you need to clear out the fog and win this thing."

"So why do *you* think she doesn't want me to compete?"

He frowns and turns back to the screen, swiping up some data again. "I don't know. But we need to figure it out. So we know how far she'll go to stop you."

I glower, but I see what he means. "We know she offered to break ascender laws to stop me." I don't mention the obvious: that she already bent the law pretty good in buying my art with untraceable chits.

"Exactly." Cyrus sighs, scanning the screens. "And we're not going to let the rules stand in our way, either."

I don't know what Cyrus is thinking. "If we get caught, I'll be disqualified. Even if I somehow manage to pull off a fugue state, they won't let me ascend."

Cyrus drops his hands from manipulating the screen and turns to me. "Don't worry about that." He has a dead serious look. "Whatever I figure out, trust me, they're not going to know what happened. You go back to the studio and work on finding your *inner ascender* or whatever Marcus was talking about. I'll meet you for dinner."

I frown. "Just be careful."

He smirks and turns back to the screen. "The shiny pants haven't caught me yet."

Which only makes my gut hollow out. I have no idea how Cyrus can rig this, but if we're caught, we'll *both* be exiled from Seattle. "Thanks, man." It feels completely inadequate to say it out loud.

He doesn't answer, just flicks his hands in angry swipes, bringing up and sifting through some kind of data that I don't understand. I back away, turn, and head toward the door.

Before I reach it, Cyrus says, just loud enough for me to hear him. "We're going to win this thing. For your mom." His eyes are still glued to the screen, but I nod anyway.

For my mom.

FIFTEEN

My inner ascender.

I need to *move* the ascenders watching the performance tomorrow. For all the time I've spent wanting to ascend, I've never really considered whether I had what it took to be an ascender. I drag my pencil in a large sweep across the canvas. It catches, leaving a smear of charcoal in an arcing line.

It means nothing to me. Yet.

My inner ascender.

I know how the ascendance procedure works, or at least as much as they let legacies know. Nanites are injected into your brain. Microfilaments intertwine with your neurons, enhancing your neural capacity. The stories from the Singularity, back when everyone could opt into ascendance, tell what happens next: those artificial neurons create an enhanced consciousness that feels like transcendence. Then there's a wild surge of... thoughts, I guess. Creativity, maybe? Some kind of mental superhumanism. The stories speak of giant leaps of insight right in the transition... and they paint a pretty horrifying picture of what happens when the procedure goes wrong. When humans burn too bright, and their minds melt down in the process. That isn't a metaphor, either: their gray matter literally liquefies into a kind of molten consciousness. It pools at the bottom, turning their skulls into custom-made urns.

I always wondered what caused some to die. Was it a flaw in their brains? Or did their neurons grasp too readily onto the change, with thoughts so transcendent they exceeded the capacity of the flesh to hold them?

I don't know. I always assumed the procedure would simply *happen*... and then I would be one of them. The nanites would take me, purify me, transform me into something... *more*.

I didn't consider there might be some part of the *more* already inside me.

The painting of Kamali stares at me from the corner of the studio. I've propped it up on one of the low cabinets. I can't stand to cover it or put it away. At the same time, I can't look at it. She's dead and broken, her blood mingling with the mud. My face burns with the shame that something inside me would envision her destroyed. Maybe that's why I can't put it away. A penance of sorts for the part of me that, for some twisted reason, wants that to happen.

My inner ascender.

A lightness infuses me. I can suddenly see it: that inner thing, the living thing that wants to beat its way out of me. *The fugue state.*

I sweep the pencil rapidly across the canvas now. The

form of the fugue is at the edges of my understanding: it feels like a tsunami of emotion, a rage and a flurry of action, but what shape is that? What color? How would it express in paint?

The pencil scrapes and carves a figure, half formed, half exploding out of the canvas.

Something pounds on my door.

For a moment, I think it's my pulse beating in my ears, but when I look, a brown face peers in my window, which I forgot to dial down.

It's Kamali.

My heart lurches. I rise so fast, my chair tips backward and falls. I look rapidly between the live, earnest, beautiful face of Kamali at the door, and the dead pallor of the one I created on canvas in the corner. My pulse races as I judge the angle, but I don't think she can see it.

I rush over to the art cabinet, use my implant to scan it open, and rummage to find a sheet. Then I hurry and throw it over the painting, hiding my shame. A brown and red edge peeks from the bottom, and I spend precious seconds tugging and adjusting and making sure there is nothing showing. When I finally stumble to the door to key in Kamali, I'm breathless and probably look as guilty as if there were bloody paint still dripping from my hands.

She frowns and takes a step back. "Are you okay? I can come back later." She peeks around me, but all she can see is the nearly blank canvas with a few lines of charcoal. And a knocked-over chair.

"No, I'm fine. Please, come in." I sweep my hand to

welcome her. The heat of my shame burns from the corner, like the painting is a roaring fire that only I can feel. I steel myself against looking at it, afraid I'll give away my own guilt.

Kamali glides in, still frowning. "You seemed, well, kind of panicked when your sponsor found you in my studio. What happened?"

I grimace. "It was just some ascender drama."

She nods. "I just wanted to see if having me model helped… you know, if you were able to access your art again." She frowns at my barely marked canvas.

"I just got started."

She looks at me, timid. "Can you tell me what it is?"

"Not really."

She nods again, but I don't think she understands.

"I mean, I could tell you, if I had any idea myself."

Her face lights up, a playful grin breaking out and stealing my breath.

"Wait." I hold a hand up, as if I can freeze her expression in place. "That is what I need, right there."

"What do you mean?" She frowns.

I don't answer, just rush over to lift my chair, whipping the pencil from where it's tucked behind my ear and starting to sketch. It's not the smile I want to capture, but the feeling that it brings out in me, like something inside has brightened. I sense Kamali behind me, peering over my shoulder as I rough out the shape of a man, only it's dominated by a bursting forth of… something. The feeling ebbs as I become more conscious of her. I stop sketching. The black smudges suddenly seem coarse and childlike.

"Don't stop," she says, behind me.

I give her a sheepish look. "It's hard for me to hold onto the feeling." Which isn't exactly true. I don't know how to directly access the fugue state, the thing I'm trying to portray on the canvas. But even the *concept* of an inner ascender feels just outside my grasp.

Her eyes light up. "I have an idea." She lifts the canvas from the easel. "I have a place I'd like to show you." She turns and heads for the door.

I have no idea what she's doing, but I tuck the pencil behind my ear and follow her out of my studio. She briskly strides down the hall, full of purpose. Her footfalls are silent in the delicate dance slippers that match the bright red of her uniform. After two turns, I'm already lost—I still don't know the layout of Agon. I make a mental note to fix that tonight.

"Where are we going?" I ask.

"Somewhere different." She glances at me. "Sometimes it helps me focus."

I nod. I'm willing to try anything, especially with her. We pass door after door of studios, mostly empty. Everyone must be at dinner.

"Thank you," I say.

She smirks. "We're not even there yet."

"Thank you for checking on me," I elaborate. "And for trying to help—" I cut off as we round a corner. Cyrus and Basha are at the end of the hallway... *kissing.*

I shoot a look to Kamali, but she appears as nonplussed as I am.

"Well," I mumble, "that happened a lot faster than I expected."

Cyrus and Basha have finished their kiss, but his hand is on her cheek, and they're whispering. They're standing in front of an open access panel with a darkened space behind it. It's about half the size of a regular door, and the panel sits propped to the side. Basha and Cyrus haven't broken out of their cozy little embrace long enough to notice us. Kamali takes me by the elbow and pulls me out of sight of the new lovebirds.

"I should warn you about my friend, Cyrus," I say in a low voice. "Correction: I should have warned you *earlier* about my friend, Cyrus."

"Why?"

"He's older than me by a couple of years," I start, wondering how much I should reveal in the interests of protecting Basha and how much Cyrus will pound on me for letting his reputation loose in the fresh hunting grounds of Agon. Not that he should be looking for girls here. He's supposed to be helping me *win*. This mollifies my conscience. Slightly.

"Basha's dated older guys before," Kamali says.

"Yeah, well..." I rub the back of my neck. "Cyrus is a great guy. A *really* great guy. He's like my brother. You should know that first."

Her eyebrows arch up. "What should I know second?"

"He's not the type to stick to one girl at a time. Or even, sometimes, two."

Kamali smiles wide. "Basha has broken more hearts

than I can count."

It's my turn to look skeptical. "Basha? Little Basha? The wide-eyed Arabic girl who hangs out around you and bumps into people when she's not looking?"

"If you think that bump was accidental, you don't understand Basha at all."

"Wait… what?" I look for signs she's pulling my leg, but there are none. "You're kidding," I try.

"I am very much not kidding." She laughs quietly. The sound is entrancing. I decide I need to find more ways to make her laugh in the future. "If social gymnastics were an Olympic sport, Basha would take the gold every year."

"Okay." I'm still not sure she's quite taken my meaning.

Kamali tilts her head toward me. "I probably should have warned you guys about *her*. Basha has this funny idea about having to kiss a million guys before she'll find the right one."

"A million." I'm not even sure what to think now. No matter how much flirting Basha does—and now that I think about it, she's friendly with *everyone*—there's no way she could take the gold from Cyrus in the love-em-and-leave-em category. For him, it's definitely all sport, and I don't know if Basha realizes that kissing Cyrus isn't anything serious… to him.

Kamali smirks and peeks around the corner. "Coast is clear," she whispers, then tugs me into the hall. Sure enough, the access panel is back in place, and Cyrus and Basha have disappeared. I can't tell if they went into the wall or retreated down another hallway. Whatever they were doing—besides the kissing—I'm sure it wasn't legal. It makes me cringe that Cyrus is dragging Basha into whatever his plans are, even as Kamali is legitimately trying to help me.

Kamali kneels by the access panel, which is now seamlessly integrated into the wall. If I hadn't seen it open, I would have never known it was there. Kamali taps the panel in four different spots with some kind of pattern that springs it out from the wall.

All right, then. I'm sure tapping into access panels breaks some kind of ascender rule, but clearly Basha brought Cyrus here, not the other way around. Then I remember what Cyrus said about Basha linking him into this darknet thing. All of which gives me a sigh of relief—maybe Cyrus isn't dragging her into his schemes after all.

Kamali opens the panel and climbs in, bringing my canvas with her. She gestures for me to follow. I hesitate, but apparently this is something the girls have been doing for a while. I hurry through before someone can catch us in the act. We're in a giant room, two stories tall and as big as the Lounge, with a black foamy material covering everything. A cluster of chairs gathers a few feet away. Kamali pulls the panel back into place from the inside, and we're left in total darkness.

A blue light appears in front of me, lighting up Kamali's face. She's grinning. "Tap your implant three times fast."

When I do, it lights up as well. It's not much, and it bathes everything in an eerie blue cast, like we're demons in an underground lair, but it's enough to see by. She glides over to the chairs, setting up two facing each other. Even those simple movements are a dance. Kamali so clearly carries her art with her everywhere, in every turn and step. When she sits, it's like a butterfly alighting on a leaf. She props my canvas on her knees and holds it with her delicate fingers on either side. Her face would seem too thin, except I know the rest of her body is pure muscle in pursuit of her art.

She's likely the most beautiful easel I'll ever have.

"Do you know where we are?" she asks.

"Um… no?" I blink and realize I've been staring at her for far too long. "I can barely keep track of where we are *outside* the walls."

Her smile is bathed in blue light. "We're underneath the stage."

"Really?" I look up as I take a seat, even though I know there's nothing but blackness above me. The weak light of our implants doesn't reach far.

"Sometime tomorrow, you're going to stroll out right above us and give the performance of your life." Her voice is quiet, almost reverent now. "I come here to picture it. Play it out in my mind. I even dance down here."

An image of that flashes across my mind like a guilty dream: Kamali shucking off her uniform and dancing in the darkness beneath the stage, lit only by the ghostly, whirling blue light of her implant. My face heats.

"Plus the darkness helps me focus." She scoots her chair a little closer, so the canvas is within my reach.

"Now... what were you trying to draw before?"

My fugue state. But I can't say that. "That thing inside me that creates my art." I reach forward and sketch lightly on the canvas she's holding. "In a way, I'm drawing *you.* You're my Muse. Or at least... you help me connect with it."

She's holding so perfectly still, the canvas doesn't move even with my faster strokes with the pencil.

"How do I do that?" She's curious to the point of intensity.

"I don't know. It just happens." I flick a look at her then concentrate on the figure taking shape under my pencil. "My sponsor says I need to bring out my inner ascender. I figure that has to be approximately the same thing."

I pause, the sketch nearly finished. I long for my paints, although the color would be completely washed out in the blue light.

Her face pinches in. "Do you think we have souls, Eli?"

I blink, hand frozen on its way back to the canvas for a couple more touches. "Uh... maybe." I haven't really thought about it, but I don't want to offend her either. "Do you?"

She nods, and her long fingers move along the edges of the canvas, flexing gently like she's searching for just the right way to hold it. The rich brown of her skin is now dark blue, and the translucent white nails at each fingertip gleam like tiny spotlights. The urge to draw a detailed sketch of her hands in the surreal lighting wells up. I realize I'm ogling her hands while she's not speaking, so I drag my gaze back up to her eyes. She locks me into an intense stare, like she's trying to pierce whatever soul I might have. I swallow, but don't look away.

"My soul is one of the few things I'm sure of," she says.

"You're a believer, then?" It's not something you normally ask someone, especially a legacy. Believing isn't a crime, but it makes you suspect... and raises the possibility you might be illegally gathering with others, like my mom and the Christians. Or any of a dozen other sects that practice strange rituals in secret to worship whatever god they think their souls belong to.

"I believe there's something inside each of us that touches the divine." Kamali smiles, and it tugs on my Muse, drawing it out. My hand itches to move across the canvas, but she's still fixing me with those eyes, so I resist. Besides, her words are tumbling through my mind, mixing and blending with the ideas already there.

"Do you think this soul, this divine thing inside of us... do you think it can control us?" I can't tell her about the fugue—she'll think I'm crazy or worse—but I can't help wondering if she has some answer for me. Some way to summon the *thing*. My inner ascender. My soul? I'm not sure what it is, but bringing it out is the key to everything.

"Your soul doesn't control you, Eli. It *is* you." She's watching me carefully, judging my response.

"But it's a separate thing, right?" I press, even though

my doubts are churning up, trying to stop my words. "I mean, there's *me*..." I gesture to my body and my head. "...who's an idiot a lot of the time and bumbling the rest..."

That draws a smile out that almost obliterates my train of thought.

I stumble into finishing. "...and then there's that *other* part. The one that can create art. It's almost as if it's outside of me. Like it comes from somewhere else."

"The artist is nothing without the gift, but the gift is nothing without work." She sounds like she's quoting someone.

"Delphina?" I ask. It sounds like her.

That smile captivates me again. "Yes. But she was actually quoting a pre-Singularity French writer, Émile Zola. He was the friend of a painter you may have heard of—Cézanne?" Her smile curls into a smirk, and I hear her French accent for the first time. English is the language of the post-Singularity world, with legacies too few to have language barriers, but I'm sure Kamali speaks French, given her family history. Her pronunciation of the famous French post-Impressionist painter is full of a lilting French accent as well as French pride.

"I hear he could be moody and bled his emotions into his work. Sounds like my kind of guy." I return her smirk.

"Yes, well, Émile could be dark as well. But he understood that the gift isn't something separate from you. It's your work that brings the gift into the world, not the other way around."

"Are you sure you're a dancer? I think maybe you

really belong in *storia*." I give her a wry grin, even though her words are sinking my heart. I want to summon the gift, the fugue, but I don't want to own it. I don't want to think the part that painted Kamali bleeding and broken on the ground is actually part of *me*. At least… it's not a part I want to keep.

Instead of smiling in return, her face falls serious. "The gift belongs to you, Eli. The ascenders don't have anything like it. That's why they seek it out from you."

I nod. "My sponsor says they're looking for that spark, that inner ascender. I know *you* have it." I smile again, but her face remains cold. "I'm just not sure I do. Or that I have it in any form that might actually show up for the competition."

"You want to win." She says it like it's not obvious. Like it's not the reason why we're all here.

I arch my eyebrows and don't answer.

"Why?" Her face is so serious that it steals some of her beauty and turns it into power.

I'm distracted once again by the idea of painting that expression, and it takes me a moment to respond. "My mom is sick." It's not like there aren't a hundred other reasons, but that's the only one that really matters. "The only cure is gene therapy."

Kamali's steely expression disappears, and empathy washes out of her in a gush. I can see it taking hold of her body, hunching her shoulders, drawing her delicate feet in. "Thompson said… I thought he was just harassing you."

My shoulders are suddenly tense. The thought of

Thompson taking the gold, ascending with his conniving parents, while my mother quietly dies in Seattle…

Kamali's watching me intently. "Eli, I'm sorry. I didn't mean to—"

"It's not you." But it comes out too rough. I lean away from the canvas and let my pencil hand fall to my lap. I close my eyes briefly and take a breath.

"You may not believe you have a soul, Eli, but I do."

I open my eyes again and look at her: all earnest beauty, believing in something that's vapor and mist and, at the same time, may be real enough to knock me out like an oncoming train.

"I don't know about souls. And I'm starting to doubt whether I have an inner ascender as well." Actually, I'm afraid my inner ascender is more powerful than I can handle. And not exactly *benevolent*, given my painting of Kamali.

"I think you need to paint to find out."

I nod my agreement. I don't know if I have a soul, but whatever is inside me is responding to her in ways I don't even understand. And painting is all I know how to do.

Kamali rises up and heads back to the access panel. I follow her out of her secret hideout, hoping that when I return tomorrow to the stage above, I'll somehow be able to paint something worthy of the ascenders who will be watching.

SIXTEEN

We've barely got the access panel back in place before Delphina shows up.

She looks affronted by my presence. All the girls must be in on the secret hideout—only it's not so secret anymore, now that I'm here. Kamali and Delphina are having some kind of wordless conversation with raised eyebrows and pointed looks.

Kamali hands me the canvas with my sketch and holds up her hands. "I was just helping Eli practice his art."

Tension hangs in the air like the static charge before a thunderstorm. It lifts the small hairs on the back of my neck. Does Delphina think Kamali brought me here to make out, like Cyrus and Basha before us? Is jealousy the thing that's charging the air? I can't tell. After a long, considered moment, Delphina nods.

"Basha was concerned," she says to Kamali. "You missed dinner."

"This was important," Kamali replies.

I like hearing those words more than I want to admit.

And Delphina seems to accept them, but I don't know what that means. Then I glimpse someone down the hall, and any warm feelings run cold.

Marcus strides toward us, six-foot-three of ascender anger. His bare feet make no noise, but my anxious stare draws Delphina's attention like a magnet. She whips around just as he arrives. Her body goes stiff, hands curled into fists, almost as if she thinks Marcus is here to physically fight her.

Me: I'm pretty sure Marcus is pissed I'm not in my studio.

Which just makes me angry right back. Maybe ascenders in their godlike bodyforms and sleepless minds can create 24/7, but I'm still human. I'm doing the best I can.

Delphina stands between us with her ripped uniform, a petite sentinel of righteous anger, determined to take on the ascender intruder.

"Elijah," Marcus says, ignoring her. "Imagine my surprise to find you here." His words are clipped. Definitely pissed, although I'm not sure how he found me at all.

"Just taking a walk," I say.

Marcus eyes Delphina and Kamali. "Time for walking is over."

"The boy decides when he comes and goes, ascender." Delphina's voice is low, but it rivets me in place.

Marcus coolly regards her. "Delphina Astoria, Paris legacy, orphan daughter of Michel and Simone Astoria.

I'm always surprised when legacies who seem relatively intelligent do not manage to keep their illegal activities more circumspect. Perhaps your parents wanted to be caught. So like an *Astoria* to make a dramatic exit, as it were. *Êtes-vous un élément perturbateur*, Delphina Astoria?"

"*Vous le saurez quand, à la force de mes seuls mots, je ferai jaillir le pus de votre âme pourrie.*" She's almost spitting the words in his face.

Marcus laughs, but it's frosted with humorless anger. "When you ascend, Delphina Astoria, I expect you will be the cause of much less trouble than you believe." Marcus turns to me. "Elijah, we have some matters to discuss before tomorrow. But only if you actually wish to take the gold."

I give Delphina a tight smile I hope she'll take for an apology. This is the second time she's stood up for me, although I'm not sure why she felt the need this time. I step away from the girls, and Marcus turns his back on them without another word.

Once we're out of earshot, Marcus says, "You need to take care with the company you keep."

I gesture with my canvas. "I thought you wanted me to work with Kamali."

"*In your studio.*" Frustration makes his voice gravelly, and black swirls of color are creeping up his neck again. "The Showcase is tomorrow. The *artem* competition is two days later. Perhaps you can stay focused for that very brief period of time."

I bite back my retort and concentrate on what matters. "I have a new idea for a Showcase piece, but it needs work." And a small miracle. Or a visit from my fugue state. Either of those will do.

Marcus glances at the canvas in my hands, which is barely more than a sketch. He's clearly unimpressed. "Is this your new idea?"

"Like I said, it needs work."

We round a corner, and before long, we're back at my studio. Cyrus is waiting outside, a scowl firmly on his face. I key us all in. Cyrus's glare is demanding an explanation for my absence, but now's not the time to tell him I was just visiting the secret hideout that doubles as his make-out spot with Basha.

I stride over and toss my canvas on top of the paint cabinet. It slides a little and jars loose the sheet draped over the picture of Kamali. I want to cover it up again, but I don't want to draw attention to it and remind Marcus how far apart my fugue work is from my regular ability to sling paint.

I cross my arms and lean against the cabinet. "You had some matters to discuss?" I'm really not inclined to paint under Marcus's supervision, so I hope that's not what he has in mind.

"The regulations surrounding the hours leading up to the Showcase and competition are very specific and very strict," he says.

"We've read the rules," Cyrus says from a spot he's taken on the other side of the room. "No leaving the building for twenty-four hours prior and no visitors, including your sponsor. Why is that exactly? I thought you were supposed to help us."

"It's an isolation time," Marcus says, "but also a last-minute precaution against fraud and other dangers. Anything that might unduly influence your performance, for better or worse."

"So they're trying to keep us from cheating?" I restrain myself from glancing at Cyrus.

"They're trying to keep you alive." Marcus looks grim. He's not kidding. "You'll go through another decontamination just prior to the Showcase."

"We just did that yesterday," Cyrus objects.

"The decon is for any illegal enhancers that may have been introduced since arrival. But it's really to your benefit. If there's any kind of slow-acting poison or device that's been smuggled into your body without your knowledge, the decon will detect and disarm it before the Showcase."

Cyrus pushes off the wall. "You think someone's trying to kill Eli."

The possibility that there might be micro devices lurking inside my body like tiny bombs makes me queasy.

Marcus coolly takes in Cyrus's clenched fists. "Kill. Maim. Even distract or disorient." He swings his attention back to me. "Just prior to the Showcase is the most dangerous time for you, Eli. After you've made an appearance in front of Orion, you are relatively safe. Any unfortunate "accidents" would not only be suspect—they would result in the immediate disqualification of all other contestants in *artem*. That protects you between the Showcase and the competition itself. But before you reach the Showcase stage, you are still vulnerable. So between now and then, it's imperative you do not interact with *anyone.*" His eyes bore into me.

This whole thing seems insane. "So anyone can kill me *before* the Showcase but not after? You realize how crazy that is, right?"

Marcus gives me a slight nod. "The Olympic committee attempts to preserve the *life-giving* nature of the games. What happens in your human lives prior to the stage is relatively unimportant. But once you enter the stadium, you are all potential ascenders. You will win the hearts of many with your performances, even if you do not take the gold. The committee would rather not have you tarnish the games by dying."

My mouth drops open, but I'm truly speechless.

Cyrus says it for me. "So it's okay for us to die, as long as no one messes with your games." He clenches his fists. "You know… I really don't like ascenders."

Marcus arches an eyebrow. "All that's required of you is to assist Mr. Brighton. If you're incapable of that—"

I throw up my hands. "Hang on! I *need* Cyrus here. Whatever you're thinking… don't."

Marcus looks us both over, me with my conciliatory hands, Cyrus still red in the face. "Our interests are aligned, Eli," he says carefully. "And I'm doing everything I can to help you ascend, inside and outside of Agon."

"All right, then," I say, giving Cyrus the order to stand down with my glare. He turns his back on Marcus and stalks to the far side of the room to lean against the wall, arms crossed. To Marcus, I say, "Just tell me what I need to know. Then I need to get back to work."

He glances at Cyrus, but continues, "In the hour before your slot, you'll be sequestered in your room. When your time comes, a security bot will escort you to the decon and staging area for the Showcase competition."

"Fabulous. Can't wait."

He gives me a steely look that kills my sarcasm. "Cooperate fully with the decontamination. I won't be able to accompany you this time."

I frown. "I don't get why you aren't allowed in. I mean, you're my sponsor. It's not like you're going to poison me on the way to the stage."

Cyrus answers for him. "They're trying to make sure *Marcus* doesn't cheat." There's still anger lacing his voice.

Marcus cracks a small smile. "If there were a way to cheat on this, trust me, I would do it. The only person who wants you to ascend more than you is *me*. But the best bet is to focus on bringing all of your talent to the competition." He turns to Cyrus. "Mr. Kowalski, please refrain from any illegal activities from now until the competition is complete."

Cyrus snorts. "I have no idea what you're talking about."

Marcus looks back to me. "In the past, some have found ways to cheat... but none of the successful ones have been humans."

"Guess I'll have to win this on talent, then." I try to say it without sarcasm.

Marcus glances at the discarded canvas of *Ascender*

Within on the cabinet, as well as the partially revealed *Broken Artist*. He may not completely realize that I can't control the fugue state, but he has to know my chances are a lot longer than whatever odds the nets are placing.

But he doesn't say anything about it—just pulls a small device from his pocket. It's a miniature holo phone. Cyrus has a few implant phones in Riley's shop, but no one has money for holo tech, even on the black market. "Use this to call me if you need anything. I'll be staying nearby, and I can be here within minutes. Just make sure it's not on your person for the Showcase or the competition."

I take the slim silver square from him. It's almost weightless, with a small indentation that makes it look like a button. I tap it, and it springs to life, floating a holo screen and an entry pad above it. I tap it again, and the image dissolves.

"Can I use this to call *anyone*?" I have no idea if holo phones can call regular phones, like my mom's back home, but my phone was confiscated when they took my clothes during decon the first time.

"If you're concerned about your mother," Marcus says, "she's well cared for. I'm receiving regular reports from her personal care assistant. Her fever has reduced, but she's been given medication to keep her sedated and calm while her *not quite legal* treatment progresses."

I swallow. Marcus knows about the gen tech circulating through my mom's system… of course. The med bot would have picked that up right away. I throw a pinched look to Cyrus, but he just gives a small shake of his head. If I win, Marcus will get his gains in social status, and whatever else he wants that's driving him to sponsor me... but if I lose, he loses, too. I wouldn't put it past him to have me exiled for possessing black market gen tech—Cyrus and my mom, too. My hands curl into fists under my folded arms.

This thing just got a whole lot worse.

"I know it's difficult, but you need to keep your focus," Marcus says. "If it helps, the fact that your mother is gravely ill makes you somewhat sympathetic in the eyes of the viewers."

"Right," is all I can manage to get out without it sounding completely hostile.

"I'll see you after the Showcase." Marcus nods and strides to the door.

When he's gone, Cyrus turns to me. "So, what do we do now?"

"Now *I* try to paint something worthy of saving my mother's life." I turn my back on him and key open the cabinet, pounding my anger and frustration into slamming the door open. My stomach rumbles from the lack of dinner. "And *you* get to find me something to eat."

"On it." A moment later, the door whispers closed behind him.

I brace myself against the cabinet, shut my eyes, and slowly bang my head against it. Then I shove aside all the emotions roiling inside me, take a deep breath, and haul out a fresh canvas.

SEVENTEEN

Each step along the length of my apartment sends another jolt of agitation up my spine.

"How'd it go in the studio last night?" Cyrus asks from the bed by the door. He perches there, waiting for the security bot to come get us for the Showcase performance.

"About as well as you might expect."

"That bad, huh?" He bites his lip.

I spent all night in my studio, going through dozens of canvases, trying to tap into that *ascender within* feeling— maybe it's the fugue, or the soul Kamali is convinced I have, but either way, no matter how hard I try, I can't seem to access it. The last two attempts at rendering it into paint sit, discarded and pathetic, on my bed now.

My Olympic-issued sneakers are wearing down the carpet in our room.

"You hungry?" Cyrus asks. "I have an extra roll from last night. Straight from the cafeteria. I can take a bite for you, make sure it's not poisoned."

"No." I don't even look at the untouched breakfast

and lunch platters on the table by the wall screen. Even if my stomach wasn't occupied by writhing snakes of worry, there's no way I'm chancing it.

"Did you make any progress in the loophole department?" I ask quietly.

"I'm working on it."

I grimace, knowing that means he's completely tapped out. If he had a glimmer of anything, he'd be boasting about how we had the gold in the bag. I glance at the screen clock. Half an hour to go. I keep pacing.

According to the schedule, Kamali's already finished her performance. I'm sure she was brilliant, but I'm itching to find her and ask. Not just because I want to know, but because I have this twitchy suspicion that I can't do this without her.

"Do you want to talk about what you're going to paint?" Cyrus asks.

"No." My nerves are like a canvas stretched too tight—my bones ache with the tension. I try to focus on Kamali and summoning that elusive feeling again, but the only sensation I muster is a dull thrumming throughout my body.

The schedule showed Thompson just ahead of me in the performance lineup. He's probably on stage right now, enthralling the ascender crowd with his skills... I wrench my thoughts away from him and try to focus on Kamali. Her ability to create beauty from movement. Her smile, which seems to reach straight inside me and tug on that inner thing, that living thing that knows how to create—

My thoughts are cut off by a chime at the door.

Cyrus is up in less than a heartbeat and at the door when it automatically slides open. The security bot is there. It bristles with weaponry and steel.

"Guess you're up," Cyrus says to me.

I nod and stride up to the doorway. The security bot doesn't step aside. It takes me a half-second to figure out that it needs to identify me.

I look it in the face. "Elijah Brighton."

"Agonite Elijah Brighton, verified. Please extend your implant."

I raise my left hand and hold it over the bot's. A blue light scans the implant, then the bot moves aside to let us out. "Please follow me to the agonite staging area," it says.

Cyrus and I fall in behind the bot as it strides quickly down the hall. I know the stage is appended to the side of Agon, near the Lounge—I was underneath it yesterday with Kamali, but this is the first time I will see it for real. The apartments and studios we pass are mostly dialed down. In one, where the window is clear, a girl is curled up in the middle of her dance floor, sobbing. I can't see her face, but it's not Kamali. Still, the sight of her heaving shoulders lurches my stomach so hard, I'm afraid I'm going to lose what little is left from yesterday's dinner.

Cyrus grips my shoulder. "Focus, Eli."

I swallow down the nausea and nod. "I'm okay."

"You're not okay, you're a freaking wreck." But his hand squeezes my shoulder in a reassuring way. "Don't worry, I'm going to tell Kamali you were all Nerves of

Steel Man, kicking ass all the way in."

My laugh is strangled, but it helps. The tension stringing my body ratchets down a little. "I don't think you'll fool her."

"I think she'll eat it up," Cyrus says. "That girl is hot for you, man."

"Shut up."

"I'm just saying."

I smile and want to say something more, but we've arrived. A bulky metal door at the end of the hallway looks more like the entrance to a vault than a stage. The security bot holds up its palm to the scanner to get us in. The door slides open to reveal a medical bay. Leopold, our original intake officer, stands next to the floating silver pod that is the decon unit.

"I'm going to have to take my clothes off again, aren't I?" I ask him.

Cyrus's expression has gone sour. I'm not sure if it's the decon itself or having to strip down for it.

"Congratulations, Mr. Brighton," Leopold says, gesturing me toward the pod. "You've made it to the competition."

I narrow my eyes as I step forward and start peeling off my clothes. "Did you lose some kind of bet on that?"

He chuckles in an indulgent way, like I'm a child. "If I were allowed to place a wager, you can be certain that I wouldn't bet against Marcus."

Marcus. I hope he's doing something in the ascender world to win me votes. Because I'm not at all sure I can bring it on my own.

"Thanks," I say with a tight smile.

I shuck off the last of my uniform and climb into the decon unit. There are no implants this time, so it goes by quickly, although it leaves me feeling like I've been slimed. I step out and hasten to get my clothes. Cyrus is already naked and ready to take my place.

While he is decontaminating, I ask Leopold, "No secret enhancements or slow-acting poisons, huh?"

He glances at me briefly, then turns back to the pod's holographic controls, checking Cyrus's readings. "Mr. Brighton, if you had been carrying illegal enhancements, you would not have emerged from the decon unit conscious. Or perhaps alive, depending on the circumstances."

I choke. "Um… thanks for the warning on that."

"Would a warning have made it less stressful?"

I guess not. Then I stare at the pod that holds Cyrus captive, hoping he hasn't done something illegal that will set it off. My pulse starts pounding while the blue light flashes through the seams of the pod, until finally, it hisses and cracks open, disgorging a naked and disgruntled but very much alive Cyrus. I have the sudden urge to hug him but judiciously hold back.

"Glad to see you made it," I say instead. I decide not to mention the hazards of the pod. I'll tell him later, after I've survived the Showcase. Assuming I'm not a sobbing wreck in my studio.

I brush that thought aside. Cyrus finishes dressing, and Leopold ushers us to a door on the far side of the room. It's another garrison of steel.

Leopold gestures to the security lock. "Your implant will grant you access to the holding room. Beyond that, at the appointed time, you'll be given access to the staging area. You will wait there until it's your time to go on stage."

I nod to show I understand.

"Good luck to you, Mr. Brighton," Leopold says. "I will be watching your performance with great interest."

That makes me frown, and Cyrus gives him a dirty look. He probably thinks Leopold is trying to play some kind of head game with me. My pulse beats in my palm as I hold my implant up to the scanner. It slides open the door for us.

Cyrus and I step into a tiny, white room. It's empty, just four walls and two doors—one in, one out. The one behind us shushes closed.

We wait.

When the other door doesn't open immediately, Cyrus says, "You can do this, Eli." He's staring at the door.

I keep my eyes there, too. "Cy, I want you to know, I never meant for this... I mean, if Marcus turns us in..." I swallow. I can't even picture what exile will mean for us.

"Shut up. No matter what happens, we'll take care of your mom. Together."

I look sideways at him, but he's still staring at the door, waiting for some signal that it's time.

Then he slips a half-grin to me. "Seattle was getting boring anyway."

I let out a breath. "You're only saying that because you've dated every legacy girl even close to legal age."

Cyrus resumes his staring contest with the door.

My heart starts to beat on my ear drums in the silence. "Which reminds me," I say, trying to keep the nerves at bay, "you should take it easy on Basha."

That rips his attention from the door. "What do you mean?"

"I mean, I saw you exchanging saliva."

His eyes go a little wide.

"Oh, come on, it's not like I didn't see it coming. Just, you know, don't treat her like yesterday's news. At least until we're done with the competition."

He frowns and looks back to the door. "I wouldn't do that."

"I'm just saying."

He strides up to the door, looking for a lock. "When do you think—"

A loud tone from the door cuts him off. He steps back as it swooshes open. There's a larger room beyond it, empty except for a couple of chairs, and on the other side of a glass wall... the stage.

Cyrus and I stride into the staging room. There's no sound from outside, but the bright daylight streams in, flooding everything. The stage is enormous, even bigger than I imagined when hiding out underneath it. Our windows must be one way, because the artist on stage doesn't seem to notice we've arrived. I expect to see Thompson, but instead it's a painter I don't recognize. I can see his hands shaking, a paintbrush in hand as he stands in front of his canvas. I can't see the work, just his face, and it's lit with glory, like he's in some kind of trance that's just now reaching its peak. Behind him, ascenders fill a stadium so huge it blocks the sky.

My mouth is hanging open.

Cyrus grabs my face in both hands, turning me away from the spectacle. "You can do this, Eli," he says again. His face is only inches from mine. "You *have* to do this. You're going to go out there, and you're not going to think about who's watching, or what's going to happen next, you're going to *focus*. You're going to do whatever crazy mojo you do to get that fugue state rolling, and you're going to paint the best freaking work you've ever done. Understand?"

I nod and pull out of his grasp.

I struggle to breathe normally.

The artist before me walks off stage, away from us, and a bot follows behind, bringing his work. Another bot rushes in with a replacement canvas and paints.

Those are for me.

The door of the staging room tones and slides open. A rush of noise, fresh air, and heat sweep in. The applause for the artist is deafening, like an earthquake of appreciation has arrived to shake all of Agon. I feel it riding up and down my bones.

I step through the door and out onto the stage.

EIGHTEEN

The sun is even more blinding on stage.

From the outside, the staging room isn't merely a bank of one-way windows—it's a towering mirror that reflects back the thousands of ascenders filling the stands. The roar of the crowd fades. My foot catches on the dull, black surface of the stage, and I stumble. I right myself just as I reach the easel. It's in the middle of a tiny platform at the focus of the stadium.

There are so many ascenders, all packed together, and the stadium is so vast, my brain has a hard time taking it in. Some of them have traveled from the other side of the globe to experience this firsthand in their custom bodyforms, but most have just downloaded to the cheaper rental bodyforms fabricated just for the Olympics. Custom or rental, their multicolored skin catches the light and glitters like a thousand angels have alighted to watch me paint.

I can't see their individual faces, but I'm sure they can see mine. All they have to do is enhance their vision, but if that isn't enough, the soft buzz of a dozen camera drones flits around the stage to capture my performance for the pleasure of all Orion. Above and below, at eye-level and hugging the floor, the insect-sized bots capture every angle of my face, the heaving of my chest, the slow dampness forming at the edge of my hair. The hum of the drones isn't enough to mask the sound of the multitudes—their rustling movements create a wind of sound that buffets me.

I stand at the focus point, the small black spot of attention at the center of the stadium, and stare back at them. The cadence of their sounds is wordless, but it still forms words in my mind. *Does he have it? Does he have it? Does he have the gift?*

I understand why the artist before me painted with his back turned to them.

I take the chair and turn it away from the crowd. The noise ceases, like a held breath, and the sound of my own breathing rushes in my ears. They still stare at me from their reflections in the staging room windows, but they're easier to ignore now that the canvas is in front of me. A palette and paints wait on a tray that floats with some kind of maglev tech next to me.

I pick up the pencil.

Focus, Eli. I hear Cyrus's words in my head. I'm sure he's watching, too.

I push all of it away and think about Kamali. I picture her human-powered flight, more like a true angel than the host of ascenders behind me. *She* has it, that ascender-within, that gift I know they're looking for. I'm merely a thief stealing a flicker of her light to ignite my own torch.

The pencil in my hand drags across the canvas, but I can see the lines before they appear: charcoal strikes against the pure driven snow. It's the work I've been trying to perfect for eighteen hours straight, dozens of tries, all miserable, but this one... I picture Kamali in her human form, a shroud of flesh covering the potential inside her. I pull that light out from within her, only it's my own body that's bursting on the canvas, rent apart by the potential trapped inside.

I sketch it quickly, just broad strokes, because I want to get to the paint. The colors are what will make this come alive, not just a skeleton of charcoal and promise, but the solidity of blues and whites and a yellow incandescence that I hadn't seen before. A brightness like the sun that's warming my face, causing trickles of sweat to creep to my jaw then itch their way down my neck. I use my shoulder to wipe it away, not wanting to stop the brush strokes, not letting the heat from the sun set this piece into finality before I'm done with it.

My strokes are rapid and getting faster. Moving the color, touching the shadow, making the light that bursts out from inside me even more eager. I stop, then touch again. I stop again and push the chair back, looking at it from several feet away. It's a boy being lifted off his feet, legs dangling in the air as his chest bursts with the brilliance of his inner ascender. The pain flings his arms wide, his body cracked open for the light to spill out. His inner self is breaking free, and the torment on his face wrenches my chest in the very same spot where the yellow-white acrylics have hollowed out his soul, baring it for everyone to see. There's something missing... something not quite right... I take the pencil and sketch the bare outline of another person in the lower right-hand corner. It's so light you almost can't see it, a pale gray wisp of a *thing*, half-formed. Incomplete. It's watching the boy.

I can't decide if I'm the watcher or the watched. I think I'm both.

I push back and look at it again. There's no question at all—it's the best work I've done outside of the fugue state. And it's reached the zenith of what it can be. *Complete.* Any more will only mar the piece as a whole. I set the pencil down and stand to face the crowd, a hot glow still burning in my chest. That's where I've pulled it from, the true source of the painting: a soul that only Kamali believes I have.

I wait.

The crowd murmurs; a slow rise and fall of wordless conversation; a smattering of applause.

My chest caves: *they don't like it.*

I stare dumbly at the crowd, at the buzzing drones, at the winking sunlight from the dustless maglev stadium seats and the beautiful perfection of the ascenders seated in them. I slowly turn back to the painting.

My finest work. It holds everything I have to give. And it's not good enough.

My head floats above my body, watching as my hand reaches to take the still-wet canvas from the easel. I automatically hold it by the frame in back, taking care with the fresh surface, even as my mind concocts the many ways in which it can be destroyed. Should be destroyed. Ought to be obliterated so it doesn't serve as a beacon for my failure for a single second longer.

I slowly walk from the stage.

A door opens in the mirrored wall, welcoming me back into the darkness. I hear a bot whispering behind me, bringing the rest of the supplies. I step across the threshold, swallowed by blackness until the door closes, and my eyes adjust to the relative dimness of the hallway.

I'm not in the staging room. I'm somewhere else inside the cloistered halls of Agon, next to some glowing-white wall just like all the rest.

And I'm lost. In every sense of the word.

My arm aches from holding the painting carefully away from my body. I set it down. Maybe the bot will take it away. Maybe not. I walk away from it, not looking back.

I wander the halls. They're empty. It's like the dream where you search endlessly for something tremendously important, but you're stuck in an inescapable maze. The maddening frustration builds with each locked door, each fruitless attempt. Only I'm awake, and the tension boiling inside me is a distant storm on the horizon, black and threatening and ready to roll in and obliterate everything that I am.

Somehow my body knows Agon better than my conscious mind, because as I near a door with the window dialed to clear, I know it's Kamali's studio. I rush to peer inside, half afraid I'll find her sobbing on the floor like the girl before, but when I get there… she's not alone.

Delphina has her arms wrapped around Kamali's neck, hugging her. Kamali has to bend down, her elegant dancer form so much taller than Delphina's short, muscular one. They're both wearing their performance outfits. Kamali's dress is barely there, long wispy strips of blue-and-white fabric that float around her body and brush against Delphina's ripped and charcoaled uniform. I want to think their hug just a comforting embrace, not the kind that comes with more at the end, but it still surges up a strange kind of jealousy. Not just that Kamali might be more than friends with Delphina, but that they both are exactly the kind of legacies the ascenders want. I can too easily see them in that same embrace, only ascended, wearing bodyforms with heightened senses that would make that touch more intimate than any human could ever experience.

My stomach wrenches with bitterness and longing, but before I can tear myself away from watching, Kamali opens her eyes and sees me staring through the door's window. I rapidly debate leaving, but she's rushing to let me in, so I'm stuck.

She keys the door open. "Eli!" She's breathless. "Are you finished?"

I have a hard time getting my mouth to form words. "Yes."

"How did it go?" Her big, brown eyes roam over me, as if the signs of my Showcase performance might leave marks on my person.

"Badly." The word is a whisper, but she hears it.

She throws her arms around my neck, and I nearly jerk back from surprise.

"I'm so sorry," she says, but my senses are filled with the heat of her bare arms touching my neck, the warm press of her body against mine, the soft tickle of her costume on my arms as they try to figure out what to do with her suddenly in them. Before I can actually hug her back, she's gone. She's pulled all the way back across the threshold of her studio, leaving me standing outside of it.

She looks earnest. "Did you hear?"

I'm still recovering from the drive-by hug, but her words don't make any sense. "Hear what?" Then my heart lurches. Was my performance so bad they've decided to actually kick me out?

Her lips press together, and she glances back to Delphina, who has stalked over to stand behind her. I work hard not to shrink away from her glare.

Kamali hesitates, then says, "Thompson is dead."

The words are like a smack to the face. "What? But he was..." ...*on the list ahead of me*. Only now I remember: he wasn't on the stage when we got there.

Delphina gently nudges Kamali aside, standing in front of her, protective. "He was found in his room. Face down in a puddle of drool and drugs." Her anger is a cold chill that crosses the air between us. "Did you do this, *artem*?"

"Do what?" I ask, confused. "Wait... you think I killed him?" I'm mystified and outraged, but a sick horror slices through me, like Delphina's cold anger has seeped into my chest. Did Cyrus do something... *terrible*... to help me? Did Marcus? It's possible. If I'm honest, it's more than possible. Cyrus isn't a killer, but I'm not sure how far he would go. And Marcus… there's no reason for me to believe that he *wouldn't* do whatever was necessary for me to win.

"I… I didn't do anything, I swear." I beseech Kamali with my eyes. "I swear, I didn't know anything about this until just now."

I think she believes me, but she says nothing, just bites her lip. Delphina is appraising me like she can't decide if I'm a fool or a viper whose head she should cut off.

"I want to win," I say to Delphina, trying to convince her, knowing that Kamali will hang me, or not, on Delphina's judgment. "I *need* to win. But I promise you, I could never do something like that." Which is true, even though I'm not at all sure it wasn't done on my behalf.

She gives me a long look, then a short nod.

My shoulders drop down.

She looks to Kamali. "Tell him."

Kamali nods.

I wait for her to say something, but she doesn't. Delphina slips past me and strides down the hallway, leaving us behind without another look.

I turn back to Kamali. "Tell me what?"

She reaches out to tug on the sleeve of my uniform. "Come inside."

I frown, but don't argue. Just inside the threshold, she uses her implant to key the door shut behind me.

She looks into my eyes. "Delphina thinks you can win."

"Okay." I have no idea why Delphina would think that, other than she hasn't seen my Showpiece yet.

"Can you keep a secret, Eli?"

I give her a sideways look. "Maybe."

"This is the kind of secret that if the ascenders knew, I could end up like Thompson."

My eyes go wide, and I flit a look to the closed door behind me. "Whatever you and Delphina are involved in... I can't believe the ascenders would kill you for it. I mean, send you into exile, sure, but they don't kill legacies."

"Someone killed Thompson."

She has a point. "Could have been an agonite," I say. "Not that I'm saying I know who did it." I pause. "Look, whatever your secret is, it's safe with me. I know lots of people who do illegal things. I may have done a few of them myself." When her eyes narrow, I speed up. "Not like *killing people* illegal. Just, you know, breaking a few ascender laws on tech and that sort of thing. Whatever you're doing, I'm not going to rat you out to the ascenders."

She nods. "I told Delphina I think you're going to win."

There's something inside me that softens with that, a melting sort of feeling. Then I realize it's not faith in my talent that makes her believe that.

"You think I'm going to win now that Thompson is dead." If he had died after the Showcase, it would have thrown everything into jeopardy—but whoever killed him knew to kill him at precisely the right time to take him out of the running and leave the field wide open for me. It turns my stomach.

She drops her gaze to her hands, which are holding each other tight. "I thought you were going to win before that." She looks up. "But yes. Now Delphina agrees. Your odds are better."

My chest feels tight. If Cyrus had anything to do with that… I'm going to have words with him as soon as I get back to my room. And Marcus as well, although I don't know what I'll do if it was him. But I don't miss that Kamali believed in me before my prime competition was murdered by someone I hope I don't know.

"What does that have to do with your secret?" I ask softly. "The one you wanted to tell me."

She straightens and takes a breath. "I think I'm going to win as well."

I nod, smiling a little. "So do I."

"And when I climb up onto the platform at the gold medal ceremony, I'm going to do something unexpected."

I draw back. "What are you going to do?" Security is pretty tight at the Olympics. It's not like legacies are allowed to attend. They view it on the net like the rest of the world, except for the few privileged ascenders who travel to be here. Only the winners are allowed into the medals ceremony, and they're the ones who've won the once-in-a-lifetime chance to ascend—there's no reason for there to be any trouble.

Kamali looks into my eyes. "I'm going to say no." It comes out in one long breath, then she darts a look around, like she thinks somehow someone has overheard, even in the privacy of her studio.

I blink. "You mean, you're going to say no to the medal?" She can't be saying what I think she's saying. It doesn't make any sense.

She stands a little straighter. "I'm going to play by their rules. I'm going to be the one person from *drama* this year they think is worthy of ascending. Of being one of *them*. And then I'm going to take that medal and shove it back in the face of the ascender presenting it to me. I'm going to turn to the thousands in the stadium and the billions watching in Orion… and I'm going to say no."

Those words sound like they came from Delphina, and it all coalesces in my head at once. "You're a *dissenter*," I say, hushed, like it's blasphemy to speak that word aloud inside of Agon. Which it is. And it's the most ridiculously implausible thing I can imagine. We're inside her studio, the one that's set up exclusively for her to train for her one shot at ascending. But dissenters hate everything *ascender*. They're exiled, but it's usually by choice. It's often like Marcus said: they want to be caught. They want to live outside the legacy cities. For a dissenter to be a competitor, an agonite striving to become one of the few allowed to ascend… it just doesn't make any sense.

"I'm part of the resistance," she says quietly.

"What resistance?" I feel like a fool for even saying those words. It occurs to me that I never thought of there being any organization to the dissenters. They were just… the exiles. The unlucky ones. The criminals and black marketers who got caught and now have to scrape together a way to survive outside the legacy cities. Or the theocrats and nomads who were never legacy to begin with.

"Delphina says we're not slaves to the ascenders. We're slaves to our own idea that somehow they're better than we are. But they're not, Eli. We..." She gestures between the two of us with her long-fingered hand. "*We* are the only thing left of humanity that's worth saving."

My mouth drops open, and I'm shaking my head now, drawing back from her. "The ascenders can be jerks, I'll grant you that. But you have to admit they're better than us... I mean, they *are* better. At just about everything."

"Not the one thing that matters."

I narrow my eyes. She's a believer. "You're talking about your soul." I don't know about souls or the afterlife or any of that religious stuff... but I know Kamali's right about one thing. This isn't just messing around with gen tech. This is something much more dangerous.

"I'm talking about *your* soul." Her dark brown eyes sparkle. "I believe you're far too important to lose to the ascenders, Eli."

My chest squeezes as her words echo my mom's, the last words she spoke to me before I left her lying feverish in a bath filled with icy water: *I can't lose you to them.*

"Win this thing, Eli," Kamali says, her voice lifting. "Then join us. Stand up there with Delphina and me on the platform and tell them all no."

"I can't do that." I shake my head, take a step back,

and bump into the door. "I... I have to go." I give the door a desperate look, like I might claw my way out if she doesn't unlock it.

She reaches past me to wave her implant. It slides open, and I spill out into the hallway. It feels like I should say something more, but I don't know what it would be. I turn to jog down the hallway, then stop and turn back.

She's still watching me from the doorway.

"I won't tell anyone." I don't know what she's thinking with this madness of saying no to ascending, but I don't want her hurt in any way. My mind can't even wrap around what the ascenders would do if they knew. There's no precedent for it. Exile might not be enough.

She doesn't say anything, just frowns as I give in to my need to flee. I recognize enough of the layout to find my way back to my apartment. Which has to be where Cyrus went after the performance.

And I have *words* yet to have with him.

NINETEEN

My apartment door slides open.

Cyrus faces the wall screen, waving his hands to operate it. I don't know what data he's diving into, but he's so focused he doesn't notice me until I'm halfway across the room.

"You're not going to believe the numbers, Eli—"

I shove him, hard. He doesn't see it coming, which is the only reason I have any impact at all on my best friend's massive body. Even so, it only knocks him off balance.

"What the—" He braces himself against the wall.

I'm in his face. "Did you do it? Did you?"

He doesn't look shocked. "Do what? Specifically."

I shove him again, both hands against his chest. He bumps the wall behind him and pushes away my hands.

"Did you *specifically* kill Thompson?" I demand. "Tell me the truth, Cyrus."

His face relaxes for a fraction of a second, then he narrows his eyes. "No, I didn't kill him. But thanks for thinking I'm a stone cold killer. I've been trying to cultivate my bad boy reputation."

I relax and take a half-step back. "It looks bad, Cy. Really bad."

"We didn't do anything."

"What if Marcus did?"

Cyrus shakes his head and pushes past me to resume his station at the screen. "Shiny pants is on his own."

"I'm calling him," I say.

Cyrus doesn't respond.

I hunt around for the phone Marcus gave me; it's buried in the blankets of my bed. I tap it, and the holo screen pops up. Before I can figure out how to navigate it, the phone is already placing a call. Marcus's face appears, a tiny floating hologram in my palm.

"Eli, how are you holding up?"

"How am I holding up?" I echo, incredulously. I wave my hand around, but that just makes his head dance and bob and probably means he can't see me. I hold the phone still and glare at his shimmering face. "The Showcase piece was a disaster, but it's okay because *someone* killed my main competition."

Marcus grimaces. "The Showcase piece isn't as bad as you think—"

"Marcus!" I cut him off, then suck in a breath. "Did you do it?"

He doesn't act outraged or offended at my accusation, but the grimace gets a little tighter. "No."

Even if he *wanted* to admit it, he might not do it over the phone. But the angry look on his face says he knows *something.*

"But you know who did," I say. Maybe someone else, someone who actually has a chance of winning, thought taking Thompson out would help them.

"I have a few guesses," he says, "but no evidence. As I'm sure there won't be, even after the formal investigation is complete."

I shake my head. "I'm the one who benefits the most from Thompson's death. That means the most likely suspects are you, me, and my friend Cyrus, who is probably betting against me right now." I glance at the screen.

"I'm not a gambler!" Cyrus calls over his shoulder. If I wasn't freaked out about this, it would almost make me laugh.

"I'm not the only ascender who wants you to win, Eli. And I'm telling you the truth—I had nothing to do with Mr. Thompson's unfortunate death. I'm not exactly pleased that it happened. While it may technically enhance your odds, it makes you less sympathetic, and that was one of your strongest features going in."

I blow my anger out in a sigh. "Maybe I earned some sympathy votes with that Showcase piece."

"I think you did much more than that," Marcus says. "But I want you to put all that aside and move forward. You've got less than forty-eight hours until the actual competition, and I want you to focus everything on that. I'll be over as soon as they open up Agon again."

"Okay." But I can't imagine any amount of practice over the next two days will be enough to elevate my skills to gold-medal-winning levels. I tap off the phone. On the wall screen, Cyrus has the odds on the agonites scrolling by.

"How bad is it?" I ask.

Cyrus swipes away one list and brings up another. "Your odds just shot through the roof."

"What? Even with Thompson gone, my Showcase piece was... did you see it?"

"Yeah." Cyrus's eyes are glued to the screen. "Pretty freaky if you ask me. Don't really want to think about what that one means."

He's not an artist. He probably can't tell how much it's just... not good enough. And Cyrus didn't see the ascenders' reaction in the stadium like I did. "I wasn't in the fugue state, Cy."

"Yeah, I got that." He glances at me. "Just because I'm not a creative like you doesn't mean I can't tell the difference."

"I didn't mean—"

He cuts me off with a wave then turns back to the screen. "Fugue state or no, you've managed to cause a giant rift on the darknet boards. Someone has access to Orion and is leaking information out. Seems the ascenders were *disturbed* by what you did. There's all kinds of commentary about what it means, why it's different from your other work, what that portends for your final piece." He looks at me. "They're talking about you, Eli. And that is in no way a bad thing."

I frown. "They're talking because Thompson is dead."

A cold flush runs through me as I think about Thompson and my painting: a boy in agony suspended in the air, blown apart, while a shadowy figure looks on. The cold flush sinks to my stomach and forms an icy pool. It's almost as if I knew. No wonder the ascenders were horrified. Thompson was a jerk, probably had been all his life, but Kamali is right: the games do that to legacies. They set up a system where a boy can be born whose sole purpose in life is to win ascendance. How does that *not* to turn you into a jerk?

And then, in the end, the games kill you anyway.

The iciness in my stomach is crawling up the back of my throat. I swallow it down.

Cyrus speaks up from his spot at the screen. "It doesn't matter *why* they're talking about you, Eli. What matters is they will be watching you in the competition. You've got a real shot at this thing."

I take a breath and try to shake off the chill of Thompson's death. "I only have a shot if I'm in the fugue state. They're not going to ascend me based on another piece like that. No matter how much they're *disturbed* by it."

"Then we better make sure you're in the fugue state for the competition." He says this like it's a switch we can just flip on, no problem. The pressure crowds down on me, like a physical thing compacting my head. I rub my temples, trying to combat it with counter-pressure from the outside, but it just makes me aware of my bunched-up shoulders. I drop my hands and roll my head, trying to work it out, but the tension just radiates down my back.

"I don't suppose there's a way to get some headache meds around here?" I ask Cyrus.

He frowns. "Are we talking black market drugs or just an aspirin?"

I give a half-smile. "Aspirin will do. Then I'll get back to work."

"You got it." He heads toward the door, dropping a hand on my shoulder briefly as he goes. I just hope he's not tempted to hack whatever med bot he finds.

When the door slides shut, I stumble to the bathroom. It takes three tries with my shaking hands to work the holo controls and order up a stream of cold water that spills in an arching waterfall from the wall. I cup my hands and splash it on my face. There's nothing to dry with, and I'm too tired to fight the bot to figure it out. I haven't slept in over twenty-four hours, and the weight of that pulls on my eyelids. The mirror reflects back a haggard face, dripping wet, eyes shot with red. As if I need another reminder of the weakness of my mortal flesh.

My hands clutch the sides of the sink, holding me up.

Thompson's dead. My greatest artwork wasn't good enough, but somehow I'm still in the running. And my muse, Kamali, is working for the resistance, whatever that is, and wants to save my soul from the ascenders.

All of it makes every muscle in my body tense up.

I used to think the ascenders were better than legacies at everything: smarter, more compassionate, more beautiful. And I believed—*believed*—what they said about being a superior form of humanity. Even when they wouldn't cure my mom, I still thought there was some explanation, obscure to me because I was merely human, that somehow, ultimately, it was for the greater good.

But they're no different than the worst dregs of Seattle.

Tightness pulls across my chest, making it hard to breathe. All I've ever wanted was to be one of them. To be worthy of someone like Lenora.

I stare hard at my reflection then wipe the water from my face.

The ascenders make us perform like monkeys on a stage, then they tear apart our performances and place their bets. Only the winner isn't who's *worthy*, it's who *survives*. The rest of us go back to sputtering along in our short human lives, while the ascenders play their immortal games. Again and again. Forever.

I don't care if they have ulterior motives, even murderous ones. I can't help that Thompson's dead. And I can't worry about whether Kamali's right, and I'm sacrificing my soul to gain an immortal life that's no better than this one. Because my mom's life is riding on this.

There's only one thing I can think about now.

Winning the games.

TWENTY

I must have fallen asleep while Cyrus was out hunting meds.

I remember collapsing into the cool embrace of the shimmering, body-adjusting sheets, staring at the ceiling, and counting the seconds as time leaked away. I don't remember closing my eyes, but they struggle to open with Cyrus's not-so-gentle shove to my shoulder. He yanks the sheet away, and the cool waft of air means I must have been under it for a while.

I open my mouth to speak, but a yawn overtakes me.

"You can sleep later," Cyrus says, "when we're done with this thing."

I force my mouth closed, though that just moves the yawn up to water my eyes. I rub them clear. "How long was I out?"

"Couple hours. They've lifted the lockdown. Marcus will be here soon."

I sit up, stretching the sleep out of my body.

"You still want those meds? I found a med bot that was just asking to be reprogrammed."

I squint at him. "Please tell me you didn't."

"I was tempted." He's leaning against the headboard of his bed, near the foot of mine. "But, turns out, I just had to ask." He holds out his hand; there's a tiny blue med tab in the middle of his palm.

I wave it off. "I'm good. Besides, I want my head clear. We have to figure out this fugue thing. I need to be able to control it."

Cyrus nods and drags a chair over opposite me. "I know." He's looking at me seriously now, more serious than I've ever seen him before. "Trust me when I say I'm going to do everything in my power to help you win this, Eli."

"I know, Cy, I know." I stare at my hands, eyes still bleary. "I just wish I had some clue how to make it happen."

"Tell me how it feels when you're in it."

"It doesn't feel like anything when I'm in it. It's like I go somewhere else. I'm in a dream or a memory or something—some other place. It's like there's another me inside that takes over and paints while I daydream about hanging out with great artists."

"So you're with other artists during the fugue?" Cyrus takes this seriously, like it's a piece of the puzzle.

"Sometimes it's my mom, sometimes I blank out altogether and don't remember anything. This last time, it was some guy I'm sure I know, some artist from the past, but I can't quite put my finger on who. Not that it matters."

"It could matter," Cyrus says, face severe. "I think you

should spend more time with Kamali."

I pull back. "What?"

"She's your muse, right? She helps you focus. I don't get how this fugue thing works, but there has to be some reasoning behind it. It can't be entirely random. Maybe she can help you draw it out."

I rub my face with both hands. "I'm not sure hanging around her is such a good idea." I debate whether my promise not to tell anyone about Kamali's secret dissenter plans includes Cyrus. I decide, with him kissing Basha, that Kamali has to know that's not likely. "There's something you should know about her."

"What? That she's part of the resistance?"

I stare at him, dumbfounded. Then anger rises up my neck, a flush of heat that makes the short hairs prickle out. "Exactly when were you going to share that tidbit with me?"

Cyrus drops his gaze, but just shakes his head. When he looks up, he says, "Eli, it doesn't matter. Whatever the girls are involved in isn't going to impact you. The only thing that matters is winning, right?"

He looks to me for confirmation, but all I hear is *the girls* part of his speech. "So Basha is involved too?"

"Basha, Kamali, Delphina... I'm not sure who else. It doesn't matter, Eli. Not to you."

Then I realize: the hideout. They weren't making out or dancing there—they were hatching their dissenter plans. *Under the stage.*

I stand up, pace away from Cyrus, then turn back. "Kamali tried to recruit me. She wants me to throw the medal back in their faces if I win." I cross my arms and lean back against the frame of the bed, avoiding Cyrus's piercing gaze. Kamali's words about my soul, about losing me to the ascenders... I don't like how they conjure up visions of my mom, thrashing in the bathtub. It makes me squirm inside, like my stomach is chewing itself into pieces.

"Well, obviously you're not going to do that."

My shoulders are tensing up again. "I'm just saying, I don't think she's going to help me."

Cyrus stands up from his chair and strides over. He hovers, like he can menace me with his larger bulk. I just glower up at him.

"You could say you're considering it," he says.

"What the—"

"Just *say* it. Then get her to do her dance or whatever else it is that turns your artistic gears."

"It doesn't work that way." I can't draw inspiration from Kamali while simultaneously lying to her and trying to con her about joining the resistance. That's not going to bring out whatever is lurking deep inside me, waiting to create great art.

But Cyrus misunderstands. "We don't know *how* it works." He's talking about the fugue now. "That's the problem."

He has a point.

Cyrus lays a hand on my shoulder and leans in. If he wasn't practically my brother, I might find it intimidating. As it is, I'm just burdened by his expectation that somehow, some way, we're going to figure this thing out.

"Tell her about the fugue," he says. "Tell her you can't win without it. It's not a lie. Ask her to help you figure it out, because God knows, I can't figure you out to save my soul."

I frown and peer up at him. "Your soul? What, are you a believer now, too?"

He steps back and gives me a hard look. "Are you going to do what it takes to win this, or not? Because we can go home now, if you want."

I don't miss that he dodged my question, but I file it under *Things to Harass Out of Cyrus Later*, and say, "Okay. I'll ask Kamali for help."

"Good man." He gives me a nod and turns to the screen. "While you and Kamali work on the fugue, I'm going to check out your competition." He brings up a page with a gorgeous girl on it. "Katya Petrova. From St. Petersburg. Works in acrylics like you."

The girl has the wintry, blue-eyed beauty of a fresh snowscape. She has to be under eighteen if she's competing, but her serious expression is that of a grown woman. And the clingy all-black artist attire in her pre-competition bio picture shows she has the curves of a woman, too.

"You've got to be kidding me," I say.

"Just doing my job, Eli." Cyrus's eyes are glued to the screen, so he doesn't see me shake my head. "Don't you have some painting to do?"

I let out a sigh and turn away. "I'll be in the studio, if Marcus comes here first," I call over my shoulder on the way to the door. Cyrus just grunts in response. I know he's shoving me out the door because he thinks my best bet is with Kamali. And I know he's still looking for a way to cheat—maybe his ability to score with every female within miles will come in handy after all. Although the idea of him *distracting* my competition, throwing her off her game with his less-than-honorable romantic overtures, still makes me queasy.

As I key open the door, I remind myself that it doesn't have to be fair.

None of this is fair.

All I need is to win.

TWENTY-ONE

My feet snag on invisible friction points on the spotless floor.

My progress toward Kamali's studio could only be slower if I was actually standing still. I've already stopped by my studio to pick up a sketch pad, but if I stall any longer, the dinner hour will be here, and I may not even catch her in time. I know Cyrus is right—she drags inspiration out of me, she's a future gold-medaling artist in her own right, and I've already painted her once in the fugue state... although I'll die before I show her that. But there's no denying there's a connection: she's somehow key to figuring this thing out.

I just can't think of any reason why she would help me. Especially after I practically ran from her revelation about throwing away her ascendance. That thought burns some kind of hot jealousy inside me: it's the one thing I've ever wanted, and she's going to toss it back in their faces.

A scuffle down the hall draws my attention as I round a corner. Two groups of red-uniformed agonites are on the verge of a fight. They each seem to be holding back an instigator. Taut, angry words are being thrown back and forth, made mostly of spittle and low-register growls. I can't make them out, but there's no mistaking their meaning. Threats. Intimidation. Beet-red faces to match their uniforms. They can't do anything to each other now that the competition has begun, or they'll all be disqualified. So their frustration bounces off an invisible barrier between the groups, spiraling the tension even higher.

Two red-uniformed ascenders appear out of nowhere, arriving with such startling speed that the human tension crumbles. I retreat around the corner before I have to witness whatever is going down next. Maybe I can take a different route to Kamali's studio... except I'm still map-stupid when it comes to the layout of Agon. After I debate and stall and consider going back for Cyrus, I peek around the corner again. The *drama* crew and their patrons have dissipated, leaving the corridor empty and silent, as if they were never there. The metallic whisper of a security bot's stride echoes down the hall just before it comes around the far corner.

I hold still, frozen as it walks toward me. But I'm not brawling in the hallway—I should have nothing to fear—so I stride down the hall as if I belong there. I pass the bot without looking at it, and it doesn't slow down as it whispers past.

When I arrive at Kamali's door, I hesitate again. Twice, I go to knock, then stop, trying to wrangle words in my head that make some kind of sense. Finally, I peek in the window instead.

She's dancing.

The tension that's locked in my shoulders eases out as my eyes drink up her movements. This is a different kind of dance than before. Sharper. Angrier. She flicks her hands while suspended in the air as if to rend the molecules apart by the splayed force of her fingers. And her costume steals my breath: it's not the nude one or the barely-there blue one, but a red-and-orange blur that makes her look more like a living flame than a person. Sheer color is painted across her limbs and floats free on wisps of gauzy fabric. She's a fire sprite come to life, burning oxygen in a blaze that doesn't consume her, but rather lifts her straight out of humanity and into something more.

My mouth is hanging open, something I realize a split second before Basha's face appears in the window. I stumble back, and the door slides open. Music spills out of the studio then cuts off as if strangled.

Basha braces one tiny hand on each side of the door frame, blocking the entryway with her slender frame and a fierce look. Her eyes glint with reflections of the hallway panel lights.

"Yes?" It's hardly a question; more of an accusation. The cheerful, bright Basha is gone. This one looks like a mother tigress protecting her cub with fangs and unsheathed claws.

I rub the back of my neck. Kamali must have told her what happened. She's standing at the music station with her back to me. "Could I... I would like to talk with

Kamali. If… if she doesn't mind." I'm convinced Basha is going to slide the door shut in my face.

Instead, she looks past me, searching the hall. "Where's Cyrus?"

"Um…" This catches me off guard. "Back in our room?"

Basha flicks a look back to Kamali, then me. Her normal smile comes back full-force. "He probably needs some company!"

"Uh…" An image of Cyrus drooling over pages of Katya on the screen pops into my head. But I need Kamali alone. "Okay."

Basha throws a look to Kamali again, then slips out the door. I grimace at her retreating back, hoping Cyrus wipes the screen before he lets her in.

Kamali arrives at the doorway, quiet, inspecting me. "Did you have some questions?"

I swallow. She thinks I'm here about the resistance. "Can I come in?"

She sweeps her hand, the tendrils of her costume following in the wake. I step inside, and she keys the door closed behind me. She remains nearby, calm, expectant.

It's causing my shoulders to hunch up again. "Kamali, I *can't* do what you're doing. I told you before. My mom is sick."

"I know," she says. "She's not the only one, you know."

I frown, not sure what she means by that.

Kamali folds her hands and stares at them for a

moment. Her flame costume extends halfway across the backs of them, leaving just her fingers bare. They're delicate and long, and I have a crazy urge to reach out and touch them to see if they're as soft as they look.

I pull my gaze back up to her eyes, blinking away my guilt for thinking about her hands instead of her words. Then I have a horrible thought. "Do you have someone who is sick, too?" I can't even fathom her choice then—giving up ascendance when it would save the life of someone she loves.

"No," she says coolly. "But there are plenty of others who get sick and die every year from diseases the ascenders could cure. I'm not doing this for myself, Eli." She's talking about refusing the medal now. "I'm doing it for every legacy. Every dissenter. Every *soul* that's kept in poverty and treated like a *thing*, a treasure that has to be locked away in a museum, instead of a *person*. Until every human has the same rights as ascenders, including the right to ascend if they so choose... until then, no one should ascend. No one should give them what they want, not while they treat us like pets. Or worse."

My stomach twists more with every word coming from her lips. It was a bad idea for me to come back. "I... I get why you want to make a statement about that," I say, even though I don't, not really. What does she think it's going to accomplish? "But this is my *mom* we're talking about."

Her liquid brown eyes warm a little. "I never knew my mom. She was banished when I was little."

My stomach wrenches some more. She's not going to

understand this. "I'm sorry about that—"

"I'm not."

"What?" I stall out.

"My mom was…" She looks at her hands again. "It's complicated." She lifts her gaze to me. "But it's good that my mom and dad left Paris. Being legacy was bad for them."

I don't understand, but I'm not going to push it. "Did the caretakers raise you, then?" I repress a shudder, and my mind skips around, wondering if that's why she's doing this. To get back at them. Legacy children aren't allowed to leave with their parents when they're exiled; the children are considered too great a treasure. That's part of the punishment actually, breaking up the families. And the orphans are usually placed with caretaker bots, raised with all the finest love that a sub-sentient machine in a humanoid body can provide. It's pretty messed up, and those kids end up being the kind you don't want to meet in a dark alley.

"No, the caretakers didn't get me," Kamali says. "There was a special circumstance in my case. I was allowed to live with an aunt."

I let out a breath I didn't know I was holding. Even so, she has to still be mad about that. "Is that why you joined the resistance? Because your parents were banished?"

She raises her eyebrows, and I guess it was kind of an invasive question. But I really want to know.

"Not directly," she says.

I wait, but that's all she seems inclined to say about it.

"Look, I'm sure you have your reasons for... doing what you're doing." I can't bring myself to say the words. I'm not even sure what the right words are for it. Throwing away your life? Committing suicide? Because that's what it boils down to: saying *no* to eternal life. "But I didn't come here to join your resistance. I can't. But I *do* need your help."

She frowns a little, like I'm not making any sense.

"I need to win this, Kamali. I need it for my mom. And I'm not going to be able to because..."

Her deep brown eyes have grown soft. I have all her attention.

"Because I can't make art when I'm conscious."

Her brow squishes up in an almost comical way. Like she thinks I've taken one of those street drugs the down-and-out legacy kids cook up in their bathrooms. Blast or Jolly or Seven or whatever the latest is that excavates their minds and makes them forget that they'll never amount to anything more than pets, so they might as well spend their lives in a blissed-out haze until they die in a drug deal gone bad or cross a police bot wrong on a dark night.

"Not being awake is going to make it hard to get up on stage," she says, like she thinks I'm kidding, but she doesn't really get the joke. "And I saw that painting you did of Thompson. You looked like you were pretty awake for that."

My mouth drops open. "That wasn't Thompson!"

She narrows her eyes. "If you say so."

I run my hand through my hair, grabbing a fistful on

the way, like I want to tear it out. "You know what? Never mind." I turn to go, but the door stays shut. She has to key me out.

Her hand lands on my arm. "I'm sorry." The steeliness is gone from her voice.

I should yank out of her grasp, but I like the feel of her delicate hand on my arm too much.

"I know you didn't kill Thompson. I do, Eli."

I let her tug me back around. "I don't know who killed him, but it wasn't me. And my Showcase piece... that's the best I can do, Kamali. The very best."

She's close and doesn't pull away, but her brow scrunches up again. "I thought maybe you were thrown off by Thompson being found dead."

"I didn't even know." I pause, trying to figure out how to explain it. "The only way I can paint something like *Lady in the Light* is when I'm in this fugue state."

The scrunch falls off her face, replaced by something a lot less charitable. "You *use?*"

"No!" I pull away this time, pressing my back flat against the door and banging my head on it. I close my eyes briefly, and when I open them, Kamali's judgmental look is replaced by one of concern.

"Tell me," she says quietly.

"Sometimes I'm overtaken by this... fit. It's like a seizure or something. I black out, or go into some alternate dream mode, and while my head is completely somewhere else, I paint. I make unbelievable art. I can't control it. I don't understand it. But if I don't figure it out, there's no way I can possibly win."

Her eyes are wide and wondering now. She probably thinks I not only use drugs, but that I'm on them right now. Or I've used *so many* drugs that it's triggered a psychotic break.

"I can't join your resistance, so I'll understand if you don't want to help. But you're the only thing that's ever…" *Inspired my Muse? Triggered something inside me?* I swallow and look away from her intense gaze. "It's like I told you before. Somehow you connect me to it. I thought maybe you could help me figure out how it works before the competition." I focus on my feet, heels nearly backed against the door. I can't look at her face. I don't want to see her expression when she tells me *no*.

"Okay."

I look up. "Okay?"

"I'll help you."

My eyebrows hike up, and for a moment, I'm speechless.

"On one condition."

My face falls.

Her full lips thin out as she presses them together. "It's not that bad. I just want you to… consider it. Think about what the resistance is really about. If I help you figure out this fugue thing, and you *win*, think about what else we could accomplish if we stick together."

"Kamali, I can't—"

She holds up a finger. It doesn't quite touch my lips, but it effectively freezes my words anyway. "And if you decide to ascend anyway… promise me you'll return the favor."

"Return the favor?" I frown, but then the light bulb goes on. "You mean... help the resistance? *After* I ascend?"

She nods.

I hadn't thought of it before, but once I'm there, once my mom is safely ascended, there's no limit to what I can do. The ascendance procedure doesn't reprogram your brain, at least, it's not supposed to. I guess I don't really know. But in theory, all it does is enhance you to the point where you are on level with the ascenders. The bodyforms come later, but even then... you're still you. Once I'm there, I can do anything any other ascender could do. And helping out Kamali and her friends would be the least of what I would owe them. And maybe... just maybe... if I win, I can convince her to change her mind and join me. Before it's too late.

I keep those thoughts to myself and smile a little. "You know what? That's definitely something I can do."

I bask in Kamali's wide smile.

TWENTY-TWO

Kamali sits cross-legged across from me.

We're in the middle of her studio, the sketchpad across my lap, blank. Our knees are nearly touching, and the only reason I'm not hyperaware of that fact is that Kamali's holding me in an intense stare-down.

"How many total?" she asks.

"Five or six." It's six, but the last fugue-state painting is of *her*.

"Is it five or is it six?"

"Five."

"Ages?"

I think for a moment. "Seven, ten, fourteen, sixteen, seventeen." And seventeen again, counting Kamali's. They're becoming more frequent, which kind of freaks me out. I don't know if it's the stress of my mom being sick or the fact that I'm trying harder to access the fugue, but something is changing. I'm getting closer to figuring this thing out... I can feel it.

"Any pattern in the kind of painting? Form? Subject? Color?"

"No."

"And you just started experiencing these hallucinations during the fugue?"

I fudged the details a little. "Just the last two. Both were hallucinations of painters. One time was my mom, and then I painted her, but the other time, the painting and the hallucination weren't related."

"You're sure?"

I shrug.

"Feelings," she says. "Before, during, after."

"After…" I take a deep breath. "I'm wrecked. It's getting worse, too. Like it takes a toll on me. During… it's like a very realistic dream. I'm happy, I guess. More like content. Like I'm right where I'm supposed to be. The hallucination feels extremely *real*, but it's actually all gauzy at the edges. And before the fugue hits…" I pause, thinking. The last two times, I've been around Lenora, frustrated with her, ashamed of wanting her when she clearly doesn't want anything decent from me. But the fugues before that… "The first time, when I was a kid, I don't remember very clearly. I just remember my mom went crazy over the painting, and I thought I had done something wrong. The second and third times, I remember not feeling well beforehand. Like I was sick to my stomach, maybe? Or just… upset about something. The *Puppet Boy* I remember clearly. That was when I figured out my mom was sick, and the ascenders wouldn't cure her. I was sixteen, and I put two holes in the crappy walls of our apartment before I finally took out a canvas. And then I blacked out."

"The *Puppet Boy*?" she asks.

"It's a painting of a boy suspended in the air by strings. It's disturbing. And brilliant. And probably pretty obvious given the circumstances. I was *consumed* with anger. Anyway, the last two times were like that, too. Anger. Jealousy. Frustration. Negative emotions, I guess."

"The last two times?" She's counting in her head, and my heart sinks as I realize my mistake. "That makes six times. You said five."

"Five or six." I stare at our knees, almost touching. I can feel the heat of her body crossing the gap between us. I lick my lips, hoping she won't ask. Knowing she will.

"You have to tell me, Eli."

I lean back and look up. "It's six. The last one's of you."

She narrows her eyes. "You didn't show it to me."

I make a mental note to destroy it as soon as I get back to my studio. "No."

She pauses. "Something about this painting makes you think I can help you with this?"

That will work as an excuse. "There's something about you that's tapping into whatever this fugue thing is about. It's... interested in you." That sounds really strange. "I mean, it's like it's a separate part of me. And if it's painting you, then somehow you've inspired it. And you're an artist. Cyrus is great, but you get this stuff better than he ever will."

"But you won't show it to me."

I shift, pull my legs in closer. "It's not that good," I lie.

"I thought you said you could only paint in the fugue."

I bristle. "I *can* paint outside the fugue. It's just not that good."

"Apparently it's not that good in the fugue state, either."

I clench up my fists on my knees. "Okay, fine. I lied. It's good. Great, in fact. Probably the best thing I've ever painted."

"But you're ashamed of it." She gives me a disgusted look. "You painted me naked, didn't you?"

Heat rushes to my face. "No!"

"You're lying."

"No, I'm not!" Sweat is breaking out on the back of my neck. "I swear."

"But you're *ashamed* of it. You painted me... and it makes you ashamed."

I'm squirming so badly I have to stand up. I throw my hands out in exasperation. "It's not like that. I just..."

She rises up and gives me a cool look. "You just what?"

"I just don't want you to think that I... that I... think of you like... *that*."

The need to flee wells up in my chest, but I stay rooted to the spot. She's studying me now, not angry, just no doubt trying to figure out why I'm freaking over her painting. Her gaze lands on my sketch pad. My grip is so hard, I'm starting to wrinkle the pages.

"You should paint it again. In front of me."

"What?" Panic seizes my throat.

"You don't want me to see it, right?"

I nod vigorously, my heart thudding out a beat that says, *no, no, no.*

"You're upset. Angry. Frustrated maybe?" She's studying me like I'm a fascinating experiment.

Some of the tension leaks out of me. "You're doing this on purpose," I say with dawning clarity. "You're trying to rile me up."

"Is it working?"

I let out a shaky laugh. "If it was, I'd be up to my elbows in paint."

"Next time, maybe we should try it in your studio."

I shake my head, relieved she was just... what? Provoking me? Although, now I'm uncertain whether she really wants to see the painting or not. Or if I'll have to show it to her "next time."

"I don't know." I smile. "I'm on to you now."

She returns the smile, then steps closer, capturing me with her wide brown eyes again. "I don't know. You're pretty easy to rile."

I can count the inches between us. My gaze pulls down to her lips, still slightly parted with her teasing smile. They're dusky pink, edged in a darker rose before they meet the creamy chocolate of her skin. The desire to paint her lips, to capture all the shades of their color on a canvas, quickly turns into the need to touch them. To see if they're as velvety soft as they look. I drag my gaze back up to hers, my thoughts full of kissing, and I wonder if she's thinking the same. If that's why she hasn't moved or spoken or breathed... her eyes are round and serious...

A pounding at the door startles us both.

It's an ascender, female, banging with a knock that sounds like it might be denting the thick metal of the door. Kamali strides over to open it. I'm frozen in place by the angry look on the ascender's face. As soon as the door slides open, she moves with bodyform-enhanced speed and stops right next to me, looming above me. I reflexively hold up my sketch pad to ward her off, but if she wanted to hurt me, I'd already be bleeding.

"Alexis, no!" Kamali says, hurrying over. "Eli and I were just... working through something for the competition."

I'm guessing Alexis is her sponsor. She eases back from menacing me with her ascender–tech bodyform, but not by much. Her lips are pursed, and a wisp of gray flits along her neck above her red *drama* uniform. It's clear that finding me in Kamali's studio is not making her happy.

"Eli's a *friend,*" Kamali says. "And he needs my help." She says this in a pointed way, like it's code for something, only I don't know what the code is. Kamali's in the resistance: is it possible her sponsor is as well? That makes my brain go sideways, but I don't know how she and Delphina could pull off their scheme without their sponsors knowing. Then again, Marcus doesn't know half of what I'm up to... so maybe not.

I keep my mouth shut.

Kamali's sponsor backs up another pace, easing the tension in the room. I don't feel in imminent danger of being crushed anymore, but that's an illusion. If Alexis wanted to hurt me, it would be done before I knew what was happening. I begin to understand what Marcus meant about too much sponsor presence at Agon leading to a loss of agonites.

Alexis shakes her head slowly. "This is a distraction," she says to Kamali, but her tone has softened. "You need to focus on your performance. The rest is… optional."

"I understand." Kamali looks me over with a narrow-eyed stare, like she's evaluating something in her mind. It's not an altogether unpleasant experience, and I'm dying to know what she's thinking, but under the circumstances, I'm keeping quiet and following her lead.

She turns back to Alexis. "There's something I need to help Eli with in his studio. I promise I'll be back by the dinner hour."

Another curl of gray wisps along Alexis's skin, but she tips her head in agreement. Kamali leads me out the door, leaving her sponsor behind, watching us go.

Once we're alone in the hallway, I dip my head closer to her and ask quietly, "Are you sure this isn't getting you in trouble?"

She gives me a small smile. "Trouble isn't something I'm exactly avoiding these days."

I grin, even though I know she's talking about the resistance and her plan to throw away the medal. That's something I still want to talk her out of, but I can't help liking this rebellious side of her, now that she's letting it show. And the fact that she's helping me… there's really a lot I like about Kamali at the moment.

When we key into my studio, all the smiles drop off my face: Cyrus is by the far wall, with Marcus pacing by the door with a murderous look.

"See?" Cyrus gestures to me. "Told you he'd be right back."

Last I saw Marcus, Cyrus was shoving him out of our apartment. And right now, I'd really rather they both cleared out—I only have Kamali's help until the dinner hour.

"What is it, Marcus?" I ask. "I need to work on my competition piece." I put a gentle hand on Kamali's back and guide her past Marcus, who seems momentarily at a loss for words. A smile plays on Kamali's face, and I send her a half-smile once my back's to Marcus. Then I stride toward the art cabinet, thinking that a show of canvases and paint might give him a hint to leave. I toss a look to Cyrus, but he's already on it.

He unfolds his arms and strides up to Marcus at the door. "How about we leave the *artistes* alone?"

But Marcus just ignores him. "Eli, I have a message from your mother."

I stop so suddenly that my shoes literally screech on the floor. "What?"

"I thought it might inspire you," he says.

I'm frozen in place. "Is she all right?"

Kamali's lips are pursed tight, and I can tell from the look on Cyrus's face that this is news to him, too.

"She's been tired, sleeping a lot," Marcus says. "But

she was able to record a short message for you."

I set my sketchpad down on the cabinet and stride back to him. "Well, let's have it."

I assume Marcus has it recorded on his person in some way. Maybe one of those fancy holo phones, like he gave me. But he simply turns to face the wall, and the screen comes to life. He must have transmitted something to activate it.

Kamali and Cyrus stand by my side as we wait for the message to start.

My mom's on her bed, blankets rumpled around her in a haphazard way that makes me instantly wonder if the low-sentience med bot is taking adequate care of her. But her face is rosier than when I left, and she's sitting up, alert, eyes bright.

"Hello, Eli," she says.

I frown. My mom never calls me Eli.

She brushes back a strand of her long, blonde hair and smiles. The treatments must be doing something because she looks better than I've seen in a long time. "I miss you, honey, but I wanted to let you know I'm feeling well. The fever's gone. I even walked for a little while this morning." She gestures off screen. "Matilda is taking good care of me." She laughs a little, but it makes my stomach bunch up. My mom hates the bots. She would never give them pet names.

Something is off. I swallow. Did the fever affect her brain? Maybe it went on too long, too hot. Maybe we didn't cool her enough, and that delirious state did something... permanent.

She coughs a little, but not long or deep. Then her smile is back, even brighter. "I watched your Showcase piece, honey. I know you can do better. I know you *will* do better. I'm so proud of you, and I know you can win this. I have faith in you, sweetie. I know you'll win this… for us. For me." She smiles shyly. "I'll see you soon, Eli."

The recording flips off.

I blink and take a half step back, my mind reeling at what I just saw. *That's not my mother.* I know this, as true as I know my own left hand. My mother doesn't talk like that. She wouldn't say those things. And most clearly, most obviously… she wouldn't be encouraging me to win. *Especially* not for her.

Cyrus's face is beet red. I don't need to say a thing to know that he knows it, too.

I turn on Marcus and shove a hand up against his shoulder. It's like smacking a brick wall, but I can't punch him without breaking my hand. I still wince as the words blurt out. "What did you *do* to her?"

Marcus glances at the screen. "What do you mean? She's doing better—"

I get in his face. I don't care if he's taller and made of mechanized power that can crush me without trying. I fling a hand at the screen while staring my hatred into his eyes. "*That* is not my mother."

His eyes go slightly wide. "Of course it is. She's just sick, Eli, maybe she sounds a little different than you expect."

"My mother doesn't like you," I say, harsh, my mind spinning to figure this out. "She doesn't like your *kind,*

Marcus. The last thing she wants is for me to ascend, so unless you drugged her or threatened her or forced her in some way—"

Marcus holds up a hand to stop me. "I wouldn't threaten your mother." He glances at Kamali, who I sense has come up behind me. I'm glad she's here. Glad she's seeing I have no love for Marcus, that I'm wise to the fact that they're not better than us... just like she believes.

It's all I can do to keep my fists to myself. Cyrus pulls me back, putting himself between me and Marcus, but mostly to keep me from doing something stupid. But the truth is, I can't imagine Marcus getting my mom to say those things by force. I have a moment of doubt tangled in a slithering snake of fear. Maybe the disease has finally ravaged her. Maybe the part that would be worth saving and ascending... is gone.

Maybe I'm already too late.

"It's a simulation, isn't it?" Cyrus says to Marcus, his voice cold as ice. "You couldn't get her to say the things you wanted, so you made a virtual."

Then I see it: a small ribbon of gray lashing across Marcus's skin. Something is causing his emotions to flux... *guilt.*

He looks past Cyrus to me. "I thought you needed some kind of reminder of why you're here. Some motivation."

I blink back tears, my anger at Marcus dissipating in a wave a relief that it was all fake. Then a new fear rises in my chest. "Is she dead?"

Cyrus's head bows in front of me, and I know he thought of that first, but wouldn't say it. Wouldn't want to believe it. Kamali's hand lands on my shoulder from behind.

"No," Marcus says, grimacing. "But she's been in a coma since shortly after we left. I kept hoping she would revive, but so far, nothing."

"But she's still alive." My voice is a whisper now. Then I realize: Marcus could be lying about this. He could be lying about all of it. "I want to talk to her!" I say suddenly. "I want to see her."

Cyrus turns to me, probably preparing to hold me back from launching myself at Marcus again.

"She's not conscious, Eli," Marcus says from behind him. "I just thought it would help if we made a simulation."

"You only care about keeping me going," I say dully, not even looking at him anymore. "Even if my mother was…" I can't say the words, but I meet Cyrus's gaze, and I can tell he's thought it all through. She could already be dead. She could have died the moment we left. And there's no way Marcus would ever tell me, not until the competition was over.

Marcus makes a sound of impatience. "I didn't want you distracted by—"

My anger surges back, rumbling like a volcano about to blow.

"Get out," I hurl at him, over Cyrus's shoulder.

"Eli—" Marcus objects.

"Get out or I'm quitting now." I stare into his cold

ascender eyes, leaving no room for misunderstanding.

He blinks. Hesitates. Cyrus moves into action, leaving my side to stride across the floor and key open the door. "Time for you to leave, shiny pants."

The hot glare Marcus gives him makes me think he might simply smite Cyrus on the way out. But instead Marcus turns on his heel and marches from the room.

Cyrus gives me a nod from the door. "I'll find out what I can about your mom, Eli." He lands an approving glance on Kamali, who's still holding my shoulder. "You focus here. I'll make sure shiny pants makes it out of the building."

I nod and Cyrus slips out. I wait until the door slides shut, then I close my eyes and let all the anger and fear and an intense glowing hatred for Marcus leak out of my body like the lava flowing after the top has blown. I take a few deep breaths, trying to tame it.

Kamali comes around to face me. "Are you all right?"

I open my eyes again. "I need to win this, Kamali."

She nods and glances at the door. "Well, I'd say if anger alone was enough to trigger the fugue state, we're going to have a hard time topping what your sponsor just did."

I let out a small laugh, then the mirth disappears, like a candle quenched with a bucket. "I think... I think there's something I need to show you."

Her eyebrows hike up, but I'm even more surprised at my own words. Because showing Kamali the painting I made of her is the last thing I want to do. There's absolutely no part of me that wants any part of that, including, I suspect, the fugue inside me.

Which is precisely why I need to do it.

TWENTY-THREE

I'm stalling, tugging at the corner of the sheet that covers the painting of Kamali.

"I'm not proud of this." I tuck and untuck the corner, revealing just a tiny smudge of blood-drenched brown in the process then covering it up again.

"Doesn't sound like you should be." Her arms are crossed, her hands hidden by the flame colors of her outfit, her face serious. She's going to make this as hard on me as possible. Which might bring on the fugue, and which is what I want, but knowing that doesn't make the knot in my stomach any less tight.

"It's just that I—"

"Show it to me, Eli."

I tell myself the harshness in her voice is calculated, but it still makes my shoulders twitch. I reach up to slowly edge the sheet off the top of the canvas. It falls away, revealing the bruised and broken image of her that I created—that the *fugue* created. I still don't want ownership of this lifeless version. Her dead eyes stare at me from the canvas. I tear my gaze away from them, searching for her living ones, just to reassure myself and erase the image from my mind.

The look on Kamali's face sends tremors racing through my body. She's shocked into stillness, except for her gaze, which roams the crumpled doll version of herself, lying in the muddy reds and bleeding oranges of the acrylic paint. I can't help but look at it again. This time I see beyond the haunting look on her face, accusing me of crimes from beyond the grave, to the details I didn't notice before in my revulsion. Her delicate hands are crooked, like cruel, pain-wrenched versions of the real ones. The blood on her feet is actually in the shape of dance slippers, her legs bent as if frozen just before a leap. With horror, I realize the slippers are the same color as she's wearing now, in her competition outfit. My gaze drops to her feet, spaced wide apart in that defiant stance she's had since I told her I would show her the piece. I slowly work my way up her body, taking in her whole painted-flame outfit anew, seeing all the colors I rendered earlier, before I had ever seen this on her, before I ever imagined her as a living flame. Or a dying one.

My gaze reaches her face. There are tears drawing watery lines from the corners of her eyes.

Breath rushes out of me. "Kamali, I'm sorry." I lurch toward her, wanting to touch her, maybe hug her, somehow erase my guilt by wiping the tears from her face. But I hold myself back, uncertain, doubting she wants me touching her in any way.

She wrenches her wide-eyed gaze from the painting to look at me. I can see her struggle to contain the emotions rippling across her face. A long, slow blink, and the dark press of her eyelashes sends another pulse of tears chasing the rest. When she opens her eyes again, she gestures to the painting, mouth working, shaking her head, like she can't find the words.

But I can. *It's monstrous. Horrific. How could you?*

Finally, she takes a breath and says, "Thank you, Eli."

It's so heartfelt, so unexpected, it feels like a slap. I stumble back a half-step. "What?"

Her sigh leaks out slow, laden with emotions I don't understand. "Thank you for showing me that this..." She gestures to her lifeless body. "This isn't me."

She's smiling through the tears now, and I'm completely confused. I look back to the painting again, but it's definitely her. Even in death, she has the same full lips, the same liquid brown eyes. I've never seen her hair outside the tightly pinned bun she keeps while dancing, but in the painting, it forms a halo of rippled black locks blending into the mud. Maybe I got that wrong? Or rather, the fugue state did? But the rest of her—lean muscles over delicate bones, chocolate colored skin stretched over hollowed cheeks—there's no mistaking it.

I turn back to her. "I don't understand."

Her smile grows brighter. "Thank you for showing me that one day, my body will be... *this*. Only this. No more. I know that I'm more than just the flesh that I push across the studio every day, but sometimes I forget." She looks back to the painting. "Sometimes I think that if I can't dance anymore..."

"That you'll die?" She told me this before. I'm held

rigid in place by her words.

She nods, still looking at her broken body. "I know it's not true. I might pour my soul into the dance. I might give everything to it. But the dancing body isn't *me*. What I have is something so much greater than that." She frowns and turns her bright eyes back to me. "So much *holier* than that. You've reminded me that I'll take that thing, that piece of me that animates the dance, along with me when I die. That even when my body can no longer dance, my soul still will."

"You're not going to die, Kamali." I say it like it's a wish... and it is. It's a hope that she'll change her mind and take the ascendance when it's offered to her. I lower my voice, pressing further than I should dare. "You don't have to die. You can still take the medal."

Her laugh is a chirp, so light, it's like a child's. "But don't you see? You've taken away all my doubts." She's elated. Her face brightens with a glow that suddenly makes me want to paint her again. But I don't want her to be happy... not about this. Not about dying, like it's some kind of release. Like it doesn't matter.

Because it does.

She must see the torment on my face because her smile drops away. She scowls at me, but it's a fake anger that's barely masking the glow that still enlivens her eyes.

"But we're not here to talk about me," she says with mock severity. "We're here to make sure you win. And I have to be honest." She glances at the painting. "If you can do this, if there's some part of you that can do this, we have to bring it out. You can't hide that away inside of you."

I step back from her, a tangle of emotions clawing at me from under my skin. I cross my arms. "It's not like I'm *trying* to hide it."

"You were trying to hide *this*." She picks up the canvas, holds it high, like it's some kind of prize, then walks it over to the easel. "Weren't you?" She sets it down, next to the blank canvas there.

"That's different."

"Paint it again." It's a command.

"Kamali, I can't."

"Don't give me that. You can. You *did*." The glow has faded, and her serious look is back. "You painted this for a reason."

I drag myself over to stand next to her as she stares at the work. "The *fugue* painted this. I have no idea if it has reasons."

She turns to me, close, trapping me with the intensity of her look. "You have to stop pretending it's not part of you."

"But it's not. I don't have any control over it."

"But you want to, right?"

I nod.

"If you're going to control it, you've got to recognize that it's part of you." She stares at my chest, like she can somehow peer inside to see the fugue-monster within. "It's in there, somewhere, waiting for you to tap into it. It's powerful." She raises her eyes to mine. "Maybe too powerful. Maybe you're afraid of it."

I throw my hands out in exasperation. "I'm *trying*,

Kamali."

"Try harder."

"I don't know how!"

She scoops up the painting again and thrusts it in my face. "Paint me again."

I turn my head away and drag a hand across it. "I don't know... I thought we were going with the negative emotion thing. Like, you're supposed to piss me off and bring it on that way."

"Am I making you angry now?"

I smile. "Yeah. A little."

"Wait till you start painting me."

I look for a smile on her face, but she's dead serious. "Fine."

More brusquely than necessary, I stride to the paint cabinet and grab a random set of colors. I don't know what she's expecting, but I know there's no way I can reproduce even a fraction of *The Broken Artist*. But maybe she's right—maybe trying will frustrate me enough to tip me into the fugue state.

I set up next to the canvas. Kamali stands behind me, so close I can feel her impatience like a heavy whisper on my neck. I flex my fingers then grab the pencil to sketch. I look back and forth between the finished fugue work and the charcoal ghost I'm reproducing, and I can already tell it's off. I smudge some of the lines, pretending they don't matter, that I'll render it in paint anyway.

"Why did you paint me this way?" Her voice is soft, close, in my ear. It sends a shiver down my neck.

I give up on the outline and reach for tubes of thick

brown and blood red. "I told you. I didn't have any reason for it."

She doesn't say anything while I mix, but once I'm back at the canvas, she's whispering in my ear again. "There is a reason. Somewhere buried deep inside. You were drawn to this."

I don't want to know the reason. The thought is strong, but I manage to keep it from reaching my lips. The feel of her breath on me, combined with the words she's dropping into my mind, sends trembles of pleasure and terror dashing through me, like warring angels and demons.

I make a fist to keep my hand from shaking then grab a brush and dip it in the colors. I sweep wide, blocking in a background of browns laced with deadly blacks.

"There's a lot of death in that picture," her angel voice says. "A lot of... broken things. What's broken inside you, Eli?"

Everything. That thought almost slips out. I press my lips together and jab the brush into the palette again. It brings up fresh blood. I blink. The paint becomes simple color again, deep crimson red. I smear a cascade of it on the canvas, blending it into the brown. It looks like a sweep of red hair floating up through the muck, reminding me of Lenora and her Spanish conquistador costume with the wig that felt so real when it brushed my face.

I suck in a breath. *So many broken things.*

"Why did you paint my dead body, Eli?" she asks.

My held breath feels trapped inside me. "We're all

dead," I breathe out, not trying to keep the thoughts locked in my head any longer. "Eventually. We're all going to return to the dust from which we came." I frown at my own words. These aren't my words, but ones I've heard somewhere else, a long ago time. It feels like they were spoken in an ancient time, before I was born. But that doesn't make any sense. I dab at the painting, adding red spots like fallen drops. Or perhaps ones rising through the mud.

"But we're more than dust, aren't we?" She's shifted sides, whispering in my left ear, angling for a better view of the work.

I turn my head to the side, catching her next to me. "That's what you believe. I'm not so sure."

"You have to know that's what you're reaching for, right?" Her face is too close, her words too much. "That soul inside you."

I turn back to the work, sweeping up more color on my brush and smearing the blood drops into lines of legs, painted and angled. Her legs, a broken flame. "My soul? Maybe it's something much less than that. What if it's a repressed thing? What if it's better if it's not brought out? Maybe it's something... not good."

"Evil doesn't create, Eli. Evil destroys."

I think of the ascenders and all the wonders they've created. "I'm not so sure about that either."

"Whatever's inside you isn't evil." Her soft voice is chastising me now. "If you think it's evil, you'll keep it at a distance. Deny it. Instead, you have to reach for it. Believe in it. Embrace it."

I close my eyes, brush hovering over the canvas. I picture the rush of the fugue coming over me, sending me to that calm place where I'm watching a master at work. I reach for it, wanting it, trying to bring it closer, but it's like a shimmering dream that you can't quite remember. I reach harder, but the more I do, the more it dissipates into mist.

I open my eyes to find Kamali kneeling between me and the canvas, watching me intently.

"Did you feel it?" she asks, face lit with hope.

I grimace. "No. If I had… well, trust me, you would know."

She rises up and glances at the faint blue glow of the *drama* implant on the back of her hand. "I have to go," she says, like she doesn't really want to. "It's almost the dinner hour, and Alexis will kill me if I don't eat. Then I have more practice tonight."

I had completely forgotten—her performance is in the morning, and here I am, keeping her from her final practice. She should be focusing on her own competition, not mine, which is pretty much hopeless.

"You're going to do great tomorrow."

"I'll always dance, as long as I have this body, at least." Her voice is quiet. She looks wistfully at the half-smeared canvas. "But tomorrow will be special. I won't ever have an audience like that again." A shy smile graces her face. "Will you be watching?"

"There's nothing that could tear me from the screen."

And that's the truth. Watching Kamali dance is one of the few things *not* broken about my life. But the idea of her never having an audience again tears at me. She's not just throwing away immortal life—who knows what the ascenders will do after she embarrasses them. Exile, most likely. She'll never dance in public again, that much is sure. Not in a legacy city or for an ascender audience. She'll have to hide her talent in some dissenter camp, if there are some that even believe in dancing. I've heard they outlaw it, like it's some kind of evil thing.

That idea wrenches my stomach. "I'm going to keep trying to talk you into taking that medal, you know. Just so I can keep watching you dance."

She smiles wide. "I'll try to stop by after the performance. If they lift the lockdown. Maybe we can paint some more then."

I try not to show how relieved that makes me. "I'd really appreciate that."

She glides to the door, and I key her out. I turn back to face my work, but everything has gone stale. Her absence has sucked the living air out of my studio. If I can't reach the fugue state with her whispering torments into my ear, how can I possibly do it without her?

I return to the canvas, determined to try anyway.

TWENTY-FOUR

With Marcus banished, and Cyrus checking on my mom and distracting my competition, along with half of Agon preparing for the first day of competition, I was able to work the rest of the night undisturbed.

Not that it helped.

I worked past midnight, digging deep into my psyche and trying to reach a state that would somehow induce the fugue. I ended up with nothing but dozens of discarded paintings, each a mockery of *The Broken Artist*. In a fit of frustration, I destroyed half of them, stopping only when I realized that wasn't working either.

When I returned to the apartment, Cyrus was snoring in the other bed, but he'd left a note: *Mom okay*. With that, I fell into my bed and passed out. After a night of fitful sleep, I'm finally up again, but I can't return to the studio with Agon in lockdown for the day's competition.

I distract myself by watching the incredible talent on the screen in my room. Cyrus is watching with me. *Drama* is up first, then *storia*. *Musica* goes first thing in the morning tomorrow, then *artems* finish up. There's an actor on the screen now, doing a Shakespearean piece. It's good, but not great. No competition for Kamali.

I mute it and gesture to Cyrus's barely touched plate of bacon, fresh fruit, eggs, and some kind of pastry that looks like they flew it straight from Kamali's hometown of Paris. Food like this would cost more than a week's worth of chit allowance back in Seattle. I wish I had more appetite for it.

"You going to eat that?" I ask Cyrus.

"Naw. You can have it." His eyes are intent on the now-silent actor, but I can tell his mind is elsewhere. Not to mention that Cyrus not eating is pretty much a first.

"How'd things go with Katya?" I leave hanging the unspoken question about what happened when Basha came to our room.

His eyes dart to me then back to the screen again. "Katya's an incredibly deep and soulful person. A fine artist."

His funk is unsettling, so I try to shake him out of it. "I thought she was hot."

"That too." He throws me a smirk. "Not that she apparently knows it. Or maybe cares."

"Meaning she wanted nothing to do with you."

He looks offended. "Meaning she didn't believe me when I said her beauty was rendering me insensibly in love with her."

I laugh, a quick snort, but it relieves me to hear him back to normal. "You know, I'm not exactly disappointed you couldn't distract her from her art. There's enough dirty business swirling around this place."

"Hey." Cyrus's look goes dark like a sudden storm blew in. "The ascenders are the ones with the dirty hands around here, not the legacies."

I nod, but can't pass up the chance to harass him. "Been spending time with Basha-the-revolutionary, have we?"

Cyrus glowers and returns to staring at the screen. Which leaves me speechless for a moment. "You like her," I say with amazement in my voice.

"She's cute," he says, but it's clipped.

"*Cute?*" I unfold my arms and drop my feet from where they're propped on the table, so I can swing around to face him. "The last time you called someone cute was Stacey Glickman in primary. As I recall, she destroyed your heart for all of sixth year."

He's back to feigning offense. "She wore braces and couldn't part her hair straight."

My grin is a mile wide. "And you wrote her poetry every day. *And* you holed up in your room all summer playing *Recon Terra* when she moved to a new complex." I nod my head sagely. "So... Basha is the new Stacey. Should I be on standby to pick up the pieces of your broken heart?" The grin is starting to hurt my cheeks. But it's worth it.

He waves me off. "Like you know anything about women."

I am so not letting this go. "Maybe not, but I know *you.* So what exactly did you and Basha do yesterday?"

He gives me an irritated look that just amps up my grin. "I was keeping my eyes on the prize. You know, winning?" He flicks a hand to the screen. "After I tossed out shiny pants, I kept Basha distracted, so you and Kamali could have some quality time. I'm assuming you didn't let that go to waste?"

I sigh, coming back down. "Not a total waste. She helped me see things a little differently."

That information finally turns him to face me. "And?" he asks, impatient.

"And nothing. She's convinced I can control the fugue if I just reach deep enough. Embrace it, instead of pushing it away. But I'm not getting anywhere with that. Although... I did show her the painting."

He looks alarmed at that. "What'd she say?"

I shake my head. "I thought she would hate me, for sure, but instead... it moved her."

Cyrus nods. "Your art seems to do that. The good stuff, anyway."

"Thanks a lot."

"Just being honest, bro. So... you're still on her good side?" He seems keenly interested, like keeping a relationship going with Kamali is key to everything. And he's probably not wrong about that.

"Yeah. I think so." It flashes me back to her studio, when we were inches away, and I thought, maybe... although after seeing the painting, I'm not sure if she would be more or less willing to let me find out how soft her lips are. At least she still wants to help with the fugue. It's in exchange for helping her cause, but that doesn't bother me. "She's coming back for one more session, after the lock down lifts."

"Good." Something on the screen catches his eyes. He pulls up the holo controls and quickly turns up the volume. "Looks like our girl is up."

On the screen, a camera bot zooms in on Kamali. She walks that purposeful dancer-walk across the stage and takes a pose in the center. I'm already holding my breath. Her fingers are splayed, reaching toward the brilliant blue sky overhead. The flames of her costume lick up her hands and down her legs to the blood-red slippers she was wearing yesterday. That gives me a twinge of guilt, but it dissipates as soon as she starts to move.

It's the living-flame dance, the one that makes her more spirit than dancer, and I can't help thinking about what she said. *When my body can no longer dance, my soul still will.* Only I'm watching her soul dance, now, on the screen. And so are five billion ascenders—a few in the stands, most over the net like I am. We're watching a living spirit leap and arch, gather up the air and toss it overhead like the elements are hers to command. It's the *ascender within* that Marcus spoke of, only Kamali would call it her soul. Whatever it is, she's baring it for everyone to see. The dance goes on for breathless minutes, and I know, without any doubt, that she'll win. Any sentient being watching her would recognize it, even if we might argue about what exactly it is.

She ends with her back arched in a pose that defies gravity for a long second.

Then the stadium erupts in applause so thunderous that Cyrus drags up the controls to turn down the volume. Kamali holds for a moment longer, then relaxes.

I expect her to walk off stage, but she doesn't. She simply stands before them, eyes closed. A cam bot zooms in on her face. The beads of sweat around the edges of her tightly drawn hair sparkle in the sun, like a cut-diamond crown. She slowly opens her eyes and raises her arms. The noise of the crowd swells.

She gives them a very small, almost secret smile, as if she's holding it back. Then she lowers her arms and turns to glide off stage.

Cyrus mutes the noise altogether. "Man, she's good," he breathes out.

I don't say anything. *Her last dance.* I could see it in her eyes, and my heart aches with how beautiful and final it was. I breathe again, almost gasping, as if I was the one giving the performance of my life.

Soon enough.

"Do you think I can go see her?" I ask Cyrus, my gaze still glued to the screen. There's no sound, but the ascenders in their rental bodies are still on their feet.

"I doubt it. They have to get through *storia* first before they'll lift the lockdown. Maybe after that."

I nod then look at him. "It kills me, what they're doing."

"What who's doing?" he asks with a frown.

"Kamali. And Delphina."

"You mean the resistance?"

"Not so much that in particular, as what she's giving up." I look back to the screen. "I can't understand it."

"Yeah, well not everyone has the choice, Eli."

His dark tone draws me back, surprises me, but it only

takes me a second to figure it out. *Of course*. Even if I win, I'm only taking my family with me when I ascend. Which means just my mom. My dad, too, if my mom would simply say who he was. Although now that I think about it, probably not, since he's likely a dissenter. "I wish you were actually my brother, Cy, not just a pain in my ass."

He waves it off. "I know. You'd take me, if you could." He laughs. "Although count yourself lucky with that. I'd just be a pain in your ass forever." Then the dark look returns. "Besides, I'd be nothing but trouble. I don't much like the shiny pants."

"I didn't notice." My smirk pulls a snort out of him.

He pulls up the controls again. "Look. It must be time for *storia*. Delphina's up first."

He turns up the sound just as a hush falls over the ascender crowd. Delphina's wearing the same outfit, the only one I've ever seen her in: the ravaged yellow uniform with the black charcoaling. She's added a few more rips across the midsection, and the sleeves are pulled up to the top of her shoulders. The closeups from the cam bots reveal the muscles in her arms flexing as she clenches and releases her fists a few times. I know she's short, but she looks even smaller on the stage, her diminutive height accentuated by the briefness of her outfit. Her black boots look like they weigh as much as she does, and she stands in a military-ease position, feet spread wide.

"I am a work of art," she starts, and I hunch forward, elbows on knees. Delphina holds her hand out like she's carrying the weight of a globe in it. "You treasure me, hold me in the palm of your hand, like a creation too precious to live. Too precious to breathe. Too precious to let go free. I am a work of art."

She raises both hands now, moving them to accentuate her words, as if she's carving them into the air. "You peer inside our souls. You seek, but you cannot find. You crave, but you cannot be satisfied. Because that thing which you seek, that precious spark which you've lost, that treasured cargo you hold in your hands, it does not belong to you."

"I am a work of art."

She takes a breath. "Fashioned and formed in my mother's womb by the random chance of DNA, the twisting strands of molecules and faith, and in that moment, with that spark, I was made. In that brilliant instant, born of love and animal lust, I stole fire from the gods and brought it down into two twirling pieces of flesh. In every cell divided, every muscle grown, every moment of screaming birth and blood and scraped knees kissed by tender lips, I was made. In each mortal moment, I am carved by grime, soaked in sweat, baptized by my hairy, ape-descended humanity. I am the full expression of that stolen fire, that spark, rendered into flesh."

"I am a work of art."

She flings her arms wide. "I live the essence of living, while you spin your simulations of life in machines wrought by genius and lust. Your lies become truth, your way becomes lost, your frittered souls slip like sand through your fingers. Billions lost to the winds of time.

You hold out the golden chalice, but it is empty. A rest stop on the way to nowhere. You sit on a bench, like a boy waiting in the rain for his lover to return, not knowing she's already been crushed by the gears of your ambition."

"I am a work of art. I am not the leftovers of humanity. I am not a vestigial organ floating inside the belly of Orion. I am meat and blood and electricity, but we... *we*, the collective breath of the human race, are more than all of that combined. We speak the language of the soul because encoded deep in that spark, we know: we are *created*. And someday the Creator will come back and say, *My children, what have you done?* And I will say, I am still here, flesh and bone and aching heart. Still sweating and fighting and making sweet love. And in that transcendent act, I have become the creator, making again in the Creator's image, reaching for a kind of perfection not free of mistakes but forged into realness through them."

"I am a work of art." Her hands float in benediction over the crowd of ascenders. "You cannot buy me at any price, for I am not yours to own, yours to covet, yours to take into the vast and teeming multitudes of the lost. I am not *your* work of art. I am not your treasure. I am the work of the Artist, and when my body has fallen away, and the Artist asks of me, *My child, what have you done?*, my answer will be: I am Your work of art." She bows her head. "Still."

The last word is soft, a hush in her voice, but it somehow manages to ring and ring over the silent stadium.

"Holy crap," Cyrus says in a whisper.

The hush draws out, the crowd motionless and staring. I'm amazed that Delphina's still standing. I expect the police bots to swarm the stage any second and take her down, crush her under their metallic feet, but it doesn't happen. The cam bots follow her as she exits the stage.

The only thing I can think is: *they're not going to make it to the awards ceremony.* Delphina's already signed their exile order.

Or maybe even worse.

TWENTY-FIVE

Agitation is a live wire inside me.

I'm pacing the length of our apartment, pounding my fists together in a beat that matches my steps, just to keep them from beating on something else.

"They've been done for an hour," I say to Cyrus, who's sitting on his bed, shoes hanging off the edge, looking relaxed, but I know he's not.

"*Storia's* only been done for ten minutes," he says. "They'll lift the lockdown soon enough."

"What do you think they'll do to them?" I can't imagine Delphina walked off that stage into anything other than the waiting arms of a police bot. Which is bad enough, but what I really want to know, *need* to know, is if they've tied her to Kamali.

The muscles in Cyrus's jaw twitch, but he's still playing it cool. "They're not going to do anything. Yet."

I give him a sideways look. "Don't tell me you're not worried about Basha. She's as deep in this as any of them."

He lets out a slow breath. "True. But I don't think

they'll make a move against the agonites until the games are over."

"Why not?" Truth is, I don't know what to think. Open rebellion, like Delphina's performance, is completely off the map of my personal experience.

He shrugs, but it's tense. "Looks bad? Throws the game? Good luck figuring out how the shiny pants think. But they sure didn't spoil the show by hauling her off in chains, did they?"

I throw a hand out, gesturing to the now-blank screen. "She completely smacked down everything they believe."

"Maybe it's like Marcus said: the more radical your art, the better."

I shake my head, pounding a fist into my open palm again and thinking it through. "Yeah. Maybe. They wouldn't want anyone to think one *storia* performance means all that much."

"Exactly." Cyrus snorts. "They're above all that, right? We're just here for their amusement."

I hope that's true.

A soft click comes from the door to our apartment. I hurry over, and sure enough, my imprint is working again, opening the door. I stand on the threshold.

"I'm going to find Kamali," I say.

"I'm coming with you." Cyrus leaps off the bed, all feigned relaxation gone. As he passes me, heading out into the hallway, he adds, "Let's just steer clear of Delphina, shall we?"

I follow Cyrus down the hall. "You know where their apartment is?"

He gives me a look like I'm an idiot. Besides, I'm sure he's been there with Basha by now. As we're taking long, hurried strides down the immaculate corridors of Agon, I figure we have a minute for me to harass him. "So, you and Basha…"

"Shut it."

I can't help chuckling. "No, seriously, what is it? The bubbly personality? The gossip? The fact that her first act was to douse you in orange juice?"

"You really need to just shut up."

I grin, but it fades as Cyrus pulls up short at the door of an apartment. His clenched fist bangs on the door. I count the heartbeats until it finally slides open. Kamali and Basha both crowd the doorway.

"You guys okay?" I blurt out as soon as I see them. That's when I realize they're both smiling, not looking anywhere near as stressed as me and Cyrus.

"Did you see it?" Kamali grabs hold of my arm and pulls me inside. Cyrus lingers behind, but only because Basha is holding hands with him at the door.

"Of course," I say to Kamali. "You were amazing."

"I meant *Delphina's* performance." Her eyes are sparkling. She gives me a small smile. "But thank you."

I glance around the small apartment, a duplicate of mine and Cyrus's. There's no Delphina present. I look back to Kamali's expectant gaze. "You're going to take the gold for sure."

The light in her eyes dims a little, probably because I'm dodging talk about Delphina. Cyrus and Basha are out in the hallway now, having an animated, low volume conversation that I don't think we're supposed to overhear. I tug gently on Kamali's arm to bring her deeper into the apartment, near the screen, which is muted but replaying the competitions in a runup to the medal announcements.

I tilt my head to the distant Cyrus and Basha. "He was a little concerned about her." I hope that's not too obvious.

Kamali smiles, but it's tight. "There's no need to worry. We all know what we signed up for."

That just makes me frown. "Are you sure? I mean, maybe they don't know you're involved yet, but at the awards ceremony, if you go through with this—"

"What can they do, Eli?" It's a challenge.

I can think of all *kinds* of things they can do, but I don't want to give voice to them. "You have to know this is dangerous. Once you're not a legacy anymore, they could do *anything*."

"Exile is a given," she says, her dark eyes growing hard. "Imprisonment? Torture? They might. There hasn't been much of that in the past, but then we haven't been much of a threat before."

I glance at the open door, nervous. Our rooms are supposed to be secure, per Agon regulations, but the hallway? It makes me drop my voice. "How does turning down the medal make you a threat?"

"It doesn't." Her eyes glitter again. "Unless it does."

She's talking in riddles, and I want to ask what she means, but at that moment, Cyrus and Basha stride back into the room and shut the door. Kamali's gaze is drawn to the screen over my shoulder, and she quickly turns up the volume.

There's a short moment where the announcer flips through snippets of each performance, highlighting a key moment. I've watched these before, in previous Olympics on the legacy net. We always get to see the competitions, the flurry of celebration, then the final tallies. Everything is done by a straight vote that comes in real-time. Ascenders don't sleep normally, but everyone on the planet, even legacies—especially legacies—are awake for this.

The *drama* competitors' faces are displayed in a grid, all thirty or so of them. This is the final tally, and all four of us are transfixed. One by one, the faces fade, disappearing in the order from least votes to most. As they fade away, the images grow larger, reshuffle, then more are lost. It's a dance of sorts, where the competitors slowly winnow down, until only one will remain. I hold my breath until we're down to the final two, Kamali and a boy I don't recognize.

The boy fades.

A grin breaks across my face, and I turn to Kamali. Her eyes are wide, staring at her image grown large on the screen.

"You did it," I say, trying to draw her away from it.

She turns and throws her arms around me. It's the second time she's hugged me, and I'm even more surprised than the first. But this time, it doesn't take me as long to figure out to hold her back. She's as tall as I am, and her frame is like silken steel pressed up against me. My hands are firm on her back, and I feel her tremble just before she releases me.

I think she must be in shock, but when she pulls back, that's not what I see on her face. She's shaking and blinking. I hold her shoulders and don't let her get too far away.

"Are you okay?" I ask, peering into her eyes.

She nods, but turns away, spinning out of my arms. Basha grabs her in a fierce hug, pulling her down to her much shorter height and whispering softly to her. "It's okay, Kam. You can do this. You're going to be okay."

I realize, belatedly, that Kamali's *afraid*. It chills me to the core.

We're drawn back to the screen by a new grid of faces, this time for *storia*. There are even more competitors here, maybe forty. I scan for Delphina's face, not finding her before the faces start to fade. I think I may have missed her, but a glance at Kamali and Basha shows them still intent on the screen. As the competitors quickly shrink in number, I find her, defiant in her ragged yellow-and-black uniform. She survives the next several rounds, until finally, before my unbelieving eyes, she takes the gold.

This time the girls shriek, making me jerk in surprise. They throw up their hands, then hug each other, then shriek again. I stare in amazement at the screen. She dressed them down, told the ascenders off in the most powerful way, and they chose her to be one of them? Even if they found her art *disturbing*, there's something not right about that.

I catch Cyrus's eye. He looks just as concerned as I feel.

But the girls are ecstatic. Apparently, things are going just as they planned. But if Delphina isn't already hauled off and exiled to the deserts outside LA, she soon will be—with Kamali alongside her. If they're lucky, the ascenders will wait until after the awards ceremony.

Kamali grabs my attention with a hand on my shoulder. "We have to find Delphina and celebrate."

"I don't know…"

Cyrus jumps in. "Eli needs to practice. He still has a competition to win."

At that, the joy drops off Kamali's face, and she instantly becomes deadly serious. "Of course." She gives me an apologetic look. "Sorry, I got carried away. We should go back to your studio. Unless…" She glances at Basha and Cyrus, like she's not sure who's in on the secret and who's not. "Unless you've already solved your problem?" she asks me.

"No. I could still use your help."

She smiles wide.

Cyrus nods to me. "Basha and I will find Delphina and make sure everything's okay." He takes Basha by the elbow, and they're out the door before I can say anything else. When I turn to Kamali, she's staring at me with solemn eyes.

"I want you to be the *artem* medalist, Eli."

"Well, that makes two of us."

In silence, we leave her apartment and head to my studio. I don't know what to say. She's a gold medalist.

She could ascend. Instead, she's going to end up in exile. Or worse. And it terrifies her… yet she's going to go through with it. And try to help me win as well.

I'm kind of in awe of her right now.

"Do you really believe all those things Delphina said? In her performance, I mean."

"Yes." She says it quietly, like she doesn't want to discuss it, so I drop it. Soon we arrive at my studio, and I key us in. I forgot that I had left the broken canvases strewn around the floor until I see Kamali's arched eyebrows.

"Going that well, is it?" She gives me a look like she's not entirely convinced I'm not doing drugs after all.

"It was a long night." I hurry around, picking up the canvases and shoving them out the trash chute. Then I set up a new canvas, settle in front of it, and just stare. This is how the last dozen have gone.

She comes to stand behind me.

"What's our strategy here?" I ask. "Because I'm all out of ideas."

She grabs a chair and sets it down next to my canvas, backwards. She sits, facing me, legs straddling the chair, arms languidly draped in front of it, studying me. The post-dance, post-win glow has returned to her face, now that the fear has passed, and I'm struck once again by her beauty. I could spend days, weeks, painting her and never grow tired of it.

But we don't have that much time. Either one of us.

She cocks her head to the side. "You're sad. Why? Are you worried about losing?"

"No," I say reflexively. "Well, yes, of course. But that wasn't why."

She waits, but I'm not sure I want to tell her. I take a breath. "I'm afraid I won't have many more chances to paint you."

I'm not sure what reaction I was hoping for, but the frown on her face wasn't it.

After a moment, she says, "Why do you paint?"

"Um... what?"

"Sometimes, when I'm stressed about a performance, I meditate. Try to restore some balance." She ducks her head, then peers shyly at me. "Sometimes I pray."

"I... don't pray." I hope that doesn't offend her. "I mean, it's just not my thing. My mom does. A lot." She always did, but it's taken a serious kick up since she got sick. It has to be a natural reaction to the fact that she might be dying. But I don't say any of that.

"You don't have to pray." Her smile is back. "Meditation works just as well. You just need a way to relax your mind. For me, most times, I focus on why I dance. What it means to me. It helps to center me again."

"Okay." I don't say that I've never meditated either. If Cyrus were here, he'd be laughing at me, I'm sure of it.

"Close your eyes."

I stare at her a moment, soaking in her lovely face, memorizing it, then I close my eyes.

"Clear your mind. There is no competition. No medals. No future. Just the present. Picture a place where you've been happy while painting. At peace while you mixed your colors and put them on the canvas."

I'm not seeing anything but the image of her face, speaking to me. But it still calms me, just like watching her dance seemed to work the knots from my shoulders. Slowly the tension eases out of my body, trickling down like a small waterfall leaking out of my feet on the floor.

"Are you picturing that contented space, where you were once happy with your art?"

I nod, even though I'm not, but then an image pops into my mind of painting with my mom. It's no different than a hundred other times, back when she was healthy, when we'd sit side-by-side, her painting something beautiful, me scrawling something passable. But I was happy. Content. It was before I had a sense there was something else, something more, lurking inside me. That I was somehow losing in a competition with my own abilities.

"You're safe in that place." Kamali's voice is softer now, floating over the scene. "At peace with your art. You let it flow from you without effort. Without thought."

I feel myself nodding slightly, and in the scene I'm lifting my brush, sweeping it across, making silly lines that make no sense, but the colors are splendid. Vivid. My mother smiles, love spilling from her eyes, like happy tears.

"Now reach deeper into that place of peace. Hold onto it. Make it yours."

My mother's brilliant blue eyes capture me. *Make it yours*, she says without sound, just her lips moving. *Make it yours*. I reach out to touch her smiling face...

The room washes away like watercolor, and in my mother's place sits a craggy-faced man with bushy hair and beret. Make it yours, *he says to me, only this time I hear it, like a clear bell has rung in my mind. I look all around the room, and I should feel panic, because the walls have transformed into ancient rock lined with thick benches, their wood seeped with a hundred days of paint, but I don't panic, because there's no room for tiny emotions here in this place, only expansive creation. Great art is made here. I can feel it, like the warmth from the nearby hearth or the sticky oil of the paints that cling to the brushes lined up in a row on the bench.*

This is all yours, *the man says again, voice ringing, vowels overlapping, all making sense, but somehow separated into pieces as small as molecules. His eyes are dark but kind, his skin lined with age, but there's wisdom tucked beneath every crevice of flesh. I know his face, but can't place it.*

Why am I here? *I ask him. My words are like raindrops on a drum, vibrating sound and mixing together.*

This belongs to you, *he says, leaning closer.* You belong to this. Dit is waar je zult vinden de meeste en de natuurlijkste beweeglijkheid.

He is speaking in Dutch now, but I understand him, because the music of his words has no anchor in language. He's saying, This is where you will find your greatest and most natural passage. *Which I both understand as some kind of instruction or map and also completely don't understand at all. Then he gestures with a wrinkled hand to the canvas which is filled with living color. It moves under his touch and seems to float, as if he has drawn out the spirit of the work to hover over it.*

I reach out to touch it, and the ghostly color draws toward my hand...

"Eli!"

My eyes jerk open. Kamali stands in front of me, towering over where I'm seated, holding my cheeks in both her hands. Her eyes are wild and concerned.

"Eli," she says again, only this time it's with relief, not panic. She's searching my eyes, still holding my face. "Are you okay? Say something, Eli!"

"I'm okay," I say, tongue thick, but only because she's holding me so tightly.

She senses it and drops her hands, stepping back from me. "You... you stopped responding to me, and I didn't know..."

I blink, still in a fog, but then I realize: *I was in the fugue state.*

I knock the chair backward with how fast I stand. There are no residual tremors, no shaking, none of the symptoms of before. I spin to the canvas next to us, but it's still snow-white. Pristine. Not a drop of paint.

My shoulders sag.

"What happened?" Kamali's voice has a tremble in it now. She's wrapped her arms around her slender frame, pulling back, afraid.

"I was there. In the fugue state," I say quickly. I turn to her. "How long was I out?"

"I don't know... it must have been five or ten minutes."

Five or ten minutes? It was mere seconds in the fugue world.

"I almost called Cyrus," she says. "I was afraid I'd—" She cuts herself off, pulling tighter with her arms.

"Kamali, it's okay." I rush over and put my hands on her shoulders. "Don't you see, you did it! You sent me there. I was having one of the hallucinations, or dreams, or whatever they are. And look!" I show her my steady hand. "No aftereffects. I don't know how you did it, but you did."

Her gaze sneaks past me to the canvas.

I drop my hands from her shoulders. "I don't know why I didn't paint this time. I mean, I was almost painting in the hallucination. Maybe if it had gone on just a little longer…"

"I don't know if that's a good idea." Her face is scrunched up. "You were… I was afraid you'd…"

I've freaked her out, that much is clear. But I'm fine, and I can't help floating with elation. I skip over to the paint cabinet, scoop up a handful of tubes and another of brushes, and bring them back to the palette.

"We *have* to try again," I say. "We are *so* close, Kamali. I can feel it."

She takes a deep breath, hesitates, then nods. I open some paints and leave the brushes and pencil within reach. We sit again, like we were before, only this time I'm in front of the canvas. I close my eyes, and she walks me through it, but I can hear the tremble in her voice. And my body is amped with excitement.

I get up, shake it off, and we try again. And again. And a fourth time, but I know we're getting nowhere. Eventually, I see her sneaking looks to the wall screen. It's almost past the dinner hour, and I'm sure she hasn't eaten all day.

And we're stuck.

"You should go," I say, finally.

"I'm fine. We can try again."

"No." It comes out too harsh, so I send her an apologetic look. "I just need a break is all. I'll try again later." Later means well into the night. Whatever it takes to figure this thing out.

She stands up from the chair she's been haunting this whole time, trying to recreate the magic of that first session. "They're going to lock down soon. I won't be able to come back and help."

I step over to her and take her hands in mine. "It's okay. You've already given me something I've never had before."

"What's that?" Her eyes are wide, but she looks tired. She needs some rest before tomorrow. The day when I'm going to try to win ascendance, and she's going to give it up.

"You made me believe I could actually do this."

She smiles and slides her arms around my neck. My body melts into hers, and suddenly I'm thinking of reasons to have her stay.

"You can do this," she whispers in my ear, and in that instant I have no doubt it's true.

She slides away from me and leaves before I can come up with a decent reason for her to stay. Which is probably just as well.

I need to practice finding my fugue state.

TWENTY-SIX

The frustration is about to kill me.

I spend the rest of the evening trying to induce the fugue… to no avail. I try meditating. I envision Kamali sitting next to me. I conjure her lilting French-accented voice in my head. I do everything that could possibly bring the fugue state back to within my reach… and nothing. I finally give up when I destroy the blank canvas in front of me instead of painting on it.

It's like I'm right back where I started. Like the fugue is some capricious demon that's taunting all my pathetic efforts and laughing in the face of the idea that I could ever control it. I leave all my canvases and paints in the studio and return to my apartment.

It's late. I don't sleep. Judging by the lack of snoring on Cyrus's part, he's not sleeping either. But he doesn't say anything. I spend the night staring at the ceiling, trying to remember why I thought any of this was possible.

When breakfast comes in the morning, I force myself to eat, although it all tastes like paste. The lockdown is in effect. *Musica* is nearly done with their competition, but it seems like the minutes are dragging by on carts made of lead.

Finally, *artems* is up. I don't want to watch my competitors, and Cyrus doesn't suggest it. After an endless wait that feels like it's eating my nerves alive, the security bot arrives to escort us to the stage. Cyrus is quiet as we trail behind our escort, letting me stew in my own anxieties.

"Thanks," I say. The word echoes in the stillness that surrounds the soft swish of our uniforms and the mechanized creaks of the bot.

It seems to startle Cyrus out of his thoughts. "Thanks for what?"

I gesture around me. "For seeing this through. For helping me, even though…" I can't say it, not yet. *Even though I'm going to lose.*

I expect him to brush it off, but instead his large frame hunches up. "Don't thank me till it's over." Which is just his way of saying he believes there's still a chance.

"When it's over, we'll party back in Seattle. I know a guy who knows a guy who I'm pretty sure can get us whatever mind-altering drugs we want."

Cyrus stops suddenly and shoves me up against a wall. My eyes go wide as his meaty hands hold me there. I don't even try to resist, more concerned about the fury on his face than anything he might do to mine. Then he's suddenly flying backwards, lifted into the air by the security bot. The bot smashes Cyrus to the floor and holds him with one hand while training some kind of open-barreled weapon on Cyrus's head.

"No!" I shout.

The bot doesn't move. "Agonite Elijah Brighton, are you injured?"

"No! I'm fine." I lurch over and hover next to the bot, hands up, unsure what to do. Cyrus is wincing in pain. "This my support team! Let him go."

The bot eases away, its weapon sliding back into one arm as it releases Cyrus with the other. I don't think he's injured. Badly.

I kneel by Cyrus's side and help him up. "Are you okay?"

He nods and gives a dirty look to the security bot.

It stands impassively, waiting for us. As soon as we're both up, it says, "Please follow me to the agonite staging area."

We fall in step, resuming our march down the spotless halls of Agon as if the bot didn't just nearly kill Cyrus.

He keeps his voice low, but I can hear the anger in it. Anger for *me*, not the bot. "You do *not* give up. You go out there, and you do everything you can to win this."

"I'm not giving up. I promise. Not until I'm walking off that stage and it's over."

I glance at the bot, but it's making no moves against Cyrus. As long as he's not physically attacking me, I guess it's okay. Still… Cyrus and I don't talk anymore. When we reach the decon unit, the security bot scans us in, and Leopold is waiting inside.

"Mr. Brighton!" Leopold says in a greeting that seems overly happy. "Nice to see you in my chambers again."

I welcome the reprieve from the tension of the walk over. "I'm starting to think you have a thing for making humans undress, Leopold." I start taking off my clothes before climbing into the decon pod.

"You'll just have to trust me when I say your legacy bodies hold very little interest for me."

The decon goes quickly, leaving me slimed, but passing their tests. Cyrus cycles through as well, and soon we're through the door that leads to the holding room.

"Good luck, Mr. Brighton," Leopold says as the heavy metal door swings shut behind us. It sounds less like well-wishing and more like an indictment. Like Leopold knows as well as I do that the chances are slim of me actually pulling this off.

Cyrus and I wait in silence in the barren holding room. The seconds tick through the stale air, each one ramping up my nerves a little more. I close my eyes, trying to focus on the calming meditation words that Kamali used to somehow induce the fugue state—but they're empty of meaning and have no weight against the tension zinging through my body.

I take a deep breath and open my eyes just as a loud tone sounds from the staging room door. Cyrus and I both jolt from the sudden noise, but he beats me to lurching through the door as it slides open.

The wall of one-way windows lets in the perpetual sun of California, flooding the staging room with light. The stadium is filled with ascenders in their rental bodies, just like before, during the Showcase competition. There's an artist on stage. I squint at the reflections coming off the stage, the ascender's bodies, the bright-white backing of the artist's canvas. My eyes adjust enough to see that it's Katya, dressed all in black. She's still working, a brush in each hand and another clenched between her teeth. Her blonde hair is pulled back out of the way, and she whips back and forth between the floating palette and the art she's creating.

I'm certain it's spectacular, even though I can't see it.

"Eli," Cyrus calls to me softly from the far side of the room. He's gone to a door, probably the exit he leaves through once I'm on stage. I frown for a flash moment, thinking he's leaving me on my own in these final minutes. Even though there's nothing he can do, that still sends a cold gush of anxiety through my stomach.

But instead of leaving, Cyrus says, "I have someone who wants to see you."

He activates the door, and outside stands Kamali.

I have no idea how he's managed it—everyone and everything is supposed to be in lockdown—but somehow she's standing there, dressed in her red *drama* uniform, her normal grace replaced by a strange awkwardness that doesn't look right on her body. Her hair is undone, and it billows around her in a halo of a million tiny black ringlets. She steps inside, and Cyrus eases out past her. The door slides shut, leaving me alone with Kamali.

"How did you—" But I cut myself off as she hurries over to me, a finger held up to stop my words.

"We don't have much time," she says, a little breathless. Then she takes my hands in hers. I'm completely distracted by how warm and soft they are, but then she drags my attention back to her face by continuing to talk. "Take a deep, calming breath."

I suck in a breath. As I breathe out, I say, "I don't think this is going to—"

She cuts me off again with a stern look. "Close your eyes," she demands.

I obey.

"Let go of the performance. Empty your mind. Think about that place you went before, the place where you were happiest with your art."

I try, but my mind is a scattering of images, rippled and distorted, like the reflection of a pond with rain pelting the surface. I try harder to clear them out, but they keep crowding in: flashes of Katya on stage, imagining myself there soon, fuzzy images of the craggy-faced man from my hallucination, and my mom... smiling in a healthful glow she no longer has anywhere but in my mind.

I gently squeeze Kamali's hands and open my eyes. "It's not going to work, Kamali. Maybe when I'm on stage, I'll be able to do it. I'll try."

She's frowning, determination still written on her face, like I'm a puzzle she wants to figure out. "Maybe if we do some more deep breathing..."

I glance out the window. Katya's still at her canvas, but she's leaning back now, examining her work. I turn back to Kamali. "There's no time. But thank you."

The frown disappears, and she gives me a small smile. "Thank *you*. I know you didn't mean to, but I think you helped me more than I helped you."

She's talking about the painting I made of her, which only reminds me that the closing ceremonies are later today, and as soon as the final tallies are made, the medalists will be called down to receive their awards. I have no idea if I'll see her again before that happens.

"It's not too late to change your mind." I hold her hands tighter and bring them up to my chest, drawing her closer. "And I could still go out there and win this. We could ascend together, Kamali—just think of what we could do then. For our families. For everyone. And we'll have all the time in the world to do it." I let go of one of her hands so I can run a finger along one long, infinitely curly strand of her hair. "Please don't throw that away."

"I'm not the one who will be throwing something away," she says, peering into my eyes. "You have something more precious than a million ascenders put together. I know I can't talk you out of ascending, but I hope you'll keep your promise to remember me after you do. And I promise you this, Eli Brighton: I'll remember *you*. I'll remember the boy you were before you ascended, before you turned into one of *them*. The boy who's scared and loves his mother and would do anything for her. That boy..." She places her hand flat against my chest, and I'm afraid she might feel my heart pounding there with every word she's saying. "...*that* boy touched my soul, and I will remember him forever. Even after he's given up his eternal life for a perpetual one."

I'm struggling for words, but the need to say anything douses as she leans forward and presses her lips to mine. They're softer than I imagined, and I don't have to think to kiss her back. My lips are already moving against hers, my hands sliding up to hold her cheeks. I pull her close and wind my fingers into the silky cloud of her hair. I deepen the kiss, and it quiets something inside me, creating a bottomless calm that wars with the pounding of my heart and the shortness of my breath. Our tongues dance together, tasting and touching each other like we're both starved for this. Like it might be the last time as well as the first.

"Eli." Cyrus's voice halts our frantic kiss, but it's not until I turn to face him at the door that I see something which makes me reflexively jerk away from Kamali.

Lenora is standing next to Cyrus.

"Your girlfriend's here," he says with cold words that horrify me.

My mouth hangs open, and I'm frozen between lashing out at Cyrus for allowing her in and asking Lenora how she could dare to be here. Her face is deeply troubled, but the look on Kamali's is what turns my insides to ice.

Her beautiful full lips turn down, hurt by my abrupt end to the kiss, but more than that... she's disgusted. She looks back and forth between me and Lenora, but my body language reflex has already sentenced me in her eyes.

"You're with one of *them*?" Kamali whispers, her face contorted in judgment.

My mouth moves, but nothing comes out. I hold my hands palm up and finally force out, "She's my patron." As soon as the words leave my mouth, I realize they only make things worse. *Of course* she would be my patron, if I were that kind of human, the one Kamali is despising with her eyes, the kind I suddenly turned into with Cyrus's words and my body's betrayal: *a domestic.*

Kamali shrinks away from me. She turns, but not before I see the shine of tears in her eyes. She ducks her head and flies out the door, squeezing past Lenora such that no part of her dancer's body accidentally touches Lenora's perfectly sculpted bodyform.

The rage inside me vents toward Cyrus. "What the hell, Cy—" But he's already out the door, and it slides shut behind him, leaving Lenora in the room with me.

Alone.

I'm speechless about what has happened. Before I can piece together why my best friend has stabbed me in the back, Lenora crosses the floor and stands before me. Her white rose skin is luminescent in the streaming sun, almost glowing like an angel.

She's no angel, my brain re-engages to remind me.

"Eli, please listen to me."

I turn away from her, shaking my head, not quite believing she's here. Through the glass, I see Katya standing and turning to the crowds, accepting their adulation for her amazing work. Work I will have to beat but have very little chance of doing so.

"Please don't go out there, Elijah," Lenora says, bringing me back.

"Are you kidding me?" The bitterness makes my mouth ache.

She looks to the door that Kamali just rushed out. "I

can see you are… attached to that girl."

"*That girl* is a gold medalist who—" I cut myself off, choking on the fact that I almost spilled Kamali's secret plans.

"Who you care about. I can see that." She pauses, and I want to read something into it. That maybe there's the slightest bit of jealousy there, but all I see is deep worry. "Cyrus said you might be having second thoughts."

"*Did he?*" My anger froths up to a new level. My friend who was supposed to be supporting me. My friend who, now that I think about it, was pushing me constantly to be with Kamali, the revolutionary. My friend who is probably sleeping with the resistance's most chatty member. The betrayal burns like acid drilling a hole through my stomach. "Well, I'm not having second thoughts. I'm going to go out there…" I fling my hand toward the now-empty stage, aware that any moment the crowd will start wondering where I am. "…and win. No thanks to you. Or Cyrus. Or, for that matter, Marcus, your ascended lover who is, I'm sure, oh so much better than I could ever be." Something tugs at me, something about Cyrus telling me, just minutes ago, to never give up. But I shove it aside.

Her eyes go slightly wide. "Eli, I do care about you. More than you can possibly know."

"Yes, you care about me so much, you want to keep me for a *pet.*" My lip curls in disgust as I say it.

"Eli, no! You don't understand. It's not like that."

"It's *exactly* like that." I turn away, but she reaches out and stops me. If she wanted to use her ascender strength, she could easily crush me. But her touch is feather-light, and I hate the way it makes my heart lurch. I hate all the times I dreamed of her touching me just this way.

I turn back to her anyway.

"Eli, I haven't been honest with you. And... I'm so sorry for that, but you see, I've been trying to protect you..." Her voice is trembling.

"From what, exactly?" My words are harsh, clipped. But whatever she's going to say is too little, too late.

"From ascenders like Marcus. From others who want to see you destroyed." Her delicate fingers are suddenly on my cheek, cool and caressing. "Please, just come with me now. I will tell you everything."

"*Now?* You want me to just walk away?" I can't believe she would even propose it.

"Yes. I promise you will understand everything, once I have a chance to explain—"

"You had your chance." I turn away from her and stride to the door. I open it, and the sun takes on a new brilliance as it blasts into the room. I glance back. She's still waiting for me, hand outstretched. "If I ascend, you and your *second*, Marcus, had better both stay far, far away from me."

I step out onto the stage.

Every step across the dull black floor just stokes my anger, jolting it with another hot electric shock up my back. Cyrus betrayed me. Kamali despises me. Marcus lies to my face, while Lenora treats me like a child to the bitter end. Meanwhile, my mother lies dying of a disease any one of the multitudes of ascenders before me could cure.

I stand before them, sensing their unease like a ripple across the stadium, a breathy wind of disapproval and concern. I hate them. *Hate* them. With every fiber of my being. And yet I've never more desperately wanted what they have. To ascend. To show them. Fix everything that's wrong. To prove to them all that I'm just as good as they are.

I feel it coming, like an undertow stealing sand from beneath my feet: *the fugue state.* I quickly spin to face it, flinging my arms wide to embrace the drowning waters.

I'm back in the master's shop. The craggy-faced man is there, working on a portrait, and a twinge of recognition whispers in my ear. He's Dutch and his clothing style is four hundred years out of date. I'm dreaming about a famous painter from the past.

Without turning, he says in his ringing thought-voice, This is not a dream, Elijah. *He turns the painting toward me, and I can see it's a portrait of me.* You are the bridge, *he says.*

The bridge between what and what? *I ask, but as soon as I do, my mind expands. I'm standing on the stage, in front of the ascenders. I sense the movement of my hands conducting a symphony of paint on the canvas in front of me. At the same time, I am standing before the master painter, staring at myself on his canvas.*

You are the bridge, *he repeats. Somehow I know his medium isn't paint, but something more.*

I'm your work of art, *I say, echoing Delphina's words.*

He smiles and shakes his head no. I lose the sense of being on stage, and at the same time, his ancient and cobblestoned room expands to hold a hundred people. They're whispering, but not to each other. To me.

What are they saying? I ask the master. As I say it, one drifts forward. She's bent with age, but her dark eyes are piercing and intelligent. Her clothing is modern, stylish, but somber. She reaches a wrinkled finger toward my forehead. When she touches me, I don't feel the aged skin of her hand, only a blinding rush of knowledge, as if she's transferred every minute of her existence into mine. It's an overwhelming flood that nearly snuffs out everything that I am. I stumble back, breaking contact, and the tsunami cuts off, leaving me woozy and aching, bruised by the encounter. I have a heaviness about me, a weight that pulls me down, like a burden I scarcely can carry.

You are the bridge, Elijah, *she says.*

I'm back on the stage, standing in front of a canvas dripping paint. I have a brush in each hand, and a roar fills my ears. I blink in the hazy-bright sun, which makes the work look as though it's glowing around the edges. That effect isn't what makes the painting transcendent, though. It's the fact that I've painted Kamali, again, only this time her broken and bruised body is lifted from the muck, carrying chains of mud around her wrists. She's breaking free from her earthen bonds as her tilted face gazes heavenward. Her hair, unbound and free, falls down her back, and her face shines with an expectant joy.

I've painted Kamali arisen… *ascended*… but in the way she wants to be.

It's the finest thing I've ever made. Only this time I know it not just as a viewer of the piece, but as the artist. I can see the details of the eyes, the glow around her wrists, the sweep of color change along the length of her body calculated in microscopic shades. It's like a veil has been lifted from my eyes, and I can see every minute stroke, every nuanced line, in a way I never have before. I look at my hands, which are smeared with her paint, and realize I know how to do this. I could paint her again. Or at least some of it. As that thought dumbfounds my mind, the sound of the crowd swells and fills my head with pounding. My body starts to tremble, and the brushes in my hands twitch with a convulsion that's gripping my body.

I only have one thought left: *get off the stage*. I drop the brushes and stumble, nearly falling, toward the exit door. I make it just as my knees give out.

I leave a smear of brown paint on the door frame as I stumble inside Agon.

TWENTY-SEVEN

The brightness of the stage is replaced by the glowing panels of the hallway.

My head is still filled with the wonder of the piece I just painted. The knowledge that I created it—that I actually have some idea how to re-create it—gives me a burning urge to find a canvas and paint it again.

Only my legs don't work right, and my hands are curled against my chest, shaking. I fall against the wall and smear paint along it, trying to keep upright. I hear footsteps pounding in the hallway ahead of me, but it takes all my concentration to shuffle my feet forward, crawling along with the wall as support.

"Eli!"

Through the fog in my head, I recognize Cyrus's voice. The footsteps pound closer, and his big, rough hands grab my shoulders, pulling me upright.

"You did it, Eli! You actually—"

I punch him.

I have no strength or coordination, so it's mostly me shoving my fist in his face and smearing it with paint before twisting and falling to the floor. I hit hard enough to pull a grunt out of me. But my swing is enough to get the message across. I think. My legs and arms are too cramped now to do anything but curl up on the floor and wait for it to pass. Then I'll give punching Cyrus another try, even if he outweighs me by fifty pounds.

He stands over me, silent. Then he bends down near my head. "Eli, I'm sorry."

"Go away," I manage to get out.

He reaches out to try to help me up, but I shove away his hands. I'm mostly flailing, but he gets the idea.

"Eli, let me help you."

"Had enough of your help."

He sighs and sits down cross-legged next to my head. I mostly see his knees near my face, and I'm well aware that he could pummel me if he wished. My body gives a violent shudder, but it seems to uncramp my hands a little. I edge away from him, even though I'm not coordinated enough to go far.

"Eli." Cyrus sighs again. "I told you… I *told* you, man, I would do anything to help you win."

My brain chews on that a moment, but it doesn't make sense to me. I roll over so I'm lying on my back, staring up at the light panels. I take a couple breaths as I puzzle it out. "You were trying to piss me off. Trigger the fugue." I say it, but it doesn't take away the sting of the betrayal.

"Well… not exactly. But yes."

My cramped arms are relaxing, so I brace against the wall and push myself up to sitting. I peer at Cyrus from across the hallway. He's using his blue *artems* uniform to wipe off the paint I smeared on his face.

"What *exactly* were you trying to do?" I ask.

He sighs again and looks away from my steady gaze. "I saw what Lenora did to you. How jealous you were. Frustrated. And then the fugue happened. I was trying to recreate that for you, and I could only think of one way to do it."

"So you brought her back." My jaw is chattering a bit, but the shakes are starting to mellow out. "And you brought Kamali into it, to make it worse." I pause and take a couple breaths, trying to calm my body. "That was a messed up thing to do, Cy."

"I know." He looks back to me. "But it worked. And now you'll get to ascend and take your mom with you, and you won't have to worry about me being a pain in your ass anymore."

I don't know if I'll actually win, but I don't have any real doubts about it. The fugue state is the best I'm capable of. If I can't win it there, I truly never had a chance. But deep inside, I know the gold is already mine. I know what it takes, and I know what I just painted. The anger at how Cyrus made it happen is still churning inside me, but it's already starting to fade. "I really hate you right now."

"Yeah, well, soon you'll get to hate me forever." He climbs to his feet. "C'mon. You're a mess. Let's get you back to your room."

This time I let him haul me to my feet. I nearly go down again, but he's got a beefy arm around my back, holding me up. It's either let him help me or sit and wait it out. I grab hold of his shoulder for support and lurch down the hallway with him.

"Did Kamali know?" I ask.

He gives me a disgusted look. "Did she look like she was in on it?" He shakes his head. "I went after her, but she wanted nothing to do with me. I'm hoping Basha can say something to make it better."

"So Basha knew."

"Well… not really," Cyrus says, quietly. "She was in on helping me get you and Kamali together. She didn't know about the rest. That's all on me. I'm sure she hates me now, too."

I squint at him, but he's staring down the hallway, avoiding my gaze. My legs are starting to get more rhythm. I loosen my grip on his shoulder, then shove away from him and use the wall for support. We keep our slow march through the winding hallways.

I realize I have no idea where I am. Again. That I'll have to rely on Cyrus to get me back to the apartment. Like I've relied on him all along.

I glance at him. "You really suck as a friend, you know that?"

"Yeah." He doesn't look at me.

"If you were any better, I'd have had no chance of winning at all."

He looks sideways at me. "You'd have had no chance with Kamali, either."

I laugh, but it's more of a snort, because my body is still a bag of trembles and shakes. "Oh, come on! She was totally into me. Not any more, mind you. But *before*."

He smirks. "Like you could have managed that on your own." Then he gets serious again. "I'll fix it, Eli. I'll go tell Kamali it's all a lie. That you're not, you know, Lenora's little love slave."

"I don't think she'll believe you." The laughter washes out of me, and I stop in the hallway. Most of the tremors are gone now, but that's not what's keeping me from moving forward. The look on Kamali's face is still etched into my mind. That look wasn't just because of Cyrus's words; it was because I pulled away from her. Because I didn't want Lenora to see us kissing. Because I was *ashamed*… and not of the right things. Kamali has every reason to believe I'm exactly what she thinks.

"Don't worry," Cyrus says. "I'll convince Kamali she got it all wrong. Basha will help, if for no other reason than she doesn't want Kamali upset any more than we do. Especially right now. Come on, their apartment is right around the corner."

"What?" But he's already slipped around the bend. I force my legs to unlock and follow after him. "Cyrus, wait." I round the corner, but he's already pounding on their door. My legs aren't quite up to fully-functional-running yet, but I arrive before the door opens and yank his arm away from pounding again. "She's got enough to worry about right now, with the medal ceremony and everything. She's probably better off just hating me and moving on."

He gives me a look like I'm pathetic. "You really *don't* know anything about women, do you?"

I give up and lean against the wall next to the door, trying to think of what I can possibly say to Kamali when she answers it.

Cyrus keeps knocking. After a minute, we both realize no one is answering.

I push away from the wall and stare at the door. "I don't like this, Cy."

"Me either." The scowl on his face is darkening by the moment. "Maybe they're at the studio." He doesn't wait for me, just takes off in a half-jog down the hallway. I lurch after him, commanding my legs to *move*. The studio isn't far, but Cyrus has pulled enough ahead that, by the time I arrive, he's already peering in the window, which is dialed to clear. His scowl is two shades worse.

"They're not here."

"The Lounge?"

"Not open." He turns away from the door. "Maybe they're at Delphina's."

Before I can respond, he's sprinting down the hall again. I stumble after and try not to lose him. Delphina's in another wing of Agon, so it seems like we go on forever. We pass a security bot patrolling the corridor on the way, but it doesn't bother with us. Finally, Cyrus stops and bangs on another door. I count my heavy breaths as we wait... but there's no answer.

"I thought for sure the shiny pants would wait until after the ceremony." His voice is tight with what we're both leaving unspoken. I press my lips together, trying to think of where they could be. Any explanation except the one that's stabbing icicles of fear into my chest. *The ascenders have already taken them away.*

"Let's go back to our room," Cyrus says, taking off down the hall again. He calls back over his shoulder, "We can find out more there."

I limp after him, winding through the hallways again. We take a different route, and this time we see more people. *Storia* and *drama* agonites, most solemn. All losers in the lottery of the games. No ascenders to be seen; they've already abandoned their agonites. Competitors who are now just legacies again, figuring out how to live the rest of their mortal lives.

Kamali and Delphina and Basha are nowhere to be seen.

When we get back to our apartment, my body is finally back to normal, or nearly so, but it feels like a vise is clenched around my chest. My mind is spinning all kinds of scenarios of what has happened to the girls. They could be under questioning about the resistance. Or maybe just locked away. Or kicked out. They could be sitting, exiled, on a crumbled road at the outskirts of LA, for all I know. But I *do* know there are nomads that lurk at the edges of the cities, just outside the police bot patrols. I've never seen them, just heard about them, but the stories aren't pretty. The outskirts are definitely no place for three underage girls.

Cyrus is at the screen, hacking in to see what he can find out, but the frustration on his face says it's not much. In one corner of the screen, the *artems* competition is winding down. It won't be long before they start the final tallies.

"Maybe they're just somewhere preparing for the ceremony," I say, more wish than actual belief it's a possibility.

"Basha would have told me," he says, still searching the pages. "She said they were supposed to stay in their rooms, for security purposes. They're medalists. They're not too popular inside of Agon right now."

"Then how did Kamali manage to get into the staging area to see me?"

"Her sponsor helped us out." He pauses. "I'm not finding any mention of anything here." He swipes the pages he was using off the screen with a grunt of frustration.

A strange toning sound starts pinging. Cyrus searches the screen, but it's not coming from there. "What *is* that?"

I scout around and find it's the holo phone Marcus gave me. I frown at Cyrus, but he says, "Answer it."

I tap the small button.

Marcus's face pops up to float above the device. "Eli!" he says, like he's surprised to actually see my face. "I've been trying to reach you. Where are you?"

"Um… back in our room?" My eyebrows lift. I expect him to say something about the painting—even if I kicked him out, he's still my sponsor. "Where are you?"

"Nearby," he says. "I'll be there soon. Just sit tight. Don't go anywhere. I'll come get you."

I throw an alarmed look to Cyrus, who is shaking his head and looks like he wants to crush the holo phone with his bare hands. "What do you mean, you'll come *get* me? We're still waiting for the final tallies."

"Right." Marcus looks off screen at something. "I'll meet you at your room. We'll watch the tallies together before we go."

With that, his holo head projection blinks out of existence.

"Something is seriously not right." Cyrus grabs the holo phone out of my hand and starts hacking into it.

"What are you doing?"

"Calling your mom."

The worried look on his face sends an avalanche of fear cascading through me. "You said she was all right."

"She was when I called her before. But that was before the girls went missing. And before your sponsor started acting even crazier than normal." Cyrus finally brings up a connection. It rings and rings. There's no answer, not even a message.

"She's not answering because she's sick." I run both hands through my hair. "Marcus said she was in a coma."

"Marcus is a shiny pants liar." Cyrus clicks the phone off. "No answer means it's disabled." His voice is quiet and dark, filled with a deep anger I'm just starting to feel.

"Why would they do something to my mom's phone?" I don't want to voice what I'm really thinking. *Why would they do something to my mom?*

"Because they don't want you contacting her." Cyrus runs a hand across his face. "This is bad, Eli."

Anxiety is climbing up my throat. "Call Riley. Get him to check on my mom."

"Right. But this thing's useless for that." Cyrus tosses

the phone to me, and I shove it in my pocket. He heads back to the screen. "I should be able to go through the darknet to reach Riley's black market net. Or reach someone who can tap into it. I'll encode a handshake, so Riley will know it's me, then have him send someone physically to the apartment. We need to get eyes on your mom without being tracked." He glances at me while his hands work the pages. "It's going to take a while, Eli."

I rub my temples with both hands, cursing my own stupidity. We should have had someone watching my mom all along. Someone *not* an ascender. Instead, I left her in the care of an ascender-controlled med bot. Why did I trust the ascenders with *anything*?

Just as Cyrus finishes with his darknet message, one of the other pages flashes an announcement about the games.

"Cy…" I say, but he's already on it.

He swipes the tallies to fill the screen. First *musica* is up, nearly forty competitors this year. They shift and sort, and the winner emerges: a dark-eyed Asian girl I don't recognize. After a small amount of commentary, the field for *artems* appears. It's the smallest cohort, only sixteen of us. I swallow as I find my picture and watch it move across the screen, surviving the winnowing, round by round. It quickly narrows to just a few, including me and the winsome Katya. I hold my breath until we're the final two… and then Katya's picture fades.

I huff out my breath, not quite believing it, even as I stare at my intake picture huge on the screen. I won. I took the gold. *I'm going to ascend.* A small, hysterical laugh escapes me. Cyrus's hand lands on my shoulder, and he pulls me into a rough, backslapping hug.

Then he grips my shoulders with both hands. "You did it, man." He's fighting a smile, like he's not sure if he's entirely won my forgiveness.

"I couldn't have done it without you, Cy." Tears prick my eyes as I realize: *we're going to save my mom.*

He breaks into a grin and grabs me for a lung-squeezing hug. Over his shoulder, I see the image of my picture flash, something scrawled across it. I pull back from Cyrus and stare at the screen through blurry eyes.

Disqualified. It's written in large red letters across my face, but a fog suddenly hits my brain, and I can't take it in.

"What the hell!" Cyrus yells at the screen. He pulls up the volume, and the announcer is saying something about information coming to light regarding the mysterious death of Aaron Thompson, seventeen-year-old agonite from Seattle, also the home of gold medalist Elijah Brighton.

I feel the blood drain from my face.

An image of Thompson on an autopsy table appears next to my picture on the screen. Then both our pictures fade, and Katya's serious artist face appears.

She's their new gold medalist.

TWENTY-EIGHT

I have to brace myself against the head of my bed.

Cyrus is cursing and stomping around our room, but all I can feel is an arctic chill settling into my bones. Someone killed Thompson and set me up for it. Someone who didn't want me to win. Someone who was willing to do anything to keep that from happening.

Lenora.

I feel dizzy, like my brain has split into two pieces, and they're both swimming in a frothy sea of surreal. Cyrus curses the ascenders in ever more colorful language, but I'm unmoored from reality. I ease to sitting on my bed.

I had the gold. And then I lost it. My one shot at ascending gone before I even had a chance to believe it. And I'll never have another one. My mom will die of the disease that's ravaging her body. I'll live out my short human life and follow after her. Being the best wasn't good enough, not when the ascenders have their own games they're playing. The bitter unfairness of it wells up to choke me. I can feel the fury growing, like a volcano building pressure under a sheet of ice.

Before it can erupt, I hear a snatch of something else the announcer is saying. I slowly turn to look at the screen. Pictures of Kamali and Delphina loom large.

"Cy." My voice is a whisper, but it cuts off Cyrus's tirade, and he takes in the screen. The announcer says something about never in the history of the games has there been such a sweeping round of disqualifications. But that the gold medalists from *drama* and *storia* have been found to have "known ties to dissenter organizations." Their pictures fade and are replaced by their runner-ups.

"Oh no." The words leak out of me, and somehow this is the final blow. I'm not going to ascend. Kamali won't get her chance to defiantly throw the medal in their faces. I'll never see her again, except maybe as cell mates in an ascender prison. My mind goes blank at that, refusing to see it. Cyrus is still staring at the screen, slack-jawed, like his worst nightmares have come true.

There's a pounding at my door.

It jolts me, and I'm on my feet. I throw a wild look at Cyrus. "Security bot?" I mumble, my heart just now jumping into my throat and pulsing there, making it hard to speak.

The door pounds again.

"A security bot would just open the door." Cyrus eyes the still-closed entrance.

I start towards it, then hesitate. "Marcus?"

Cyrus nods. "He must have already known. Maybe shiny pants will be good for something after all, if he can keep us out of prison." He tilts his head toward the door for me to answer it.

I hurry over and key it open. But it's not Marcus.

Lenora pushes past me so fast I've barely registered that she's no longer in the doorway when she calls from deep inside my room, "Close the door, Elijah!"

I don't close the door, but I turn wide-eyed, looking for Cyrus, afraid she's going to do something to him. Or me. She could kill us both before we even knew what was happening.

Cyrus edges away from her, positioning his large body between me and her. A nice gesture, if I wasn't more worried about her taking him out.

"Eli, please!" Lenora says, and I decide she's not here to kill us. Not yet, at least.

I slide the door shut. I'm speechless, but I can see Cyrus putting it all together.

"You murdered Thompson as a backup plan, in case Eli won," he says, voice full of restrained anger.

"I didn't murder Thompson," she says, but the guilt on her face tells me Cyrus isn't that far wrong. "But I did arrange for some new evidence that connects Elijah to the murder. I'm sorry, but I had to do it. Eli, I tried to warn you—" She cuts herself off and strides over to me, brushing past Cyrus like he doesn't even exist. Which ramps up the anger building inside me.

"You got what you wanted," I say bitterly. "I guess I shouldn't be surprised."

Her perfectly sculpted face draws down in sadness. "This isn't what I wanted. But I couldn't let them kill you. And that's what would have happened. They would have pretended to let you ascend, but you would have been part of the one percent who didn't make it. If by some chance they allowed you to ascend, it would only have been because the most important part of you had been destroyed in the process."

My stomach bunches up. She's sounding like Kamali, and it's sending my head sideways. "What are you talking about?"

Lenora takes my hand in hers. It's cool and soft as a newborn's cheek. I'm so thrown by all of it, I let her lead me to the bed, where she sits and beckons me to sit, too. She's wearing a thin, blue jumpsuit, the fabric of which resembles my sheets, shifting to fit her bodyform no matter which way she moves. Cyrus frowns from across the room, but he's waiting to hear what she has to say.

"Eli, you're the most important thing in the world. Not just to me. To the world."

"I... don't understand what you're talking about." She is crazy talking.

Lenora turns over my hand, so it's palm up, then traces the lines in my palm up to my fingertips. "You are unique, Elijah. Your body is human.... Well, mostly human."

I blink. "*Mostly* human?"

She smiles a little. "Do you remember the last time you were sick?"

"It's been a while." The truth is, I don't get sick. I mean, I get tired sometimes, run down. But I don't get the standard virus that floats through Seattle every year.

Her smile grows. "You're lying. You've never been

sick a day in your life. I would know. I've been charged
with tracking your progress from the beginning."

"The beginning of *what?*" But the shivers are raising
goosebumps on the backs of my arms. I'm not sure I
want to hear what she's going to say.

"We simply called it *The Question*," she says, and
there's a weird glimmer in her eye, like she's glad to be
finally saying it out loud. "And you were going to be our
answer."

I jerk my hand out of hers and stand up. "Either start
making some sense or get out." I fling my hand toward
the door.

She stands and calmly regards me. "You were born
seventeen years ago, through natural birth to Agatha
Brighton. There is no recorded father on your birth
record, Elijah, because... you don't have a father. At
least, not the way most humans do."

I seriously consider whether ascenders can go insane.
Like, literally, have a mental illness or malfunction or
whatever.

Before I can think of something coherent to say, she
continues, "You were part of an experiment to create a
new Singularity, a second one, one that would fix the
errors, the mistakes, of the first. One where human and
machine would be seamlessly integrated at the molecular
level to bond them together in a way that would sustain
the one thing we lost the first time around. Or at least
may have lost. That's The Question, you see. Is that one
thing, the only real thing that matters, still present within
us? Or was it forever lost in the Singularity? There are

many among us who believe in it, but we can't prove it. And not for a lack of trying."

"A soul," Cyrus says. "You're talking about your soul." But he's looking at her like she's crazy, too.

"Your soul." Her eyes glitter again. "Your spirit. That spark of the ineffable that is more than just mind or personality or creative impulse. It's your connection to the divine." She trains her gaze on me. "You, Elijah, are that connection. A bridge, not just between human and machine, but between our existence and a higher plane."

A bridge. I take a step back, the weight of that word thudding into my stomach like a punch to the gut. "I'm not... I'm not that..." I struggle to deny it, but the words are getting tangled up on the way out.

"You think Eli is a bridge? Between you and... God." Cyrus says it like he's quite certain she's mentally ill now. And I want to believe he's right, but the coincidence... that the craggy old man in my vision or dream or whatever it was called me *the bridge.* Then I realize... *the ascenders have done something to me.* They could have programmed these dreams in me, making me have the fugue in the first place. Whatever delusional ideas Lenora has about why they did it—or how I'm her answer to *The Question*—she obviously believes I'm not entirely human. And that the ascenders made me that way.

I can't think of any reason for her to lie about that.

"What did you *do* to me?" I ask in a whisper, horrified. My legs feel weak, and I brace myself against the wall. My mind is still grasping at it. Casting back. Thinking about how long the fugue has been going on. How long I've been… *different.* "You said you did this experiment. When?" I lurch toward Lenora until I'm staring her in the face. "*When* did you do this to me?"

"Eli." Cyrus pulls me back from her, talking quietly. "Eli, she's crazy. Something's misfired in her brain. Don't tell me you're buying any of this."

I don't want to believe her, but there's some part of me that *knows*… there's something different about me. Something that's wrong or changed or tampered with.

"You were created in your mother's womb, Elijah." Lenora's voice is soft, almost reverent. "It was an act of love, even if not the natural kind, the way human babies are normally made. But your mother knew about The Question. She was a volunteer."

With that, even Cyrus turns to glare at her.

I shake my head. "Now I know you're lying. My mother hates you. Hates all ascenders. She thinks—" *She thinks you have no souls.* I stall out. My mother was convinced there was something special about me. Something she didn't want me to lose to the ascenders. I thought it was just a mother who believed in God and souls and hates ascenders… but what if *she knew?*

My stomach lurches. I'm going to throw up.

"You don't know jack about Eli's mother." Cyrus's cold hatred is served in words. "She's a better person than all of you put together. Take your shiny pants delusions and peddle them somewhere else."

"I understand this is hard to believe, Elijah." She's ignoring Cyrus again, and that just brings my anger roaring back.

"*You think?* I don't know what your game is, but you destroyed my only chance to get the one thing I needed. The one thing I had to have. Cyrus is right. You need to get out."

Her lips press together, but she doesn't move. "We do need to leave, but you need to come with me. You're in grave danger, Elijah. I have a place we can go where you'll be safe. I've already moved your mother there—"

"*You what?*" I rush up to her again, anger balling up my hands. "What have you done with her?" I'm shouting in her face.

She touches my arm, but I recoil. "She's safe, Elijah, I promise. But I couldn't leave her at your house, not with you going through with the competition. They would have taken her, maybe used her against you."

"Where did you take Eli's mom?" Cyrus's words are clipped.

She finally looks him in the eye. "You don't want me to tell you. If you know, and you fall into their hands, they'll extract that information from you, and she will no longer be safe."

I throw my hands wide. "Who are *they?*"

Before she can answer, the door to my apartment suddenly slides open.

A security bot—six feet of ascender-designed killing technology—stands at my door.

TWENTY-NINE

Lenora blurs past me and attacks the security bot.
By the time I turn, she and the bot have both gone down, rolling out the door with a screech of metal-on-metal echoing off the walls of the hallway. They tumble out of view, Lenora with one hand already deep in the security bot's head. The bot has a grip on her that would easily crush a human.

I lurch toward the door, but Cyrus holds me back. "This is our cue to leave." He pulls me close to his side, like somehow he's going to shield me from the security bot once it breaks loose from Lenora.

"How are we going to get out of Agon?" My harsh whisper is just loud enough for Cyrus to hear me over the mechanical grinding and metal-death sounds coming from the hall.

When we reach the doorway, Lenora is rising up from the twisted body of the security bot. Its head is practically riven in half, and one of its arms lies dangling from a foot-long set of whitish filaments. Lenora steps over the bot and strides toward us.

"Be cool," Cyrus whispers.

I pull my gaze from the mangled bot and scan Lenora: her thin blue jumpsuit is rumpled and torn, but there's no other sign of damage.

"We have to move," she says crisply, but she waits to see if I'm going to come along.

I glance at Cyrus, but he just gives me a short nod.

"You can get us out of here, right?" I ask.

"Yes, Elijah, please. Let's go."

"And you'll take us straight to my mom?"

"That would be the safest place for you as well."

I shouldn't trust her. I *don't* trust her. But that security bot was coming for me, and I'm sure there will be more on the way. And whatever crazy ideas Lenora has, they don't seem to include killing me or dragging me off to an ascender prison. "Let's go, then."

Her eyelids flutter—she's communicating with someone. Or something. "The main entrance is heavily guarded. This way." She turns, and in a flash, she's at the end of the hallway. Cyrus and I dash after her. She's checking around the corner, waiting for us. Then she gives us the signal to follow and disappears in another burst of ascender speed.

Cyrus shakes his head. I'm sure he's never seen ascender tech in action before. We run after her, playing tag as she leads us through the Agon maze.

We're breathless trying to keep up with her, but Cyrus pants out, "Once we're out of here, we make a break for it."

"What about my mom?" I whisper back.

Cyrus winces. "Okay. We stick with Lenora until we find your mom. Then we leave."

I nod.

Cyrus stops me as Lenora disappears around another corner. "Promise me, Eli. Say you're not going to sign up for whatever crazy ascender game she's playing."

"I promise," I say, even though I have no idea what I'll really do. There are too many questions swimming around in my head right now. "Let's just not lose her, okay?"

We round the corner and pull up short.

Lenora is grappling with Marcus, and it's a replay of the fight with the security bot—the two of them on the ground, death grips on one another. Suddenly Lenora's bodyform twitches and spasms, and Marcus shoves her away from him. He climbs to his feet, some kind of silver device in his hand, small and square and featureless. But he's holding it like a weapon.

Lenora's body stops twitching and lies still.

"No!" The word is out before I can think.

My body surges forward, but Cyrus grabs my arm and tries to drag me back around the corner. Before we get more than a few feet, Marcus is at our side. He grabs us both, a hand on each of our shoulders, and the crush is insanely painful. Cyrus and I drop to our knees.

"I'm sorry, Eli," Marcus says. "But I can't risk you running off before we're done here."

I'm not sure what he means by *done*, but I'm certain I don't want to find out. Cyrus tries to twist out of Marcus's grasp, but he just ends up gasping in pain as

Marcus tightens his grip.

"Cyrus, don't." Whatever game the ascenders are playing, it's all because of *me*. Cyrus doesn't need to be involved in any of it. "Marcus, let him go. You don't need him, right? Just me."

Marcus doesn't loosen his grip, but he does glance back down the hall at Lenora's inert bodyform. "Had time for a little chat with your patron, did you?"

Cyrus is still cringing under Marcus's ascender-tech hand.

"Please," I say. "Just let my friend go."

Marcus releases both of us and steps back. A squad of five security bots marches around the corner. Most skirt Lenora's body on their way, but one stays behind with her. Cyrus and I are still on our knees, rubbing our shoulders where Marcus held us.

"I think we'll keep Mr. Kowalski around, just to ensure your continued cooperation." Marcus turns to stride toward the oncoming security bots. He doesn't even bother to warn us that they'll catch us if we try to run. The bottom sinks out of my stomach as I realize at least part of what Lenora said was true—that ascenders like Marcus are definitely not on my side. He's giving instructions to the bots, but they're not verbal, so I have no idea what he's saying. One picks up Lenora's body and carries it off, back the way they came. Marcus confers with two others. After a moment, they head our direction.

Then the world explodes.

A concussive boom knocks me off my knees,

throwing me into Cyrus. We both tumble backward around the corner as a cloud of debris and smoke envelopes the hallway. I can't hear anything in the wake of the explosion, just a high pitched ringing that also feels like someone is stabbing a pick through my eardrums. My hands automatically press to my ears, but it doesn't ease the pain. I'm lumped up against Cyrus, awkward in trying to untangle from his body, when I realize he's not moving. I twist around until I'm facing him, pushing myself up on my knees to get a better look.

His eyes are closed, and he's jammed up against the wall.

"Cyrus!" I yell in his face, but I can't hear my own voice—it's just a vibration through my head. I shake him and yell some more. I quickly check his uniform, but I don't see any bleeding or cuts or shrapnel from the blast.

The blast. I look back over my shoulder. The two bots that were coming for us are slumped against each other on the ground. I can just see the edge of Marcus's head lying on the floor, his body pushed up against a wall. Whatever caused the blast must have had some kind of anti-ascender tech, because there's no way a simple bomb would have knocked them out.

I turn back to Cyrus. Breath rushes out of me as he stirs.

"Cyrus! Come on, man, wake up! Wake up!" I'm relieved to hear my own voice again.. My eardrums are still tender from the overpressure, but the shock is wearing off. I shake Cyrus again, and he flails around, pushing me away.

Finally, he cracks open his eyes. "Eli?" he says blearily. "What happened?"

"I'm not sure, but we need to clear out of here. Can you get up?"

He struggles up. The way he's holding his head worries me. But for now, we need to *move*. I'm just getting Cyrus on his feet when I hear voices shouting down the hallway followed by pounding boots. I try to boost Cyrus with my shoulder under his arm, but he's ridiculously heavy. He sways dangerously as we shuffle down the hall. We make almost no progress before someone comes around the corner behind us.

"I have them here, sir!" a rough voice shouts.

I try to shuffle faster, hazarding just a glimpse back to see how hopeless it might be.

I stop in my tracks, and Cyrus nearly trips and falls. As I keep him upright, I stare at the black-garbed figure standing next to the fallen security bots.

He's human.

He hurries toward us, combat boots marring the spotless floor. He's covered head-to-toe in body armor of some kind, black and dull and riddled with armaments strapped to his chest and sides. He's toting a weapon bristling with tech—it looks less like a gun and more like a bot taken apart and reassembled into a hand-held device. His combat helmet covers his head, and a shimmering shield obscures his face, but there's no mistaking it: he's definitely human.

"Mr. Brighton," he says when he reaches us. "Would you come with me, sir?"

I don't move, not because I'm afraid, just because I'm stunned. Cyrus twists around to see him, but he's even more out of it than I am.

"I… um… who *are* you?" I ask.

He doesn't answer, just glances over his shoulder at the sound of mechanical footfalls in the hallway. My heart is already pounding, but it lurches out of rhythm when I imagine more security bots about to descend on us. Instead, around the corner strides Leopold.

I blink. *Leopold.*

The intake officer who watched me undress before sliming me with blue goo for decon.

"It's alright, Gretsky," he says, not to me, but to the black-garbed, heavily-armed human. Leopold looks us up and down. "Are you all right, Eli?"

I nod, still stunned.

"What about Mr. Kowalski?"

"Leopold?" Cyrus says, like he's not sure his eyes are working right. "What are you doing here?"

"Rescuing you, it would seem." He gives a small smile. "Although I had assumed you would have Lenora with you. What happened to her?"

I'm just now finding my voice. "Marcus stunned her or something. One of the bots took her away."

Leopold does not look pleased to hear this. "All right, we'll have to go without her." He shakes his head, but I think it's more to himself than anything. "We need to leave immediately, Eli. It's not safe for you here."

"You were working with Lenora?" I guess, still foggy on what exactly is happening.

"How do you think she was able to get in to see you at the last minute?" Leopold gestures to the black-garbed human to help me with Cyrus, but Cyrus just shoves him away. He makes an effort to stand on his own, but it seems like his balance is off, and he might topple over any second.

"Mr. Kowalski could use some medical attention," Leopold says. "I suggest we leave before Agon security reaches us." He sounds surprisingly calm, but there's an underlying tension. I still don't entirely understand what's happening, but I'm not going to argue.

"Okay," I say. "Where are we going?"

"Somewhere beyond Marcus's reach." He doesn't add any more, just turns away. Cyrus gives me a nod that he's okay, so we do our best to keep up. Leopold has a small army of black-clad humans, several of whom fall into formation around us, a human shield to conduct us away from Agon.

We climb through a ragged hole left in the side of the hallway by the explosion and out into the brilliant California sun.

THIRTY

The garrison of human militia hustles me and Cyrus away from Agon.

Leopold leads the way. We're on the backside of the building, with the stadium looming to our left and the city of Los Angeles's apartment towers to the right. A flurry of bright specks in the air and the tall space port spire catch the sun. They seem as foreign as the off-planet outposts that are their destination.

I can't imagine where Leopold thinks we're going to escape to.

We scurry in a tight formation past several disabled security bots lying crumpled on the ground. It appears as though their insides were blown apart. The men who provide a human shield around us bristle with more tech weapons. Cyrus stumbles over some bump in the hot white pavement, and I grip his arm to keep him moving with the group. His eyes are nearly squeezed shut, his lips pressed in a thin line, and his face is pale and sweaty.

I'm about to ask how far we have to go—I'm not sure if Cyrus can keep up this pace—when two hover

314

transports appear out of nowhere. Like they literally weren't there a moment ago. Before I can wonder at what kind of cloaking tech they have, the group breaks into two, with Leopold leading Cyrus, me, and four of the militia men to one ship, while the rest board another. The air sizzles next to me, and some kind of blue energy pulse sweeps across the hull of the ship as we climb into it. Leopold yanks me clear of the entrance, and a door appears behind me. The ship leaps into the air, leaving my stomach behind.

Cyrus slumps over and throws up on the dull, black flooring. I can't help him because the ship is pitching wildly, and I'm clinging to the gray netting that covers the walls of our tiny transport compartment. It's barely large enough to hold the seven of us.

The militia are holding tight to the netting, too, but the one closest to Cyrus leans down and grabs hold of the back of his shirt, I think to steady him. Leopold seems to have no problem navigating the rocking ship. He shifts past me to a forward door that I think must lead to the pilot's cabin. Suddenly the pitching stops, and we drop like a stone. At least I think we've dropped—there are no windows in our transport—because I'm momentarily weightless. Cyrus floats up, but the militia guy has a hold on him. Cyrus's arms flail, and his vomit slowly drips *up* from the floor in long gravity-inverted strings. Then we hit bottom or something because gravity crashes us down again. Cyrus's face smacks into the mess on the floor, and I'm glad to hear him curse, just because that means he's still conscious.

We're not moving anymore.

My legs are like rubber, and I keep my grip on the netting, but we must be down because the militia guys are moving again. I avoid the muck on the floor and bend next to Cyrus. He's trying to wipe his face, so I just put a hand on his shoulder.

He crawls up to sitting, back against the netting wall. His eyes are squeezed shut, and his face starts to go slack. I don't know if he's just resting or passing out. The militia guy who had a hold on Cyrus before must be a medic—he slings his weapon around his back and digs out a tiny tube with a light beaming from it. He deactivates his helmet shield, so I can see his face for the first time. He's young, but his face is lined, like he's lived a hard life or maybe seen too much death.

"Please open your eyes, sir," he says to Cyrus.

His eyes stay shut. "Eli."

"I'm right here." I'm relieved to hear his voice. "But you need to stop being such a baby and open your eyes." My stomach lurches from the sour stench of the sickness and the pale sweatiness of Cyrus's face. And from my worry that something much more serious than airsickness is making him throw up.

"Let's not do that ride again." A shudder captures him, but he forces his eyes open.

The militia medic flicks the tiny light back and forth across Cyrus's eyes, while the rest of the militia cluster by the spot where the door appeared. I know the medic is looking for a concussion, but my fogged brain can't remember the symptoms. Dilated pupils? Undilated pupils?

The medic looks to me, his expression betraying nothing. "We need to keep your friend awake, sir, until we can get a med unit to examine him."

I nod. The medic stands and joins his comrades in a ready stance by the door. Leopold reappears from the cockpit and strides over. The door blinks out of existence, and the entire squad leaps out, weapons ready. Beyond them is a spotlit section of concrete floor, past which I can't see anything due to the curtain of darkness. The militia slip into the dark, disappearing from view, then one of them calls back, "Clear!"

A moment later, the medic appears in the spotlight again, weapon slung low behind his back. He climbs back into the transport and bends down to Cyrus. "Can you stand, sir? We'd like to get you inside."

Cyrus nods, very shakily, and the medic and I help him up. As we step out of the transport, the light above begins to dim. I look up to see two halves of an overhead door sliding closed, blocking out the blue of the sky and taking the sun with it. We're plunged into darkness, and it takes a moment for my eyes to adjust. The medic and I half-carry a limping Cyrus across a dim, concrete-lined garage. It's small and crammed with a couple more transports, but they don't look like ours. The second transport must have gone somewhere else. Leopold quickly moves ahead of us, waving a hand at a steel door in the wall, which then slides open.

Once inside, I realize the other militia have stayed behind in the garage, and this place, wherever we are, looks more like an apartment than anything else. We stumble into the center of a huge, immaculate studio, with white flooring and couches, and a giant screen at one end. It's almost like walking into a hazy, glare-filled dream with the sunlight streaming in the wraparound windows.

We're somewhere in the middle of the city with the towers of ascender apartments surrounding us, all looming higher than we are. The thin spires are a holdover from the pre-Singularity era when these buildings were offices or businesses where humans used to work. Now the ascenders live here, their work done mostly from their spacious and spotless homes.

Which makes me realize: *we're in an ascender apartment.*

I throw a quick look of panic at Leopold, but he's striding toward a group of militia-type humans in a hallway off to the side. I rein in my concern that Leopold's just taken us from one ascender captor to another and focus on getting Cyrus to one of the couches. The medic leaves, and Cyrus leans back, sinking into the body-conforming cushions like he's never going to leave.

I bend down next to him. "Hey, this is no time to get lazy on me."

"So tired," Cyrus says, and I can see his face start to go slack again.

"Cyrus!" My voice hikes up with concern. I snap my fingers in front of his slowly closing eyes. "Man, you have to stay awake."

He frowns like he's not quite sure why I'm bothering

him. "Just going to rest for…" His voice fades.

I grab hold of his cheeks and smack them. Not too hard, but enough to make him flail against me. "What the—"

I let out a breath. "No sleeping, man. I mean it."

He glares at me. "Okay. Right. No sleeping."

The medic is back, followed by a med bot. Leopold is a half-step behind them. I stand up to give the med bot room. It's humanoid, low-level sentience, like the one Marcus left caring for my mother. Which is pretty good treatment for humans, and I'm shocked there's one here in the city. Then again, I'm shocked that militant dissenters are hiding in an ascender apartment, as well. I need to understand what's going on here.

"I have questions," I say to Leopold, who's standing next to me.

"I can imagine." He measures me with his ascender eyes, then gestures me away from Cyrus and the couch, as if he doesn't want too many ears overhearing his answers.

I'm hesitant to leave, but Cyrus is speaking in mostly coherent sentences now, replying to the med bot's queries. He's probably in good hands for the moment.

The medic notices my hesitation and gives me a nod. "I'll stay with him, sir."

"I'll be right back," I call to Cyrus over the med bot. He waves, which actually makes me feel better. I follow Leopold to the far side of the room, next to the windows blaring LA sun and heating the room in spite of the environmental controls' attempt to keep it ascender-cool.

I can't see Agon from here, so we must have traveled a ways during that brief, hectic trip in the transport.

"Why?" I ask Leopold.

"Why are we staying in this well-appointed ascender apartment?" Leopold asks with a small smirk. "Or why did I rescue you from Agon before Marcus could get ahold of you?"

"Why are you involved in any of this?"

Leopold's eyebrows lift, like he's amused by me. "Well, that's a more complicated question. With an equally complicated answer."

"Try me." I glower at him, then glance back at Cyrus. He's propped up now on the couch, probably so he's less likely to drift off.

"The real question isn't why or how we got here, but what to do now."

"Look…" I turn back to Leopold and cross my arms. "I don't understand any of this. So how about if you tell me what's going on? Who *are* these people? And how are you connected to Lenora? Marcus zapped her with some kind of electric weapon. Does that mean… is she…" I swallow. I'm furious about her lies and getting me disqualified, but I don't want her dead. And with Lenora gone… I have no idea how to find my mother.

I brace my hand against the hot glass, suddenly feeling woozy myself.

"I highly doubt Marcus killed her." Leopold's face loses its humor. "He *was* her second, not that someone like Marcus would allow that to stop his ambitions. I've had my suspicions about him from early on, but Lenora refused to believe he had turned."

My hand on the glass is heating to a painful level. I pull it away. "The Olympics are over. None of that matters anymore. I just want to find my mom and go home. Lenora said she had hidden her away somewhere. Do you know where?"

"I'm afraid not." Leopold frowned. "And you're very wrong that none of this matters, Eli. This is just beginning. Now that they have Lenora, your mother may not be as safe as we had hoped for. They're probably trying to crack her personal key right now."

"Her what?" My head is starting to throb.

He peers at the mirrored windows of the ascender apartments surrounding ours. "Ascenders are all connected through Orion. But that connection can be... overwhelming. Our personal keys are what allow us to keep our individuality. You can think of it as a kind of barrier or encryption. It keeps us secure whenever we transport or download or upload. It ensures that our backups remain untampered with, so no one can destroy the thing that allows us to have this perpetual life of ours." He pauses to turn back to me. "It also allows us to keep secrets. For example, *your* secret. I assume Lenora has told you?"

"She told me *something*," I say, my voice rising. "Not sure I believe any of it. And if there's any truth to it, why not tell me sooner? Why wait until I'm about to ascend and then snatch that away?" The bitterness is still strong in me. I don't know what I believe about Lenora's crazy story, but I know *for sure* she's responsible for getting me disqualified.

"She didn't tell you precisely because you couldn't know and still remain the person you are," Leopold says gently. "Lenora was convinced that your path needed to unfold organically. That to tamper with it would seriously compromise your development." He pauses. "How do you tell someone they're the answer to a question they aren't even asking?"

Leopold is talking in riddles, and I'm dead tired of ascender nonsense. "All right, whatever. I really don't care about what Lenora thinks right at the moment."

"I can understand your anger." His voice is still calm, not at all disturbed by the rising heat in mine. "But you are still mostly human, Eli. And as you can imagine, humans have few resources for keeping secrets from ascenders. There have been many who have taken substantial risks to keep your existence a secret, including myself. At the moment, I'm completely disconnected from Orion. I personally destroyed my backup to eliminate the risk of the secrets therein being revealed. So, as of right now, I'm as isolated and vulnerable as an ascender can be. In this state, I'm nearly as mortal as you are. One wrong encounter with a security bot, and the only life I have could be snuffed out." He lifts one eyebrow. "I sincerely hope the risk is worth it. That Lenora is right about you."

My stomach is slowly curling into knots. The idea that ascenders like Leopold are taking this so seriously... it's sinking the conviction deeper and deeper into my mind that they actually *have* done something to me. It *feels* like the truth. But when I consider what that might mean, my mind flies away from it. The ascenders could all be straight-up crazy. I need to just get out of this mess and back to Seattle and my mom.

"Look, whatever Lenora thinks I am... I'm not," I say with conviction.

Leopold narrows his eyes, regarding me. "What makes you so sure of that?"

"Um... because it's *insane*?"

"The Question has been called worse things." He smirks. "I have to admit, I'm not sure she's right about you being our answer. But there are some questions worth asking, even if you're unsure if there will ever be an answer."

"Yeah, well, I don't really care about any of that." The nauseous feeling is coming back, like the world is spinning, only just for me.

He nods, but not like he agrees with me. Like he's reached some other conclusion about me. It irritates me, turning the acid in my stomach into a roiling torment.

"Look, I just want to get my mom back. Are you sure Lenora is the only one who knows where she is?"

Leopold is about to reply, but a woman's voice cuts him off. "That is not our largest concern at the moment, but, as far as we know... yes." Her lilting French accent draws out the *yes*, and I turn, half expecting to see one of the girls. Instead, there's a middle-aged woman standing next to us. Disappoint rushes out of me, and I remember I'm not likely to see any of them—Kamali, Delphina, or Basha—again, unless it's inside an ascender prison. The woman's dark, intense eyes are familiar, though. She's short, barely reaching my shoulder. Her commanding stance, feet planted wide, plus the same black-garbed outfit as the rest of the militia, makes me take a guess.

Leopold beats me to it. "Eli, meet Simone Astoria."

"You're Delphina's mom," I say quietly, not sure if she knows yet that her daughter is missing. That the ascenders likely have her.

"*Oui*," she says. "You have perhaps seen her performance?"

"She helped me once," I say, not sure I want to tell her the whole story about Thompson, especially given that I now stand accused of his murder. "And she wanted me to join, well, their plans. For the ceremony." It occurs to me that I still don't know anything about the militia or why they broke into Agon to get me. Maybe Delphina isn't the only one who wants to recruit me to their cause. But still... I hate to be the one to break it to her that her daughter is missing. I stall by glancing at the other militia members still gathered in the hall on the far side of the room. "Are Kamali's parents here too? And Basha's?" I throw a quick look at Cyrus, but he's being fussed over by the med bot and doesn't hear me.

Mrs. Astoria raises her eyebrows. "No. But I see you have had some experience with the girls."

That was one way to put it. "I went looking for them after my performance. To check on them." I shift from one foot to another. "I'm afraid I couldn't find them, Mrs. Astoria. I don't know what happened to them."

"I am quite sure they are in ascender custody," she

says calmly.

My eyebrows fly up. "So you know?"

"Of course." She dismisses my surprise with a small, black-gloved hand.

Leopold tilts his head to the diminutive Mrs. Astoria. "Lenora said she was keeping Eli ignorant until he was ready to know," he tells her. "And Marcus is unlikely to have furthered his education in any substantial way. I doubt Eli understands much about the resistance."

Mrs. Astoria looks me over in a harsh way that reminds me of Delphina and her initial belief that Cyrus and I were nothing but trouble. When she speaks, it's to Leopold, "And you think he can be trusted?"

Leopold smirks. "I think Eli's interests align with ours for the moment. And I trust Lenora's judgment."

"You've broken into Agon to snatch me away, and you're wondering if *you* can trust *me*?" I'm still kind of lost as to everything that's in play here. I glance at Cyrus, wishing he was up to helping me sort it out. But the bot is administering some kind of meds, and Cyrus is lying down now. I'm on my own with this.

"Ah, well, that is where you are wrong," Mrs. Astoria says. "The objective of our mission had nothing to do with you, Elijah Brighton. You were, as you say, a last-minute change in plans."

I frown, even more confused. "What was your real mission?"

She gives a small smile. "To send a message to the ascenders that we will no longer allow them to play their games."

THIRTY-ONE

I stare at Delphina's mom.

"You want to shut down the games. Permanently." I have to look down to peer into her eyes, to see that she's serious. I'm in awe that she thinks she can do this. Or maybe she's crazy, just like the ascenders themselves.

"Oui," she says. "The games provide a relief to the ascenders." She nods to Leopold, who is quiet, waiting for her to go on, but it's clear this information comes from him. "We are more than just entertainment to them. More than just a possible source of fresh minds to ascend into their ranks. The games are a way of confirming their own righteousness. They tell themselves they cherish us, all while they oppress us and keep us like pets." She sounds a lot like her daughter now, which I guess is no surprise. "They tell themselves we are happy in our legacy city cages. That we wish to be like them. So much so, that we will send our children to Agon, to risk their lives in the fierce competition of the games and in the ascendance procedure, just to secure one of the few slots available each year. It allows the ascenders the illusion that their choice is the preferable one."

"But the ascenders know dissenters exist," I say, not really getting her point. "I mean, *you* were exiled, right? And the original dissenters were all about disagreeing with the choice to ascend. Especially the believers."

"But then the choice was taken away, no?" she says. "Do you know why?"

"Because there's only so much room on the planet?" I stall out, realizing that doesn't make sense. Not completely. Especially with ascenders having outposts throughout the solar system for decades now.

"It's true, there are only so many resources on Earth," Leopold says. "Which is why ascendance was originally removed as an option. If humans continued to reproduce, providing an endless supply of new candidates for ascendance, our numbers would quickly outgrow the planet's ability to support them. Especially given the energy- and material-intensiveness of the ascender way of life. But the settlements on Mars and Jupiter's moons are well established now. The asteroid belt provides more metals than we'll use in a thousand years. And the best estimates put interstellar space travel within a few years reach."

"Do you see, Eli?" Mrs. Astoria draws my attention back. "There is no longer a plausible reason to deny ascendance to any human who wishes it… save one."

"What's that?" I frown, not entirely tracking all this. My mind is still spinning with how fast everything is changing.

"The Question." Leopold watches me to see if I get it,

but I still don't.

"You mean, whether they have a soul?" I ask. "But… what does that have to do with anything?"

"That is everything, Eli," says Mrs. Astoria.

"Well, sure, for *believers* it is, but ascenders aren't believers…" I trail off because Mrs. Astoria and Leopold are sharing a sly smile, like I'm a child who's finally figuring out something the adults have known all along. I feel like an idiot, because that's exactly what Lenora was saying. "You're a believer," I say to Leopold, a little stunned. "But… you're… I don't understand. You *chose* to ascend. I mean, maybe it was a long time ago, and now you're… wait… *have you changed your mind?*" This thought stuns me so badly, I step back from the close huddle I have with the two of them and bump into the red-hot glass behind me. I flinch from it. The sensation of dangling over the city, about to tumble hundreds of feet to the sparkling clean streets below, makes my stomach lurch.

"Ascenders are not a homogenous lot." Leopold says this like it should be obvious, and I suppose it should, but it honestly never occurred to me that there could be disagreement on something so fundamental. "There are many thoughts, many perspectives. The people who ascended came from all possible religions and countries and philosophies. Ascendance brought all of those into a giant rushing discourse that lasted many years. The early days of Orion were fraught with discord until a consensus emerged that finally swayed the majority. That was when ascendance was cut off, and while I agree with my compatriots in the resistance that ascendance should be reinstated as an option for all…" He inclines his head to Mrs. Astoria. "…I am profoundly glad that you, and your fellow legacies, have been preserved. Until we could come to our senses about The Question. However, that time is not yet here. The Question is still whispered in secret. It remains a dangerous idea. But, perhaps, the time has come for it to come out into the open."

"But why now?" My head is still wrapping around the idea that there might be ascenders who think their ascendance was a mistake. "I mean, what does all this have to do with the games?"

"Our original plan," Mrs. Astoria says, "was to wait until the gold medalists took the stage. We could not be sure that my daughter would be counted among them, which was why we were quite blessed that her friend came to understand the worthiness of our cause. Of course, with Delphina taking the gold as well, we were very excited. Our message would be even stronger when my daughter and her friend made their defiant statements from the stage. It was then that we planned to amplify that statement with an assault on Agon that would be shown worldwide across the nets, human and ascender alike. We would pluck our defiant medalists from the stage, saving them from the ascenders' judgment while at the same time destroying that symbol of our oppression, our status as puppets for the amusement of the ascenders… along with as much of the stadium and the bodyforms therein as possible."

"You were planning on killing the ascenders at the

games?" I draw back from her again, my mind reeling with all she's saying.

"There would be no deaths," Leopold says. "At most, we would have destroyed their bodyforms—a violent, and perhaps painful, disruption, but ultimately a small inconvenience in their perpetual lives. They would download their backups to new bodyforms within days, if not hours. But it would have been an elegant and pointed demonstration."

"It would have clearly said, *Your games are unworthy of us.*" Mrs. Astoria's shoulders are thrown back, and I can easily picture Delphina on the stage with the same look of disdain for the ascenders just before her militia blew them to bits. "And it would show the legacy humans watching that we exist. That we are strong. And that they can join us and do more than scrape out a living in dissenter camps run by the backward and the brutal."

"*And* it would have put pressure on the ascenders who have thought The Question long settled," Leopold added. "Unfortunately, someone found out what the girls were planning. The last transmission from their sponsor indicated the police bots simply seized them in their apartments."

"Last transmission?" I grimace. Alexis, Kamali's sponsor, must have been involved in the resistance after all.

"Their sponsor wisely made sure her bodyform was destroyed before she could be captured," Leopold said. "I've confirmed her backup has been activated. The rest of our operation should not have been compromised, but the girls remain in custody."

Mrs. Astoria takes a step toward me. "Someone turned them in. Perhaps someone who knew their intentions, but did not agree with them." Her small stature doesn't keep me from being intimidated by her stern look.

"Wait… you think *I* told them? I wouldn't do that! I would never do that to Kamali. She was helping me." Mrs. Astoria looks unconvinced, so I quickly sweep my hand to the prone Cyrus lying on the couch. "My best friend is practically in love with Basha. And Delphina helped me already, like I said before. I swear, I'm not the one who turned them in."

"It's all right, Eli," Leopold says. "We believe you. It was likely Marcus, or someone else who caught wind of their plans. Regardless, their capture has disrupted our plan."

"Once we realized they had been detained," Mrs. Astoria says, "our plans shifted to breaking into Agon to free them. But we were unsuccessful in locating them."

"And then you complicated matters further," Leopold says. "Lenora alerted us that Marcus was likely on his way to seize you—"

A pinging sound interrupts him. Leopold and Mrs. Astoria both frown, look at each other, and then to me. I realize with a start that the sound is coming from my pocket. I reach in and pull out the holo phone.

Leopold's eyes go wide, and he shoots a look to Mrs. Astoria.

"He has been *tracked*," she hisses. "I told you this was

a mistake!" She wheels around and charges off to her fellow militia in the hallway, spewing French.

"It's Marcus's phone." I hold the small, silver square out to Leopold. It's still pinging.

His face settles into a scowl. "I guess you had better answer it, then."

THIRTY-TWO

The apartment is in chaos.

Mrs. Astoria is shouting orders in French to the militia who are scrambling around to gather items from the apartment and rushing back out to the rooftop garage. Cyrus and the med bot are still at the couch, but the medic has disappeared.

Marcus's phone is still pinging in my hand while Leopold looks on.

"Are you sure this is a good idea?" I ask, glancing at the decampment in progress and thinking we should be moving as well.

"Marcus is no doubt on his way here," Leopold says. "At the minimum, he has sent a squad of police bots. I would like to know what he has in mind before they arrive." Leopold steps back, like he wants to be out of range of the holo capture.

I tap the button-sized phone, and a holo image of a head appears above it. I don't recognize it. In fact, it looks... blank. Like the face is bland somehow.

"Eli," the head says in a surprisingly even, calm voice.

"Whatever you think you're doing here, you need to stop and consider the consequences."

"Um, who are you, exactly?" I ask.

The bland face shifts into a half-frown, but it's off somehow. Like that's all the bodyform is capable of producing. I realize belatedly that it must be a rental. "It's me, Marcus. Your little friends have inconveniently disabled my normal bodyform."

"Yeah, well, I still have a bruised shoulder from your last bodyform." I glance at the final militia members clearing out of the apartment. "Nice chatting with you, but I've got a ride to catch." I make a move to tap off the phone.

"Eli, wait!" Marcus's voice strains against the limits of his generic bodyform. "You can run off with your resistance friends, but the police will find them eventually. And I don't want you getting caught in the crossfire when that happens. That's not your fight, Eli. We both know that. And all I want is what I've said all along: to help you ascend. That's still possible. We can fix this with the Olympic committee. Just come back in, and I'll help you."

"Funny, I don't remember you offering to help while you were attacking Lenora."

He grimaces, as much as his face will allow it. "Lenora caught me by surprise. And I only stunned her. Her bodyform's intact, and she's fine."

I hesitate and bite my lip. "I want to talk to her." I have no idea if Marcus is telling the truth, but Lenora's the only person who knows where she stashed my mom.

"I can arrange that for you, no problem. Just come back to Agon."

A black figure runs into the room from the direction of the garage. His face shield is back on, but I can tell it's the medic. "Sir, your friend insists we can't leave without you."

Leopold gives me the sign that it's time to go.

"I'll get back to you," I say to Marcus, then tap the phone off and toss it to the floor. Leopold is gone with ascender speed before I can look up. The medic and I dash across the apartment and out into the garage. It's empty of vehicles and personnel. The last transport waits for us, hovering in the spotlight of California sunshine beaming through the rooftop entrance. We sprint across the concrete and climb inside. Our feet are barely past the entrance before it materializes, and the transport shoots into the air.

I crawl across the floor, keeping low as the ship bucks and rocks. I don't know if we're dipping and weaving in pursuit of something or being pursued. Cyrus is laid out on the floor. His eyes are open, but they're glazed, staring at the ceiling. He looks like he might be sick again. The medic is kneeling next to him, one hand on his chest to keep him from sliding. I work my way over and reach past Cyrus's pale face to grip his uniform at the shoulder, holding him steady.

The medic has his face shield off again. His unusually green eyes are shooting looks to the pilot's cabin, where I assume Leopold must be. Otherwise, there's just the three of us in the transport hold.

"You can go," I say to the medic. "I've got him." He nods, but before he can leave, I add, "Hey. What's your name?"

He stops and twists back. "Tristan. Sir."

I hold out my hand. "I'm Eli."

He gives me a small, amused smile, but shakes my hand with a firm, black-gloved grip. "I know, sir."

A lurch in the transport breaks our handshake and wipes away the awkwardness. "Thanks for taking care of Cyrus."

He gives me a nod, then turns away and fights the rocking of the ship to disappear into the pilot's cabin.

I shift around so I can face Cyrus. "How're you doing?"

His gaze doesn't waver from some point on the ceiling. "I'll let you know if I'm about to spew again. So you can take cover."

I smile. The rocking of the ship suddenly ceases. I think for a second that we've landed, but the humming of the dull black flooring under my hand seems to indicate otherwise. Cyrus's face relaxes a little, so I'm glad for the reprieve, however long it lasts. I don't know where we're going, but I hope we get there soon.

I loosen my hard grip on Cyrus's shoulder, but keep my hand close, in case we start rocking again.

"I got a call from Marcus," I say to him.

"You've got to be kidding me."

"No," I say with a sigh. "He wants me to come back to Agon."

"What?" Cyrus struggles to lift up from the floor.

I shove him back down. "Stay down!" I command. "That knock on the head's making you stupid."

His shoulders ease back into the floor. "Stupid is you taking a call from Marcus. I'm out of it for one minute—"

"He's got Lenora."

Cyrus tilts his head to scowl at me, cringes, then goes back to staring at the ceiling. "She got you disqualified for the gold. What is it going to take for you to get over your crush—"

"Cy, she knows where my mom is."

He closes his eyes. "Right. I keep forgetting that part."

"Don't worry about it," I say, hand back on his shoulder. "You need to rest."

He opens his eyes again. "Eli. You can't believe anything she says. Or Marcus either. None of the shiny pants give a crap about us."

"We wouldn't be here if it weren't for Leopold," I point out.

"Yeah… well… give me time. I haven't figured out his angle yet."

"I think I know. At least part of it." I drop my voice, even though there's no one to overhear. Mostly the turmoil inside me is making my voice weak. "They did something to me, Cy."

He squints and turns his head to look at me. "What, just now? While I was out?"

"No." I swallow. "Before. I think Lenora was telling the truth when she said they… *tampered* with me. There's something wrong with me."

"Man, don't do that to yourself."

"C'mon, Cy, think about it." Now that the words are out of my head, they seem to gush even faster. "The fugue? The hallucinations? That's not normal. And the art I can make while in the fugue… it's like they've implanted some hidden ascender parts inside me. Inside my *head*."

"Or you could just be a whacked out creative. It's not like the fugue is the only way you're messed up in the head." He tries to smirk, but it dies as he winces and returns to staring at the ceiling. It's a nice try, but I know it doesn't get at the truth.

And the truth is settling into me like a dripping black ooze invading my body. "I'm not entirely human, Cy." I whisper it, and the ooze fills up my lungs, choking me. "What does that make me?"

"An idiot." But he's frowning when he twists his head to look at me. "Don't believe it, Eli. They're messing with you."

"That's just it. Even if I don't believe it… *they do*." I swallow down the choking feeling. "They may be totally wrong about the result, but they wouldn't be saying any of it, if they hadn't done *something* to me."

Cy grimaces but doesn't say anything.

"I need to go back." I say it quietly, hoping Cyrus will talk me out of it.

"No you don't. We'll figure this out some other way. Going back to Marcus will just get you killed."

"He's right about that." Leopold's smooth voice makes me jump. I twist to see him standing just behind me. "I don't know how much Lenora told you, but Marcus never intended to let you live."

That doesn't add up for me. "He could have killed me at any time."

"I'm not saying I entirely understand his plans," Leopold says. "But I assure you he is not on your side."

I know he's right, but I also know that whatever the ascenders have done to me, it's as important to Marcus as it is to Lenora. And Leopold. I'm about to argue further, when Tristan, the medic, pops his head out from the cockpit.

"Grab hold of something," he says. "We're almost there." He disappears back inside.

I have just enough time to grab hold of the wall netting with one hand and a fistful of Cyrus's uniform with the other. The bottom drops out of my stomach again. The ship rocks and lurches, but in short order we've landed. When the door winks out of existence, I see we've landed outside this time. A makeshift camp of a half-dozen nomad tents sits twenty feet away in the middle of a clearing. On two sides are clumps of purple-flowering scrub brush, the kind that survives in the desert mountains of California, and straight ahead a rock wall rises as far as I can see from inside the transport. I'm guessing we're outside the city, but not far, just to the ring of low-lying mountains that surround the LA basin.

Tristan rushes out of the cockpit, tells us to sit tight, and leaps down to the hard-packed dirt of the encampment. He runs straight for the rock wall… and disappears through it.

I throw a puzzled look to Leopold.

He arches an eyebrow. "I'm not the only ascender who supplies aid to the resistance, Eli. Without our cloaking shields, weapons, and transports, I'm afraid your dissenter friends wouldn't stand much of a chance of eluding detection."

Which makes all kinds of sense. I figured the transport must be ascender tech—even back in Seattle, all the transit systems were—but this is something way beyond anything I've seen. "So, you give military-grade ascender tech to the resistance, but legacies are banned from using even the simplest gen tech?" I don't bother trying to hide my anger about that.

"If we distributed technology to every human who needed it, our aid wouldn't stay secret for long, now would it?" But he has the decency to look less than happy about that. "Our goal is not to supply you with technology, but to liberate you from oppression."

I frown, thinking that one would serve the other. But I know that's not what Leopold's after, and I think Cyrus is probably right: the ascenders really don't give a crap about us. They're all in it for their own agendas. Leopold's agenda just happens to be served by supplying the dissenters with weapons and secrecy.

And using ascender tech to experiment on human babies.

Which springs a thought loose in my head. "Am I the only one?" I ask Leopold.

He's watching the fake-rock cloaking shield, waiting for something. "Only one what?" he asks distractedly.

"The only human whose DNA you've tampered with."

He turns sharply to face me, and I give him a cold stare. "You would have to ask Lenora about that."

I'm sure he knows, but he doesn't want to tell me. "All the more reason to go back to Agon and pay Marcus a visit."

A furrow carves in Leopold's forehead, but then he's distracted by Tristan reappearing through the rock wall, pulling a maglev stretcher behind him. When he arrives at the transport, he slides it in, adjusting it to sit low to the floor. Between the two of us, and with only mild protests from Cyrus, we haul him into it. I walk the stretcher back with Tristan, hesitating only slightly when we reach the rock wall. It looks completely solid, even up close, but I know it's some kind of projection. I'm a little relieved when the foot of the stretcher breaks through before I plunge face-first into the resistance's mountain hideout.

THIRTY-THREE

The dissenters' hideout is part cave, part high-tech hanger.

The cavernous space seems carved from the granite of the mountain, and the security shield certainly makes it look like rock from the outside. But the shield is one-way, letting the brilliant California sunshine flow in. The cave is big enough to act as a hanger, housing several transports, racks of bunks, stacks of shipping containers, and several silver pod-like structures. They remind me of Leopold's decon unit only they're not floating and they're twice the size of my apartment at Agon.

Leopold breaks away from us to stride over to one of the pods, but Tristan directs the stretcher to a different one. Inside is a full med suite. We transfer Cyrus to one of the three beds, and a med bot immediately takes over, putting him through a battery of scans and tests. Cyrus grumbles but quickly closes his eyes and submits. Tristan and I stand back and let it do its job.

"He'll get a full work-up now," Tristan says, "but I'm pretty sure all he needs is rest. His concussion doesn't seem too severe."

"Looks like you've got top flight med care here." I scan the other medical equipment crammed against the walls and on shelves. I wonder how much of it is illegal, then I realize it *all* is: no ascenders should be giving the dissenters anything. Which means they could have gen tech as well.

Tristan gestures to the other two beds, which are empty. "We expected to have more casualties. Assuming we'd carried through with the mission."

I frown. "You mean blowing up the stadium?"

Tristan grins. "We don't have quite the munitions for that. But the stadium's over fifty years old, and we have the original plans. There are some structural weaknesses that ascender buildings today don't have. A few well-placed bombs would have brought down a good section of it."

"But you thought people might get hurt? Meaning resistance fighters."

Tristan's grin is replaced by that sober, seen-too-much look from before. "There's always that risk." He pauses. "I'm glad we were able to extricate you, sir. Hopefully, the commander will have a new plan to rescue the other agonites as well."

Tristan must think I was fully on board with Kamali and Delphina's plans. "I hope so, too."

He nods like this is a given.

"And," I say with a pained voice, "you really don't have to call me *sir*. I mean, I'm younger than you are, and I just got here."

"Yes, sir." He grins. "Should I call you Eli, sir?"

I just shake my head and swing my attention back to checking on Cyrus. "Hey, lazy. How're you doing over there?"

I frown when Cyrus doesn't answer, but then his snore rumbles across the pod.

"The commander wants me to bring you to the command center as soon as you're done here," Tristan says. "Are you ready, sir?"

I give him a look like, *are you serious with this sir business?*

Tristan relaxes his military-level politeness. "Eli, he's going to be fine. And you're wanted in command."

I peer at Cyrus, but he's out. Which is probably for the best. He wouldn't like the trickle of a plan that's forming in my head. I nod and follow Tristan out of the med bay pod. We stride toward a silver pod against the back wall, dodging militia using maglev skids to move crates. The transport we brought with us is slowly being guided into the cavern. I'm once again struck by the scale of the operation and the sophistication of the tech. The militia has access to serious resources, which makes my trickle of a plan solidify with the icy realization that it actually might work. The only trick will be convincing Leopold.

We reach the command pod, and the inside is jammed with more tech and black-garbed personnel. A large screen floats at one end, but smaller ones line the sides, with militia attending to the data streams on each. One monitors a contour map that looks like it could be the mountain range we're nestled in. Another scans pages of data on a holo screen, pulling out individual threads by waving her hands in a complicated dance. Tristan and I only garner brief glimpses as we pass, heading toward the large screen where Mrs. Astoria and Leopold are having a hushed but animated argument in French.

Before we reach them, Tristan leans back to whisper to me, "They're arguing about you. Something about going back to Agon?" His look is questioning, but I don't want to explain that he may have just rescued me for nothing. Because I need to find my mom and get her a cure, which means getting Lenora back. And to do that I'll have to face the ascender that Tristan and his fellow dissenter militia just risked their lives to liberate me from.

Tristan catches my arm, holding me back before I bust in on Mrs. Astoria and Leopold's urgent French conversation. "Commander," he says quietly to Mrs. Astoria, "if this isn't a good time…"

She turns and waves off his concern. "No, no. This concerns Eli as well."

Tristan takes a step back, but doesn't go far, watching us.

Leopold's scowl grows deeper. "We can find another way to get them back, Simone," he says to her. "Involving Eli will put too many of our objectives at risk."

"Too many of *your* objectives, perhaps." Red splotches rise up in her cheeks. "Mine are simple: to retrieve the girls."

This makes my heart lurch. "Do you know where they are?" That wasn't part of my plan, but it could be.

Leopold gives me a dark look which immediately tells me that they don't, but then he just shakes his head at Mrs. Astoria—*Commander* Astoria. "I know this is personal for you—"

"*Of course* it is personal." Her body stiffens, and the small rustling noises of the command center fall silent. I'm holding my breath, too. "She is my *daughter*, Leopold, something I do not expect you to understand. But that is far from my only concern. The girls won the gold. You understand what this means as well as I: they won the hearts of a majority of the ascender world, and no doubt the legacy world as well. Then, while the whole world was watching, on nets both legacy and ascender, it was taken from them. They were *denied* the gold, Leopold. It is not quite the statement we wished to make in refusing it, but it could possibly have an even more dramatic effect. The Olympic committee denied the will of Orion, all because the girls were associated with *us*, the resistance. It is unprecedented, and it makes us appear strong. A true threat that must be quashed. But if we allow the girls to disappear into ascender custody, it will prove our weakness to the world. And it will strike a demoralizing blow that no one in the movement will forgive us for. Nor should they. We must strike back. We must use every resource to retrieve the girls and not allow them to become sacrificial lambs to the ascenders' games."

She glances at me, but then returns her steely-eyed stare to Leopold. "In spite of our attack, the ascenders are proceeding with the medals ceremony. We must not allow that to continue unanswered. We should strike at the heart of the Agon, just as we originally planned, regardless of who is on the stage."

"If you simply commit the act of terrorism," Leopold says, his voice tight, "without the defiance of the girls, you will not have the intended effect on the sentiments within Orion, I can promise you that. And it will be even more difficult to retrieve the girls then, if not outright impossible." The way he says it makes me think it's already an impossible task to get them back.

"Perhaps," Commander Astoria says. "I do not wish to make martyrs of our children. Better to retrieve them, so they can become living symbols of what we are fighting against. But the ascenders must pay a price."

Leopold fists one hand and presses it to his forehead, like he's run out of arguments for the small but fierce Simone Astoria. Given she's Delphina's mom, I'm surprised he's held out this long.

"Let me help," I say.

Leopold points an angry finger at me. "Stay out of this, Eli."

"No," she says harshly. "If the boy can help, you will not stand in his way." She definitely sounds like Delphina now, and even Leopold seems to cringe a little.

"Marcus wants *me*, not the girls," I say to Mrs. Astoria. Then I turn to Leopold. "He doesn't need Lenora either, right? Just me. So, it's simple. We make a trade. Me for all of them." I leave out that Marcus probably most wants for me to be *dead*. Although I'm not really sure of that, given he could have killed me before now.

Leopold is shaking his head, like he's already thought

of all the ways this isn't what he wants. Mrs. Astoria is sizing me up.

Before they get too far, I say, "I just want one thing in return." They both wait to hear what I have to say, but I direct my words to Leopold. "I want you and Lenora to find my mom and get her the gen tech cure she needs."

Commander Astoria gives me a sharp nod. That she doesn't even question the gen tech part confirms my suspicion that the resistance has access to that and probably a whole lot more.

Leopold crosses his arms and stares at the giant screen. It's a map of the city, crisscrossed with lines that might be roads or train lines or ancient sewer pipes, for all I can tell. But it's clearly a level of knowledge that the dissenters wouldn't have without the help of ascenders like him.

Finally Leopold turns back to me. "If I trade you for Lenora, she will never forgive me."

"And if you don't, Marcus may crack her personal key," I say. "What happens then? How much does she know about the resistance? You could lose a lot more than just one human experiment." I'm reaching here—I have no idea how tightly Lenora is involved in the resistance. Leopold's grimace gets darker, and he turns back to examine the screen again, but I don't think he's looking for something there. More like he's running a thousand scenarios in his ascender brain, trying to find a solution to this situation. But I'm pretty sure the one I've laid out is by far their best option.

Finally, he turns to Mrs. Astoria. "If we get the girls

back, will you hold off on blowing the stadium? There will be a proper time for that, Simone, but it's not now."

"We will not have another chance for a demonstration like this," she says tightly. "If we wait until the next games, it will not have the impact we desire. I will mobilize the forces needed to execute the mission. If you fail to liberate the girls, I will proceed."

I have no doubt she'll carry through with that threat, even though it would make getting Delphina back nearly impossible... and I'm kind of aghast at her willingness to put her own daughter at risk for the cause. I glance at Tristan behind me, but his face is blank. His words from before float back to me. *There's always that risk.*

"Well, now, that doesn't give us much time, does it?" Leopold's sarcasm actually makes me relax. Makes me think he has a plan. He turns to me. "Eli, I have no intention of losing you to Marcus."

"Okay." I have no idea how he plans to manage that, but I'm all for trying.

"I've suspected all along that Marcus wasn't a true believer. But the things he's managed... getting Thompson killed, influencing the Olympic committee to get the girls disqualified... I knew he had influence, but I didn't know how far it reached."

"Are you sure he did those things?" I say, although I wouldn't be surprised.

"No," Leopold says. "But I'm certain now that he's not acting alone. He's part of some larger force at work here. One that wishes to destroy what Lenora and I and the rest of the group have been working toward."

I wonder just how many ascenders are involved in this experiment they've been running, but I don't ask. I may not live long enough for any of that to matter.

Leopold continues. "I need to know who else Marcus has been working with. And handing you over to him just might be the only way to do that."

That gets my attention. "What do you have in mind?"

He holds me with a long look. "I want you to crack Marcus's personal key."

THIRTY-FOUR

Less than an hour later, I'm on a one-way ride back to Marcus.

At least, that's what I'm assuming at this point. Whatever Marcus has planned for me, I'm not likely to come back from it… *unchanged*. My stomach churns on that, even though the transport flight across the LA basin is utterly calm. At least, by the end of this, my mom will get the cure she needs and the girls will be safe. Lenora will be freed as well, although I'm a lot less willing to risk my life for her.

Riding in the cockpit is definitely an improvement over the transport's cargo hold, and the view is better, too. The afternoon sunshine turns the ascenders' glass and metal spires into blazing torches as we fly over them. Leopold sits next to me in the copilot seat, with the pilot being one of Commander Astoria's troops. The 360 degree flying helmet obscures her face, but her battle armor is the same as the dozen militia crammed into the hold, waiting to ensure the exchange goes according to plan.

In the distance ahead, the Pacific Ocean winks reflected sunshine off a million rolling waves. The ascenders' aversion to water relegates the beachfront to the seagulls and crabs. We're headed to some abandoned pier. I think Leopold called it Saint Monica. I wasn't listening to that part, more keenly interested in the exchange that is scheduled to happen there. What happens after that—the part where I somehow crack Marcus's personal key—seems ridiculously half-baked.

Like I said, one way ticket for me.

Leopold is holo programming something into the tiny button that he says is my weapon to use against Marcus. The pilot heels the transport over in a slow sweep that angles us down the coast. The cloaking device for the ship must be working, or we'd already be intercepted by police bots.

"Are you sure Marcus isn't going to meet us at the pier with a hundred tactical weapons bots?" I ask Leopold. "If he's as well connected as you say, I don't see why he wouldn't just set a trap for us and spring it once we get there."

"Probably because I told him I would kill you if he brought more than the girls, Lenora, and two personal security bots."

"Okay," I say, drawing the word out.

He looks up from programming the button and smirks. "He didn't believe me either. But I know Marcus. If he brings a small army to this exchange, he'll simply be broadcasting what he's doing. Which is not legal on several fronts. But most importantly, he's not going to want to risk losing you in a melee."

"You're sure?" I ask. "Because as far as I'm concerned, this is all for nothing if you don't get Lenora back and hold up your end of the bargain."

He looks me in the eyes. "I gave you my word on that, Eli."

My frown probably gives away that I'm not too sure how much that's worth.

He sighs and looks out the cockpit window at the vista below. "I have my own reasons for wanting Lenora back."

"So Marcus doesn't crack her personal key and find out what she knows?"

"That, and I quite literally owe her my life." He looks back to me with a small smile. "Can you guess what I was before the Singularity?"

The original ascendance was so long ago, a hundred years and counting, that it's hard for me to remember the ascenders came from that time period. That they were ordinary people once, all different ages and races and occupations. Intellectually, I know they're all over a hundred years old, but they seem so timeless in their bodyforms. Eternal. Like gods.

I try to picture Leopold in that long-ago time of personal automobiles, incurable diseases, and excessive pollution. "Heart surgeon?" I guess.

His smirk grows into a grin. "Almost. Tibetan monk."

I choke on my surprise. "I thought all the religious were dissenters." Although, technically, I know this isn't true. A lot of people who belonged to religions still ascended. At the time, it was like a religious calling of its own.

"Oh, I had my doubts. About everything. That was the problem, really."

I don't understand what he's saying, but I nod anyway.

"For a long time, it was everything promised and so much more. I thought it was the true awakening." Leopold gazes out into the brilliant blue sky ahead of us. "I believed that quenching the fires of ignorance would eventually lead to nirvana here on Earth. But instead of stillness, the passions of self and suffering were even more inflamed. When the realization that I had been wrong came creeping in, it was more devastating than you can imagine." He glances at me. "I nearly became one of the scrubbed."

"One of the what?"

He gives a sad smile. "I withdrew from Orion and destroyed my backup. I was daring the world to destroy me. To let me see if I truly had a soul that would live beyond this earthly world. I thought I might reincarnate into one of you: a legacy or a newborn dissenter. It wasn't until I found myself back at my old temple, destroyed in the religious purges, that I realized I was just warming up to the idea of self-termination.

I listen wide-eyed to his words. "You were trying to kill yourself?"

"I coated my bodyform with the few chemical reactants powerful enough to reduce it to elemental sludge. I shut down my sensory inputs, so the pain wouldn't weaken my resolve... then Lenora arrived at the temple." Leopold holds me with an intense look. "She promised an answer to the question I had given up asking. It was literally the only thing that could have stopped me."

"So, you owe her," I say.

"Yes, I owe her, but it's more than that. Lenora thinks you're our answer. She'll hate me for putting you at risk, but I don't need her to love me. I just need her to keep asking The Question."

I nod, finally convinced, then gesture to the tiny silver button still lying in his hands. "Tell me how this is going to work."

"Give me your hand."

I frown, but offer my left hand to him, palm up. He pulls out a thin, tube-like device and uses it to suck up the button. Then he holds the tube to my middle finger and taps it. A small pinch makes me twitch, but then the pain is instantly gone. When he pulls the tube away, there's no mark or any indication that he's done anything.

"You'll need to be close enough to touch him," Leopold says. "Once you press your finger against Marcus's bodyform, the device will be drawn out and transferred to his skin. Make sure you're not touching clothing because that won't be enough to activate it."

"Okay." I have no idea if I'll have the chance to touch Marcus, but it's at least worth a shot. "What happens then?"

"Possibly nothing. If he was in his normal bodyform, his automatic defense systems would quickly detect the intruding program and destroy it. But if he's still in a rental body, it's possible it won't have the more sophisticated defenses. They aren't standard in that level of tech."

"And if it works… how long until I know?"

"Minutes, possibly longer. If it succeeds in cracking his personal key, I've enabled a basic immobilization routine." He frowns at me. "It's important not to kill Marcus, or at least, not to destroy his bodyform. If that happens, his backup will be automatically activated, he'll change his personal key, and we won't be able to access what he knows. I need for you to disable and capture him, understood?"

I nod, but this seems as half-baked as the first time Leopold explained it to me. "And once I've disabled him, how do I get him out of… wherever we're going to be?" I have no idea what Marcus's plans are.

"The device has a tracker as well. We'll know if you've successfully deployed it."

"So you'll come for me?"

"That's the idea."

The transport heels over again and starts to drop toward the water. The shining sea surrounds the broken skeleton of the pier lying in the water. It's wide at each end and narrow in the middle. More than half of the broad wooden planks have fallen away, but a forest of concrete pilings has survived the onslaught of weather and years. Most of the pilings serve as perches for seagulls, but a string of the concrete stubs are still connected, forming two slim walkways on either side of the pier. It's maybe fifty feet across in the narrow section and several hundred feet long. The pilot steers us toward the wide end jutting over the water, while at the beach end, I can just make out the glint of another transport with several figures standing nearby.

From this distance, I can't tell who they are, but one figure is laid out on a stretcher… which makes my chest tight. I take a breath and let it out slow to steady my nerves. We swoop down and hover over the pier. A walk plank extends from the ship to the barest sliver of pier that still exists at the end. There's enough room for the dozen troops, plus Leopold and me, but only because we're spread out, like birds on a wire. I have an uneasy feeling, like we're exposed, even with the transport hovering at our backs.

Leopold is whispering into a communicator, setting up the exchange. I can barely make out Marcus's transport at the other end. The haze of sea spray and glinting sun make it appear to be a mirage.

Leopold steps up to my left side. "You'll be using the south side of the pier. The girls and Lenora will use the north side. The exchange will occur in the middle. I'll meet the girls, while Marcus will meet you. I'm sending Tristan with you, but if there are any problems, I'll be able to span the gap and come to your aid. Marcus has agreed to only send one security bot to escort the girls."

I nod and notice Tristan in his full body armor has eased up to my right.

"Are you ready?" Leopold asks me.

"Yes."

"I'll be in contact with Tristan at all times." Leopold

heads for the broken walkway along the north side, while Tristan and I pick our way across warped planks to reach the south end. The thud of Tristan's combat boots gives rhythmic punctuation to the dull roar of the distant waves crashing on the shore and lapping at the pilings. I glance across the span of the collapsed pier to Leopold to make sure we're matching speed. We start our march down the walkways together. We have almost two hundred feet to go to reach the center, but I can already see Marcus's bodyform in the distance, catching the summer sun.

There's barely enough room for Tristan and I to walk shoulder-to-shoulder, but he hunkers close to me, scanning the walkway in front and the water below, like he expects an amphibious assault or a land mine at any step along the way.

We walk in silence for half the way. I can see Marcus more clearly the closer he gets. The girls are matching pace with him on the north side. Sun glares off the security bot behind them, but I can see the three of them: Kamali and Basha in front, holding onto each other; Delphina behind, pushing a maglev stretcher holding Lenora's body; and the bot bringing up the rear. The tightness in my chest pulls harder.

I lean over to Tristan. "Ask Leopold if Lenora's okay. Deal's off unless we know."

Tristan relays the message, his face stoic, and listens to the reply. "Lenora is immobilized but conscious, sir," he tells me, still listening. "Leopold confirms he has spoken to her."

I nod my head and keep walking steadily forward.

After a moment, Tristan says, "It's an honor to know you, sir." His green eyes peer into mine, and it makes me cringe. Because I'm not doing this for his cause, or even for the girls, although I'm glad they'll be free. I'm doing this for my mom, plain and simple.

I shake my head. "You're really not going to stop calling me *sir*, are you?"

He grins.

We're getting closer, so I look over to the girls again. Delphina looks undaunted, but the other two look like they've been through hell: I can see the dark circles under their eyes from here, and Kamali's soft cloud of hair hangs limp around her head like it's been beaten and kicked into submission. Angry bile rises up in my throat, but even worse… I'm not going to have a chance to say even two words to her.

I turn back to Tristan. "Will you do me a favor?"

One of his eyebrows quirks up. "Yes, sir."

"If I don't come back from this…" I swallow and look to Kamali again. Her arm is wrapped so tightly around Basha, it's like the two girls are melded together. I say the words as I look at her face, even though the sea breeze has no chance of carrying them to her. "Tell Kamali I'm not what she thinks I am." I gaze at her, imagining saying the words straight to her, then I look back to Tristan.

He's frowning, looking back and forth between me and Kamali, no doubt wondering what in the world I'm talking about. But I don't need him to understand. Cyrus, when he wakes up to find I've gone off and gotten myself killed without him, will probably tell her he lied about me being Lenora's domestic. But I'm not sure Kamali will believe him. Maybe from Tristan, with my own words, and what I'm doing now… maybe she'll believe it. Maybe not.

It's all I have to offer.

Finally, we meet Marcus in the center. Leopold has reached the girls. Tristan hangs back as I take the final two steps to come face to face with Marcus.

He still has the rental body, which gives me an internal sigh of relief, but his smile hollows out my stomach. "You made the right choice, Eli."

"Wouldn't be here if I didn't agree." My anger leaks out in my words, but I figure there's no sense in being polite. Marcus glances over to the security bot still hovering over the girls. He must have transmitted some instruction because it turns back toward the beach. Marcus gives me room to pass and falls in step with me as I keep pace with the bot.

I take one last look back over my shoulder, just to make sure Leopold has them. Tristan is watching me go, not moving from his spot. I look forward again, wondering if it's too early to try to touch Marcus. I decide to make sure the girls are safely away first. Breaking Marcus's personal key is Leopold's goal, not mine. I want Lenora out of Marcus's reach first. Then I'd prefer not to die, if that's an option. Last place comes capturing Marcus to further Leopold's grand schemes.

"So, where are we going?" I ask Marcus, keeping it

light until we're off the pier and Leopold is away.

"Somewhere we can properly ascend you, of course."

I shoot a look at him, but Marcus just grins and faces our awaiting transport.

THIRTY-FIVE

Marcus and I don't talk on the ride to wherever he's taking me.

I'm still trying to wrap my head around what's happening. Is Marcus really going to let me ascend? How will that work? What about breaking his personal key, like Leopold sent me to do? Do I even *want* to ascend?

It's that last one that's gumming my throat shut, stopping me from asking all the obvious questions. It lodges there, choking me with all that's changed in the last short hour. Since I gained and lost the gold. Since I was attacked, rescued, then ransomed to save Lenora and the girls. Since I found a potential way to save my mother, even without ascendance.

Since I found out I'm not truly human.

And that's it… a feeling settles into my bones, that dark, creeping ooze that says something is terribly wrong with all of this. With *me*. I'm swimming upside down in a pool of darkness with no compass to tell me which way is up.

Marcus's transport gently glides between the towering

spires of LA. There's no lurching back and forth, no threat of losing my lunch while fleeing to the mountains. The resistance's transport was military grade in amenities and comfort, while Marcus's ship has luxuries I've never seen. It's a small, flying apartment, with the floor covered in some kind of misty carpet that gives gently under my regulation agonite sneakers. The seats are body-contouring maglev, apparently thought-controlled, at least for ascenders, as Marcus glides effortlessly from one end of a wall-sized display of the rainforest to the other. It's so realistic, I could swear the wall was a portal to South America rather than the back of the cockpit.

My thoughts are drawn to the dull rainforest painting I made for Lenora, a mockery in paint of the scene I see before me now. *You can do better*, she had said. And she was right. I could do better, but only in the fugue. And now... now I have some idea of how to do it even outside the fugue. Now, retroactively, I can see in my mind's eye the flaws of that work and how to fix them. All because some woman in a fugue hallucination touched me... and infused me with knowledge I never had before. The dark ooze is filling my lungs again, whispering the woman's words. *You are the bridge.*

I blink and shake myself, physically trying to rid my body of that creeping feeling that something is horribly wrong. Marcus is watching me from the door of the ship, which is now open. Outside is a short, well-lit walkway tunnel made of glass. Somehow the craft stopped without me noticing. I rise out of the infinite comfort of the body-contour seat and cross the floor.

"Where are we?" I ask, even though a thousand other questions should be coming out of my mouth right now.

His rental body sweeps a hand to the hallway. He's slightly awkward in it, like he's still adjusting to his bodyform. "Welcome to my home."

I step into the glass tunnel. We're impossibly high in the air, thousands of feet. A wispy puff of white cloud whips around the building a hundred feet below us. A wash of vertigo makes me pull my gaze from the dizzying height below to the building above, but it appears we're at the top. A lush domed garden covers the roof, but we're on the floor directly below that. Looking out over the city, I'm fairly certain there are no towers higher than ours, not even the space port, with its nearby launch arm ready to slingshot ascender flights into orbit. As I walk through the tunnel to Marcus's apartment, I try to piece together how much power he has to live here, in the clouds, like a god.

And what his real reason is for wanting me to ascend.

We reach the end of the glass tunnel, and the door winks out of existence with a wave of Marcus's hand. Across the threshold, there's more of the misty, softly-giving flooring that his ship had, only now it's spread across a huge living area dotted with a couple of couches and what looks like a medical bay at the far end. Floor-to-ceiling windows span one side while the other has a long hallway that appears to lead to rooms in the back. Brilliant sunshine streams in and filters through the swirling mists of the floor, creating the impression that we're literally walking on a cloud.

I'm still stunned out of words, but when we reach the windows, I manage, "You live here?"

"When I'm in LA, yes." He's watching me with an amused expression. Like he expects me to do something more serious than ask about his apartment. His expression dredges up an annoyance that cuts through the fog in my brain.

Marcus sweeps a hand to encompass the city. "All of this and much, much more will rightfully be your domain once you ascend, Eli."

"I don't understand," I say, the understatement of the year. "I lost the gold. How exactly are you going to ascend me?"

"It's a simple matter to clear you of the charges. Especially since I know who actually did kill the boy." Marcus waves away Thompson's death as if he were an annoying bit of trash swept into the bin. It adds barbs to the growing ball of annoyance inside me. "Convincing the Olympic committee that they should find you innocent of Thompson's murder and reverse their decision to disqualify you will take a little more bribery and possibly a few well-placed threats. But having the official cover of you ascending as a medalist is worth the trouble. It will make it easier for Orion to accept you. Besides, the committee has already disappointed Orion by disqualifying your rebellious little friends, so I imagine it won't take much prompting."

"Was it you?" I ask. "Did you kill Thompson so I would have a better shot at ascending?" Lenora confessed to framing me for Thompson's murder, but she claimed she didn't kill him herself. Which I want to believe, but I honestly don't know what to think anymore.

Marcus's limited bodyform still manages a small scowl of annoyance. "I told you before. I would have preferred if Thompson hadn't been killed. I thought it might turn Orion against you. But I'll admit to not foreseeing Lenora's last-minute sabotage, planting evidence against you. That was highly inconvenient."

"She says she didn't kill Thompson."

"And she didn't," he says. "One of my associates did, someone I would prefer not to be put to storage. So we'll find someone else suitable to take the blame."

"Wait… you're going to frame someone *else* for the murder? To clear the way for me to ascend?" The black ooze feeling squirms around in my stomach again, forcing me to swallow down a sour sickness in the back of my throat.

"Don't worry, it's no one you know. And once you ascend, none of this will matter."

I narrow my eyes. "Lenora said you want to kill me."

His nearly emotionless face manages to contort into something close to anger. "I imagine Lenora told you a great many lies. The very last thing she wants is to lose her precious experiment." He means it as an insult, against me, I think, or possibly Lenora. All I hear is the word *lies*. There are so many of them, I'm losing track.

"I know all about the experiment," I say, although I'm not sure how much of it I believe. "I know what she thinks she'll lose if I ascend. What I don't understand, is why it's so important to *you* that I do. Why not just kill me?" The sick feeling in my stomach is urging me on. I lightly rub my thumb across the middle finger on my left hand. I can't feel the device there, embedded in my flesh, but I know it's there. I just can't decide if I should use it.

Marcus's scowl takes a darker turn, his dull eyes turning more menacing. "You weren't supposed to live in the first place."

The sickness crawls back up my throat. "What do you mean?"

"Did Lenora tell you how many *experiments* there were?"

I shake my head, fighting the sickness again.

"Dozens," he says. "And that was just in the first round. None of them took. And do you know why?"

The shake of my head is more flinch than anything else. *Dozens.* Babies that Lenora and her cohort experimented on, trying to produce their hybrid bridge or whatever—their ascender baby with a soul. *All dead.* My stomach is in full rebellion.

"Because I made sure they weren't viable." He takes a step forward, and I edge back.

My disgust finally reaches my face. "You killed them *all*?"

"I made sure their design was flawed. Lenora is a brilliant geneticist... *now*. But she was an artist before the Singularity. Worked in acrylics just like you. Did you know that?"

I look at him like he's crazed. I'm convinced more than ever that all ascenders are essentially insane. At the very least, completely without morals.

"Given where she started," he continues, calmly, "Lenora was always a bit more talented in rendering in paint rather than DNA. I, on the other hand, was doing genetic studies well before I ascended. It didn't take much to make sure her little experiments never came to fruition. Until, somehow, to my extreme annoyance... *you managed to live.*"

The look on his face sends chills down my back, and I'm acutely aware that he could crush the life out of me at any moment. I curl up my left fist, protecting my middle finger, keeping it ready in case he makes any sudden moves. I'm tempted to reach out and touch him now, anyway, but I'm sure that would destroy any chance of me ascending. And I'm still wavering, uncertain.

Marcus pulls back a little and affects a more casual air. "Lenora was elated. She thought she had finally succeeded. And in a moment of weakness, probably because I enjoyed being her second just a little too much, I allowed you to live."

"So there *was* something different about me." My voice is weak, and I can feel my fisted hand shake slightly. I edge farther away from him and the windows and glance behind me to the med bay. It strikes me suddenly that an ascender would have no need for a med bay. Certainly not in his apartment. Is this where all the experiments took place?

Another wave of chills sweeps across me. I look back to him.

Marcus smirks. "There is precisely *nothing* unique

about you, Eli. That's the curious thing. Of course the first thing we did was examine your genetic composition. There was absolutely no difference between you and all the others. You had the same interweaving of ascender tech at the chromosomal level. The same genetic code. Identical to the others. And yet you lived. Once you were born, of course, Lenora tried to duplicate her success. First with another round of freshly conceived specimens. All were failures. Then she became convinced it was your mother's contribution that mattered. So, naturally, we cloned you."

"You… cloned me?" My jaw drops open, but I quickly shut it. "Are there… do I have…" I'm gibbering like an idiot, but my brain is working overtime to keep up.

Marcus looks unimpressed. "No, there are not clones of you walking around, if that's what you're thinking." He gives an elaborate sigh that comes out slightly jittery with his rental body. "All the clones failed to thrive as well. It turns out that you are, in fact, unique. But for reasons I still do not understand." The hard look comes back to his dark eyes. "As you grew, your talent for acrylics, combined with the fact that you lived when you shouldn't have… well, it fostered an unnatural fondness for you in Lenora. And a little too much hope in her fellow acolytes of the search for an "answer." But her Question is backward-looking, Eli. We left that behind, shortly after the Singularity, yet it's gaining purchase again. Spreading like a virus. Lenora and her group of believers are the only ones privy to the experiment, but they're not the only ones asking The Question. And resurrecting that is like falling back into those dark times when chaos reigned in the ascender world. Before Orion. Before the social stability that allows us to move forward. To explore. To create the wonders of our world." He gestures to the glittering city outside his windows, then swings his dull, menacing eyes back to me. "It has to be stopped, Eli. Before something much worse than a few renegade experiments happens."

He's creeping forward again, nudging me toward the med bay. Swirls of mist stir up as I stumble slightly in my step backward. "I still don't understand. Why don't you just kill me? You could have done it at any time along the way." It seems crazy to be asking this, but I need to know. Like there's some missing piece I need to figure out.

"It's easy to kill a man, Eli. It's much harder to kill an idea."

I swallow. "The idea that you… that ascenders are… missing a soul."

"The idea that there could ever be a bridge to find out."

A bridge. That sweeps a fresh chill through me that saturates me head to toe. Of course he would use the same word as Lenora. They worked together on the experiment. But, as far as I can tell, they didn't program me to have the hallucinations. They didn't… *force* me to dream about people who called me that. Who insisted on it. Who gave me an ability I didn't have before.

I shake my head to clear it of the thought that

somehow the hallucination isn't a hallucination at all. That it's not some figment of my subconscious. Because it has to be.

Marcus smiles a little, like he thinks I'm agreeing with him.

I stop my slow backward creeping and stand strong against him. "And if I ascend? Will that kill the idea?"

A smile tugs at the corner of his mouth, unsuccessfully, like he can't quite control it. "When you ascend, your mind will be open to every other ascender. It's part of the process of your first upload to Orion, before your personal key allows you to lock everyone out. Anyone who cares to can peer into your ascended mind and see what I already know: *there is nothing special about you.* You're not a bridge to anywhere: you're an ordinary legacy who happens to occasionally sling paint better than the current crops of agonites at the games. And, on the off chance that I'm wrong, I'm quite sure the ascendance process will cleanse your mind of any abnormalities that Lenora has managed to introduce with her experiments. She and her fellow believers can believe whatever they wish about you, but they will no longer be able to whisper in the dim corners of Orion that a savior is coming. An answer to The Question. I can expose what they've done and hold you up as the failed experiment that you are." His intense gaze, which is boring holes into me, suddenly softens. "And you, my little human oddity, will have exactly what you've wanted all along: to ascend. To save your mother's life." He smirks. "Perhaps you can have Lenora as well. I will certainly have no use for her once we're done." He holds his hands out, palm up. "So, you see, Eli, we both get what we want. In a rather amusing touch of irony, our interests have been aligned all along."

My chest is tight. He's not going to kill me. He's actually going to ascend me… so he can kill the hopes of Lenora and every other believer out there, human and ascender alike. And when those ascenders stop believing, stop hoping, what will become of the resistance? What happens to people like Kamali and Basha and Delphina? Cyrus and my mom, too, because there's no way they'll be able to return to Seattle now. Not if Leopold cures her. Even if Lenora's wrong about me, even if I'm not what she thinks, if I take what Marcus is offering, I'll destroy the one thing that's holding the dissenters and their ascender-enablers together. *hope.* Tristan's words fill my head again. *It's an honor to know you, sir.* Only his faith is misplaced. What will happen when I destroy the hope he and the others have? Will Leopold still keep our bargain and cure my mom, if I ascend?

The answer to that can only be *no.*

Marcus is watching me, waiting.

"No," I say. Then I clear the tremor from my voice and say it again. "No. I don't want your ascendance."

Marcus takes a deep breath and gives a long, well-of-patience sigh. The kind that has always signaled his true feelings of disgust for humans.

"Well," he says lightly. "The procedure would have gone much smoother with your cooperation." Then his voice drops. "But you're very much mistaken, Eli, if you think I need your approval to proceed."

THIRTY-SIX

"What?" It's a gasp more than a question.

My brain doesn't want to believe I heard Marcus correctly.

"You're going to ascend, Eli. If it was voluntary, you'd have a much higher likelihood of surviving. And I would very much like you to survive. Your cooperation would have made things so much simpler, but I should have expected as much from you. You've been trouble since the moment you were conceived." He grabs my arm, and in a small stroke of great good luck, it's my right arm. I clamp onto his exposed hand with my left one, making sure that my middle finger makes contact. A small pinch tells me Leopold's device has left my finger and adhered to Marcus.

He shows no sign of any effect.

Meanwhile the pain of him crushing my arm makes my knees buckle. He drags me toward the med bay, my hand clawing uselessly at his, my feet kicking up puffs of mist as we go. Black stars zip across my vision as Marcus nearly wrenches my arm out of its socket. He throws me into a reclined seat that's half stretcher, half luxury body-conforming chair. The cushion absorbs the blow of my body so I don't recoil back out again. I recover from the stun and try to climb out, but the seat has grabbed hold of me, like an enormous suction cup, and the more I struggle, the deeper I sink into it.

I force my frantic movements to still, breath heaving out of my chest in ragged gulps. I can still turn my head, if I move slowly, but the rest of my body is held fast by the cushion. I ease my head to the side, straining to see Marcus. I can't, but I hear his bodyform shuffling to the cabinets behind me, the swish of one opening, the dull click and scrape of something he's taking out.

"Marcus!" I yelp. "Marcus, don't do this!" I know it's useless, but I can't help saying it. I pant, struggling to control the panic that's threatening to strangle me. *Time*. I need time. What did Leopold say? It might take *minutes* for the device to break Marcus's encryption key. If it's going to work at all. If it doesn't... I can't think about that. I have to stall him. Talk to him. Get him to slow down. Anything.

"Marcus, I... I changed my mind!" I try to clear the hitch out of my voice. "If you're going to ascend me anyway, I just... give me a minute to prepare, okay?"

Marcus appears with ascender speed at my side, causing me to jerk, which just makes the chair grab tighter. The cushion somehow seeps through my agonite uniform to my skin, cool and clammy on my back and shoulders. I shudder, but that just makes it worse.

Marcus's cruel smile makes my heart seize up. He has

a small silver tube in his hand identical to the one Leopold used on me. I can't help staring at it.

"I would like you to survive, Eli," he says matter-of-factly. "Although I will admit to a certain level of annoyance about all the trouble you've caused. If you should die during the procedure, it won't break my heart. I'll be sure to explain to Lenora that you were a willing participant all along. Just to wipe away any faith she might still have in you."

I force words out of my mouth, saying anything, just to keep him talking. "Wait... okay... I can see you're serious about this. And, you know, on further thought, you're right. I mean, I never believed what she was saying. It's crazy, right? I'm just a legacy from Seattle. I'm nothing special." I gulp. I'm completely rambling now, and Marcus is ignoring me, checking his tube for something I can't see. It must contain the nanites or whatever the first step in the procedure is. I have no idea. "Is that... are you going to knock me out first? Is it going to be painful?"

He gives me an amused look, like he knows I'm stalling. "No, the procedure works best when you're awake. And unfortunately, it will be quite the opposite of painful."

Unfortunately? Some part of him must like watching me squirm in the chair. He's relishing it too much. Maybe I can work with that. "What do you mean the opposite?"

He gets a faraway look, gazing past me out the windows to the city. "Ascendance is like every pleasure you've ever known multiplied together. It's been a long time since I experienced it myself." His gaze zooms back down to me. "But trust me, it's not something you'll forget."

"Are you sure? I mean, if I'm not ready for it, you said it might kill me. Last time I checked, dying wasn't a pleasurable experience." I don't have to try to put fear into my voice.

He leans casually against the back of my prison-chair and smirks down at me while he dangles the tube near my face. My heart-rate kicks up as I alternate between staring at the open tip of the tube and Marcus's sneering rental face just past it. "No, I imagine it's quite painful as your brain rejects the nanites. As your neurons fight a losing war against the invading filaments. You begin to die, one neuron at a time, until your basic systems stop functioning. Your brain swells as your autoimmune response system floods your skull, trying to fight off an enemy it cannot recognize but knows is killing you. It's your own body that finishes the job, crushing your brain tissue with the pressure until your brain matter, blood, and all those complicated but ephemeral and ultimately inferior organic tissues simply leak out of your body through every orifice in your head."

He's definitely enjoying this.

Meanwhile, I'm working hard not to lose the contents of my stomach.

"Okay, so... you've convinced me, all right? I don't want to die, Marcus." The truth of that rings in my voice. It's strong enough that it may have convinced him, because he pulls back slightly, and the leer drops off his face.

"Just give me a minute to prepare, okay?" I say. "Just a minute. I want this to work." There's a jittery fervor in my voice. I'm pleading now. And hoping like crazy that he will buy it.

He frowns slightly. "One minute." He taps the tube lightly against the back of my chair then eases away from it.

I nod my appreciation. As he drifts toward the cabinets, taking that tube with him, I close my eyes and try to quell the shaking that's taken hold of my body. I think of Kamali and her meditation techniques. Breathe in. Breathe out. One minute… one minute… I'll have to think of something else to stall him after that, if the decryptor hasn't done its work by then. And if it doesn't work… or it doesn't work in time…

I really *don't* want to die.

I have no doubt that everything Marcus has told me is true, and I don't want the end of my life to come while I'm strapped to an ascender chair in the clouds. Maybe I really should accept it, if the ascendance is going to happen anyway. It's what I've wanted all along. To be like them. To be stronger, faster, more intelligent… better than human in every way. For as long as I can remember, I've wanted to join their pantheon of gods-on-earth, so I could have everything they have: all the tech, the riches, the spoils of the world. Their beautiful, perpetual bodies. Their incredible talents. But now I know the truth: they're ruthless killers who will stop at nothing to achieve what they want. They're not gods—they're not even close, with all their conniving and striving and murder. Now Marcus is going to force me to join them, and I won't even reap the one benefit that meant anything at all: saving my mom.

An intense bubbling of hatred wells up in me. I would give anything to be *merely* human. To erase this *thing* that Lenora has made inside me, this monstrosity that her ascender ambition has created and that fuels all the scheming. My hatred for the ascenders and all their games boils up and forces my eyes open. Angry breath leaks slowly out of me.

I would rather die than become one of them.

A dull roar fills my ears. It sounds like the waves at the pier, distant crashing against the shore, only it's rushing, rushing, rushing towards me.

I suck in a breath and struggle, trapped in my chair. "No, no, no—"

Not now, not now… but it's too late. The rushing roar keeps going then slowly ebbs. I'm on the shore of a sandy beach that's somehow familiar. Like a beach I know back home in Seattle, except it's empty now. Kayaks drift by themselves, blankets lay crumpled and abandoned, shovels and toys sit next to a half-built sandcastle. I walk toward the water. The lapping of the waves dims, and a woman in a red swimsuit appears in front of me. I stop. She's facing away, looking across the water. When she turns to smile at me, I don't recognize her, but she's beautiful even in middle age. Large chocolate brown eyes, long cascading hair falling down her back. She stands to face me.

I step toward her. Who are you? *I ask.*

I'm waiting, *she says. Her voice is sad music, each letter a note so lovely it makes me ache.*

Waiting for what? *I'm suddenly closer to her now, as if I moved without thinking.*

She smiles kindly at me, like I'm a child. She's my mother's age, beautiful like her, before the disease ravaged it away. Waiting for you, *she says. She reaches her hand toward my forehead. I want to lean away, but I'm frozen. I sense the chair holding me, back in Marcus's apartment, but at the same time, it's the music of her words ringing in my head that keeps me still, entrancing me.* You are the bridge, *she says. Her lips shape each word slowly, and she finishes them just before her finger touches my forehead.*

A tsunami of images, sounds, and feelings buries me. I see a man that she embraces in passionate love, a sister dead and buried, a baby snuggled in her arms. Days and years and sounds and memories flash by. It's a flood that I can't keep out. Just as I'm swept under, I see an image of a handsome, dark eyed boy with a scraped knee that she kisses... It's all right, Marcus, *she tells him, but it whisks away like the rest, and I'm drowning in all of it, a dark, dark hole of nothingness closing in over my head...*

"Eli!" Something slaps my face. "Eli, wake up!"

My eyes jerk open. Marcus's face looms above me, holding as much panic as can be apparently wrought with his rental body. I'm still in the haze of the fugue state, the overwhelming sense of it still drowning me. I'm a glass jar filled to the brim with everything that was her life, the woman's life, so full that I'm bursting with it. Her name comes to me—Lilith—along with every small thought and feeling and wish she had.

I look up into the dull, flat eyes of Marcus's rental body, but somehow I see beyond them. I see the dark eyes that belonged to the boy. "She's your mother." My voice is rough with the aftermath of the fugue, and already the tremors ripple through my body. "Lilith is… so beautiful." The tremors work into my voice. "She… loves you… so very much."

Marcus's eyes go wide, and he leans away from me. "What are you talking about?" But his voice is weak. Surprise mixed with a kind of horror.

I fight against the growing shakes in my body, which just sink me deeper into the chair, but my mind calmly sorts and files all the knowledge that has been given me. *Gift* feels like the right word, even though it's nothing I asked for or wanted. I blink and look at Marcus again. He's scowling at me now.

"She believed you," I say, with the certainty that comes from having every moment of her life poured into me. "She believed *in* you. She wanted to ascend because of you." As I say it, the images flash in front of my mind's eye: his impassioned pleas; his convincing arguments; his impossible promises. He was always so smart, her son, so clever. And he loved her, she knew that. He wouldn't say it if it weren't true. Then the pain and the darkness…

Marcus's mouth hangs open. "How do you know about…" He looks at me like I'm a horrible nightmare come to life in front of him. Then the anger rises up and takes hold of him. "This is some kind of trick or… I don't know what you think you're playing at, Eli, but nothing's going to stop me from—" He cuts himself off, and his face goes blank, slack for a moment, then true panic contorts his features. "What have you done?"

He casts about the room, looking for something, moving so fast I can barely track him. Then he disappears from my view, and there's a tremendous crash from the direction of the wall of windows. The jitters that wrack my body make it even more difficult to fight the chair. I slowly twist my head to the side. Finally, I can see it: a whole section of the window wall is missing. Streams of mist fly off the carpet and whip out into the free air outside the apartment. Wind howls past the gaping hole, and my eyes are blinking fast from the sudden frigid breeze, the post-fugue shaking, and the realization of what the hole must mean.

Marcus just jumped out the window.

THIRTY-SEVEN

"**B**ut he's dead, right?"

I can't help asking it again, even though Leopold already assured me that even an ascender body wouldn't survive a fall from that height. The shakes from the fugue were mostly gone by the time Leopold arrived in his transport and freed me from the chair, but the wind is still howling around the hole in the window, and the cold makes me shiver.

"His bodyform is dead," Leopold says. "But that will only trigger the release of his backup. As I told you before, it would have been much better to capture him."

I gesture to the chair, my hand still showing the tremors. "I was a little short on options."

Leopold smirks, then gets serious again. "We should go, Eli. I don't know how quickly Marcus will resurrect, but we certainly don't want to be here when he does."

I nod, jerkily, and follow him and the heavily armed resistance militia he brought with him back out to the transport, which is hovering in the whipping winds outside Marcus's broken window. The walk plank extension isn't as steady as I'd like for a thousands-foot-drop, but we manage to get across it and safely aboard.

I think I'm still in shock as I sit on the floor of the transport and stare at the cockpit wall, one hand clinging to the wall netting. Every time I try to think about what just happened—Marcus, the fugue, his mother—my mind recoils from it. Like it's too much for me to take in. I take several deep breaths, trying to clear it and focus on what's next.

"Did Lenora say where she's hiding my mother?" I ask Leopold, who's standing at the threshold to the cockpit.

"I didn't have time to ask. But since Marcus only had her for a short while, he wasn't able to break her personal key. So it's safe to return to the resistance's mountain station, which is where she and the girls are now, recovering. You can ask her yourself when we get there."

I nod, then resume staring at the wall. Time passes, but it feels suspended for me. Like I'm waiting for something to descend upon me and explain what happened in Marcus's apartment. And when nothing does, and the miles pass silently underneath the transport, I slowly begin to think it wasn't real. It *happened…* but it doesn't mean anything.

I know this is wrong. But I can't think about it anymore without feeling like my grip on reality is slipping away.

A jostle in the ship tells me we've landed. I follow Leopold to the door, and when it winks out of existence, I see the pilot has actually landed us inside the dissenters' hideout. It's crammed with militia, most changed out of their black-clad battle armor and back into regular clothes of all shapes and colors. Commander Astoria and Delphina stand off to the side of our craft, waiting for us, but as we debark down the walk plank, they don't say anything or smile, they just start to clap. Leopold glances back to me, and as we keep walking, others join in, standing up from their bunks or stopping in their purposeful strides. It takes me a moment to realize they're clapping for me, and I have no idea what to do with that.

I'm not a hero of their resistance. I'm not even *in* the resistance.

I'm not sure what I am.

I duck my head, avoid Delphina's steady gaze, and catch up to Leopold. "Where's Lenora?" I say in a harsh whisper so it won't carry, but he'll hear me over the subsiding applause. "I want to leave as soon as possible."

He frowns. "Probably in the medical pod. I ordered the bot to do a work-up on her bodyform to make sure Marcus hadn't tampered with it."

"Great." I glance around, and I'm relieved to see the militia members going about their business again.

When we reach the medical pod, I'm all set to demand Lenora tell me where my mom is and then leave as quickly as possible. But there are far more people inside than I expect.

Of course Cyrus is there—a surge of guilt spears my gut that I had completely forgotten about him. He's sitting up, smiling and holding Basha's hand. She must have forgiven him for everything that's happened, what seemed like a million years ago, but was only earlier this afternoon. She looks a little better than on the pier, mostly because of the smile beaming from her face.

"Eli!" she says in her over-excited voice. But she stays by Cyrus's side as he struggles to get up off the bed.

Kamali's not far from Basha, and next to her is Tristan. They're standing close, like they've been talking amongst themselves, but when he sees me, Tristan breaks out a grin. Kamali's harried demeanor stays even. I can't face her chocolate brown eyes for more than a second before I have to look away.

Then I see Lenora on one of the beds with the med bot nearby. She leaps off it with ascender speed, and she's the first to reach me at the door, where I'm standing frozen.

"Eli," she says, and it's a gasp of relief. She scans me up and down like she can't believe I'm standing in front of her. When her gaze finally comes back to meet mine, she puts her soft hands gently to my face. "I thought I had lost you."

I wrench my face free of her grasp. "I'm fine."

She frowns, chastened, and drops her hands.

I step back to put space between us. "Tell me where my mother is."

"Eli, I'm sorry for…" She stalls out, looks to Leopold for help, but he's standing coolly next to me and offers none. "Did Marcus tell you—"

"Where *is* she?" I shout her down. My voice bounces off the hard surfaces of the pod, making it even louder in the silence that's fallen. I drop my voice low again. "Tell me now, Lenora."

She nods, biting her lip. "I'll take you to her."

"No," I say, shaking my head so there's no confusion. "Give Leopold the coordinates. If she's not there or anything has happened to her—" I'm biting my words off in angry chunks and throwing them at her. My blood pounds in my ears, and my head feels like it's full to brimming again. I'm venting at Lenora, all the anger and confusion and... *fear*... about what she's done to me. I struggle to rein it in. I'll have all the time in the world to tell her what I think of her and her experiments and her pursuit of The Question *after* I have my mother safe again. She'll have to come back here for the gen tech cure anyway. "I'll be back later," I say simply and leave it at that.

I turn away from her, fully planning on marching out of the pod and waiting for Leopold in the transport, but Cyrus is by the door. I nearly run into him. I force myself to peer up into his face. His concerned look deflates all my turmoil in one sweep.

"Cy, I'm sorry, I had to—" He cuts me off with a hug that squeezes all the air out of me. I blink back tears, and thankfully, he releases me before I have to figure out whether I need to hug him back.

He holds me by the shoulders. "Oh sure, run off, be a hero, and take all the glory for yourself. Have I told you how much of a pain in the ass it is to be your friend?"

A strangled laugh escapes me, in spite of feeling like I might break down at any moment. But I can't look him in the eye right now. "I'm going to get my mom, Cy. I'll be back."

"The hell you are. I'm going with you."

I ball up a fist and press it to my mouth. I'm desperate to be alone right now, simply because I'm barely holding it together. But I don't think I can argue with him, not without breaking down. And my mother is his mother, at least in all the ways that matter. I relax my hand and peer up to look him in the face. "Okay."

He frowns, and I know he knows: that something's not right with me. That something's not ever going to be right with me again. He puts his heavy hand on my shoulder, but it doesn't weigh me down, it lifts me up. He pulls me into a one-armed Cyrus hug and gives me a sharp nod.

"Let's go get your mom," he says.

We leave the pod, Cyrus's arm holding me up all the way to the transport.

We fly to Seattle. It's just me, Cyrus, Leopold, and the pilot, with a mini med bay set up in the hold, complete with the dissenters' med bot. I'm sitting in the third seat of the cockpit, staring out the window. I don't speak. The ride is smooth, and there's nothing but fertile restored habitats and the clear blue sky to look at, broken up by the occasional ascender city, each a major metropolis shining in the sun. As we cross Oregon, it gets darker, both due to the writhing storm clouds ahead in

Washington, and the sun sinking lower in the West, adding a fiery red to the mix.

By the time we land at the coordinates Lenora gave us, the sun is hovering above the horizon, a churning orb that lights the hanging dark clouds from below. I don't realize exactly where we are until we step out of the transport… onto the beach.

I freeze in place, my sneakers digging into the sand. Cyrus nearly runs into me from behind. I blink and look around, but it's not the same beach. The kayaks and abandoned blankets are gone, and I can see the skyline of Seattle in the distance. In my fugue hallucination, there were only rolling hills over the water. I shake my head to clear it and force my legs to unlock and march forward. Leopold has skirted around me and Cyrus, leading the way to a small bungalow set back from the water. It's separated from the sand by a narrow concrete walkway that's broken into uneven bits, the waterfront having been long abandoned since the Singularity. It makes sense to me that Lenora would stash my mom here for safe keeping—somewhere no ascender would naturally stumble upon.

There's no one visible in the adjacent abandoned bungalows, and most of the buildings here are in the same state of disrepair as the sidewalk. The one next door has a roof caved in, and the wooden porch of the house we're approaching looks like it will barely hold me or Cyrus, much less Leopold's more substantial ascender weight. He looks skeptical of it, too, but he gingerly crosses it and pulls open the screen door. It comes off in his hands, which makes him frown in an almost comical way. He sets the screen aside, knocks, then pushes open the door.

He peers inside, decides it's safe or something, then lets me go first.

Cyrus shadows me on the way in. My heart has jumped up into my throat and starts pulsing there as I pick my way around the musty abandoned furniture that crams nearly every inch of floor space in the main room. I peek into the kitchen, but there's nothing there. Cyrus is ahead of me, heading toward the back bedroom.

My heart is knocking in my ears by the time I reach the back. Cyrus is kneeling by my mom's bedside. A rush of breath I didn't know I was holding washes out of me when I see her.

She's sleeping. At least I think she's sleeping. I stumble to Cyrus's side and work hard to keep the tears out of my eyes. We both watch as her chest slowly rises and falls.

Cyrus stands and puts a hand on my shoulder. "She's okay."

I nod, too much. Then I squeeze his shoulder. "Can you give us a minute, Cy?"

He lets out a long breath, but I think he's relieved. "You got it."

I wait until he leaves and slides the door shut behind him. There's a small med bot, the non-sentient, non-android kind in sleep mode in the corner. A shallow dish next to my mother's bed has remnants of oatmeal, with a half-filled glass of water nearby. My relief that she's actually eaten something recently fills me with a kind of glowing joy that almost starts the tears again.

I am such a mess.

I take a couple deep breaths before I kneel by the bed and gently place my hand on hers to wake her. It takes a full heart-stopping minute of gentle taps and calling her name to rouse her.

When she opens her eyes and smiles, I give up the fight and bow my head, pressing her hand to my forehead and letting the tears fall.

"Elijah," she says, surprised. Her voice is stronger than I expect, and she pats my head with one hand before pulling the other from mine and struggling to sit up. I duck my head away, wipe my face as quickly as I can, and have a smile for her when I turn back.

"How are you feeling?" I ease up to sit on the creaky mattress next to her. She adjusts a pillow, propping herself up, so she can sit next to me.

"Good. You know," she says. "How long have you been gone? I've been sleeping a lot. Kind of lost track of the days."

How long? *Forever. A lifetime.* I think back on it. "About five days."

She nods like this makes sense, even though it seems crazy to me. Then she frowns and studies her hands. "I didn't watch the competition, Elijah," she says quietly. "I couldn't. I just—"

"Hey," I cut her off. "Don't worry about that."

"Lenora said you were doing well, when she arranged to have me moved. And now... you're already back." She hesitates again, staring at her hands. "Did you win?" Her question is a whisper.

I let out a small laugh. "Yes."

She looks up, a dire look on her face.

"And no," I add quickly. "I'm not going to ascend, Mom. But I am here to take you somewhere you can get a cure. A real cure. The kind that will actually work."

A kaleidoscope of emotions cross her face, and she seems to struggle for words. Finally, she says, "Lenora said it would be better for me to rest here by the seaside…"

"Lenora's not in charge of this." I wait for her to look up at me. "I know, Mom. I know everything."

She looks genuinely puzzled, and for a moment, I think, maybe, she doesn't really know. Maybe they drugged her and made her pregnant without her knowledge or consent. That springs up an anger that chokes me, but then I know that can't be right. She had to know, even if only afterward. And if she doesn't… she should.

"I know about Lenora and the experiment," I say quietly, watching her reaction.

Her eyes widen, and she drops her gaze.

She knows.

"I just… I just want to know *why*, Mom," I say, my voice cracking. "Why would you let them do that?" *Why would you let them put something not human inside you?* I can't force it from my lips.

Her face scrunches up, like she's trying not to cry, and it just about kills me. I want to take the question back. I want to erase all of it and just hug her. But, at the same time, I have to know. I *need* to know—like my sanity is hinging on her answer.

She twists and twists the sheet in her lap, starts to speak a couple times, then stops.

I wait, unable to say anything more.

Finally, she looks up at me, eyes shining, and says, with a small shrug, "I did it for love."

I pull back. "For love." I have no idea what she means.

"I was in love with my patron." She says it like she's surprised I haven't guessed it already.

I'm genuinely shocked. "I didn't know you even had a patron."

"Well, it *was* before you were born." She gives a teasing sort of smile that slowly melts into sadness. "He was brilliant and charming and... well, you know how they are."

I do, but my brain is overwhelmed with the idea of *my mother...* as a domestic. My throat is closing up.

She keeps talking. "I was convinced he loved me. That he saw something special in me. I was too old for the games, but I was sure that one day he would find a way for us to be together. Because we were meant to be together. That was obvious to my twenty-year-old heart." She shakes her head and gives a dry chuckle that makes her cough. "I was a fool, of course."

I can hardly listen to this. The agitation is crawling up my legs, and I have to stand. I pace to one side of the tiny room, cross my arms, and stare at her, waiting for her to go on.

"Eli, you have to understand. I was young. I was in love. And when he asked me to… well… basically carry his child, I didn't hesitate. I thought he wanted it because he wanted *me*."

I fist up both hands and press them to my forehead. I don't want to hear this. I don't want to *know* this.

"I thought, once the baby was born, that he would find a way to ascend me, and we would raise our child together. But once I was pregnant with you…" She looks away quickly, but I see it: the pain in her eyes. It makes me want to hunt down and kill the ascender who did this to her. She clears her throat and looks back to me. "After that, I found out he had taken a second. Soon after, he left Seattle. I've never heard from him again."

I turn away from her and drive my fist into the flimsy paperboard wall of her room. It hurts, but nowhere near as bad as the pain I want to inflict on this… *patron*. This ascender who used my mother like breeding cattle for his experiment, breaking her heart in the process.

I lean my forehead against the wall and pull my fist from it, breathing out the anger in short bursts. Someday, I vow to myself, someday… I'm going to find that bastard and make him pay. Meanwhile… my mom needs me.

I turn away from the wall. My mom's shoulders droop with the burden she's laid on me, this knowledge of how I came to be. And why. I rush over and hug her as hard as I dare with her disease-ravaged body. A disease this patron of hers doesn't know or care about, having abandoned her… and me… long ago. She sobs quietly into my shoulder, and I feel her tears through my uniform.

When she pulls back, she puts a cool hand to my cheek. "I never once regretted it, Elijah. Never once. Because I have *you*. And I love you so much."

"I know, Mom," I say, barely choking it out. "C'mon. I have a place I'm going to take you. Somewhere they can cure you."

I help her up from the bed. She's so unsteady and frail in my hands, but I can see her determination to stand on her own. I think about how much she's had to do on her own, all this time. Raising me. Worrying about me. Not wanting to lose me to the ascenders who created me in the first place.

She holds tight onto my arm for balance. "Lenora said she would look out for you." She gingerly works her way across the room with my help. "She said she would bring you back to me." She pats my arm. "And she did."

In that moment, I forgive Lenora just a little—for taking care of my mom in a way I didn't even understand she needed.

I shift forward to open the door for her, and Cyrus is waiting just outside.

"Mrs. B," he says. The tear tracks are still wet on his face. "I've got a stretcher waiting right here for you." He shuffles into the furniture-stuffed living room, where Leopold is waiting for us with a solemn face, a militia member, and a maglev stretcher.

"We're going to see Lenora now," I say quietly to my

mom, holding her arm as we slowly walk the hallway. "But we're going to have to leave Seattle to do it. And once we leave, we're not going to be able to come back."

I nod to Cyrus to let him know we're ready.

"Where are we going?" my mom asks, taking in Leopold, the stretcher, and the black-garbed dissenter pilot holding it with surprising calmness.

"Somewhere safe," I say. "Somewhere you don't have to ascend to live."

She smiles at me. It's weakened by sickness and takes as much effort as her slow steps across the floor.

But it's the most beautiful thing I've seen in a long time.

If you enjoyed *The Legacy Human*, please leave a review—even just a few words about your response to the story is incredibly helpful in spreading the word about it.

Want to know when the next Singularity book is out? Subscribe to Susan's mailing list
http://smarturl.it/SKQnewsletter

If you liked *The Legacy Human*,
check out the Mindjack series (three novels, five novellas, and more to come…)

Mindjack Trilogy
When everyone reads minds,
a secret is a dangerous thing to keep.

Susan writes YA SF, steampunk, urban fantasy and more…find all of Susan's books here:
http://smarturl.it/SKQwebsite

A NOTE FROM SUSAN KAYE QUINN

I've been working on Singularity for nearly two and a half years.

My original idea was to write a reverse Pinnochio story about a boy who wants to become a machine—or, more precisely, a reverse Bicentennial Man (apologies to Mr. Asimov), where the pinnacle isn't attaining humanity, but transcending it. The idea of humanity's future evolution has intrigued me for some time (see my Mindjack and Debt Collector series), and technology is already changing how we interact with the world (and each other). I was fascinated by the question of what would cause humanity (or even a single human boy) to choose to leave his human-ness behind. I had no question that the technology to advance human intelligence (or create from scratch a machine intelligence) would eventually arrive: the true question was, what would we do with it? Would we use it to ascend into something greater? What did that even mean? And what could possibly motivate us to choose that option, if it were presented?

One thing I knew: the answer (and there wouldn't be just one, but a multitude) would involve the intersection of everything we knew about the mind, conscious and subconscious, creativity and the soul, and all of our philosophies about what it means to be human. It would be far more than a tale about technology—what was *possible* –and much more a story about the choices humanity would have to make in the face of those possibilities.

Needless to say, I was hooked.

Of course I was vaguely aware of the Singularity as a concept—the idea of a time when computers would become sentient—but I already knew that my version of the Singularity would be nothing like Terminator and Skynet. Our real world was hurtling forward with robotics and nanotechnology and artificial intelligence in everything from our browsers to our games—the idea of an AI rampaging against humanity was already long overdue for a reimagination. I had my own ideas, but I didn't get far in my research before stumbling upon Ray Kurzweil's *The Singularity is Near...* and found myself nodding at nearly every page. Ray's optimistic view of the future was only one of its allures—it was Ray's vision of the nature of the Singularity and what it would mean for humanity's soul that captivated me. Because what is Pinnochio's quest to become a real boy other than the desire to claim that quintessential thing that makes us human? And how does that thing change when we become *more* than ourselves, as Pinnochio wished? These are the questions we face when we peer into a future where organic-only humans are but one of the options for intelligence on our planet.

Two years ago, I set about building a fictional world based on the idea of enhanced intelligence as the basis for the Singularity. I drafted the prequel (Day Zero, which covered the Singularity event) as a screenplay at roughly the same time that I wrote *The Legacy Human* (the first novel in the post-Singularity world). The two stories were inextricably linked, and writing them together was illuminating to both. (I'm in the process of converting Day Zero to a novel, which will be published later in 2015.) Meanwhile, I watched the movie industry begin to reimagine the Singularity as well, moving beyond Terminator and into stories like Transcendence and Her and Lucy (and soon Ex_Machina and Chappie). I cheered this development, even as Hollywood seemed to stumble a bit, trying to wrap their storytelling minds around this new idea. But each story added to the lexicon of our imagination (something I hope mine will do as well).

My children are growing up in a world where Artificial Intelligence isn't about science fiction—it's about the technology in their present and near future. In the end, it will take the form of a question: what exactly do we mean when we call ourselves human? It's a question humanity has been asking for a long time, and one that will continue to challenge us.

This series is one attempt to answer it.

ACKNOWLEDGMENTS

This book has been a special, terrifying, and amazing journey. The people who helped make it happen were equally special and amazing (but not terrifying, except for Bryon Quertermous and his teaser emails about impending editorial letters). It feels like the universe sent me just the right people at just the right time to help me bring this story into the world the way I originally envisioned it, way back in the fall of 2012.

The Editor: Bryon Quertermous. I first contracted with Bryon to freelance edit this book… then promptly forced him to edit an entirely separate trilogy first. (This is partly his fault, for insisting I should expand on the first book and make it into a series.) When we finally got to work on *Legacy* together, we were a seasoned team… which was exactly what this book needed. Thank you, Bryon, for sticking with me until we could get here.

The Artist: Zachary Mueller. Zack was an actor on the Mindjack trailer, volunteering his time to help bring that story to life. When I noticed some artwork on his phone in the cast room, we quickly dived into talking about *Legacy,* even though it was just a glimmer of an idea at the time. As we spoke about his art and my story, it was as if the two were destined to cross paths. Zack's critique of *Legacy,* two years later, reassured me that I had captured the essence of Eli's artist nature the way I had wanted. Thank you, Zack, for having an open heart for this story.

The Cognitive Scientist: Daniel Smith. A recent friend, brilliant mind, and invaluable discussion partner on the finer points of philosophy, religion, duality, and artificial intelligence. Beyond the sheer pleasure of our conversations, and my frequent trips to the dictionary and Wikipedia so I could keep up with him, Daniel helped me take the raw stuffs of theme that were rife throughout the story and work through all the myriad implications. Thank you, Daniel, for jumping in with both feet. I can't wait for your thoughts on Day Zero!

The Treasured Writer-Friends: Adam Heine and Rebecca Carlson. When the prospect of writing this story was terrifying me—not just the complexity of the topic, but the hot-button issues of religion and spirituality—Rebecca and Adam gently encouraged me to have faith, work hard, and write it anyway. And once it was written, they both lent their considerable talents in the craft of storytelling to make it better. Thank you, Rebecca and Adam, for having faith that I could actually pull this off… and for helping me get there.

The Borrowed Husband/YA Reader: Tim Sussman. The husband of a writer-friend, Tim is an avid YA reader as well as enjoying SF, which put him square in my "adults who read YA and/or SF" target audience. Tim was my mini market-test of both the story and the cover, seeing whether they had crossover appeal for adult readers (especially males) and if the story left them wanting more (always key). Thank you, Tim, for being my guinea pig!

The Kid: Adam Quinn. My sixteen-year-old son is a seasoned writer in his own right, with a trilogy of novels and two novellas under his belt. (I highly recommend raising your own critique partners. There are many benefits to this.) Not only is Adam in my target audience now, but his notes are always insightful and entertaining. You have't been properly critiqued until you've been taken to task about the viability of your world's monetary system! Thank you, Adam, for being willing to read your mom's stuff and for catching my plot holes before they make it out into the world!

The Alpha Reader: Liz Masterson Searle. A good friend and fellow writer, Liz is relentlessly supportive in all my publishing antics. This kind of moral support is invaluable to writers. The fact that she loved Eli as much as I did from that very first, raw chapter flung across email, just solidified her as a treasured *alpha reader* (the one who gets everything *first*). Her encouragement and enthusiasm have been a constant source of inspiration over the long stretch of time it took for this story to come into the world. Thank you, Liz, for being Eli's first and best fan!

Some projects feel like there are larger forces at work, nudging it into the world. This was one of those.

Final thanks go to Dale Robert Pease for the gorgeous cover and Jason Anderson at Polgarus for the formatting. Thanks especially to my readers for taking a chance on Eli's story.

I promise you, there is much, much more to come.

ABOUT THE AUTHOR

Susan Kaye Quinn is the author of the *Singularity Series*, the bestselling *Mindjack Trilogy*, and the *Debt Collector serial*, as well as other speculative fiction novels and short stories. Her work has appeared in the *Synchronic* anthology, the *Telepath Chronicles*, the *AI Chronicles*, and has been optioned for Virtual Reality by Immersive Entertainment. Former rocket scientist, now she invents mind powers, dabbles in steampunk, and dreams of the Singularity. Mostly she sits around in her PJs in awe that she gets to write full time.

CPSIA information can be obtained at www.ICGtesting.com
Printed in the USA
LVOW12s1543260116

472354LV00008B/930/P

9 781508 557494